Hear My Voice

Marcia R. Rudin

Give ye ear, and hear my voice;
hearken, and hear my speech.
Isaiah 28:23

ISBN: 154269440X
ISBN 13: 9781542694407
Library of Congress Control Number: 2017903152
CreateSpace Independent Publishing Platform
North Charleston, South Carolina

Foreword

HEAR MY VOICE follows fifty years -- from 1940 to 1990 -- in the lives of my three protagonists, Sister Mona Sullivan, Rabbi Sandra Miller-Brownstein, and Reverend Elizabeth Adams. While these three women are fictional, the public figures mentioned in the novel are real, and at times my characters interact with some of them. The real people with whom they have contact include Sister Ann Gillen, Sister Gloria Coleman, Rivka Haut, Francine Klagsbrun, Rabbi Helene Ferris, Russian "refuseniks" Masha and Vladimir Slepak and Ida Nudel, Sister Margaret Ellen Traxler, Rivka Aleksandrovich, Rabbi Malcolm Stern, Rabbi Alfred Gottschalk, Dr. Rosemary Radford Ruether, Archbishop Vincenzo Fagliolo, Sister Mary Linscott, Frances Kissling, Barbara Ferraro, and Patricia Hussey. But of course, their interactions with my fictional characters did not take place.

The activities of the real people I include in the novel are historically based; many of their speeches in the story are taken verbatim from the books listed below and from other documents. In addition, some of the courageous and significant actions I attribute to my characters were in reality done by historical figures. By crediting my characters with these accomplishments, I do not mean to take away from those of the real people who deserve our applause.

For example, Sister Mona did not head the Women's Ordination Conference, nor did she sign her name to the important *New York Times* 1984 statement "A Catholic Statement on Pluralism and Abortion," thereby becoming one of "The Vatican 24". She did not appear on the Phil Donahue Show with these other brave women. She did not deliver a speech at the Baltimore Harbor the night before the 1978 Women's Ordination Conference. Sister Mona's fictional friends, former nun Luella and former priest Peter, were not part of the "The Plowshares Eight" who protested the Vietnam War by breaking into the General Electric facility in King of Prussia, Pennsylvania, earning prison sentences. Her Mother Superior, Mother Patricia Luke, did not found NETWORK.

Reverend Liz Adams did not contribute a chapter to Dr. Rosemary Radford Reuther's book *Women of Spirit: Female Leadership in the Jewish and Christian Traditions* and did not travel to the Soviet Union in 1978 with Sisters Gillen and Coleman or participate in other activities of the Soviet Jewry movement. She did not serve on the Presbyterian Church's Committee on the Status of Women or hear Rivka Aleksandrovich speak. Sister Ann Gillen did not lecture at her church.

Rabbi Sandra Miller-Brownstein was not the sixth woman to be ordained by Judaism's Reform Movement and was not part of Women of the Wall movement or other Jewish feminist activities. She did not attend CCAR conferences or Women's Rabbinic Network meetings. The rejection letters Sandra receives in the novel from the Hebrew Union College-Jewish Institute of Religion were sent to Rabbi Sally Priesand before she was finally admitted to the rabbinical program. Sandra's fictional friend Carolyn Schwartz was not one of the co-founders of the magazines *Davka, Lilith,* and *Ms.*, and did not participate in the Women of the Wall activities.

The towns of Elmville, Illinois and Stewart, Maine are fictional, as are the West Virginia compound, WomanSpeak: Voices of Faith and its award and awards dinner, Reverend Adams' churches, Rabbi Miller-Brownstein's synagogues, and Sister Mona's convent.

Many thanks to the following individuals who aided me in writing this novel with information and advice: The Reverend William Hall Harter, Dr. Thomas E. Bird, Sisters Celia Deutsch and Gloria Coleman, Rabbis Sally Priesand, Myra Soifer, James Rudin, Eve Rudin and Elliott Kleinman, and my friend Muriel Berger. If there are others I failed to mention here, please accept my apologies and thanks. I also want to acknowledge the information I received from the archives of the American Jewish Committee regarding its important role in the Soviet Jewry movement. I also apologize to and thank those women rabbis whose personal anecdotes regarding their challenges and struggles I heard or read about and "stole" to enrich my novel.

Finally, I want to thank my husband Rabbi James Rudin for his love and support over the many years it took me to write *Hear My Voice*, and to express my love and appreciation to our two wonderful daughters, Rabbi Eve Rudin and casting director and writer Jennifer Rudin.

By setting my characters in this fifty-year time-period, I needed to extensively research the events that impacted them in order to be as historically accurate as possible. These momentous changes included both religious and general feminism, especially the changes in the role of women as ordained Jewish and Protestant clergy. I devoted much of my research to an exploration of traditional Catholic convent life and the effects that radical change brought about predominantly by Vatican Council II had on Women Religious, including the rise of the Catholic Women's Ordination Movement.

The books I consulted include:

- *Women Who Would be Rabbis: 1889-1985* - Pamela S. Nadell
- *Deborah, Golda, and Me: Being Female and Jewish in America* – Letty Cottin Pogrebin
- *The New Nuns: Racial Justice and Religious Reform in the 1960's* - Amy L. Koehlinger
- *Judaism and the New Woman* - Rabbi Sally J. Priesand
- *The Sacred Calling: Four Decades of Women in the Rabbinate* - Edited by Rabbis Rebecca Einstein Schorr and Alysa Mendelson Graf.
- *Women & Religion in America: A Documentary History*, Volume 3, 1900-1968 – Edited by Rosemary Radford Reuther and Rosemary Skinner
- *The Catholic Revolution: New Wine, Old Wineskins, and the Second Vatican Council* - Andrew Greeley
- *Sisters in Arms: Catholic Nuns Through Two Millennia* - Jo Ann Kay McNamara
- *A People Adrift: The Crisis of the Roman Catholic Church in America* - Peter Steinfels
- *The Habit: A History of the Clothing of Catholic Nuns* - Elizabeth Kuhns.

- *Women of Spirit: Female Leadership in the Jewish and Christian Traditions* - Edited by Rosemary Radford Reuther and Eleanor McLaughlin
- *American Women in Ministry: A History of Protestant Beginning Points* - Virginia Lieson Brereton and Christa Ressmeyer Klein
- *The Church and the Second Sex* - Mary Daly
- *Women in the Pulpit: Is God an Equal Opportunity Employer?* - Priscilla and William Proctor
- *The Nuns* – Marcelle Bernstein
- *Women of the Wall: Claiming Sacred Ground at Judaism's Holy Site* - Edited by Phyllis Chesler and Rivka Haut
- *Unveiled: The Hidden Lives of Nuns* – Cheryl L. Reed
- *Sisters: Catholic Nuns and the Making of America* – John J. Fialka
- *When Everything Changed: The Amazing Journey of American Women from 1960 to the Present* - Gail Collins
- *When They Come for Us We'll be Gone: The Epic Struggle to Save Soviet Jewry* – Gal Beckerman
- *The Faithful: A History of Catholics in America* – James M. O'Toole
- *Double Crossed: Uncovering the Catholic Church's Betrayal of American Nuns* – Kenneth A. Briggs
- *No Turning Back* – Barbara Ferraro and Patricia Hussey, with Jane O'Reilly
- *Changing Habits: A Memoir of the Society of the Sacred Heart* – V.V. Harrison
- *Standing Again at Sinai: Judaism from a Feminist Perspective* - Judith Plaskow
- *On Being A Jewish Feminist: A Reader* - Rachel Adler and Paula Hyman
- *WomanSpirit Rising: A Feminist Reader in Religion* - Edited by Carol P. Christ and Judith Plaskow
- *Lesbian Nuns: Breaking Silence* – Nancy Manahan
- *The Struggle for Soviet Jewry in American Politics: Israel Versus the American Establishment* – Fred A. Lazin

Mona: 1958

AM I GOOD enough?

Will I ever be good enough?

Is it only the sin of pride making me think I'm worthy of becoming a sister?

I lie motionless in the silent darkness, a white muslin curtain hanging from the high ceiling separating me from the other new postulants. Room in my tiny space only for this narrow bed with its hard mattress and for the small chest to hold the few belongings I brought into the convent this morning.

Never have I been so frightened. Never have I felt so alone.

But I know my Lord Jesus will protect me and Mother Mary will watch over me. Yes, for the rest of my life as a sister I will lose myself in God. I will let the Holy Spirit touch me and guide me.

I will find certainty.

I will find peace.

Sandra: 1945

Is this the eye of God?

The eye is the only thing that is a real picture in windows in the big room in our temple where we have our services and Sunday School assemblies and where Rabbi Kahn gives his long boring speeches. I am always looking up at this scary eye in the window that stares right back at me as I wiggle in my seat waiting for the services or assemblies or Rabi Kahn's long boring speeches to end.

Even though I'm only five years old, I'm pretty sure it's the eye of God. Can't hide from it. I'm pretty sure it watches me all the time. Probably will watch me for my whole life.

The scary eye can see and remember everything I do. It wants me to be a good girl. It wants me to always be a good Jew.

Yes, scary eye, I promise.

I will always be a good Jew.

Forever and ever.

Liz: 1960

WHY?

How could God allow this to happen?

Hunched under my umbrella in the pounding rain, I stand at Jack's grave praying I can find the strength to sustain myself. Hoping I can restore my religious faith shaken that night two weeks ago when a drunk driver crossed the median line on the hilly New Hampshire road and instantly killed my seventeen-year-old brother.

Now my life is in turmoil. I want to reverse time, to go back to my safe existence where I lived an orderly life in an orderly world governed by an orderly and logical and predicable God.

Suddenly I feel an overwhelming sensation of peace. I turn and try to flee from Jack's gravesite and from this mysterious feeling, but something compels me to stay. This strange feeling…is it Jack, or maybe Jesus or God, telling me to accept my brother's death? To get on with my life?

Is this God calling me to serve Him?

I am somehow transformed.

At this moment I choose to serve God.

1990

WomanSpeak: Voices of Women of Faith
cordially invites you to honor the outstanding contributions to the advance-
ment of women in religion and in society by celebrating the lives of

Sister Mona Sullivan

Rabbi Sandra Miller-Brownstein

The Reverend Elizabeth Adams

As we bestow upon them
The WomanSpeak Let My Voice Be Heard Award

March 22, 1990

The Grand Ballroom
The Plaza Hotel
Fifth Avenue at 59th Street
New York, New York

Cocktail reception: 6:00 p.m.   Dinner: 7:00 p.m.

$100 per person
Table of ten: $900
RSVP to Norma Appelbaum,
Executive Director, WomenSpeak:Voices of Women of Faith
212-679-4876

Dietary laws will be observed.

Part I

Mona: 1990, 1958

THE ELEGANT GRAND Ballroom of the Plaza Hotel is dark except for the dais table.   I sit in the center of the table next to the podium, leaning slightly to my left to avoid being captured in the spotlight because now I realize I'm not dressed correctly for this posh dinner.

I've never known how to dress. Always depended on my best friend Kathleen to help me, especially after Momma died. Then when I took the veil I didn't have to worry about what to wear because all the girls in the convent looked the same. That was the whole idea. Part of our lesson in humility, Mother Patricia Luke always said. Back when we called her Mother Patricia Luke. Back before she was Sister Phyllis. Before she was Phyllis Wartofski.

As the waiters pour coffee and tea and deliver chocolate mousse, the well-dressed president of this organization wearing what I am sure is a real diamond pin on her expensive black suit rises from her seat. She waits patiently for the large crowd to quiet, then begins to speak.

"I want to welcome all of you to the annual banquet of WomanSpeak: Voices of Women of Faith." She pauses, looks out at the crowd. "The purpose of our organization is to help women find and assert their voices in their lives and in their careers in the field of religion. Tonight we honor three outstanding individuals who have truly found their voices.

"Each has been a pioneer," the president continues, "breaking down boundaries, struggling to shatter old stereotypes in their respective faiths. But this can often be a frightening endeavor. In doing so, these three women have confronted anger and hostility from others that this risk-taking can engender because these activities shake up the religious power structure, the traditional male hierarchy thought to be the natural order of things ordained by God. Each woman we honor tonight has forged new role models for future generations of women following in her footsteps. Each carved a path breaking career for herself, beginning her endeavors at a time when women in the clergy were rare birds and sisters in the Catholic Church knew their place and didn't speak out. The lives of our three honorees reflect the momentous changes in both society at large and in their faiths, as well as in the lives of all women throughout these years."

My mind begins to wander, and I gaze around the room. I see Vivian and Sluggie and Janet and Muriel and Joe and Peggy and David at that nearby table. So sorry Dad didn't live to see this day.

"Our first honoree tonight is Sister Mona Sullivan," the woman announces.

I focus again and smile at the speaker. After all these years, I can still hear Dad saying, "Smile, Mona, whatever happens. Keep smiling, no matter what."

"Sister Mona took her final vows in 1966," the president of WomanSpeak is saying. "And for the next twenty-four years her life as a sister has reflected the turbulence of the rapidly-changing Catholic Church and of our rapidly-changing society."

Yes. Turbulence. How did it happen? Turbulence -- and recognition like this award -- this was not what I had planned.

All I ever wanted was to find stillness and calm. So I could quiet my mind and receive the Holy Spirit. So I could really hear God. So I could listen to God and serve Him. All I wanted was certitude and calm and peace and quiet.

My first night as a postulant, lying in my bed in my little cubicle, alone and frightened, I convinced myself I would find certitude and calm and peace and quiet in my convent. How could I know then how wrong I was?...

...Mona Sullivan said her goodbyes to Sluggie, Peggy, Rory, and Muriel that morning before they left for school. After the half-hour subway ride, now she stood with her father and the other new postulants and their families gathered on the front lawn of the small convent in Queens nervously sipping punch and nibbling on small tasteless chocolate chip cookies.

She was already dressed in the mid-calf-length black dress with white collar and cuffs, short black cape, narrow black bow tie, small black cap, black heavy hose, and black oxford shoes she would wear until she was professed as a novice. Only the short mesh black veil was missing. A sister seated behind a long table nearby handed her one from a stack of folded veils.

Mother Patricia Luke approached Mona and her father. "Hello, Mona," she said. "Welcome."

"Thank you, Reverend Mother."

She turned to Patrick Sullivan. "And you must be our proud father."

He nodded.

The Mother Superior turned back to Mona. "Well, my dear, the day has finally come. Let me help you with your veil." Mother Patricia Luke shook open the veil and secured it onto Mona's cap with large pins.

Mona reached up to her head and touched the veil with her fingers. It was a symbol of her separation from the world. Proof she really was going into the convent. Proof she was really leaving her old life forever.

She saw tears in Dad's eyes when he stared at the veil. He faked a cough, lowered his head. Tears, this would never do, Mona knew he was thinking. Not in front of a woman. A sister, no less, the convent's Mother Superior. Mona had never seen her father cry, not even when Momma passed away. This was the way he'd been raised. Irishmen didn't cry. But now he knew he wouldn't be able to see her for at least three months. Perhaps longer. That was harsh.

"Seems like only yesterday she was my baby," Patrick Sullivan mumbled to Mother Patricia Luke. "My girl is so young…only eighteen. A good daughter…a big help looking after the other kids and doing the household chores. You know her mother passed in childbirth three years ago?"

"Yes, a tragedy. Well, God has his reasons, Mr. Sullivan. It is not given to us to understand."

"And my Mona kept up so well with her studies, too. Just graduated first in her class."

"Yes, Mona is a good girl, and very intelligent. She will be an excellent sister. But it's a difficult road, Mr. Sullivan, especially at first. She must pray for strength. You and your other children must also pray to God to give her strength and courage."

Mother Patricia Luke turned away from them, clapped her hands to get everyone's attention, and announced, "Time for our class photograph."

All ten of the new postulants entering the convent together that afternoon gathered into a group and smiled bravely as a young sister snapped three photographs. Out of the corner of her eye Mona saw Dad and the other parents taking photos with their own cameras. Another sister shook a brass bell.

"Line up, girls," Mother Patricia Luke ordered. "It's time to go inside."

Patrick Sullivan clasped Mona's hand and whispered, "Smile, Mona." He patted her shoulder. "Always remember, keep smiling no matter what."

"I will, Dad. I will. Goodbye for now."

Mona squeezed her father's hand, clutched her small suitcase, joined the line of nine other girls in her band of new postulants, and, smiling bravely as Dad had instructed, marched through the iron convent gates into the grey stone Gothic building.

"You said goodbye to your families this morning," Mother Patricia Luke told the girls at the orientation session in the convent's parlor after a quick lunch. "Now you must forget about them. This is why you are not allowed to bring photographs with you. You must not speak of your families or of your past lives to each other here because you must break your attachments to the outside world."

The new postulants listening to their Mother Superior sat up straight on the hard wooden folding chairs, hands folded in their laps. The young women had already been warned to never let their backs touch the backs of their chairs.

Mona stared at the woman who would now have total control over her life. She estimated Mother Patricia Luke to be about forty years old. The same age as Momma when she died. Tall. Momma would have described the woman as big boned, her polite way of saying someone was overweight. But in spite of her large body accentuated by the formal habit she wore, the Reverend Mother glided slowly and effortlessly back and forth in front of the new postulants, her arms folded beneath her scapular. She spoke quietly but firmly with a flat Midwestern accent.

Mona glanced around the room. Faded flowered wallpaper. A frayed Persian carpet. Two worn couches and five groupings of mismatched easy chairs. Hanging over the stone mantel of the fireplace a portrait of Our Blessed Lady holding the chubby rosy-cheeked baby Jesus. A heavy scent of furniture and floor wax blended with the odor of cabbage and corned beef prepared in the kitchen for the lunch they had just finished.

"You must die unto your old selves," Mother Patricia Luke was saying. "So you may be trained to serve our Lord."

But as Mona struggled to fall asleep later that night she wondered if she could ever be trained to serve her Lord.

No, she was selfish. Proud. Worst of all, weak. Maybe too weak to live without Dad and her brothers and sisters. Maybe too weak to give up marriage and motherhood. And her girlfriends. She'd miss their giggling and their movies and parties and gossip about boys and the Elvis Presley records they played in secret because their parents warned the outrageous singer would lead them straight into a life of mortal sin. She'd miss her best friend Kathleen Reilly's experiments with Mona's long red hair, pin curling and then brushing it into the latest style. And attempting to remove Mona's freckles with the latest magic concoction Kathleen swore would work. Mona would miss the bright red or orange or pink lipstick from Woolworth's she and her friends smeared on their lips after they left their houses in the morning and rubbed off with a tissue before the sisters at school saw them. She'd miss the cigarettes she and Kathleen smoked every day on their way to and from school.

Well, no more cigarettes, Mona.

She had smoked her final Lucky Strike last night when she and Kathleen snuck out to her back porch out of sight of the others at the big sendoff party Kathleen's mother threw for her.

"You'll never be able to give up ciggies," Kathleen warned as Mona took her last furtive puffs.

"Yes, I will. I gave them up for Lent this year, so I know I can. Watch. This is my last one." Mona took a final long drag, closing her eyes to savor it. She and Kathleen ground out their cigarettes in the ashtray her friend usually hid under her bed. "It's a small sacrifice to make for following my dream. A small sacrifice for our Lord."

"You'll never be a good sister, Mona. You'll get yourself in real bad trouble. Maybe not right away, but someday. You'll never do the vow of obedience. You'll end up leaving the religious life and disgracing your family."

"No, I won't leave. Never."

"Besides, your dad needs you at home."

Kathleen had hit a sensitive spot. Since Momma had passed away Mona had cooked the family's meals, done all the washing, and cleaned their three-story house. She had nursed her siblings and her father when they were ill. Helped her brothers and sisters with their homework. All while keeping up with her own schoolwork and stealing time with her friends.

"Dad says he can manage the other kids alone," she answered Kathleen with more certainty than she felt. "Since we gave up eating meat two other nights besides Fridays we have the money to hire Mrs.Wizniewski."

"The Polish widow from down the street with that ghastly mole on her chin? Huge hair sticking out of it? Ugh. I can barely stand to look at her," Kathleen said.

"She'll cook and clean. Dad says he can get along without me."

"He's lying, Mona, because he knows this is what you want."

Maybe Kathleen was right. Maybe Dad did need her at home, in spite of his assurances. Maybe she *was* doing the wrong thing.

Mona's English teacher Sister Martha Joseph had also expressed her doubts. "Of course we want as many girls as possible to go into religious life," she said when Mona asked her to write a letter of recommendation necessary for admission to the order. "But there's a bit of a stubborn streak in you, Mona. The vow of obedience is the most important thing, you know. And the most difficult. You will have much to overcome in your formation."

"I know, Sister Martha Joseph."

"Why did you decide to take the veil? Is it just because your mother passed?"

"I wanted to serve our Lord way before Momma died. Since the day of my first communion when I was seven. I felt so close to our Savior that day. So peaceful, even though I was just a little girl. I long to find that peace again, keep it for my whole life."

"The religious life is not as easy as Sister Maria Del Rey makes it out to be in her book *Bernie Becomes a Nun*," Sister Martha Joseph warned Mona. "I'm afraid you girls think becoming a sister is romantic. It is not. Far from it. You must learn to keep The Rule. You must submit yourself completely to it. To the Mother Superior who represents The Rule and who herself submits to the bishop, who in turn submits to the rule of Rome, who follows St. Peter and our Lord Himself. Are you prepared to do this without questions, Mona, no matter how senseless what is asked of you may seem at the time?"

"I will try my best."

Sister Martha Joseph and the sister who headed Mona's school wrote letters of recommendation for her. So did her parish priest Father Connell, who assured Mona she was well suited to the religious life. She went on a weekend retreat to another order in Ohio to see if she liked it better, but she chose the one in Queens because it was a teaching order and because it was closer to home.

"I want to be near my family," she explained to Kathleen. "Though I know I won't be allowed to see them often."

Sister Martha Joseph helped her complete the detailed application form and answer the questionnaire accompanying it. She wrote a brief autobiography explaining why she wanted to take the veil. She passed her physical examination. The doctor wrote a statement saying Mona Sullivan possessed the necessary mental ability to enter religious life. She passed her five-hour behavior assessment and her family and background check. At the end of this long procedure Mother Patricia Luke interviewed her.

Mona was overjoyed the day she received her letter of acceptance to the order.

Fortunately by the late 1950s Mona's family was not required to provide a financial dowry. Her father didn't have extra money to give to the church, and in earlier times this might have prevented her acceptance into the convent. Now Mona would have to bring with her only her postulant's outfit and enough black wool serge to sew her habit and muslin for her veil when she became a novice. In addition, following the imagery of becoming a bride of Christ, she'd need to bring what was called a trousseau. For her community that included underclothing, nightgowns, shoes, rubber boots, an umbrella, blankets, sheets, towels, soap, toothbrushes, toothpaste, bedroom slippers, a bible, dictionary, rosary, and other personal supplies to last at least two years. Mona would have to sew nametags into every item of clothing and linens.

"I'll help you do the nametags," her sister Muriel had offered. "You're hopeless at sewing."

Although Mona's family and friends were proud of her, her friend Kathleen was still skeptical.

"You'll never make it, Mona," she warned one last time.

"You just don't want to lose me."

"You've been my best, best, best friend for my whole life. Since we played nun together when we were three years old. How do you expect me to feel?"

"We'll be able to see each other after the first couple of months," Mona assured her.

But now as the hours crept by that first night in the convent, as Mona lay in her bed alone in the small cubicle motionless in the silent darkness, a white muslin curtain hanging from the high ceiling separating her from the other new postulants, doubts overwhelmed her. Maybe Kathleen was right. Maybe she didn't have a vocation.

And she needed a cigarette. How she needed a cigarette, would give anything for a cigarette.

No, Mona, no more ciggies. Never again for the rest of your life. Try to go to sleep.

But sleep was out of the question now. Mona's mind raced as she lay in the darkness recalling how she had reached this moment, how she had come to be here in this dark tiny rectangular space big enough only for her uncomfortable bed and for the small chest to hold the few belongings she had brought into this big cold grey building.

Mona thought back to her first communion. She had felt so close to her Savior, wearing the white lace dress and veil she loved Momma had sewn for her. She thought about her special personal relationship with the Blessed Virgin Mary, telling her things before she went to sleep every night she'd never tell another living soul, certainly not Father Connell. Mona remembered how she struggled to memorize her catechism for her confirmation. Thought about the awe she felt every time she went to Mass.

It was so quiet here in this tiny space in the convent. So different from the struggle and conflict of the world and the commotion of Mona's family and the confusion of growing up. Things always changing. Why was this, she had frequently asked herself. Why can't things just stay the same? Why can't we all just be still and quiet and happy and at peace?

Mona's childhood and teen years had been just one big blast of change and confusion and noise. Sluggie screaming when he was a toddler craving attention from Momma as she tried to get dinner on the table for seven hungry people. Muriel wailing when Dad spanked her for marking up their living room wall with a purple crayon. Rory sobbing inconsolably the day his pet gerbil died. Dad shouting at her the night she went to Kathleen's Halloween party with Frankie Ryan and came home after eleven even though she knew she was supposed to be home by ten.

Sister Martha Joseph and her friend Kathleen were right. She was rebellious. And disobedient. Like the time she stayed out too late with Frankie Ryan. She didn't even like Frankie Ryan. His breath smelled of onions and his hands were clammy when they danced. If Mona couldn't properly obey Dad, how could she ever properly obey God? How could she ever obey the sisters and their strict rules…?

…The sudden clanging of a loud bell jolted Mona back into the present.

Five a.m. already? Impossible. She hadn't slept at all. She was exhausted. How would she ever get through the day?

Mona heard the other girls stirring and a novice shaking a hand bell from outside their curtained cubicles calling out, "Blessed be to God." As Mother Patricia Luke had instructed at their orientation session yesterday, the new postulants responded together, "Blessed be His holy name."

She got out of bed, stood by it for a moment, then knelt in prayer. "Please, Our Blessed Lady. Please, God," she whispered. "Please my Lord and Savior Jesus Christ. Help me. Grant me the courage and strength I need. I am so scared. I feel so alone. God, are you listening to me? Are You here with me? Tell me I've made the right choice. That I'm doing the right thing, that this is Your plan for me. Tell me You really want me to leave my life and my friends and Dad and my four brothers and sisters who need me so much since Momma passed away."

Mona received no answer to her prayer, but reciting it calmed her. She rose, armed with new courage. She was ready to begin her new life. Her real life. What she had hoped and planned and prayed for. She would be with her Lord Jesus and with the Blessed Mother and with God. This was what God wanted for her. She was sure. Yes, Mona was sure this was her special destiny.

She would find answers to all her questions.

She would find certainty.

She would find peace.

Sandra: 1990, 1945

I PICK MY way carefully through the darkness of the Plaza Hotel's elegant ballroom until I reach the head table on the dais.

A woman is speaking into the microphone, probably the president of WomanSpeak. She's welcoming everyone. Good. The formal program's just beginning. Made it just in time. It's not my fault I'm late. Not my fault Isaac Strauss finally died and I had to take a later plane so I could officiate at his funeral. Or that heavy air traffic forced the pilot to circle LaGuardia for an hour.

I slip into the empty seat at the dais table as unobtrusively as possible. Drink from the water glass. I reach up and brush my hair out of my eyes. It's a mess, as usual. I tried to freshen my makeup in the taxi, but it was too dark. And my contacts are killing me. I need to take them out and give my poor tired eyes a rest. Well, you can't, Sandy. Make the best of it. Deal with it.

I compose myself and peer through the darkness at the round tables below the dais. Yes, I can see Mom and Joanie and Carolyn.

Robert should be here. He could have rearranged his important meeting with those clients or pawned them off onto another partner. But that meeting was just an excuse. My husband didn't want to come. He says I don't deserve this award. Says I'm a fraud and a hypocrite.

He's probably right. I have been living a lie. I have failed. I haven't kept the promise I made to that eye in the stained-glass window in my synagogue when I was a child that I'd be a good Jew forever. I've tried to keep that promise to that frightening eye, but it's been a long and challenging journey.

A waiter skillfully negotiates a path through the tables and brings my dinner. He sets down the plate carefully in front of me and refills my water glass.

I whisper my thanks. I try to eat discreetly because the others have finished their meals. I raise my eyes between bites of food to focus on the president of WomanSpeak and what she is saying. She's talking about me now. I smile out at the crowd modestly.

"Our second honoree tonight, Rabbi Miller-Brownstein, was only the sixth woman ordained by the Reform movement's Hebrew Union College-Jewish Institute of Religion in New York City." The president stops, looks at me, as if for verification. I nod, and she continues. "Rabbi Miller-Brownstein completed her five-year rabbinical training and was ordained in 1977. She has served congregations in Philadelphia, Milwaukee and Chicago, at the same time becoming an activist in the Soviet Jewry movement and a prominent pioneer in Jewish Feminism. All, mind you, while successfully balancing her role of wife and mother with a challenging career on the pulpit and on the national and international religious scene."

Successfully balanced? Hah! If they only knew. Constantly exhausted. I could work twenty-four hours a day and still never be finished. And never enough time for Robert and the kids.

Why did I choose such a difficult path? All I wanted to do was carry on my Jewish heritage. To be a good Jew. To keep my promises to the eye in the stained-glass window.

It all started with that frightening eye. Yes. I blame it all on that eye...

...Even though she was only five years old, Sandy Miller was pretty sure the eye in the stained glass window in her temple in her hometown of Elmville, Illinois was the eye of God.

So, Sandy reasoned, since Rabbi Kahn says God sees us all the time and knows everything we do and wants us to be good, for sure the eye in the window with all the pretty colors saw her and knew how bad she was sometimes. Well, of course she was better than the bratty boys in Sunday School who punched each other and giggled all through class. All the girls were better than those horrible boys.

But Sandy could be bad, too. Like yesterday when she was burying the turtle she bought at the dime store in a hole she dug in the backyard and the icky thing started to move so she knew it wasn't dead yet but she buried it real quick anyway. Did God see her do this? Did the eye in the window escape from Sandy's temple and follow her home? Did it watch her in the Millers' backyard when she dug a hole with a wooden spoon behind the old maid's rhubarb patch and threw in the turtle even though she knew it wasn't dead yet?

Now the president of the temple with his big booming scary voice was talking. Sandy stopped looking at the eye in the window. She straightened up her body and looked at the president, who always came to every Sunday School assembly to talk to the kids, no matter what.

"Page ten, boys and girls," the temple president shouted in his booming voice. "Let us sing together the song on page ten."

Sandy knew this man with the scary loud voice got to be the president of their temple because he was rich. His daughter got to be Queen Esther at the Purim carnival because he gave so much money to the temple. That's what Mommy and Daddy told Sandy when she complained she never got to be Queen Esther. Sandy's daddy couldn't give a lot of money to the temple because he didn't have a real job yet. He was still going to school at the big university in Elmville to learn how to teach kids in college and to learn how to be a sociologist. Whatever a sociologist was. Probably Daddy didn't want to be president of the temple anyway. Too busy going to school.

The president scared all the kids in Sunday school because his voice was very loud, and he was always shouting at them. Was God's voice loud and scary like this? Sandy wondered. Was this God talking, not the president? Did that loud scary voice come from the eye in the window?

The kids all sang the song the president chose, sounding terrible, as usual. They hated the songs the president told them to sing. None of them could sing anyway.

When the kids were finished trying to sing, the president said, "Boys and girls, now Rabbi Kahn wants to talk to you for a few minutes about something very, very important before we adjourn. Remember, there's no Sunday School next week."

"Yea!" the bratty boys shouted.

The rabbi got up from his seat, moved to the center of the big room, and held up his hand to quiet the bratty boys down. The president with the scary voice sat down on one of the hard benches in the front row.

Sandy didn't like Rabbi Kahn. He was always patting her on her head and saying, "Little Sandra Miller." Then he would sort of laugh his creepy laugh, "Heh, heh, heh."

When Sandy told Mommy and Daddy she didn't like Rabbi Kahn, Daddy said that's because she probably sensed that he didn't like kids.

"Of course, he has to pretend he likes kids," Daddy explained to her, "because rabbis are supposed to like them. Educating youngsters about our religion is an important part of a rabbi's job."

Mommy told Sandy that Rabbi Kahn was just a student rabbi. "Our temple can't afford a real rabbi," she explained. "There aren't enough Jews in Elmville. Most of the Jews in Illinois live in Chicago. All we can afford is for Rabbi Kahn to come every two weeks from Cincinnati, where he goes to a special school. Rabbinical school."

"You mean he's going to school to learn how to be a real rabbi, like Daddy's going to school to learn how to be a real college teacher?"

Mommy laughed. "Yes, Sandy. You've got it."

"So, if Rabbi Kahn isn't a real rabbi," Sandy said slowly as she thought about what her mother had just said, "why do we have to listen to him?"

"He's a brilliant young man," Daddy answered. "He'll be an ordained rabbi soon. So you have to listen to him. Even though the bible stories are all fairy tales. Of course, fairy tales are very important. Story telling is important in all societies. But remember, Sandy, the stories aren't true. Most sociologists don't believe in religion, God, or in bible stories. At least I don't."

"So," Sandy answered, "if those boring stories aren't true, why do we have to learn about them? Why do we even have to go to Sunday School? I hate it."

"To learn about your Jewish heritage," Daddy said.

Sandy didn't know what "Jewish heritage" was, and she didn't know what a sociologist was. But she knew being a sociologist must be something important, and that's why Daddy was still in school even though he was a grownup. To learn how to be a real one. And this was why the Miller family had no money. Why she couldn't ever have any new dresses of her own and had to wear her sister Joanie's hand-me-downs. Sandy hated this because Joanie was four years older than she was, and by the time Sandy grew into her clothes, they were already old fashioned or worn out. And it was why Mommy sewed her own clothes even though she was so busy typing things for the college students. So she could save money so she could buy food because the Miller family had no money because Daddy didn't have his degree yet.

"What's a degree, Daddy?" Sandy finally asked one night at supper.

"I'm getting what's called a Ph.D.," he explained.

"What's that?"

"It means piled higher and deeper," Mommy said.

Her parents laughed, but Sandy didn't get the joke.

"It's like a license to teach in a university," Daddy explained after he stopped laughing. "You have to have it if you want to have an academic career. And once I get it, if I ever get it."

"You'll get it Leon," Mommy said. "Someday soon."

Daddy sighed. "God, I hope you're right, Helen. Sometimes I'm not so sure." He turned to Sandy again. "Well, honey, once I get my Ph.D. our lives will change forever. You girls and your mother will watch me march down the street near the big university wearing a cap and gown. And we'll have more money because I'll be promoted in the sociology department to Assistant Professor, or else I'll get a good job at another university."

"And then maybe you won't have to spend so much time in your little room reading and typing so loud sometimes it wakes me up at night?" Sandy asked.

"I'll have to work just as hard," Daddy said. "Maybe even harder."

Even though Daddy complained when Sandy interrupted him while he was typing in his little room, he always let her come in to talk to him anyway. Sometimes he let her sit on his lap and punch the keys on his black shiny typewriter. When Daddy wasn't reading or typing in his little room he taught classes about sociology to students in the university. He hated to teach them because they were the beginning classes in sociology, and Daddy said it was boring to teach beginning classes...

"…Boys and girls…"

Now Rabbi Kahn was talking to the kids in the Sunday School assembly. Sandy sat up straight on the hard bench and looked at him.

Rabbi Kahn was skinny. He was already losing his hair even though he wasn't very old, and he wore big ugly glasses. Sandy got dizzy watching him pace back and forth in front of them as he said, "Boys and girls, you need to be very quiet today because I'm going to tell you something very, very serious. I don't want any giggling or moving around in your seats. To do so would be a terrible sign of disrespect for the dead."

Now the kids could see this was for sure going to be a serious talk. So they all got quiet, even the bratty boys. Sandy glanced at the big eye in the window. Oh yes, for sure it was watching them all now. Especially her.

"Boys and girls," Rabbi Kahn said again, "we are beginning to hear stories of what the American soldiers have found out in Europe about what happened to Jews there during the war. Remember, I told you very bad things were happening to the Jews in Europe during the war, which, thank God, America has won? Remember I told you how lucky you are to be in our wonderful America where we Jews are so safe? Well, our soldiers have found camps where the Nazis put Jews from everywhere in Europe. Not nice summer camps in Michigan and Wisconsin like some of you go to. No, what we call 'concentration camps.'"

Rabbi Kahn stopped talking for a minute. Sandy thought he was going to cry, even though he was a grownup, and grownups usually didn't cry. "Many, many Jews have been killed in these camps by the Nazis," Rabbi Kahn continued, "or they died of bad diseases or because they didn't have enough food to eat. We don't know how many yet. Perhaps millions. Children just like you, too. So, boys and girls, this is why you must come to Sunday School and study your Jewish heritage. There are so few of us Jews left, especially now since the war. It's bad enough so many Jews in America are marrying Christians or don't want to be Jewish anymore. Many go to church instead of temple. And now we are finding out how many of us were slaughtered in the war in Europe."

Rabbi Kahn was walking up and down across the big room. Sandy was afraid he'd come over to her and pat her on the head and laugh and call her "little Sandra Miller." But he didn't. No. Now he was too busy being sad about the kids in Europe Sandy's mother always said were going hungry. That was why she and Joanie always had to eat up all the food on their plates. Because kids were starving in Europe.

"We must never forget our Jewish heritage," Rabbi Kahn was saying. "An evil man, Adolph Hitler, wanted to kill all of us. Thank God our brave soldiers fought hard. Thank God they won the war and defeated Hitler. Many, many people have tried to kill all of us throughout our long history. You remember how Haman in the Purim story wanted to kill all the Jews?" All the kids nodded solemnly. "We must never die out," Rabbi Kahn continued. "Each and every one of you must be Jews forever."

Sandy was only five years old, but already she knew it was hard to be a Jew, even though she wasn't really sure what a Jew was and what being one was because almost everybody in her town in Illinois and all over the world were Christians. Already Sandy knew Jews were different from everybody else, and she didn't want to be different. No, she wanted to be like everybody else. Why did she have to be different? She was afraid being a Jew might keep her from having friends. She didn't have many friends anyway, probably because her hair was straight and all the pretty girls in Elmville had curly hair. Or maybe other kids didn't like her because she wore Joanie's old hand-me-downs?

Sandy knew it was selfish and bad to not want to be a Jew just because it was hard and it made you different from almost everybody else and maybe you won't have many friends. She knew the eye in the temple window would be mad at her for not wanting to be a Jew, and so would Rabbi Kahn. So would the president of the temple with the loud scary voice. If so many Jews in Europe died in those camps and Jews were dying out anyway because Jews were marrying Christians and going to church instead of to temple, then she must be a Jew forever.

As Rabbi Kahn continued to give his long boring speech, Sandy looked up at the eye in the window again and said silently to it, "Yes, scary eye of God, I will always be a Jew. For my whole life. I will always be a good Jew. I promise."

Liz: 1990, 1960–1961

WHERE'S ALICIA?

From the dais table I look out at the ornate Plaza Hotel ballroom and peer through the dark at the round tables, searching for my best friend. Where's Alicia?

There she is, sitting with Harry at the table on the left, sipping from her glass of wine.

I look down at my empty wine glass. Would love a glass of wine, but I don't dare. I promised Father Tony. And lunch was hours ago, and I didn't get a chance to eat anything at the dais reception. Certainly don't want to drink on an empty stomach. Not the time to get looped. Not when I need to be at my best tonight, when everybody can see me sitting up here at the dais table. When you're the pastor, everybody is always scrutinizing you. You're "on" twenty-four hours a day. Especially if you're a woman.

What will I tell Alicia and Harry if I don't go back with them to their apartment tonight? Should I tell them the truth?

Alicia looks fabulous as usual, another stunning new dress and expensive understated jewelry. Probably Cartier. Probably a perfect French manicure. Harry looks great, too. He always does. Gorgeous as well as rich. Alicia hit a home run when she snagged him.

Alicia beams up at me and gives me the thumbs up sign.

After all these years she finally approves of my strange profession. My oldest friend is proud of me at last. She was so horrified when I told her, a million years ago when we were twenty years old, that I planned to be ordained.

"You've always been the world's worst prude, Liz," Alicia shouted that day thirty years ago in Edinburgh. "And now you'll be the world's worst freak…"

"…Our third honoree tonight is the Reverend Elizabeth Adams," the president of WomanSpeak announces. "One of the first women Presbyterian ministers, she was ordained in 1965. Reverend Adams currently serves the First Presbyterian Church in Stewart, Maine. But her influence has reached far beyond this charming New England town. She was active in the interreligious Soviet Jewry movement and has become an important figure in the religious feminist movement with the recent publication of her book *Lillith and Eve Revisted: New Jewish and Christian Perspectives.* Reverend Adams has been a real pioneer and an inspiring role model for the many young women who have since followed her career path."

Role model. Pioneer. Who could have predicted it? I always thought I was dull. That's what Alicia told me. Drab. Prude. No sense of adventure.

Well, I certainly turned out to be far too adventurous for my parents. They never wanted this career for me. They never wanted me to be ordained, never accepted it. They've always been embarrassed. Women preachers. An unladylike profession. Not respectable.

That's why I never told them about that day in the rain at Jack's grave. What happened to me there was neither respectable nor ladylike. No, my parents never understood my decision to be ordained because I never told them the real reason. I never told my parents about that mysterious feeling.

My mysterious calling…

…When Elizabeth Adams suddenly felt an overwhelming sensation of peace at her brother Jack's grave that day two weeks after he'd been killed on a small New Hampshire country road by a drunken driver, she tried to leave the gravesite to escape from the strange feeling. But her legs wouldn't move. She stared at the gravesite. She wondered if this strange feeling was God telling her Jack was with Him now? That her brother was happy and at peace? That she should get on with her life?

Was it God calling her to serve Him?

Liz Adams told no one what she had experienced that day. She tried to forget about it because she needed to get on with her life. She had an important decision to make immediately. She and her best friend Alicia Spencer had been planning for a year to go to the University of Edinburgh for their Junior Year Abroad. They were scheduled to leave in only a month. Should she go?

"My brother's just been killed, Alicia. How can I run off to Europe when my parents need me here?"

"But Liz, we're going to be roommates there. I don't want to go alone. Please?"

"No. I'm going to stay at BU so I can be near my mother and father and go home and see them frequently. Boston's only an hour away from New Hampshire. Not half a world away like Scotland."

Liz' mother agreed with her friend. "You must go, Elizabeth," she argued. "Alicia is counting on you. Nothing can bring our Jack back."

"I don't want to leave you now. Since Jack."

"We'll be okay. Your father and I have each other. We have our friends and our church and our faith."

It was true. Her parents' faith seemed as strong as ever in spite of their terrible loss. But Liz wondered if they really were okay. They hadn't cried since Jack's death. Dad had gone right back to work at his insurance company after the funeral as if nothing had happened, and her mother had resumed her usual activities. Her parents kept their sorrow bottled up because that's the kind of people they were. But they had to crack sometime, didn't they?

"You're young, Elizabeth," her mother added. "You can't stop living. You must go ahead with your plans."

Liz didn't know what to do, so she sought advice from their pastor, Reverend Oliver Davis. She made an appointment to see him in his office three weeks after he had officiated at Jack's funeral at their Presbyterian church packed with stunned mourners.

"You should go," he said. "I'll watch over your parents. I'll keep your mother so busy with church work she won't have time to think about Jack."

"But why?" she asked Reverend Davis. "Why did God take him away from us? A drunk driver killing a wonderful boy like Jack."

"We can't question God's motives. We can never know what's in the Almighty's mind or why we have suffering and pain in our lives. God has reasons for everything He does, Elizabeth, even if we don't understand them. Jack is with our Lord. He is at peace now. Your beloved brother has found his eternal rest. God will help you through your sorrow and grief."

"I know I'm not the only person to face this crisis of faith. Jesus and the Church Fathers and the Old Testament people struggled with the problem of evil also."

"Everyone on earth has suffered in some way," Reverend Davis reminded her. "I hope you don't think I'm callous by telling you this. There's a reason why the Book of Job is included in the Old Testament. And remember the story of the mustard seed? If we allow ourselves to love, then we must face the loss of this love, sometimes sooner rather than later. Being human and feeling love means having to feel pain, too."

Liz wanted to be convinced by Reverend Davis. She had always liked him, although she thought him a bit cold and slick, more concerned about his thick salon-cut silver gray hair and with his large LL Bean wardrobe than with communicating with his flock. His platitudes, obviously memorized well in Divinity School, didn't comfort her. But she couldn't fault Reverend Davis for not being able to console her. Even at age twenty Liz knew there weren't any satisfying rational or intellectual answers to these questions. There was so much we didn't know, so much we human beings could never fathom.

Liz decided to go to Edinburgh for the year as she and Alicia had planned.

Was it God's plan for she and Tom Hagerman to meet? Is that why she had given in to her parents and to Alicia and gone to Europe in spite of her qualms? And had God placed Liz and Tom at Melinda Martin's party? How else could they explain why they were both there, they wondered later. It couldn't just have been chance.

Melinda's party was the first and only one Tom went to in Edinburgh. His classes were at the theology school called New College near the famous Edinburgh Castle about a mile away from the main campus. He rarely came to the common room in the Old Quad where they heard about the parties students threw almost every night in their grubby flats for which sweet little Scottish landladies charged outrageous rents. Tom wandered into the common room for coffee that day because he needed a book from the library upstairs. Melinda, a big flirt, plopped down at his table, introduced herself, and invited him to her bash that night.

Liz rarely went to these rowdy parties. She felt uncomfortable because everybody drank too much and behaved badly. Just one week before Melinda's party Charlie Spitovsky had been arrested after Lynn Rankin's drunken brawl because a busload of tourists passed by at the very moment he chose to urinate on a tree. He was deported back to the States the next day.

"Come on," Alicia had begged Liz. "Come with me. Melinda's party's going to be a blast." She added sarcastically, "You can take your knitting."

"I have to study," Liz had argued.

"You're such a grind. Got to loosen up and have some fun. Have a drink once in awhile."

"I don't think those parties are fun. I don't drink because I don't like to lose control, and when you're sober and nobody else is, it's disgusting. They're worse than those frat parties at BU. You know I wouldn't be caught dead at one of those."

"God, Liz, You're such a prude."

"Because I don't make out with every boy I meet? Well, then, I guess I'm proud to be a prude."

Alicia and Melinda and some of the other American girls in Edinburgh were striving to lose their virginity during their mad European fling, shocking in those days before the era of free sex. Two roommates from Florida were making a list of their conquests, competing for the highest number. Alicia thought it was hilarious. Liz was appalled.

"You're such a prude," Alicia kept saying.

"You just don't understand my values," Liz explained to her friend.

"Yes, I do," Alicia countered. "They date back to the Middle Ages."

"Old Testament, actually."

"God, Liz, you are just hopeless. You're going to die a virgin."

"Okay, okay, I'll go to the party."

"Good. Try to look sexy. Do something with yourself for a change. Try to do something with your terrible hair."

Alicia was always attempting to spruce Liz up. Her brown hair was frizzy, so even when she tried to grow it long it just curled up more, especially when the humidity kicked in. Alicia advised her to brush it all the time, maybe that would straighten it, but brushing never helped. Alicia also constantly nagged Liz to wear those new contact lenses. Liz wouldn't because the idea of sticking something into her eyes revolted her.

For Melinda's party, Liz did allow Alicia to put her black eyeliner on her eyelids and to brush mascara on her lashes. But it didn't matter because it was so dark in Melinda's flat nobody could see Liz' face, let alone her eyes. Nobody could ever see her eyes anyway because of her thick glasses.

Soon after they arrived at the party Alicia deserted Liz, disappearing with the cute Irish guy she'd met in her psychology class. Liz stood alone in the darkness trying to look as if she fit in. She sipped a Coke in lieu of the warm Scottish ale from the barrel Melinda had ordered.

A tall, thin boy with dark brown hair trimmed neatly and heavy brown horned-rimmed glasses approached her, appearing, like Liz, to be sober.

"Tom Hagerman," he shouted, pointing to himself.

"Liz Adams," she shouted back.

"You know this Melinda?" he asked.

"Not very well. My friend talked me into coming."

He cupped his hand to his ear. "Can't hear you. Music's too loud. Let's get out of here."

Liz searched for Alicia and found her in one of the bedrooms entwined with the Irish guy.

"I'm leaving with a nice boy I met," she said. "Don't worry about me, I'm sure he'll take me home."

Alicia came up for air, grunted, and waved her away.

Tom and Liz strolled in the chilly late autumn night, then wandered into a coffee house near her flat. They ordered hot orange drinks, popular in Edinburgh at that time, a good way, Liz discovered that year, to warm your entire body. They talked all night. Discovered they were both Presbyterians.

"I plan to go to Union Theological Seminary in Manhattan after I finish Grinnell," Tom told her. "I want to have my own church." He sipped his hot orange drink. "Religion is what keeps things in moral perspective. The church is the only social institution whose purpose is to present the moral alternative."

"Hmm. I guess that's true."

"God wants us to be moral. Above the animals. We are His masterpiece of creation because we have moral sensitivity. This is why I want to preach. So I can bring out the best in others, help change the world. Spiritual changes, not just physical."

"I'm active in our church at home," Liz told him. "I teach Sunday School and work with the youth group. Last year I was in charge of collecting food and old clothing. We have a lot of poverty in New Hampshire."

They talked about God, what He could be like if He exists, which, of course, He does, or else how could you face the vicissitudes of life? They speculated about why He permitted suffering and pain. Liz told him how her brother Jack had been killed, how she couldn't understand how God allowed this. Then, before she could stop herself, she told him about the mysterious feeling that had come over her at Jack's grave. That perhaps something was telling her she should keep on living.

"I tried to ignore whatever it was, tried to shake off what happened because it just doesn't fit into my experience," she told Tom. "But I couldn't. The sense of peace was just overwhelming. I thought, this is silly, it's nothing, just my mind playing tricks on me. I'm not cut out for mystical experiences. But whatever happened that day felt real. I couldn't deny it."

Liz thought Tom would laugh at her. He didn't. Instead he kissed her gently, told her he thought God had touched her. That God wanted them to find each other.

"You really think God controls our lives?" she asked.

"You're a Presbyterian. The doctrine of predestination?"

Liz laughed. "I know, I know. But would God invade my rational orderly life this way?"

"Yes. When you least expect it."

"Perhaps." She paused. "Tom, I didn't tell you everything that happened that day. I think whatever it was, that mysterious force or energy or being, the sensation I felt at Jack's grave was also telling me to serve God. Calling me. Maybe urging me to seek ordination."

"If you're considering ordination you should take classes at the theology school here. New College is one of the best seminaries in the world. You shouldn't waste this opportunity."

"I haven't decided whether or not I'll give in to this voice. Or whatever it was. Presbyterians have been ordaining women for only five years. This would be a radical career choice, especially for someone like me. I'm too conventional. Dull, according to my best friend Alicia. I'm not sure I'd have the strength to follow such a difficult path.

"And my parents would be horrified. I've never told them what happened at Jack's grave. They think, as I do, the purpose of religion is to bring a calm structure to your life. It's not supposed to turn your life upside down. Respectable girls don't become clergywomen. Mother would say this profession is undignified for a well-brought up girl like me. She's always telling me above all I must always be a lady."

Tom laughed.

"I don't want to upset my parents. I can serve God without being ordained. Be an active layperson."

"Preaching God's word is the best way to serve Him," Tom argued. "You're a strong person, stronger than you think. And you have high standards of morality. God calls those of us with a higher moral sense to show the way to others. Very few people are blessed with this gift. Even though I've just met you I sense you are, too, Liz, if you answer His call."

"I can't believe you stayed out all night with this guy," Alicia shrieked after Liz told her all about her night with Tom a few hours later when her friend woke up. "I mean it wasn't even really a date! Are you going to go to bed with him?"

"I just met him. And Tom agrees sex should be saved for marriage. He's going to wait, too."

"Oh, my God. Leave it to you to find a male virgin. God, Liz, you're hopeless!"

As Liz thought over their special night together, she couldn't believe she had told Tom about that mystical experience at Jack's grave. She'd always been cautious in her relationships, especially with boys. She was amazed she'd been so open and trusting with a boy she had just met.

Liz and Tom studied together every day and held hands in church every Sunday morning. They went to foreign films and concerts of the Scottish National Orchestra and saw every Gilbert and Sullivan operetta in the D'Oyle Carte's repertoire when it toured Edinburgh that winter. They took a bus trip up to the Scottish Highlands and explored London over a long weekend. Much to Alicia's dismay, they always stayed in separate hotel rooms.

At first Liz scoffed at Tom's idea that she should pursue ordination. But then she realized maybe he was right. She was blessed -- or cursed, she often thought later in her life -- with a strong sense of right and wrong. That's why she was such a prude in Alicia's eyes.

As the months in Edinburgh passed, gradually Liz became comfortable with her decision. It was daring, but in time it became more natural to her. She decided God really had called her that day at Jack's grave. It had been a rather polite request, not a lightning strike like Paul's epiphany on the road to Damascus. No, hers had been a calm, respectable orderly mystical experience. If there was such a thing. Liz had always believed in a personal God, but never would she experience Him in a sudden blinding mystical flash. To Liz God was civilized order and progress. She would help Him bring civility and progress into the world.

As Tom had suggested, she decided to attend the theology classes at New College for the rest of the year.

"I'm bored learning about the Mende of Sierra Leone in my Social Anthropology class," Liz wrote to her parents, *"and I hate reading Beowulf. I'm just not cut out to be an English Lit major. You know I've always been interested in religion anyway. I'm finding Tom's classes at New College in Old Testament and Church History much more interesting than my own. The Old Testament professor is very nice and he says I'm welcome to sit in on the class. He's the private Chaplain to the Queen.*

"I love being at New College. I feel transported back in time when I walk through the narrow cobblestone streets of old Edinburgh, take a shortcut through quaint alleys the Scots call 'closes'. The statue of John Knox glares at you as you pass it to get to the front door of the theology school. We sit on hard backless benches hunched over a long table to take our notes. It's always freezing in the classrooms. There's no central heating anywhere and I wear my coat in class and wind my blue and

green striped University of Edinburgh scarf around my neck to keep warm. The pro-
fessors lecture in academic robes. Probably so they can add another layer of clothing,
though Tom tells me wearing those academic robes while they teach is a tradition here.

"I'm going to switch my major from English literature to religion when I get
home. BU has a good religion department. Is majoring in religion isn't any less practi-
cal than majoring in English lit or anthropology?"

What Liz didn't tell her parents was that she had decided to seek ordination. She didn't want to break this upsetting news to them just yet. And she didn't tell them she and Tom were on the verge of getting engaged. She was sure they'd approve of him, but she didn't want her parents to know how serious their relationship was until they met him.

In the living room of the small flat she shared with Alicia and a skinny English girl who giggled too much, sitting on the shabby brown couch in front of the electric heater in the fireplace in which they had to insert shillings to keep warm, Tom and Liz planned their future.

"After we finish college we'll go to Union Theological Seminary together to get our Bachelor of Divinity degrees," he said.

Liz nuzzled her head against Tom's shoulder. At this moment life seemed almost perfect to her.

"I'm so happy you've finally decided to be ordained, Liz. It's a great choice for you. In spite of your doubts, your faith has been made stronger by your brother's death. Don't you see? It was meant to be."

Yes. It was meant to be. Everything was settled. Her future was secure. Her life with Tom was all planned out. Everything was in order.

There would be no surprises.

Mona: 1958-1959

His Holiness Pope Pius XII died a month after Mona entered the convent. She was shocked. She couldn't imagine her Church without the steady guidance of this stern man. He had been the representative of Christ on earth for nineteen years, her entire lifetime. A few weeks later the College of Cardinals gathered at St. Peter's Basilica in Rome and chose a new pontiff to be known as Pope John XXIII.

"The new Pope is a kind and gentle man. You shouldn't worry, the Church will be in good hands," Mother Patricia Luke assured them. "You should just focus on your new lives as postulants."

The discipline for postulants was strict.

"You are on trial to see if you are fit to become novices next year," Mother Patricia Luke had explained to Mona and the other new postulants on their first day in the convent. "This is when you will take temporary vows and your real Sister Formation will begin. Now I am training you to break away from your past lives and prepare yourselves for your new ones. You are to carefully examine your reasons for taking the veil. You are to learn The Rule. There are over two thousand regulations in our canon law, all known as The Rule, all designed to bring you to a state of perfection. Obedience is the key to your Sister Formation. Our spiritual exercises are designed to assist you."

They couldn't go home unless there was a death in the family. No visitors for at least three months. They could write to and receive letters only from their immediate families, and those were to be kept to a minimum. Mother Patricia Luke read their letters before she sent them out and perused all incoming mail. Their Mother Superior allowed no radio, television set, newspapers, or magazines in the recreation room because she reported to the girls the news and world events she deemed necessary and appropriate for them to know.

Mona knew she was supposed to be psychologically and emotionally removing herself from the outside world, but she missed her father and siblings desperately. She looked forward to their letters so she could catch up on their lives.

Dad wrote that he was fine. He worked long hours in the sanitation department and was active in his labor union.

"I'm enjoying my Knights of Columbus charity work," he wrote. *"Mrs. Wizniewski makes lunches for me to take to my job and for the kids to take to school. She cooks supper every night and does the wash. Her ironing is lousy, my shirts don't come out good like when you or your mother of blessed memory ironed them. But I don't complain, no use. She's teaching Muriel to cook, but your sister will never be as good a cook as you were. Don't tell Muriel I said this, no sense in hurting her feelings. And Sluggie is still loving his baseball."*

Mona's brother Sluggie's real name was Timothy. Everyone called him Sluggie, short for Slugger, because he was such a good baseball player. Her mother had been proud of him, even though she was always nagging him to tend to his homework more and to baseball less. Baseball was his whole life.

"I hit a home run yesterday," Sluggie scrawled in his nearly illegible handwriting in his first letter to Mona. *"So we went on to win the game."*

"You still want to play for the Yankees when you grow up?" she wrote back.

"Course I do," he answered.

"Then I will pray God will grant you your dream, as He has now granted me mine," she replied. *"But just to be safe perhaps you ought to have a fallback career plan."*

The most important news Mona's family wrote was that her best friend Kathleen Reilly suddenly married her boyfriend Dickey Donovan. According to Mona's sister Muriel, Kathleen was gaining weight and her stomach expanding rapidly.

"A very premature baby, Mrs. Wizniewski says," Muriel wrote. *"A mortal sin."*

"And gossiping is a venial sin, Muriel," Mona answered in her next letter. *"Maybe even worse, I'm not sure. You better mention this to Father Connell in your next confession."*

Mona felt sorry for Kathleen. Her friend had planned an exciting life for herself. She was going to get a job in the city after she went to business school and learned typing and shorthand. Even though Manhattan was just a few subway stops away from their homes, in their experience and in their dreams it may as well have been a thousand miles away. Kathleen would live in one of those residence hotels for respectable single working girls until she could afford her own apartment. She'd be able to smoke cigarettes whenever she wanted, yes, right out in the open, away from her strict parents and the sisters at their school. She'd work until she met the perfect man. Then she'd wear a beautiful long white gown and veil in her perfect wedding and they'd move out to New Jersey so their perfect children could romp in a big backyard. Well, a baby now was lovely also.

> *"A baby is always a gift from God, isn't it?"* Mona wrote to her family. *"And Dickey Donavan is a decent boy in spite of his wayward family. Good looking, too. Kathleen gave in to temptation, which comes from our fallen nature, but don't you ever give in to it, Muriel and Peggy. Remember what Momma has taught us. Perhaps God will forgive Kathleen if she goes to confession with a pure heart and says enough Our Fathers and does her proper penance. This will be Kathleen's responsibility after Father Connell shows her the way."*

Mona would never admit it to her younger sisters that she understood the temptation her best friend had faced because she knew how wonderful the caresses of a boy could be. It only happened once to her, one Saturday in her last year of high school when she and Kathleen went to the movies. She never forgot that afternoon.

She usually did her family's wash on Saturdays, but that day Dad encouraged her to go to the movies with Kathleen instead. "You need to have a little fun once in awhile," he said. "The wash can wait until tomorrow."

"I'm meeting Dickie Donavan inside, up in the balcony," Kathleen whispered as they paid their admission. "Ma's forbidden me to see him 'cause she says his father's a lazy drunken bum. So you can never tell her I'm meeting him, Okay?"

"It's wrong to lie and use me for an excuse," Mona scolded Kathleen.

"What are you complaining about? That dreamboat Will Matthews is coming with Dickie. You get to sit with him."

Will Matthews! The cutest boy in their neighborhood. All the girls were madly in love with him, and she was going to sit next to him in the movies today. They climbed upstairs to the balcony, searched through the darkness until Kathleen found Dickie and Will Matthews sitting in the back row. Dickie grabbed Kathleen and they began to make out.

Will Matthews glanced at Mona, mumbled, "Hey, you're Mona Sullivan, right?"

He knew her name?

"My bratty brother knows your little sis Muriel."

"Oh," was all she could manage.

"Popcorn?"

They munched on stale popcorn as Mona pretended to watch the movie. She couldn't concentrate because Will leaned in so close to her she could barely breathe. Suddenly he reached his arm around Mona, pulled her to him, and kissed her. A sensation she never before experienced, sort of like electricity, ran through her body. As if under a magic spell, Mona kissed him back. Her first kiss. Then Will stuck his tongue in her mouth. A French kiss.

When Kathleen had told her about French kisses on one of their sleepovers, Mona thought they'd be disgusting. But it wasn't. No, even though Mona could sort of taste the butter in the popcorn Will had just eaten, the long wet kiss was great.

In the dark of the last row of the balcony of the movie theatre, as Will kept kissing Mona he opened the tiny buttons of her blouse. She tried to stop his hand but it was already inside her bra. His other hand was pulling up her skirt and moving up her leg.

"No," she protested.

"Come on, uh, Mona. Everybody does it. All your virtuous girlfriends." He nodded toward Kathleen and Dickie, now nearly on top of her friend.

The other girls do not do this, Mona thought. She glanced over at Kathleen and Dickie. Well, maybe Kathleen does. Not the others. But maybe they were lying to her. Maybe they did do these things with boys. Here was Kathleen, making out like mad with Dickie Donavan in the dark balcony of this movie theatre right here in front of everybody.

In her mind Mona could hear Dad asking her, "Would you jump into a lake just because all your friends did?" whenever she begged him to let her go somewhere or do something because all the other kids were going there or doing it. She'd answer "Yes," and then she and Dad would have a good laugh together. She could also hear her dead momma's voice in her mind as Will's hand stroked her body. Never let a boy touch you, Mona. It will ruin your reputation forever. There's no going back, and nobody will ever marry you. Save yourself for the holy sacrament of marriage. God will know what you have done. Remember, Mona, you can never hide from God.

"Stop it, Will," she pleaded.

"Come on, baby. Let's have a little fun."

She pulled his left hand out of her bra and wrenched herself away from the grip of his right hand. Sat upright in the seat. Smoothed down her skirt.

"Fucking cock tease," Will shouted.

Heads turned. Everyone stared at them. Mona jumped up and rushed up the aisle and down the stairs and out of the theatre and ran the mile home.

It had taken every ounce of her physical and emotional strength to resist this handsome popular boy that afternoon. Although she was angry with Will because he never even looked her way again, Mona had to admit his kisses and caresses had been wonderful. These were the feelings and sensations her girlfriends talked about. That Momma hinted at before she died. The feelings and emotions you got married for and had children for and made all the other sacrifices for, Momma always said.

But these feelings were also frightening and overwhelming, and Mona didn't want to be scared and confused. She wanted to feel secure and calm. She yearned to be at peace with herself and with God. That's why she had decided to take the veil.

Well, it didn't matter now because now Mona was in the convent. All those confusing feelings and sensations were behind her. Dead to her, in the past. She'd take her temporary vow of chastity when she became a novice and her final vow of chastity when she became a fully professed sister. It would be a relief. Never again would she have to feel this uncertainty and anxiety.

Now Mona didn't have time to think about love or sex. She was too busy and too exhausted.

After the postulants knelt in prayer by their beds at five a.m., they waited in line in silence to use the toilet in the bathroom down the long corridor. In the darkness of their own sleeping spaces the girls dressed quickly. They walked to the chapel for the morning meditation and prayers, then filed into the refectory to eat their breakfast of oatmeal and hot water, the only hot liquid allowed.

Their work assignments changed every week because, as Mother Patricia Luke had explained, she needed to constantly shuffle their duties so they wouldn't fall into a comfortable routine. One week Mona would mend or wash and iron bed linens. The next she might work in the kitchen. Every day they cleaned the toilets and staircases and mopped and waxed the floors because their community was too small to have what in those days were called "house nuns," sisters who only did menial housework. If Mona was lucky she got to polish the silver candlesticks and carefully dust the Stations of the Cross in their chapel.

These mindless repetitive chores were designed, Mother Patricia Luke explained, to free their minds so they could be open to God. The convent's bells announcing when it was time to move on to their next duty regulated their entire routine. Their full schedule of work was interrupted only for a fifteen-minute lunch and five other prayer periods throughout the day. They prayed for a total of six hours each day. Whenever the parish priest Father Vertucci visited the convent, he heard their confessions if they had fasted the required three hours beforehand. After supper they were allowed a half-hour recreation period in their community room, but Mother Patricia Luke gave them special sewing projects to do at that time so they wouldn't be idle. They meditated for an hour before Compline, their last prayer session in the chapel at 8 p.m. Then they sank onto their cots for lights out at nine after a short final bedside prayer on their knees and after they had questioned themselves, what they called *examens*, to ascertain if they had committed any sin or infraction of the rules that day.

Mona especially enjoyed working in the convent's small garden in the inner courtyard where they grew vegetables to supplement those donated by parents of the students in their parish schools. Those contributions and what they could grow in the garden helped feed their community of forty women. Each convent was responsible for its own budget, and they were dependent on the meager earnings of their teaching sisters who turned over their salaries to the order. Mother Patricia Luke was always telling them how tight their finances were.

But Mona's gardening assignment didn't last long. She knew she was in trouble when she saw a note in her mailbox from Mother Patricia Luke. A slip in the mailbox from the Mother Superior always meant trouble.

"You will no longer be permitted to work in the garden, Mona," Mother Patricia Luke said sternly when Mona hurried to her office as she had been instructed in the note.

"Why not, Reverend Mother?"

"Why not?" Mother Patricia Luke repeated. "You are asking me 'why not'?" She rose from the chair behind her desk and walked slowly toward Mona. "You are not permitted to question the decisions I make for you. I carry out the policies from Rome, from the hierarchy of our Church, which is the embodiment of our Lord Jesus Christ. Through my Grace of Office my word is as though you are receiving the word of God Himself. I will make every decision for you until you come under the training of Novice Mistress Sister Agnes Brigid. Is this clear?"

"Yes, Reverend Mother."

"I will tell you this. Yesterday when you were weeding the garden I saw you very nearly spoke to the man who delivers our milk as he passed through the courtyard. You know we do not talk to seculars."

"He asked me a question, Reverend Mother. I did not want to be impolite."

"You must never answer back. Thankfully you caught yourself at the last moment. Also, your walk was not properly modest. I need to remove you from all temptation. Most importantly, I noticed you were taking pride in your gardening work. Is this not correct? You were being singular. All sin stems from the sin of pride, Mona. You exist just for the community. You work here as a postulant for the community, not for your enjoyment. You are free to leave any time you wish, without even giving a reason, because you are only a postulant. But if you stay, you must fit completely into our community and conform to The Rule. This is the purpose of the Sister Formation you will undergo in earnest when -- or should I say *if* -- you are accepted into the novitiate."

"I don't think she's going to ask you to leave," her new friend Luella McBride assured her that night during recreation period when Mona asked her if she thought Mother Patricia Luke was giving her a warning. "She likes you, I can tell, though she can't show it."

Luella, whose sleeping cubicle was next to Mona's, was the one real friend she had made in the convent so far. It wasn't easy to make friends here because it was nearly impossible to have private conversations. Mona's order didn't operate under the complete Rule of Silence, as many others at that time did. But the girls could speak to each other just twice during the day, after lunch and during their recreation period after supper, and then only in groups of at least three. They couldn't talk during their meals. Instead, as they ate they listened to one of the novices read from scripture or from the writings of the Church Fathers or the saints. During their work assignments they could speak only when necessary to carry out their tasks, and then softly and using as few words as possible. Of course they were silent during their prayer and meditation sessions. They could not talk at all after the lights out at the nine p.m. bedtime, a period known as The Great Silence. They were forbidden to enter another postulant's cubicle and were not allowed to touch each other, even if they were joking.

Three months after Mona entered the convent, one morning after breakfast she noticed two of the girls in her class were not in the refectory.

"Where are Antonia and Evelyn?" Mona asked Luella that night during recreation period.

Mona's friend put her fingers to her lips, moved closer to her. "Gone," she whispered. "Particular Friendship. Even though Mother Patricia Luke warned them, they disobeyed her. I heard Antonia sobbing in her cubicle at night. Our Reverend Mother gave them another chance, but Antonia decided to leave, and when she left, so did Evelyn, this morning before we even got up."

On their first day in the convent Mother Patricia Luke had cautioned the new postulants against forming Particular Friendships, known in their convent shorthand as "PFs." They realized later the prohibition of close friendships was designed to prevent lesbian relationships. But in those days this forbidden love was never mentioned. The ban on Particular Friendships was justified as part of their training in self-denial and discipline.

"Friendship is based on selfishness, a fulfillment of desire that focuses us on our selves as individuals," Mother Patricia Luke had told them during the orientation meeting in the parlor that first day. "We are no longer individuals here. We must direct our desires for individuality and attachments and love away from specific individuals toward our Lord Jesus and God and the greater good of the Church, the embodiment of Jesus on earth. Caring for one person takes away from our love for everyone in our community and from our love of God."

Although Mona understood why they couldn't form close friendships, she missed the companionship she'd known with her friends in school. She missed Kathleen especially. And she still missed her family. She was happy when Mother Patricia Luke gave them permission to receive visits from their families three months after she had entered the convent.

The first meeting with her family was awkward. As Mona walked into the parlor her father jumped up from his chair, a wary expression on his face. Sluggie, Rory, Muriel, and Peggy stared at her. Mona wanted to run to them and hug them, but she was forbidden to touch them. They must have been told about this rule because they didn't try to hug her.

There was a long moment of silence. Clearly Dad and her siblings were ill at ease. Probably they were wondering how much she had changed. If she was still the same Mona. Probably they were wondering what they'd talk about after three months of communicating only through letters.

Mona scrutinized her brothers and sisters. Sluggie, now eleven, had shot up the most. Rory was a handsome sixteen. Momma always said he'd be a heart-breaker. Muriel and little Peggy, the spoiled baby in her family, were fifteen and thirteen. On the brink of womanhood. Such a difficult time in girls' lives, especially with no mother and now no older sister to guide them.

"My word, you're so thin," Patrick Sullivan said finally. "They feeding you here?"

"Yes, Dad. We work off our calories."

"Sluggie's got a gift for you. Help fatten you up."

Her youngest brother thrust a box of Whitman's Assorted Chocolate toward her. Mona took the box and without taking a piece of candy set it on the mantel of the fireplace, saying, "Thank you. I will share it with the others."

Mona didn't want to be rude and tell her family she would never eat the chocolates. She had to repudiate pleasures, offer them up, give them over to her Lord.

The Sullivan family settled onto the couch and chairs nearby.

"Are you taking care of Dad for me?" Mona asked Muriel.

"I don't need taken care of," her father protested. "I'm managing on my own."

"We wish you were home with us," Muriel complained. "Dad's no good with girl things."

"I'm sorry I'm not there to help," Mona said. "You're a big girl now. You must fend for yourself."

Mona knew Muriel wasn't trying to make her feel guilty. But she did. She had always taken care of her brothers and sisters, even before Momma died. Now she knew believing she was so important to her family, thinking she was irreplaceable, was a sin of pride.

Mona's little sister Peggy looked as though she might burst. "Where's your hair?" she blurted out. "Did they chop it all off?"

"Not until I become a novice." Mona laughed. "It's shorter, but it's still there." She pointed to her head. "Under my cap."

"Your hair's always been so beautiful," Peggy protested. "It's a shame nobody can see it."

Mona didn't want to admit to her sister how difficult it was for her to hide her hair. Even though she knew she wasn't pretty, she'd always been proud of her long red hair. Momma told her to brush it one hundred times every day to make it shine, and she have given Mona a silver matching comb and hairbrush set on her twelfth birthday. Her hair was her one area of vanity.

"Vanity," Mona told her sister. "We must triumph over vanity. We have no mirrors her, or combs. We must ask Reverend Mother's permission for everything we have here, and she'd never allow combs or mirrors. So, long hair would be hard to take care of, wouldn't it, Peggy? And it's dark in our cubicles. We have no windows. You can't tell day from night. How could we fix our hair in the morning?"

"How come no mirrors?" Peggy asked.

"Sin of pride. And we have no need of them. In this convent and in our cubicles we have only the objects we really use. You'd be surprised how little you need in life. Freeing ourselves of personal possessions frees us to listen to God."

"Well, at least I can still see your freckles," Peggy said.

"Nothing I can do about them," Mona quipped.

Rory and Muriel laughed in spite of themselves. Mona's father glanced warily around the room at the clusters of other postulants and their families, not sure if laughter was allowed within these intimidating walls.

As happy as Mona had been to see her family, she was relieved when they left that day. The visit had been stressful for everyone. Talking to them tired her out because now she wasn't used to long conversations.

The Sullivan family visits became more relaxed. Time began to pass more quickly for Mona. Her friend Kathleen gave birth to a beautiful boy they named Richard Donavan Jr. Mona was officially accepted into the convent, and the six remaining postulants -- two more girls had left since Antonia and Evelyn had gone -- prepared themselves to become novices at the end of their first year there.

They would each take a new name in order to be reborn as a new person. Mona Sullivan would be no more. Although Mother Patricia Luke did allow them to submit a list of three names they would like to have, the Mother Superior made the final decision. Mona's new name would be Sister Thomas Marie.

After much anticipation, the day of her Clothing when she became a novice arrived. She was to become a Bride of Christ, so for the Mass that day she wore a long white dress made of gauze and silk sewn by the new class of postulants. They wore white high heels donated to the convent or worn by new postulants when they entered. The shoes pinched Mona's toes because she couldn't find a pair in the pile to fit. The night before the clothing ceremony they all giggled as they practiced walking in the high heels none of them had worn for a year. For the ceremony they carried bouquets of white carnations. Mona's hair was not covered, but it was now trimmed even shorter than before.

She glanced at her father and brothers and sisters as she marched down the long chapel aisle to the choir's solemn *Ave Maria*. Muriel and Peggy were weeping, Dad smiled wanly. Her friend Kathleen and her parents seemed proud, though Mona knew Kathleen still didn't approve of her decision to take the veil.

As the postulants marched down the chapel aisle, they were handed habits and short white veils. When they reached the altar they knelt before the bishop. He blessed their habits, then said to each of them, "The religious habit is the garment of your salvation." Next the bishop cut a lock of hair from their heads with a large scissors.

It was the most beautiful moment of Mona's life. She knew God was with her here. She could feel His presence. He would always be with her.

They rose, and, still holding their new clothing close to their hearts, hurried to a small room at the side of the chapel. There the new postulants helped Mona's class remove their bridal clothing and uncomfortable high-heeled shoes and put on the heavy black hose and oxfords they usually wore.

Mother Patricia Luke helped them put on their habits, slightly different from those worn by sisters who had taken their final vows. Before they put on their new caps and veils, they sat on a low stool as the Mother Superior shaved off their remaining hair. Mona understood shaving her head was an important act of self-effacement and contrition, but still she felt a pang of regret as she watched the last strands of her red hair drop onto the floor near the stool.

The sin of pride Mona had not yet overcome.

Wearing their symbolic new clothing, they reentered the chapel to watch the class of novices ahead of them become sisters and take their temporary vows of poverty, chastity, and obedience. Then they watched as one by one the novices who had been temporary professed sisters for five years recited their final vows.

God would guide Mona to the day in six years when, like these sisters who lay prostrate before them, she would take her final vows. She would be happy and fulfilled in the life she had chosen. Her life would be peaceful and secure and serene.

Her journey would be complete.

Sandra: 1948–1957

NINETEEN FORTY-EIGHT WAS an important year in Sandy Miller's life.

In May the United Nations made a new country just for Jews. It was called Israel. Rabbi Kahn told the kids all about this new country of Israel in one of his speeches in a Sunday School assembly in the sanctuary of Sandy's temple. By this time Rabbi Kahn was a real rabbi, not just a student one anymore.

"Now we Jews will have a land of our own," Rabbi Kahn announced, beaming as he walked back and forth in front of the children. "The great Theodor Herzl, the founder of what we call Zionism, proclaimed, 'If you will it, it is no dream.' Remember this, children. Where there is a will there is a way. Now we Jews have the land God promised to Abraham. Remember that bible story?"

All the kids nodded. Sandy knew most of them didn't remember it. For sure the bratty boys didn't because they never listened in Sunday School. But Sandy did. She remembered all the bible stories, even though Daddy still insisted they were all fairy tales. She thought about those stories and remembered them because she had promised the eye in her temple's red and blue and green and yellow glass window she'd always be a good Jew. And Sandy knew being a good Jew included remembering all those bible stories in our Sunday School book called *When the Jewish People Was Young* with drawings of wandering nomads wearing what looked to her like bathrobes walking through what was supposed to look like a desert.

"Especially now that so many Jews, perhaps millions, were killed by Hitler," Rabbi Kahn continued, "especially now we Jews need a land of our own. Where we can create our own destiny and never again fall prey to a maniac's desire to kill us. Now, boys and girl, we have our own land. Now we must always be good Jews and be thankful God has given us the land of Israel. The land of milk and honey."

And in 1948 Sandy's father finally got his Ph.D. But the Millers' lives didn't change much. They still didn't have enough money because even though Leon Miller was now an Assistant Professor, his salary was low. Her mother still needed to work. But now that Sandy was old enough to stay alone for a few hours in the afternoon after she walked the three blocks home from school, Helen Miller was a secretary in the math department at the university instead of typing things for college students in their house. Helen still sewed most of her own clothes. Sandy still wore her sister Joanie's hand-me-downs.

And Sandy still felt different because she was Jewish. She even had a personal experience with what her mother told her was called anti-Semitism.

She'd been playing with Betsy Smith at her house one day after school.

"You know, Sandy," Betsy said when they stopped jumping rope and sat down on the Smith's front porch steps to eat the delicious oatmeal raisin cookies Betsy's mother had just pulled from the oven, "all Jews are rich. All they care about is money. There are way too may of them, and they're taking over the world. My parents think Hitler should have come over here and finished the job."

When Helen picked Sandy up from Betsy's house, she told her mother what Betsy had said.

"What did you say to her?" Helen asked. "Did you answer her?"

"No. I sort of pretended I didn't hear what she said."

"Probably Betsy doesn't know you're Jewish because you have blonde hair and blue eyes. Or she wouldn't have said those things. What she said to you was anti-Semitic." Helen stopped at a four-way stop sign, looked carefully in both directions, then continued driving again. "I don't really want to tell you this Sandy, it isn't pleasant, but you need to know, even at your age. There's a lot of anti-Semitism in the world. Look what Hitler just did. Tried to kill all the Jews in Europe. Lots of people don't like Jews, hate us, even. Unfortunately, this is the way it's always been and probably always will be. We just have to learn to live with it."

Yes, now Sandy knew for sure from her personal experience that day that Jews in Elmville, in fact, Jews everywhere, lived in a Christian world where anti-Semitism would always exist and Jews would always be talking about it and trying to live with it and trying to keep themselves safe. Because they were Jews, they would always be sort of left out of things. For example, Christians celebrated great holidays with Christmas trees, pretty songs, chocolate bunnies, and beautiful colored eggs. Christians' holidays were much more fun than Jewish holidays.

For a few years the Miller family did have a Christmas tree in their living room, but even Leon realized this was wrong. And when Sandy was younger, at Easter time she and Joanie helped their mother dip hardboiled eggs into colored food dye and then searched for the hidden eggs all over the house on Easter morning. But by the time Sandy turned nine, they didn't hunt for Easter eggs anymore because her family knew they shouldn't be celebrating Christian holidays. They knew as much as they tried they could never really be part of the Christian world. The most they could do was to learn how to live in two worlds at the same time, their Jewish world and the Christian world. Sandy was only nine years old, but already she was learning how to do this. Already in her short life this was a difficult balancing act. She had her friends in town and at her public school, nearly all of them Christians. And then she had her Sunday School friends, the other Jewish kids.

When Sandy was fourteen, she joined the Reform Jewish youth group called the National Federation of Temple Youth, known as NFTY. Twice a year the kids went to various towns in central Illinois for a weekend to go to what were called conclaves, a fancy word Leon Miller said meant "getting together." She met Jewish kids from other small towns who also lived the same strange double lives. Then Sandy came back to her regular school Christian-world friends in Elmville.

Sometimes she had dates with Jewish boys for the Saturday night dances at those youth group weekends, but Sandy's real boyfriend was Jeffrey Shoemaker. He was a Lutheran. The Jewish girls in Elmville never went out with the Jewish boys there because they had grown up with them and they were just friends. They could never be boyfriends. Years later Sandy discovered what a mistake this was, because those Jewish boys, even the bratty ones in Sunday School, grew up to be terrific men.

There were very few *Bar Mitzvahs* in their temple, and *Bat Mitzvahs* were unheard of in Elmville at that time even though in 1922 Rabbi Mordecai Kaplan, the founder of the Reconstructionist branch of Judaism, had instigated the coming of age ceremony for his daughter Judith. But when Sandy was fifteen, six of the kids who survived Sunday School were confirmed. This took place in the late spring, at *Shevuot*, the holiday commemorating Jews receiving the Ten Commandments from God at Mount Sinai.

"You know this never happened," Sandy's sociologist father reminded her. "What we call The Ten Commandments evolved gradually, when society discovered through trial and error that in order to survive it's necessary to create strict rules of behavior to control people. Those rules enable society to function."

She sighed. "Yes, Daddy, you're right."

"But even though religion is all nonsense, confirmation is still a big deal. It's what we sociologists call a *rite de passage*. Something that marks an important transitional moment in our lives. Every society has them in some form."

Sandy got a new dress of her own instead of having to wear one of Joanie's hand-me-downs. The dress had puffy short sleeves. It was made out of white organdy decorated with tiny velveteen flowers. Sandy loved it, and wore it as often as she could before she grew out of it.

Her best friends from school, including her boyfriend Jeff, were coming to her confirmation. This was going to be an awkward mixing together of the outside Christian world and the inside smaller Jewish world, the two lives Sandy usually kept apart. At the end of the ceremony the president of the temple was going to give each of them a little white bible with their names in gold engraved on the cover. Sandy knew this from when her sister Joanie was confirmed. They would get lots of presents from the congregation. They were, of course, eagerly looking forward to the presents.

All six wrote confirmation speeches. The topic Rabbi Kahn assigned for their speeches was "Why I want to be a Jew." Sandy liked to write, and she worked hard on her presentation. She didn't mention her promise to the eye in the temple's colored glass window because she knew everyone would laugh at her. She just wrote she wanted to be a Jew for forever and help her people keep their heritage and maybe even go to the new country of Israel some day.

Leon and Helen Miller thought Sandy's speech was great. She turned it in to the rabbi three weeks before the big day. The following week Rabbi Kahn returned their speeches to the confirmation class. Or, rather, he returned *his* speeches to them. He had rewritten all of them.

"This isn't anything like the one I wrote," Sandy complained.

"He shouldn't have done that," Helen fumed. "He really insulted you."

"Your speech was a hundred times better than the one Rabbi Kahn wrote," Leon insisted. "I'm going to call him to complain."

The next day Leon slammed down the telephone after he finished talking to Rabbi Kahn. "Well, he admitted Sandy's speech was excellent," he told Sandy and Helen, "but he said the others were terrible, and since he rewrote theirs, he had to rewrite hers also in order to be fair. So I said, 'Why did you have to rewrite any of them? They're kids. What difference does it make how good the speeches are? The parents will think they're brilliant, no matter what.' Damned rabbis. Arrogant assholes."

"Watch your language, Leon," Helen said.

"I would be a better rabbi than he is," Sandy said to her parents. "Maybe I'll be a rabbi when I grow up."

Leon laughed and said, "God forbid."

"Can girls be rabbis, Daddy?"

"No, honey. Only boys can be rabbis."

"Why can't girls be rabbis? Who says?"

Leon thought for a long moment. Sandy was surprised Daddy thought for so long because usually he came up with an answer for everything right away. "I don't know," he admitted finally. "Ask Rabbi Kahn."

One day Sandy did ask Rabbi Kahn why girls couldn't be rabbis, and was that ever a mistake. He threw back his head, laughed for about five minutes. Like this was the funniest thing he ever heard. Then he said, "Heh Heh. Little Sandra Miller. Always full of excellent questions. Perhaps someday you will marry a rabbi, Sandra, but you can never be one."

"Why not?" she asked again.

"Well, I'm pretty sure it is forbidden by *halachah*. You know what *halachah* is?"

She shook her head.

"Jewish law," he explained. "From the *Torah*. The Book of Leviticus, rules given by God. Plus law added in the commentary to the *Torah* we call the Talmud. There are 613 ritual and other laws, what we call *mitzvot*. They are the basis of our religion. Nobody can do all of them, of course, we just do our best. Women are not obligated to do some of the 613. You are excused from what we call 'time-bound positive ritual commandments'. Those things that have to be done at a specific time during the day or evening."

"What does the 'positive' part mean?" Sandy asked.

"Things you are ordered to do, not forbidden from doing. You shall do these things, not you shall *not* do these things. For example, Sandra, telling you to make your bed as opposed to forbidding you to listen to certain radio programs."

"Why are girls excused from them? Doesn't this kind of leave us out of some really important things?"

Rabbi Kahn frowned. Her questions were obviously annoying him. None of the other kids ever asked him questions like this.

"Well," he said after thinking for a minute, "no one knows for sure. There are many theories. Some think it's because the purpose of these *mitzvot* is to make people more aware of the cyclical nature of time. But women don't needed to be reminded of this because of their, uh, physical cycles. Some rabbis said it's because women are of a high spiritual nature, higher than men, so they don't need to do them. Probably the best theory is that performing these *mitzvot* would interfere with your many household and motherly and wifely duties, and this would upset your husband."

"But just because we don't *have* to do these things, does that mean we *can't* do them?"

"Oh, very good question, Sandra. Very good question, indeed."

Sandy noticed Rabbi Kahn didn't answer her very good question. Hah, she thought, I really stumped him, Daddy will be proud of me when I tell him. He'll laugh really hard. She pressed on. "So," she asked Rabbi Kahn, "it says in the Bible girls can't be rabbis?"

Again Rabbi Kahn thought for a long time. "Um, well, I'm not sure it actually says this. Of course, there were no rabbis then. They came later after the destruction of the Second Temple when there was no longer a priesthood. But we can infer from *halachah* that women can't be rabbis." He paused. "Do you know what the word 'infer' means?"

"Sort of like a good guess?"

"Yes. Such a bright girl." Rabbi Kahn patted her head. "And, Sandra, women can never be rabbis because of their, uh, limitations."

"What limitations?" she asked. Sandy's parents never told her she had limitations. Even though it was only the mid-'50s and the new wave of feminism hadn't yet begun, her parents were, as Sandy looked back on it later, way ahead of their time. They always told her she could be or do anything she wanted.

"Well, Sandra, you know about the monthly blood flowing from women when they are not going to have a baby?"

"Oh. Yeah. Our periods. The curse. Menstruation," she said, relishing Rabbi Kahn's embarrassment.

"Uh, yes. Well, rabbis have to touch the Torah, right?"

"Right."

"It is forbidden for women who are, uh, menstruating to touch the *Torah*."

"But that's just a couple of days out of the month. We could touch it the rest of the time."

Sandy couldn't believe she was discussing menstrual periods with Rabbi Kahn.

He quickly changed the subject. "Sandra, women can express their Judaism in other ways. By making a fine Jewish home. Transmitting our heritage to your children. Working in the many wonderful women's organizations like Hadassah and Sisterhood and the National Council of Jewish Women. There are many other volunteering opportunities for women. You'll marry a nice Jewish boy. Raise a fine family. You won't have time to have such an important job, anyway."

"Couldn't I get married and have children and work, too, like Mom does?"

Now she could see Rabbi Kahn was getting really aggravated.

"Frankly, Sandra, allowing women to be rabbis would cause a rupture among the Jewish people. It would create a terrible ruckus. Upset four thousand years of tradition."

Well, nothing was more important than their tradition, and Sandy certainly didn't want to upset four thousand years of it. Still, she couldn't get the idea of being a rabbi out of her mind. Rabbi Kahn hadn't given her good reasons why she couldn't be one. She got the feeling he didn't know the answer, but just wouldn't admit it. Rabbis never had to admit they were wrong, did they? At least Rabbi Kahn never did.

When Sandy told her friend Susan Kleinman she wanted to be a rabbi, Susan was horrified. They were juniors in high school now. Susan was from nearby Decatur. Sandy knew her from their Jewish youth group. Sandy was regional first vice-president, a very important job. Next year she'd be president of the region, and Susan would move up from being second vice-president to first vice-president. She was Sandy's best friend in all the world.

"Nobody will ever marry you if you're a rabbi," Susan screamed. "You'd be an old maid. Jeff would never marry you."

"I can't ever marry Jeff anyway. He's not Jewish."

"Well, nobody else would marry you, Sandy. Trust me. Then where would you be? Look at my homely cousin Roz. She's so alone. I really feel sorry for her."

"Roz has a great apartment in Chicago and a good job," Sandy pointed out. "And beautiful jewelry. Tons of cashmere sweater and skirt sets."

"So what? You're nothing without a husband."

Sandy knew not getting married was the worst fate a girl could imagine. If girls even considered a career, it would be as a teacher or social worker. And then only until they got married. Or if, God forbid, something happened to their husbands, all their mothers added. Because then they would need what the mothers called "something to fall back on."

Susan was very smart, and usually Sandy took her friend's advice. But she was not going to be just a housewife. She was going to have a career, too, like Susan's cousin Roz in Chicago, who didn't seem all that unhappy to Sandy. Nobody with an apartment like hers and all those beautiful clothes could be unhappy.

In April of that year, Sandy's Midwestern region of the Jewish youth group NFTY held its annual sermonette contest. Her parents drove her to Davenport,

Iowa where the temple there was hosting the event. The topic of the contest was "The Teen Commandments." How to be a good teenager according to Jewish teachings. Right up my alley, Sandy had said to herself when she learned of the contest topic, since the eye in the stained glass window was always watching her and judging her behavior.

As Sandy delivered her short sermon, she felt very proud of herself. She couldn't really explain it, but somehow she felt empowered, sensing an inner strength she never knew she possessed as she stood behind the pulpit and gazed out at the few parents and youth group advisors that made up the small audience in the sanctuary. Everyone clapped when she finished. After the judges took a few minutes to make their decision, they proclaimed Sandy the winner, and she accepted the little brass trophy graciously.

She felt ten feet tall. People listened to her. She could influence people. She was good at this. She was born for this. Why couldn't she do this all the time when she grew up? Write sermons. Speak from the pulpit. Have people listen to her, look up to her. Help people, maybe change their lives. Teach them about their heritage, like Rabbi Kahn said, so they would all be a part of their past generations of Jews. Why not? Why couldn't girls do what boys do? She was as smart, actually smarter, than most of the boys she knew. Except maybe for her boyfriend Jeff, who was the smartest boy in school.

That day Sandy made her choice. She realized she was probably crazy. Nobody would believe her. In fact, Sandy decided she wouldn't even tell anybody because they'd just laugh at her, or be horrified, like her friend Susan Kleinman.

A girl rabbi. Impossible. It was unheard of. Unthinkable. It could never happen.

But Sandy would prove everybody wrong.

Someday she was going to be a rabbi.

Liz: 1962-1965

"I SUPPOSE IT will be all right, Elizabeth," her mother said after Liz worked up the courage to break the news to her that she planned to be ordained. "As long as you don't turn into one of those bible-thumping lady evangelists who dunk people into rivers."

"You have my word, Mother."

Her parents were more enthusiastic about her engagement to Tom. They approved of him wholeheartedly. Solid, they declared. Serious. Dependable. The kind of young man who would never let her down.

They'd been saving money for years to put toward a large wedding for their daughter. But Liz and Tom decided instead to use that money for living expenses while they attended Union Theological Seminary, so their wedding was small and simple. Tom's parents and siblings from Indianapolis, Liz' parents, aunts, uncles, first cousins, and a few friends from their church attended. And of course her best friend Alicia and her mother. Reverend Davis performed the ceremony at her family's church in August. In September they went down to Manhattan for school.

At that time the seminary didn't have apartments for married students, so the administration allotted two floors of Hastings Hall, the men's dormitory, to them. Each couple was assigned what was euphemistically called a suite, a large room and a smaller connected room. Tom and Liz used the small room as their bedroom, sleeping huddled together in a twin bed. They used the larger room for their study, living, and dining space.

All Tom cared about was having enough space to set up his beloved Hi-Fi system, an elaborate combination of the latest giant speakers and woofers and tweeters or whatever those components were called, Liz wasn't sure, all connected by thick unsightly cords. Liz never understood the complicated sound system Tom was always tinkering with, expanding, and perfecting in spite of the fact they didn't have money for anything she wanted to buy.

They hiked to bathrooms and shared a communal kitchen in the middle of the dormitory's long corridor. From their suites the girls wheeled food carts containing their shiny new wedding-gift cookware to the kitchen. They retrieved the food purchased from a nearby store that passed for a supermarket in Manhattan from the group refrigerator. After the women prepared their meals they wheeled everything back to their suites where they ate.

The night Liz met Tina Bell she had fallen asleep early, exhausted after a full day of classes. Tom woke her up when he climbed into bed later. She needed to go to the bathroom, so she threw on her robe and slippers and tramped down the corridor to the women's bathroom. Tina was standing by the mirrors, one hand cupped on each breast. "God, they're huge now," she said to Liz as she entered the bathroom.

"Pregnant?" Liz asked, still half asleep.

"No. The pill."

"Tom wants me to get on it, but I heard they make you fat."

"And the bosoms humongous." Tina cupped her hands around her breasts again. "So, what are you doing for birth control?"

"Diaphragm."

"Otherwise known as motherhood." She extended her hand. "Tina Bell."

"Liz Hagerman."

The following night in the kitchen the brides shared, Tina watched Liz trying to cook. "Your chili would taste better if you used tomato sauce instead of Campbell's tomato soup," her new friend advised. "It costs a little more, but it gives it more flavor. Add a bay leaf, too." She appraised Liz sympathetically. "Just learning to cook?"

"Yes."

"I've been making meals for my father since I was fourteen when my mom died," Tina explained. "I'll teach you. It's easy. Have you joined the Divinity Dames yet? We're all going to exchange recipes."

"Divinity Dames?"

"The student wives' group."

Liz became acquainted with all the wives on the floor she met either in the kitchen or in the bathroom. Most were struggling to learn how to cook as she was, and Tina cheerfully helped everyone. The other girls worked to support their husbands in menial jobs the seminary found for them. They worked at the seminary, at nearby Columbia University, or in the National Council of Churches building across the street from Union known as the "The God Box" because of its unimaginative square architecture. Liz was the only wife aiming to be ordained. She and Tom didn't have to work because he received financial assistance from Union and from his home church and Presbytery in Indiana. And they had the money her parents gave them in lieu of a big wedding. This set Liz apart from the other wives. But they did accept her, especially after she offered to teach knitting classes in their Divinity Dames sessions.

Even though they were tired after long days of working or studying, they always joked and laughed while they cooked or waited their turn to wash dishes in the one sink. The only wife who never joined in the laughter and gossip was an exhausted-looking girl named Louise with small wire-framed eyeglasses and a pale pinched face.

"Her husband's getting his Masters in Sacred Music," Tina told Liz one night after they watched her glumly stir a stew, load up her cart, and drag herself out of the kitchen. "If he doesn't like the supper she's prepared, he makes her start over again from scratch."

When Liz reported this to Tom, he said, "Well, that's his right. Wives should try to please their husbands."

"She works all day."

"Doesn't excuse her from her domestic chores. All the rest is secondary."

"You mean cooking for you is more important than getting my BD and serving a congregation? You told me in Edinburgh that was what God wanted for me."

"This is a silly discussion, Liz. You can easily do both."

Over the long Thanksgiving weekend, they visited Liz' parents in New Hampshire. Even though they needed a break from studying, they took their books on the bus with them. Each had to finish two term papers and start preparing for the first semester's final exams. Liz was trying to read Paul Tillich's *Systematic Theology* for one of her term papers. The bus kept lurching, and a baby in the back wouldn't stop wailing.

Tom looked up from Hegel's *Phenomenology of Spirit.* "I can't concentrate," he complained. "I'll never get all my work done. We should never have planned to go see your parents."

Tom made the visit difficult, complaining that he missed his music and there wasn't one decent reading light in her parents' house.

"I'm sorry. They don't read much," Liz said.

For Liz the best part of their trip home was seeing Alicia. Her friend had returned to their hometown after college to live with her mother because her mother's breast cancer had returned. She took a job as a buyer in the one department store in town. Alicia hadn't planned on retail as a career, but this job suited her for the time being. She had always had a flare for fashion.

Tom strongly disapproved of Alicia. "I don't understand how you two can be friends," he argued. "You're so different. She's a tramp."

"She's seeking a father figure," Liz explained. "Her dad deserted them when she was a baby. I think that's why she's so boy crazy."

"Well, she's a bad influence on you. I don't understand why you need Alicia now you have Tina."

"Can't I have more than one friend at a time? I'll meet her for lunch alone, so you won't have to deal with her."

"Good. I need that time to finish this Hegel paper."

Liz drove through a light snowfall to her favorite restaurant. From her seat, Alicia looked Liz over critically as she walked into the restaurant. They hugged. Alicia sighed as Liz sat down, and said, "God, you still haven't done anything with your hair. There must be a beauty parlor in New York that can straighten it."

"Starving students. Can't afford a beauty parlor."

"Try a little more makeup."

"Yes, Master."

"Have you given any more thought to getting contacts? Those glasses are dreadful."

"No contact lenses, Alicia."

"And I see you're still wearing those drab colors."

"So I can wear everything I own with everything else. It's sensible. Saves money. Tom and I don't have any."

"And you never will, kiddo. Your brilliant decision to become preachers."

After they ordered their meals, Alicia asked, "So, how's the sex life? Now that you waited until you were an old married woman to lose your virginity."

"Alicia!"

"Hmm. Not so good, I see."

"We're tired all the time. Besides, I don't think sex is all it's cracked up to be."

"Bullshit."

"I suppose this is my cue to ask you about your no-doubt fabulous sex life."

"Yup. It *is* fabulous. Gary. He owns the department store. Really, really rich. And really, really well hung."

"And probably really, really married," I said.

"Suits me fine. More exciting. Motels."

"God, Alicia. How sleazy."

"We're not all prudes like you."

"You're going to be sorry."

"No, I'm not. I know the score."

A week after they returned to New York, Liz realized she had missed her period.

"You probably didn't put your diaphragm in right," Tom shouted that night in their tiny bedroom after the doctor the seminary recommended confirmed she was indeed pregnant. "I told you to go on the pill. It's your fault."

"Is it so terrible? Cynthia Almond's pregnant, and they're delighted. We're talking about a baby, Tom. A miraculous new little human being."

"This isn't the right time. We've just started school. We don't have any money. How are you going to finish your BD?"

"Maybe one of the other wives can babysit while I go to classes and at night so I can study in the library for a few hours. It'll be a good way for them to pick up some extra money. I'll ask around at the next Divinity Dames meeting."

"No, don't tell anybody about the baby."

Liz stared at her husband. "What do you mean?

"Not even Tina. And certainly not that slut Alicia. Don't tell them until later. If we decide…"

"…What are you talking about, Tom? An abortion? They're illegal."

"We can find a doctor. I have a cousin who's a social worker. They have a network, I'm sure. I can rely on her not to tell my parents."

"Tom. This baby growing inside me is a creation of God. We're married. It may not be the best timing, but we'll manage."

"I can't deal with a baby now. I've got so much work to do."

"God has planned this, just like He planned for me to go to Edinburgh and for us to meet at Melinda Martin's party. This is God's will."

"You believe that, Liz? Come on. He gave us free will, too. Brains."

"And the moral sensitivity to make good ethical decisions. God creates life, Tom. We can't end it for no reason."

"We have good reasons."

They argued for two weeks. As Tom had requested, she didn't tell anyone else about the baby. When Tina heard her throwing up one morning in the bathroom, Liz denied she was pregnant, said something she ate the night before didn't agree with her. She knew Tina probably didn't believe her, but tactfully her friend didn't mention it again.

Finally, exhausted from arguing, Liz gave in to Tom. Their nightly fights were disrupting their lives. An unhappy husband would not be a good way to welcome a child into their lives. It would make things very difficult financially, he was right about that. They'd have plenty of time later to start a family after they were working and earning steady incomes. From his cousin, Tom got information about a doctor on Park Avenue. He went to the bank and took out one thousand dollars in cash from their account.

"That money was nearly all we had," Tom complained when he returned to their room with the cash hidden in his shoe. "Now both of us will have to get jobs. I won't have as much time to study as I need."

"Neither will I."

"Well, you should have been more careful. Gone on the pill."

"You're blaming this on me? I think you had something to do with it. And you're getting your way." Liz began to cry. "We're getting rid of it."

The next morning as Liz rushed to get dressed Tom said, "I don't want to miss my Church History class. You don't really need me there, do you? The nurse can put you in a cab to come home."

"You're coming with me," she shouted.

Tom stared at her. Liz had never raised her voice, even during their few arguments. He nodded reluctantly, sighed, then grabbed Reinhold Niebuhr's *Moral Man and Immoral Society* from the bookshelf. They rushed out of the dormitory.

Liz had never known anybody who had had an abortion, or, at least, anyone who admitted to it. She harbored images, mostly from movies, of evil back-alley criminals wielding unsterilized rusty knives. She certainly didn't expect to see a well-decorated waiting room in an old Park Avenue building on Manhattan's affluent Upper East Side.

The attractive receptionist nodded when Liz gave her name. She picked up the telephone, dialed, and spoke softly into the receiver. Five minutes later a young girl entered the room, and the receptionist nodded toward Liz. The girl told Liz to follow her. As Tom rose to come with them, to Liz's dismay the girl said he had to remain in the waiting room. Tom appeared to be relieved, and Liz saw him calmly open his book and begin to read.

The girl shepherded Liz down a long corridor, made several turns, then unlocked a door at the end of another hallway. They walked through the door and entered an examining room at the far end of another corridor. She gave Liz consent forms to sign, took her blood pressure and temperature, handed Liz a hospital gown, and instructed her to remove her clothing. Then she left. Liz waited nervously, shivering alone in the cold room. Finally a slim man with an expensive haircut strode briskly into the room. He shook her hand. Liz looked down and noticed his fingernails were impeccably manicured.

"You have discussed this with your husband, Mrs. Hagerman, and you're certain you want to do this?" he asked.

"Yes."

"It's a simple procedure. However, as with any medical procedure there are risks, primarily infection. I will write you a prescription to prevent that. You will have some discomfort and cramping afterwards. I suggest you rest in bed for the remainder of the day."

It was over quickly. After Liz awakened from the light anesthesia and sipped ginger ale and ate two crackers, she put on her clothes. The girl led her through the network of long corridors back into the waiting room where Tom was reading Reinhold Niebuhr. They rode in silence in a taxicab back to the seminary. Liz was woozy and in pain from the cramping the doctor had warned her about. She stayed in bed for the rest of the day while Tom went to his afternoon classes and then to the library to study.

That was that. The baby was gone. There was no going back.

It was a decision and a day Liz would regret for the rest of her life.

Second-year students at Union Theological Seminary were eligible for real apartments in McGifford Hall, a Tudor-style building a block from the seminary but connected to it by an underground passageway. Their two-room apartment there was the smallest in the building. There was only one closet and no bathtub, just a cramped stall shower. Their rooms were dark and gloomy because they directly abutted the famous Riverside Church. Tom and Liz set two alarm clocks to wake them up in case, because of the darkness, they slept through one of them. They couldn't assess the weather, couldn't see if it was raining. Often Liz would trek from McGifford Hall to the seminary via the indoor passageway only to find she wasn't dressed correctly for the outside temperature.

They heard loud organ music frequently from the church's world-famous organ, and on Sunday mornings the bells in the Riverside Church carillon chiming popular songs and Christmas carols during that season jolted them awake.

> *"At least I don't have to run down the hall to the bathroom or cook in a communal kitchen,"* Liz wrote to her mother. *"I have my own kitchen. Well, sort of. There's a little sink, a little stove, and half-size refrigerator in one area of the wall in the small room we use as our living room. You can close the whole thing off if you want. It's very efficient. I can make a meal without moving a step. My cooking's improving, with my friend Tina's help."*

Tina and her husband Charlie lived one floor below. They went out for pizza together, went to movies, or bought the cheapest back row Broadway theatre tickets. They often ate dinner together and played long Monopoly games. Or agonized over thousand-piece jigsaw puzzles taking up their entire dining tables and forcing them to eat sitting in the olive green and orange Danish-style chairs, the then-fashionable dreary furniture the seminary provided. Neither couple had a television set. When President Kennedy was assassinated they watched the funeral on a small black and white TV the seminary administration placed in a student lounge.

Liz spent ten hours a week filing in the bursar's office. Tom found a part-time job in the gift shop of the nearby Episcopalian Cathedral of St. John the Divine.

"This job cuts into my study time," he complained constantly.

"My job cuts into mine also. Everybody here has a part-time job, Tom. We all have to juggle our time."

"If you hadn't goofed and gotten pregnant we wouldn't have to work, and we wouldn't have had to use up our savings for the abortion. It was all your doing. You should have been on the pill."

They had the same argument over and over.

And gradually Liz began to realize that Tom seemed to be trying to sabotage her studying in subtle ways.

"He's probably not even aware he's doing it," she told Alicia in a long telephone conversation. "He interrupts my reading to engage me in a long discussion about eschatology or some esoteric Biblical criticism dispute."

"What's eschatology?"

"Or, he puts a record into his huge Hi-Fi system and blasts Mahler or Schumann while I'm trying to study. He can study with the music blaring, says it helps him concentrate."

Finally, Tom purchased a headpiece with two large earphones. He plugged the headpiece into the Hi-Fi system and listened through the headphones, his head bobbing and nodding to the music. If he finished studying and wanted to relax he'd pump himself back and forth in their rocking chair, blissfully transported by the music, cut off from the world.

They obsessed about politics, as did the entire liberal Union Theological Seminary community, and became involved in the civil rights movement. Throughout the winter of 1964, the Presbyterian Church spearheaded marches by rabbis and Presbyterian and Episcopal clergy in Hattiesburg, Mississippi. Tom and Liz went down for two of them along with other Union Students. They celebrated when Lyndon Johnson shepherded his Civil Rights Act through Congress in July 1964.

But in September Tom and Liz needed to focus on their own lives. They had to secure permanent positions. They'd graduate the following May, although they would not be ordained until they were called to their first church. All that the prospective churches needed to know as they considered them for employment was that they had fulfilled the requirements for ordination. Liz and Tom had met the requirements for the Presbyterian Church because they'd also taken courses at Auburn Seminary, the official Presbyterian seminary now part of Union, and during the previous summer had taken a six-week intensive course in Hebrew. This past summer they had taken a six-week Greek course so they could read the Gospels in their original language and fulfill that language requirement for ordination.

They met with Union's placement director for his advice, but had to follow Presbyterian Church job placement procedures. They filled out a personal information form, distributed by and processed in the Louisville, Kentucky Presbytery. On these forms they indicated their personal preferences and requirements. These forms would be matched up to the requirements and preferences of the churches seeking pastors. Of course the most important requirement for Tom and Liz was to be employed at a church together or in churches near each other.

"This will be difficult for you," the placement director advised them. "There are so few women, fewer clergy couples. Let's hope for some good luck. But I have to warn you. If you are co-pastors at the same church you probably won't get two salaries." He turned to Liz. "Or, if you do, yours will be much smaller than Tom's."

"Not fair," she protested. "I'll be working just as hard."

"When did you become such a pain in the neck?" Tom complained after they left the placement office. "You embarrassed me in there."

"I just don't think it's fair you might get more money than I will."

"I should never have let you read that awful Betty Friedan book."

"*Let* me read it? We discussed *The Feminine Mystique* in our Divinity Dames meetings. We little wives can read whatever we want. *I* can read whatever I want."

There was only one church with an opening that year willing to consider a clergy couple. It was in Reno, Nevada.

"Reno? Nevada? With all the gambling?" Tom protested to the seminary's placement director. "Quickie divorces?"

"Lots of counseling opportunities," the placement director joked. "Seriously, Reno is a regular little city. It's a nice place. There's a large university there. It's near California, Lake Tahoe is gorgeous I understand. You'd probably have a nice parsonage because housing's reasonable."

To Liz's dismay the church's form indicated they would hire her only as the education director.

"I don't want to be an education director," she complained to Tom. "I'll have a BD."

"We don't have any alternatives. Don't be difficult, Liz. We'll be co-pastors, but you'll be in charge of education and the youth activities."

"Because I'm the girl."

"Education and youth work is very important. We'll work together. On everything."

Since there were no other job alternatives that could accommodate both of them, they formally applied for the positions in Reno. The church flew them out for personal interviews, and Liz saw for herself Reno wasn't so bad. The wife of the minister who was leaving showed her around the parsonage. It was a sweet little three-bedroom cottage not far from the church and near the university's botanical gardens.

"Look, Tom, a real kitchen," she said as they explored the house. "Even a dishwasher."

"I can use the third bedroom for my Hi-Fi equipment," Tom said. "Could be my music room. I can go in there and listen to my albums in peace."

"I was thinking we could use that room as a nursery."

Tom didn't answer her.

The church elders interviewed them together. Tom had warned Liz to be silent about her complaints of inequality in their duties if they hired them.

"Do you think you can handle working and marriage at the same time?" the Stated Clerk of the Session asked Liz.

"Oh, yes," Liz assured him, remembering to smile sweetly. "I've managed a difficult work load at Union along with my cleaning and laundry and cooking."

"You might want to re-think your situation when you have children," he advised her.

The elders asked Tom to deliver a sample sermon for the congregation on Sunday. Liz was upset they asked her only to present the scripture reading, not a full sermon. They were both happy they'd taken a good hermeneutics course that trained them to write and deliver effective messages.

In January the church in Reno offered them the jobs. They would pay Liz a separate salary, much smaller than Tom's. But Tom was right. They had no alternative. Liz kept her mouth shut. There was no use complaining.

On March 7th, Tom, Tina, Charlie, and Liz went with other Union students in chartered buses taking them to Selma, Alabama to join the march for voting rights from Selma to Montgomery that became known as Bloody Sunday. Tom got a concussion when a policeman hit him with a club. Liz narrowly escaped injuries by running away as fast as she could. Tina collapsed from tear gas.

Liz was worried about Tina because she'd just told Liz she was pregnant. It wasn't an accident. She and Charlie had decided to stop playing it safe. They wanted to start their family now since he'd soon be earning a salary. Liz was happy for her friend. Envious, too, she confided in a letter to her parents.

"You have plenty of time, Elizabeth," her mother replied. *"You and Tom have many happy years ahead of you. Don't worry. Plenty of time for you to have your own family."*

Liz and Tom and Tina and Charlie shared one last dinner in the Hagerman's small apartment in McGifford Hall before Liz and Tom left for Reno and Tina and Charlie moved to South Carolina for his first pulpit. Tina and Liz prepared dinner as Tom and Charlie talked theology over their wine. Tina stopped chopping the vegetables she'd been preparing, laid down the sharp knife, hugged Liz, and, fighting back tears, said, "I'm really going to miss you, kiddo."

"I know. Me, too."

"We can visit often."

"Of course I'll come to see your baby. But it's pretty far from Nevada to South Carolina."

"We'll find a way," Tina said as they embraced again.

In early September, the church in Reno formally installed Liz and Tom in their positions. During the installation ceremony the outgoing minister, the elders, and representatives from the Presbytery ordained them by laying on of hands. Tom's parents flew out from Indianapolis and Liz's from New Hampshire.

Her mother, still wary of Liz' strange career, focused her disapproval on the size of their small house.

"Where's your antique pewter collection?" she asked.

"Still in a box in the garage, Mother. I don't have room to display it."

"Everything in its own place," she advised her daughter. "If everything has its own place you'll have room for all of your things." She looked around the small living room again. Sighed. "Well, it's a start. You're young. You'll have a bigger house someday." She paused. "Well maybe, and maybe not. Neither you or Tom will ever make a decent salary."

"I'm doing what I want to do, Mother. What I need to do. Money has never been very important to me."

Her mother sighed again.

The Hagermans were deluged with dinner invitations from their new congregants. Everyone was eager to meet the new pastor and his wife.

"New pastor and other new pastor," Liz said to Tom. "Don't they get that?"

"It's hard for them to get used to the idea. You're a rare bird. They probably haven't read The Feminine Mistake out here."

"Mystique."

"I was joking."

"I don't think it's very funny."

"You've always been completely humorless, Liz. You should work on that."

They divided up their responsibilities. Liz would run the Sunday School and Wednesday night adult bible study group. Head the exploratory committee looking into establishing a pre-school and work with the lay chairs of the book review and adult education committees. The youth group meetings and special activities and field trips would take much of her time, and she'd organize the summer camp teen retreats to take place in June. She planned to start beginning and advanced knitting groups. Tom would do most of the personal counseling, hospital and home visits to the ill, and conduct the worship services, baptisms, confirmations, weddings, and funerals.

Three weeks after they began their jobs at the Presbyterian church in Reno, Tom came down with the flu.

"You better officiate at the Dodson funeral today," Tom croaked from the bed. "I can't do it."

Liz entered the small lounge next to the sanctuary where the family was gathered an hour before the service was to begin.

"Where's Reverend Hagerman?" the wife of the deceased blurted out.

"I'm Reverend Hagerman," Liz said quietly.

"No, I mean your husband. That Reverend Hagerman."

"My husband is too sick to even get out of bed," she explained. "I'm sorry, I didn't have time to call you to tell you I'd be substituting. We thought he'd be able to come, but when I realized how sick he was, I barely had time to get dressed."

"I want him to do the funeral," Mrs. Dodson protested.

"I'm afraid he can't. Unless you delay it for a few days, which I don't think you want to do. I'm a trained and ordained Presbyterian minister. Fully qualified to officiate at a funeral."

A burly man stepped forward and glared at Liz. "I'm Jimmy's brother," he said. "We don't want no woman, see. We want our Jimmy to have a proper send-off."

"I assure you I will give your brother a proper funeral," she responded firmly. "I'm sorry, I don't think you have much choice."

The family exchanged looks. Jimmy's wife nodded tentatively. The brother grimaced but after a few moments agreed. Liz conducted the service.

"Needless to say, the widow did not invite me back to her home for the funeral repast," Liz told Tom when she returned home.

"You didn't handle it well," Tom said. "You should have been more sensitive to their needs."

"I was sensitive to them. What should I have done? Grovel? Keep apologizing for myself just because I'm a woman?"

"Don't start this Betty Friedan crap with me. People can't accept a woman burying their loved one or comforting them. Don't push them during one of life's most painful moments. They'll come around in time."

"If you let me do more life-cycle events like baptisms and weddings they'd get used to the idea of women officiating."

"I don't want to blur our roles. It would confuse people."

"When we took this church you promised we'd work together on everything."

"We are. We're a good team," Tom insisted.

"I don't understand it. You encouraged me to become ordained when we were in Edinburgh. Without you I might not have had the guts to. You shouldn't have encouraged me then if you don't want me to share your responsibilities now."

"I'm just trying to deal with reality. Now get out of my bedroom, Liz. I need to go back to sleep."

Liz did not share with Tom her next uncomfortable pastoral experience because it involved a sensitive topic for them.

One day a lovely seventeen-year-old girl in her youth group from one of Reno's most prominent families came to her office with her mother to seek her advice. The young girl was pregnant.

"Jerry and I want to go college, like we planned," the girl told Liz. "We've already been accepted into good schools. We don't want to get married now. Maybe someday because we really love each other. But not now."

She started to cry quietly. Liz handed her a tissue from the box she always kept on her desk.

"I wouldn't know how to get an abortion even if we decided to," the girl whispered.

"You must know I cannot help you with that," Liz said. "But even if you could arrange it, you might have difficulty living with that decision because it appears to me you and your boyfriend share a relationship of integrity. You might later regret it. Bitterly." Liz paused, trying not to let her feelings show on her face. "For the rest of your life."

It was all Liz could do to keep from spilling out her own story of her abortion, and the regret it had caused her. Was still causing her. Especially regrettable since she and Tom were married at the time and could have managed the complications to their lives a baby involved.

"Yes. Yes, she and Steven are serious about each other," the mother said, "and we love him like a son. We certainly don't want to do anything illegal. And we don't want to put the child up for adoption." She paused. "It's my grandchild, after all." She began to cry also. Liz handed over another tissue.

"Think carefully what you want to do," Liz advised. "Examine all your options. Pray on it."

"Thank you, Reverend Hagerman," the mother said. "I am so grateful we have a woman pastor to talk to. I could never have talked my daughter into confiding in your husband." She laughed nervously. "Oh, no offense."

"None taken. I understand completely."

The following week, the mother pulled Liz aside after Sunday morning services and told Liz the young couple had decided to marry.

"My husband and I will help take care of the baby while the kids go to school and get on their feet. To tell you the truth, I'm looking forward to it. I love babies. This one is just a little ill-timed."

"I think that's a wonderful solution," Liz said.

Liz begged Tom to allow her to perform the brief marriage ceremony in her office, and finally he relented. Liz unwrapped her antique pewter sugar and creamer set from the box in their garage she had never emptied, and presented it to the young couple as a wedding gift.

In October either the Klan or the local White Citizens Council bombed Tina and Charlie's parsonage in South Carolina because they were outspoken in their support of the civil rights movement. Fortunately Tina and Charlie weren't home at the time. A few brave congregants offered their spare bedrooms to them. When Tina delivered her baby girl in November the church found them a small temporary parsonage until the damage to their house could be repaired.

"Please let me fly to South Carolina to see their little Charlotte?" Liz begged Tom. "I miss Tina so much."

"We don't have the money. Tina sends you photos. That'll have to do. Anyway you can't take time off now. We've just started here."

Liz mailed off the tiny sweater she knit as a gift for Tina's child and settled for ogling the photographs Charlie snapped of his beautiful daughter. Whenever she received a new batch of photos of Tina's daughter Charlotte, she thought about the child she and Tom didn't have. Somehow she was convinced that baby would have been a boy, perhaps sent by God as partial compensation for so cruelly snatching her brother Jack from them in the automobile accident more than six years ago.

Once Liz shared these thoughts with Tom. He was relaxing after dinner, listening to Mozart's Mass in B Minor through the headphones connected to his Hi-Fi set. She poked his arm and signaled him to remove the headphones. He reluctantly took them off and turned down the volume.

"Forget about that baby," he said when Liz finished expressing her regret about the abortion. "It wasn't the right time."

"When will be the right time? You have a job now."

"We need your salary, too. You don't want your education to go to waste."

"I could still work. One of the youth group kids could baby sit after school. I've heard Kathy Lehrman is a great baby sitter, and she seems desperate to earn money. The janitor's wife could help with the cleaning."

"You're not ready for motherhood."

"Ready? I am, Tom, I am. I long for a baby."

"I don't think you understand what parenthood means. It's a huge responsibility. You're not mature enough."

"I was born an old woman," Liz snapped. "Just ask Alicia. I'm not getting any younger. Every time we have a baptism I look at the happy mother holding her new child and wonder when will that be me?"

"I'm done with this discussion," Tom said. Frowning, he put the headphones back on his head, blocking her out. He turned up the volume on the Hi-Fi, closed his eyes, and began to conduct in the air.

Liz tried to bury her maternal instincts by focusing on her work and on their political causes. The Stated Clerk of the Session had warned Tom and Liz not to be too overt about their opposition to the war in Vietnam because some in the congregation still supported it. So instead of going to anti-war demonstrations taking place throughout the country, they contributed as much money as they could afford from their paltry salaries to the interreligious organization Clergy and Laymen Concerned About the War in Vietnam.

It appeared the congregants and the townspeople were getting used to a woman pastor in Reno's Presbyterian church. Liz and Tom had settled down into a comfortable routine.

Liz's well-organized life was proceeding according to her plans.

Mona: 1960–1966

LIKE HER SAVIOR on the cross, Mona lay prostrate on the floor in the doorway to the refectory with her arms outstretched. The others were forced to step over her as they entered the room. Three sisters stepped on her habit. She was in pain from lying in this uncomfortable position, but she was forbidden to cry out because she was giving over her pain to Jesus. Her own pain was nothing when compared to that of her Savior who had suffered for all mankind.

Mona knew she deserved this strict penance. She was trying to do her best, but failed constantly and needed God's assistance. This penance would help teach her the humility she lacked and help bring her the perfection she sought.

When everyone was seated for the meal, Mona's friend Luella McBride, now Sister Theresa James, began to read Psalm One Hundred. "Make a joyful noise unto the Lord, all ye lands," she recited. "Serve the Lord with gladness: come before his presence with singing."

Mona got up slowly, nearly tripping on the hem of her long habit. When she regained her balance, she approached the dining tables. She knew the others were trying to ignore her as she lowered herself to the floor again. She carefully lifted up her habit and the petticoats underneath so the bulky clothing wouldn't be in the way as she crawled under the U-shaped table arrangement.

"Know ye that the Lord he is God: it is He that hath made us, and not we ourselves; we are his people, and the sheep of his pasture," Sister Theresa James was reading.

As her friend read aloud and the others ate in silence, Mona inched her way on her hands and knees under the table, kissing one by one the shoes of every postulant, novice, and fully professed sister. She had barely finished when the half-hour supper period ended and the others filed out of the refectory to go to the recreation hour in the community room. Of course Mona would not be allowed this privilege tonight. She stayed under the table until everyone left the room and she could see only the polished black shoes of the postulant clearing away the dirty dishes.

The young postulant glanced at Mona sympathetically as she crawled out from under the table. She walked from the refectory to her tiny room in the novitiate where another postulant had delivered her meal. She could barely swallow her supper. As Mona tried to eat, she thought about what she had done to deserve this painful penance.

Her infraction of The Rule this morning had been so serious that the Novice Mistress Sister Agnes Brigid had bypassed the usual penance system, in which each novice was assigned one night a week to ask for penance. If their names appeared on the bulletin board near the refectory on the penance list for that night, they would line up at a long table in the parlor, Sister Agnes Brigid sitting at the head of the table, glaring. When they reached the head of the line, they would plead, "Sister Agnes Brigid, please may I ask forgiveness?" After they admitted their infraction, the Novice Mistress would assign a penance. They would thank her for the privilege of punishment and the opportunity to admit their sins. They would kiss the floor, then hurry out of the parlor to carry out her orders. But if they realized they'd done something really serious, they were not allowed to wait for the weekly penance session. They'd have to tell Sister Agnes Brigid immediately. Or, at any time the Novice Mistress could tell them what they had done wrong and demand penance immediately, as she did with Mona today.

This morning, Sister Agnes Brigid and Mona had scheduled consecutive appointments for their twice-yearly dental checkups. The sister who drove the convent's clunky automobile chauffeured them back and forth together to save gasoline and time. During Mona's appointment, the Novice Mistress sat stiffly in a nearby yellow plastic chair watching the dentist scrutinize her charge's mouth. But Sister Agnes Brigid didn't say anything until she and Mona were in the car on the way back to the convent.

"Sister Thomas Marie, you walked into the dentist's office too quickly, and you did not keep your arms under your scapular," the Novice Mistress began.

"You violated Custody of the Eyes by looking directly into Dr. Malloy's. A man. This is forbidden."

"It was hard to avoid looking at Dr. Malloy when he examined my teeth."

"We do not make excuses. You have not yet overcome your pride. You have broken The Rule. Is this not correct?"

Mona nodded solemnly.

"The Rule is sometimes difficult to keep, especially when we are forced to venture out into the world. But it is a good test for us. Obedience is the key to your Sister Formation. During your novitiate you must correct all of your faults." She paused and her steely blue eyes peered into Mona's. "You are aware, are you not, I can dismiss you from the convent at any time? Without even giving you a reason?"

"Yes, Sister Agnes Brigid, I am aware of that."

Then The Novice Mistress ordered Mona to perform the suppertime penance she had just completed. To help her overcome her prideful focus on herself, she explained.

Perhaps, Mona thought as she picked at her food tonight alone in her tiny room, yes, perhaps after all I am not suited to the religious life. Maybe, after all, I do not have a vocation? Maybe Kathleen and Sister Martha Joseph at school were right when they warned me I'd never be able to follow the rule of obedience.

Once again the doubts that had tortured Mona during her first long sleepless night in the convent and many times since overwhelmed her.

The two years of novice training were designed to force the women to confront such doubts. They needed to face their spiritual shortcomings and recommit to God, to their Savior, to their Holy Mother, and to their Sister Formation.

The novices were socially isolated from the postulants and the professed sisters. They ate with the others only because there was just one kitchen and one refectory in the modest convent. They were allowed even less mail from their families than before. During Mona's first year as a novice, known as the canonical year, she studied only theology from the other sisters in classrooms inside the novitiate section of the convent, where they slept. In her second year, teachers came from outside the convent to teach them other subjects. During the last sixty days they studied only the history and rules of their own order. Then they went before Mother Patricia Luke and asked to be professed.

But Mona experienced many happy times in those two years also. In spite of the difficulty of cultivating relationships with the other sisters, she had made good friends. Things were going well with her family. Sluggie's mind was turning from baseball to girls. Muriel had a boyfriend named Joe who Dad actually approved of. Her friend Kathleen Reilly Donavan gave birth to a beautiful second son. And in November 1960, they were thrilled when handsome young Senator John F. Kennedy became the thirty-fifth President of the United States. Every Catholic in America was proud. Mona's father displayed a photo of President Kennedy on their living room wall, as did most Irish Catholic families in America. The same photo hung in the convent's community room, next to the colored portrait of Pope John XXIII.

"Who would ever have believed a Catholic could be elected President of our marvelous country?" a giddy Mother Patricia Luke raved the morning after the election. "Perhaps this election signifies the end of anti-Catholic and anti-Irish sentiments we've fought so long in this country. This is an amazing time for us Catholics. Our people have made great economic progress. Our churches and parochial schools everywhere in the country are bursting at the seams. There are no limits to our growth.

"But the soaring popularity of our Church and our parochial schools is a double-edged sword," she warned. "It's difficult to accommodate so many children and to keep the schools adequately staffed. Because our bishop keeps requiring more teachers for our parish's schools, immediately after you have completed your novice training and taken your temporary vows, I will assign teaching positions to those of you I choose for this task." She paused. "I know you have had no college or specialized teacher training, and you probably fear you are not qualified to mold the minds of our precious children. However, you will be fine. You girls have the natural gift. I will send you all to summer school every year to get your college degrees." She laughed. "What we Mothers Superior call our twenty-year plan. I will try to convince the bishop to send you to college full-time as soon as possible."

On the first day Mona entered her classroom, sixty third grade girls wearing the school uniform stared up at her from their desks crowded together in the stuffy room.

"Good morning, girls," Mona said.

"Good morning, Sister Thomas Marie," they responded dutifully.

As Mona led them in recitations of the Pledge of Allegiance and the Our Father, she hoped she was successfully hiding her terror from the youngsters. She tried to emulate the authority the sisters in her schools had displayed when she was a child. Mona wondered if those sisters, no older than she was now and also untrained and uneducated, were as frightened as she was today. Probably.

There were so many students, Mona could barely remember their names. She kept the alphabetized nametags on the front of their desks far longer than other teachers did. When a new girl came into her friend Sister Theresa James' class a month after school started, there was no space for an extra desk. Sister Theresa James gave a new child her own desk at the front of the room and stood on her feet all day for the rest of the year. The desks in Mona's classroom were so crowded together, the aisle between them was barely wide enough for her to walk to supervise written assignments.

Sometimes for no apparent reason the bishop switched them to different schools or different classrooms and they had to get to know a new batch of students just when they'd been making progress with the others. Or, in the middle of the year, the bishop transferred them to another grade, doubling their preparation time.

Mona and the other teaching sisters were constantly exhausted. They had to push themselves because Mother Patricia Luke told them if she couldn't staff their parish schools, their convent would have to pay the salaries of public school teachers brought in to fill the gap. And they could barely make ends meet as it was. Mother Patricia Luke, in charge of their finances as were all the Mothers Superior in those days, insisted their convent couldn't afford to bring in extra teachers. Fortunately they were aided by a few laywomen who volunteered to help in the classrooms.

Mona struggled with the conflicting demands of her teaching and the prescriptions of her Sister Formation. Throughout her training to take the veil she'd been striving to empty her mind so God could enter it. But when she taught school, she needed to think for herself and make quick decisions based on her own judgment. As a sister she had to sublimate her selfhood to the vow of obedience and put the needs of her convent and her order and the Church over her own. At the school she needed to assert herself with the children, parents, and other staff members. It was confusing.

Mona could sense she was beginning to change.

She was beginning to question.

Mona's doubts began during her first visit with Kathleen. They hadn't seen each other alone since Mona had entered the convent. Kathleen's appearance shocked her. Her friend hadn't taken off the weight she'd gained during her back-to-back pregnancies. She'd always been careful about her appearance. But today Kathleen's eyeliner was smeared, her fading blonde hair a mess. It was a shock to Mona because Kathleen had always spent so much time fussing with it. It was obvious her friend no longer bleached her hair, and today she hadn't even bothered to set it into the bubble cut style popular at the time.

"Come, Kathleen, sit over here," Mona urged after they greeted each other in the convent parlor. Mona steered her toward two easy chairs near the highly polished oak sideboard, away from the other groups of visiting friends and families. "You look like you can use a rest."

"Exhausted. No sleep. Never," Kathleen complained. "The baby cries all night, and he wakes up Dickie, Jr. 'cause their cribs are next to each other. Now they're both up, and then Dickie starts yelling he has to get some sleep so he can go to work. He's still working the early morning shift at the plant. Starts at six. So then I say to him can you give Sean his bottle and I'll try to quiet Dickie, Jr. and he says, 'I have to get some sleep so I can go to work,' and then he starts yelling and calling me a bitch."

"Kathleen," Mona said gently, touching her arm.

"Oh, Mona…I mean Sister Thomas Marie… I'm doing the best I can. Nothing I ever do is enough for him. The kids are never quiet enough. The apartment's never clean enough. When he's not working he's at the Dublin Bar on the corner." Kathleen lowered her voice even further. "You know his dad's a hopeless drunk now. Maybe Dickie's headed that way, too."

"Perhaps he just needs to relax with his friends after a hard day's work," Mona tried to assure her.

"When do I get to relax with my friends?"

"You have a husband and children now. More important things to do."

"Dickie never helps with the babies. My job, he says. He has his job, bringing in money for the family, and I have my job, taking care of the kids. Oh, Mona, I'm so miserable."

Mona didn't want to correct her friend when she called her by her birth name. At that moment it didn't seem important.

Kathleen burst into tears. "And now I think there's another baby coming. I'm pretty sure. I've missed two periods," she whispered.

"Oh, no. Can't you, you know, keep Dickie away?"

"It's the only happiness we have together. It's so wonderful…" Kathleen clamped her hand over her mouth. "I'm sorry. I shouldn't be talking to you about this. Not here. Your vow of chastity."

"I do have a dim memory of the outside world. Will Matthews?"

This coaxed a smile out of Kathleen. They laughed, and together recalled that afternoon in the movie theatre that seemed so long ago. Her friend was almost like the old Kathleen. But then she began to sob again.

"Maybe this time you'll get a girl, Kathleen. You've always wanted a little girl to dress up and do her hair, haven't you?"

She nodded, sniffled, then pulled a tissue from her purse and wiped her nose. She moved closer to Mona, leaned over, whispered in her ear, "After this one I'm using something. I'll take that new pill in secret. I don't care what Dickie says. I don't care if I rot in purgatory forever."

"Birth control is against Church teachings."

"Lots of Catholic women are using something in secret. You don't live in the real world anymore, so you don't know what it's like."

"Momma managed all of us," Mona argued. "Five kids in seven years. She was happy."

"How do you know?" Kathleen straightened up. She looked Mona in the eye. "And, Sister Thomas Marie, just how did your mother die?"

Mona stared at her. "Having a baby."

"Exactly," Kathleen said.

"It was an accident. She hemorrhaged and the doctors couldn't stop it. Momma was happy she was going to have the baby."

"How do you know? Did you ever ask her? Did you ever talk about it?"

"But it's Church *law*," Mona reminded her. "Transmitted from the Holy Spirit to the Pope."

"The Holy Father, when has he ever had a huge stomach and screamed bloody murder from labor pains? When's the last time he's been up all night changing diapers and sterilizing bottles and trying to keep a cranky husband happy?"

"We can't go against Church law," Mona insisted.

"That's easy for you to say. You'll never have to worry about having a million babies, losing your figure and never having a second for yourself and not enough money in the house and a mean husband who calls you a bitch and a lazy slut."

What Kathleen said was true. Mona wouldn't have to face those things. She knew that's why some girls took the veil, so they wouldn't be tied down all their lives to a mob of children and a difficult husband like Dickie Donavan. And so they could have a meaningful job and do something important and fulfilling with their lives.

After Kathleen left that Sunday, Mona thought about what her friend had said. Mona had never questioned why God took her mother from them. God knew what's best for everyone. Mona had never questioned whether or not it was safe for her mother to be pregnant when she was forty. Now she wasn't so sure.

"Maybe Kathleen's right," Mona whispered to Sister Madeleine John a week later during the recreation hour after supper. "Maybe Momma would be alive today if she'd been able to use something to keep her from getting pregnant again."

"Sister Thomas Marie, God decrees how long we have on this earth. He has His reasons."

"Last night before I fell asleep, I remembered a day I caught Momma weeping in the kitchen when she was cooking supper. I asked her what was the matter. She said 'nothing', then she changed the subject and asked me about my school day and did I have any homework. This was just a few days before she told us kids about the new baby coming."

"She could have been crying about something else," Sister Madeleine John argued.

"Momma never cried or complained. Maybe she *was* unhappy about her last pregnancy. Maybe she would have used some kind of birth control if it didn't go against Church teachings. Momma never went against Church teachings."

But Mona's mother's Catholic Church was beginning to change.

As early as 1951, Pope Pius XII had called for modifications in the habits sisters wore so their clothing would be more hygienic and more appropriate for their work in the outside world. He also made some changes in the Holy Week liturgy and in the way Catholic scholars studied scripture. In 1950 and 1952, he called Mothers Superior together to begin to examine what he termed outdated rules and practices of their orders and to explore ways in which their convents' work would be more relevant to the outside world.

In the past, convents had operated independently, with little if any communication among them. Sometimes they were suspicious of each other and competed to recruit girls. Each order functioned according to its own constitution, under the total control of and subject to approval by the male hierarchy and the Vatican. In 1952, the Conference of Major Superiors of Women Religious began to break down the orders' isolation and stimulated communication and cooperation among them. The Sister Formation Conference, founded in 1954, continued this process. Mother Patricia Luke attended some of these conferences and was now networking with other Mothers Superior.

During the recreation periods the sisters now read and discussed important articles in The Sister Formation Conference newsletter, *The Sister Formation Bulletin*. They were beginning to think differently about their daily rituals. They started to question the elaborate and cruel system of penances, whispering during recreation periods that these severe measures seemed extreme in this day and age.

The most important transformation in the Church, although they didn't know it at the time, began in 1959 when Pope John XXIII called for the establishment of Vatican Council II, the first Church Council to be held since the 1800s. The Holy Father insisted he wanted concrete changes in the Church, not just abstract philosophical or theological discussions. He officially convened the Council in Rome on October 11ᵗʰ, 1962.

Mother Patricia Luke had been excited about the new Vatican Council. But at Mona's convent's first meeting after the Council began, she paced back and forth in front of the women instead of gliding in her usual slow gracious manner.

"No Mothers Superior, no other sisters, and no Catholic laywomen have been included in the Council's important proceedings, as I had hoped," she complained.

Mother Patricia Luke had never before questioned the Pope or the hierarchy in Rome. Never before wavered from her image of serenity even when her community of sisters had faced difficult circumstances. Mona glanced over at Sister Theresa James. She could see by the expression on her friend's face that she also noticed the change in their Mother Superior's demeanor.

"No women have been asked to participate even as observers," Mother Patricia Luke continued, waving her arms as she spoke instead of resting them under her scapular as was the proper position. "They have invited many others to observe. Catholic laymen. Protestants. Even a Jew and Russian Orthodox clergy from the Soviet Union. The Council is truly an amazing international mix of bishops. However, not one woman."

Mother Patricia Luke raised her voice. "Who is speaking up for women religious and for Catholic laywomen? Now we have only the male hierarchy representing us at the Council. How much do they know about our lives and the challenges we confront?"

Racial justice became an important issue for the Church when in April 1963 Pope John XXIII released his Encyclical known as *Pacem in Terris*. For the first time a Pope spoke officially to the world at large rather than just to Catholics and spoke about issues affecting everyone, not just those having to do just with Catholics and Catholic doctrine. He called for economic and social justice for all people in the world. Including women. Citing the existence of human rights for everyone, the Holy Father urged governments to insure racial justice and harmony for those he called members of "minority groups".

Civil rights became an important issue for all Americans when on August 28, 1963, approximately 250,000 people marched from the Washington Monument to the Lincoln Memorial in the nation's capital and heard Martin Luther King, Jr. deliver his eloquent "I Have a Dream" speech. Although Mona's convent still didn't have a television set in the recreation room, Mother Patricia Luke allowed them to read newspaper accounts of the historic march and to read and discuss Reverend King's inspiring speech.

In late November, Mother Patricia Luke did rent a small black and white TV set so they could watch the funeral and burial of their beloved President John F. Kennedy.

Everyone was devastated. The loss of this great man was a tragedy for the country and for his beautiful young wife and small children. Pope John XXIII had died in June, but he was eighty-two years old. While the women in Mona's convent mourned this gentle man's passing, his death followed the natural course of things. And there had been a smooth transition to his successor Pope Paul VI.

The death of young President Kennedy meant for the country and for Mona personally the end of the naïve belief that America was different. That it was not as violent as other countries. The ground beneath everyone's feet seemed to be crumbling. The country had irrevocably turned a corner.

Nothing would ever be the same again for America.

At the second session of Vatican Council II in 1963, Cardinal Leon Joseph Suenens, Archbishop of Malines-Brussels and one of the four moderators of the Council, had publicly stated women should be invited to participate. So when the Council reconvened in September 1964 for its third session, fifteen representatives from prominent Catholic women's organizations and religious orders traveled to Rome. The delegation included one Mother Superior from America.

Mother Patricia Luke was still not satisfied. "It's just for show," she grumbled. "Cosmetic. We won't have any real influence. Those women can attend only as auditors. They will not be permitted to speak or have other input into the proceedings."

Mona's Mother Superior was also losing patience with the local bishop. "He promised me he'd send you girls to college to improve your teaching skills. But he hasn't," she complained. "I've reminded him of this promise politely, as sweetly as possible. To no avail. So now I'm taking matters into my own hands. I've spent hours poring over our convent's financial records, and I've trimmed our budget enough here and there to be able to finance books and tuition for one of you to go to St. John's University in the fall to earn your degree. You'll eat and sleep at our convent so there will be no additional living expenses. Your delicious lunch will of course be packed in our kitchen every morning."

Everyone laughed. The meager lunches those who worked outside the convent brown-bagged every day consisted of one small dry egg salad or bologna sandwich sliced neatly into quarters and one piece of fruit. The lunches were a standing joke in their community.

Mother Patricia Luke tuned to Mona and said, "Sister Thomas Marie, I've chosen you."

"Thank you, Reverend Mother," Mona said. "I promise I will study hard and justify your faith in me."

Shortly before Mona began her first semester at St. John's, her father informed the Sullivan children he was getting married.

"Her name's Vivian," he told Mona. "A widow I met in church. She came back to Queens from Atlantic City when her husband passed from a heart attack on his way home from work at one of those big hotels on the boardwalk. Don't know how anybody can gamble away all their hard-earned money. It just isn't right."

Their father's remarriage was just one change Mona's brothers and sisters had to deal with. Their own lives were changing rapidly also. They were growing up. Sluggie was now seventeen, still hoping for a baseball scholarship to college. Peggy planned to become a nurse. Muriel had gone out to work right after finishing high school. She commuted into Manhattan every day to her job as an executive secretary in a Wall Street brokerage house. When Dad and Vivian got married, Muriel would move out of our house and share a small apartment with her best friend from school. Mona's brother Rory had enlisted in the Marines, hoping to be sent to Vietnam because President Johnson was increasing troop commitment there to stop a Communist takeover of Southeast Asia.

"I want to pay this great country back," Rory explained to the family.

"We're all proud of you," Mona told her brother. "I'll pray every day that God will keep you safe."

Yes, her family was changing. It was normal. Kids grew up and left home and faced the challenges and dangers of the frightening world. Lonely widowers' grief gradually faded and they found new companions.

Mona's life was changing also.

Because she was going to college she had to adjust her strict prayer schedule. She couldn't follow the times set aside in the convent and in the school where she had taught. She could still do morning meditation and prayers and evening meditation and Compline inside the convent, but not the other four prayer periods of the day.

Mona quickly recited the prayers in the subway or bus or as she walked to school or in the moments or hours between classes. She discovered if she concentrated she could pray anywhere. She began to feel God was inside of her and she could communicate with Him on her own personal level rather than just during the established prayer and meditation periods of the convent or in a chapel or church.

And since Mona was enrolled at a university, she had to take courses in all the required subjects leading to her degree. In the convent she had studied only subjects pertaining to the Church and to her Sister Formation -- scripture, the writings of the saints and the Church Fathers, Church history and Church law. Plus the bare basics she needed for teaching her young students. Suddenly Mona had to broaden and deepen her intellectual interests. Stretch her mind. Pursue and refine and learn again to value the thinking process. This was contrary to her Sister Formation, which had forced her to curb her reasoning abilities. Humility had been the goal of Sister Formation. Service to the group, to the Church, to the Lord Jesus Christ. To rely on the intellect was to focus on the individual, on herself. To become what sisters called "singular," which led to the sin of pride.

But now Mona had to open her eyes, take in new thoughts and new ideas, take in the entire world. And what a world she was suddenly thrust into! She felt like an alien a space ship had dropped off onto this strange planet earth, and it was sink or swim. This was Mona's first extensive contact with the outside world and with non-Catholics since she had joined the convent. She realized now what a sheltered life she led even before she took the veil.

On the campus she felt like an awkward teenager, a wallflower at a party where she knew nobody and didn't fit in. She wasn't familiar with the music the students, only a few years younger than she was, after all, listened to and talked about. Who were these Beatles anyway, and why did girls scream when they saw them? They couldn't compare to her Elvis Presley. She didn't understand the other students' slang. The ease with which the girls in black eye makeup and teased heavily hair-sprayed bouffant hairdos wearing short skirts flirted with the boys now sporting long tangled hair and beards was foreign to her. Something called free love had broken out by 1964.

The most practical problem Mona now faced when she went to classes at St. John's was the cumbersome full habit she wore. Every day she had to make sure she didn't trip on her long skirt when she climbed stairs going up and down to the subway and buses or in the buildings on the campus. The starched white linen wimple covering Mona's cheeks, neck, and shoulders interfered with her full range of vision. The veil could be dangerous. It could get caught in something. The coif, a tight white cap, and the guimpe, the white head binding holding her waist-length veil in place, were hot in the summer as was the entire long-sleeved black wool tunic. All the under slips she wore made the heat worse. Washing and ironing her habit and the long procedure of dressing in it every morning, including reciting special prayers as she donned each piece to remind her of her vows, stole precious time away from her studies. And Mona felt the formal habit separated her from people in the outside world she was now part of.

Women religious had already begun to discuss the possibility of modernizing their habits. Pope Pius XII first brought up the subject in 1951. In 1962 Cardinal Suenens had published an important book in which he argued the Church needed to make sweeping changes, especially in the lives of sisters. They should no longer be treated as minors. Convents should be more democratic, and sisters should not be isolated from the world. Outmoded customs should be done away with. Their habits should be modified because they hindered their work.

Cardinal Suenens' book caused a sensation.

"He's right," Mona's friend Sister Theresa James had argued during recreation period. "My habit's still wet when I put it on after I've washed it. It never dries overnight. I spend way too much time starching my wimple. Our habits are a fire hazard. Last week when I was sitting in the parlor visiting with my family a spark jumped from the fireplace."

"But we can never change our habits," Sister Madeleine John insisted. "They remind us we must obey The Rule. Our Church and God. We could never go against such an important tradition. What would the laypeople think? They expect us to be different. Besides, what else would we wear?"

Just as Mona began to question the practicality of her habit, at Thanksgiving time that year two Ursuline Sisters from a convent in Paola, Kansas teaching in a Catholic high school in Oklahoma City appeared in public wearing modified habits. They had received permission from their Mother Superior to fashion the new outfit themselves. They wore black skirts, white blouses, and black vests decorated with their order's insignia. They tied their hair back with white ribbons. They removed the coif, the guimpe, and the wimple, and shortened the long skirt.

Furious laypeople complained. Otherworldly sisters in traditional habits symbolized the Church to them, and this new clothing was a disgrace. They barraged the Ursuline order with hundreds of letters. Newspapers and television reporters rushed to cover the story. The Vatican commanded the Ursuline sisters to return to their old outfits, but it was too late. Other orders were already debating possible changes in their clothing. Only a year later, Vatican Council II sanctioned radical re-thinking of all their traditions, including the design of their habits.

Catholic women hoped Vatican Council II would also modify the Church's strict stand on the prohibition of artificial birth control by approving use of the pill, now the most widely used contraceptive method since coming onto the market in 1960. This would help overwhelmed mothers like Mona's friend Kathleen and perhaps save lives, as Mona was now convinced it might have saved her mother's. Instead, in June of 1964, Pope Paul VI created a Papal Commission on Population, the Family, and Natality, widely known as the Birth Control Commission.

"Mother Patricia Luke says the Council didn't want to cause a big ruckus by taking up the birth control issue," Mona explained to Kathleen. "So they passed it off to the Pope, and he's passed it off to a committee to study. There's even a married couple on the committee. But that's an old trick of bureaucracies, Mother Patricia Luke says. Keep tossing the hot potato to somebody else."

"Why do a bunch of celibate old men get to decide how many kids I'm going to have?" Kathleen complained.

The key theme of Vatican Council II was *Aggiornamento*, which meant adaptation to and dialogue with the modern world. This was a tall order, because the modern world was indeed rapidly changing. To help the Church adapt, in November 1964 the Vatican Council promulgated an important document called *Lumen Gentium*, Pastoral Constitution on the Church in the Modern World. Included in it were statements on the status of women religious.

Their position in the Church had never been clearly defined. The hierarchy didn't consider women religious to be clergy. Their recitation of vows was not sacramental. But the Church had always ranked sisters above Catholic lay people. They existed somewhere in between these two categories, and, although they knew they were flirting with the sin of pride, sisters enjoyed their special status as sort of mysterious perfect beings. They felt this prestige made their hard work worthwhile.

Lumen Gentium called into question even this vague advantage. Now, the Council proclaimed, holiness was no longer solely the domain of sisters and clergy. Every Catholic should aspire to be holy and special. Everyone should search for spiritual fulfillment. According to this document, baptism made all Catholics and the Church as a whole into the "People of God." Part of the human presence of a loving Christ rather than the transcendent and impersonal God. The Church was now a dynamic spiritual entity. God was in history. He worked in history. So, too, the Church exists in history and is subject to fluid historical processes.

The Church could change. The Catholic Church was no longer the static perfect institution it had been in the past. And sisters were no longer models of perfection.

Then who were they?

What made them special? Were the sacrifices they were making worth it? Were the Church's doctrines the Truth? Was the authority of the Pope and the hierarchy beyond questioning?

If people could now question the Catholic Church, could they now question other social institutions? The answer was "yes."

Many Americans began to seriously criticize the U.S. involvement in the war in Vietnam and to challenge the very basis of political power itself. In March 1965, the Students for a Democratic Society sponsored its first teach-in at the University of Michigan. In the same month in Detroit a Quaker woman, Alice Herz, set herself on fire to protest the war. Another Quaker, Norman Morrison, would follow her example eight months later. In April the SDS and the civil rights activist group Student Nonviolent Coordinating Committee led the first of several anti-war marches in Washington, D.C. In October there was an International Day of Protest Against the War In Vietnam. Students everywhere began to burn their draft cards. Prominent Rabbi Abraham Joshua Heschel, Richard John Neuhaus, a Lutheran pastor who later became a Catholic priest, and Father Daniel Berrigan founded Clergy and Laymen Concerned About the War in Vietnam.

The civil rights struggle grew more tumultuous. In March 1965 after the "Bloody Sunday" demonstration in Selma Alabama, Jewish, Protestant, Catholic, and Greek Orthodox clergy travelled to the southern town to show solidarity with blacks there. Fifty-six sisters, including Mona's friend Sister Theresa James, joined them. They stood together for days, praying and singing, in rows against police barricades, bravely facing armed police and other hostile whites. The national media, both Catholic and secular, extensively covered the sisters. For the first time sisters were publicly featured as social activists.

"Bloody Sunday" transformed Sister Theresa James. When she returned from Selma she asked Mother Patricia Luke's permission to leave her teaching in the parish school to devote herself to working for racial equality.

"*Lumen Gentium* has changed the concept of our apostolate," Mona's friend pointed out. "Now our work must be more relevant to the problems of the world. It must be the focus of our religious lives. We can no longer separate the realms of the secular and the sacred. Jesus and the Holy Spirit will surround me in my new tasks."

Sister Margaret Ellen Traxler, Executive Director of The Department of Educational Services of the National Catholic Conference for Interracial Justice located in Chicago, was organizing several new social programs. President Johnson's War on Poverty, through the Office of Economic Opportunity, largely funded them. Sister Margaret told Sister Theresa James she hoped to get a new program, Project Cabrini, underway by summer. The Sisters of St. Francis from Minnesota planned to turn an abandoned Catholic school near Chicago's infamous Cabrini-Green high rise public housing project into a summer enrichment program for poor African-American children in the area. They were willing to accept volunteers from other orders. Although Sister Theresa James didn't have a college degree, the Franciscan sisters gladly welcomed her into the daring program because of her teaching experience.

Mona's friend left their convent in June to tackle her new challenge. In September Mother Patricia Luke gave Sister Theresa James permission to stay in Chicago to join Sister Margaret's office to help the outspoken progressive sister plan other civil rights programs.

Six women auditors at Vatican Council II were present at the adaptation in December 1965 of *Gaudium et Spes*, the Pastoral Constitution on the Church in the Modern World. This document asked how the Church could be more "present" in the modern world and commit itself to racial equality, human rights, and justice.

A week later nearly 1,000 Catholics, including seventy-five priests, signed a full-page ad appearing in the December 12, 1965 issue of *The New York Times* as a response to what many considered to be Father Daniel Berrigan's "exile" from New York by Francis Cardinal Spellman because of the radical priest's increasing anti-war activism. The Open Letter to the Authorities of the Archdiocese of New York and the Jesuit Community in New York City proclaimed freedom of conscience in opposing the war in Vietnam. It cited the recently promulgated *Gaudium et Spes*, which supported Catholic pacifism and conscientious objection.

Mona's father was furious. "Those people are ruining our troops' morale," he shouted. "Saying bad things about our land of opportunity. How do you think our brave Rory serving his country feels when he hears about this? Shame on those priests."

"President Johnson knows more than we do," his wife Vivian added. "He's got information we aren't privy to. We have to trust our government to do the right thing."

"And those hooligans," Patrick Sullivan continued, "those lazy good-for-nothing bums marching around having sex everywhere in public and smoking dope. Rich college kids, nothing else to do but get into trouble. They should all go out and get a job."

In addition to the social upheavals in the country and the world, sisters every-where were confused about changes Vatican Council II had ordered them to make. In October Pope Paul VI had proclaimed *Perfectae Caritatis*, Decree on the Adaptation and Renewal of Religious Life. This document called upon women religious to renew themselves by returning to their sources, primarily the Gospels, so they could adjust their communities to the changing conditions of modern life. It asked them to examine why and how their orders came into existence and how they defined their aims and missions. To reevaluate their priorities and revise the rules and regulations of their orders, especially the way they were governed. But Vatican Council II closed suddenly in December 1965 without clarifying how it intended for women religious to carry out these reforms and without clear boundaries regarding the authority of the Pope and the male hierarchy to monitor these changes.

"They tell us to rethink our procedures," Mother Patricia Luke told Mona in her office after she studied the document carefully. "They order us to modern-ize ourselves, but they didn't have time to give us guidance. I'm going to confer with other Mothers Superior to find out how they're planning to handle these changes. I want you to accompany me. Be my secretary. I'll need your help keeping track of these ideas."

At the first convent meeting after Mona and her Mother Superior returned from their travels, Mother Patricia Luke announced, "We need to have better communication. We're doing away with The Great Silence at night and our practice of silence throughout the day. However, I still want conversations kept to a minimum. No frivolous chatter to clutter up the mind and close off our receptivity to God. And we need more discussion about matters concerning our convent. We should meet at least twice a week, not once. This is what other Mothers Superior are doing."

Mother Patricia Luke had always made all of the decisions for the community and for each of them in it. She had always had the final word, which none of them could question. Now, Mona asked herself, they were going to have input into Mother Patricia Luke's policies?

Except for Rory who was off fighting in the dangerous jungles of Vietnam, Mona's family was present on the day in June 1966 when she and the five others remaining in her class took their final vows. Muriel's fiancé Joe and most of Mona's friends came also.

As they had carefully rehearsed, the six who were becoming fully-professed sisters lay face down in front of the altar, their arms and habits spread out at their sides forming the shape of a cross. The bishop walked among them. He gave each of them a large crucifix and rosary. Holding their hands, he blessed gold wedding bands and gently slipped the rings onto the women's fingers.

The bishop then covered them with what was known as a pall made out of linen to symbolize they were now dead to the world. Altar boys placed tall candles at each corner of the pall and lit them. The choir sang the *Deus Irae* as if this was a funeral mass, also signifying their individual selves were now dead to the world.

"When you enter the chamber of the Bridegroom," the bishop intoned over them, "you may carry a shining lamp in your hand and meet him with joy. May he find in you nothing disgraceful, nothing sordid, nothing dishonorable, but a snow-white soul and a clear and shining body. Thy beauty now is all for the King's delight. He is thy Lord and God."

However, as the choir sang the *Deus Irae* and Mona lay under the pall, she didn't feel dead to the world. No. She was very much a part of it. Now it was her mission to be part of the confusing and chaotic world and to struggle to improve it. The confusion and chaos and flux and uncertainty of the world, with all of its possibilities for progress and all of its pitfalls and tragedies, would be part of her life. God didn't want them to flee from the world to serve Him. He wanted them to serve Him by embracing it.

And during this ceremony full of mystery Mona didn't feel transformed and exhilarated as she had anticipated for the past eight years. She had always thought taking her final vows would mean she had attained her final personal goal.

But now she wasn't even sure what her goal should be. She was now a fully- professed sister, but she was far from done with her Sister Formation. Her character training was not complete. She wasn't "finished."

As Mona lay under the pall, she realized she would never be "finished". She would always be searching and growing and becoming.

Her journey had not come to an end.

It was just beginning.

Sandra: 1958–1972

"WHY DO I have to wear my sister's hand-me-down dress on the biggest night of my life? My senior prom?"

"It's lovely," Sandy's mom assured her. "Take a deep breath, honey."

Sandy sucked in her stomach and held her breath as Helen Miller carefully zipped up the strapless baby blue taffeta formal with net covering the entire full ankle-length skirt. She stood back and assessed her daughter.

"You look beautiful. Joanie only wore the dress once. Four years ago. It's practically brand new."

"Nobody at your stupid prom will know it was mine," Joanie said as she grabbed the can of hair spray from the dresser and aimed it at Sandy. "Shut your eyes."

Sandy squeezed her eyes shut as Joanie sprayed her hair.

"You know it's hopeless," Sandy said. "It'll be straight again by the time we even get to the prom. I hate my hair."

Sandy waved away the hair spray lingering in the air as Helen tugged at Sandy's strapless bra and hiked it up, saying, "I hope this darned thing stays up. Don't make any quick moves."

"The wires are digging into me. This bra is torture."

"Well, you wanted breasts, and you finally got them," Joanie said. "The God you're always talking about must have heard your prayers."

Yes, Sandy had finally gotten breasts, and they were pretty big. Too big already. Probably it served her right for wishing for them. Since she was eleven years old, whenever she went into the Sears store downtown, she'd head for the bra department and gaze longingly at what in those days were called "starter bras," a thick band of elastic for girls with teeny bumps where breasts would hopefully someday sprout. Joanie was right. Sandy had prayed this would happen to her. Well, it had. Big time. And now she had to suffer in this horrible strapless contraption.

Helen grabbed Jeff's big gold senior class ring hanging from a long gold chain around Sandy's neck. "Don't wear this ugly thing tonight. It ruins everything. You can borrow my fake pearls."

"Jeff and I are going steady. I'll never take off his ring."

"Jeff's a nice boy, honey, but you know how we feel. He's not Jewish."

Sandy rolled her eyes at Joanie. Not this discussion again.

The doorbell rang.

"Oh, God. He's here. I'm not ready yet."

"You make your dates wait for you," Helen Miller reminded her. "Even if you're ready. And you always wait upstairs, never downstairs. You don't want the boys to think you're too eager."

Sandy's mom was always dispensing advice about etiquette, especially concerning the opposite sex. For example, you never stood at the ticket window when your date bought the movie ticket. Instead you meandered off to the side of the theatre and pretended to look at the movie posters. And Jewish girls never, never, *never* sat at bars.

Leon Miller shouted up the stairs in his fake English accent, "Madam, your prince and his carriage have arrived."

They fussed some more until they decided Sandy was as ready as she'd ever be and they had kept Jeff waiting a respectable amount of time. Sandy walked down the stairs slowly, teetering in her new blue satin high heels that matched Joanie's dress perfectly after the woman at the shoe store dyed them.

Jeff looked great, even though his rented tuxedo was a bit too short for him because he was now six feet tall. His light brown hair was styled into a crew cut all the boys sported in 1958. It felt like a soft brush when Sandy ran her hands through it. No matter how many milkshakes, French fries, and cheeseburgers Jeff Shoemaker devoured at the drive-in Steak 'n Shake, he never gained an ounce.

"Probably burns off the calories in basketball practice, running track, and riding his bike to school every day instead of taking the bus like you do," Helen had speculated. "And," she added, "Gentiles are thinner than Jews. Just another of God's tricks."

Jeff was sitting erect on the couch, holding a box containing her corsage from the campus florist. Sandy's dad liked him. He knew and respected Jeff's father, who was head of the geology department. But Jeff looked uncomfortable because Leon had no doubt been grilling him about driving slowly and carefully. He stood up when Sandy entered the living room. He awkwardly thrust the corsage box toward her. She opened the box and pulled out the white gardenias arranged into a wrist corsage.

"Wow, beautiful," Sandy said. "Thanks."

"Drive carefully," Leon reminded his daughter's boyfriend.

"Yes, Dr. Miller. Always do."

"Daddy, I've told you a million times Jeff took Driver's Ed from the gym teacher."

"I just don't want you two to end up like those five girls who got killed last summer in that yellow Cadillac convertible when they tried to beat the train at the railroad crossing."

"Leon, stop being so morbid," Helen said. "It's their prom night."

Sandy had spent most of the day helping decorate the gym. They tried to mask the smell of sweat from PE classes and basketball games with the cloying scent of cheap lilac toilet water from the dime store they squirted everywhere. "Spring Has Sprung" was the theme the prom planning committee had chosen. Sandy chaired the committee, one of her most important duties as president of the senior class. Twisted light purple and white crepe paper streamers hung down from the basketball hoops. The decorating committee had tied groups of three or four yellow and purple balloons to the railings of the bleachers and to the backs of chairs distributed around the room.

The big moment came when Miss Leighton, the vice-principal, was to announce the prom king and queen selection. Jeff and Sandy assumed they'd be chosen because he was captain of the basketball team and editor of the school newspaper and yearbook and Sandy was senior class president, president of the student council, head cheerleader, and chair of the very important student council activities budget committee.

When Miss Leighton proclaimed Sandy and Jeff king and queen of the prom, they tried to look surprised. Under a bright spotlight Jeff and Sandy sat on two metal folding chairs wrapped in purple and white crepe paper in the middle of the gym as Miss Leighton crowned them. Then they danced alone in a spotlight to Nat King Cole's beautiful "Unforgettable" as everyone watched enviously.

The senior class parents had carefully planned after-prom parties to keep the kids out of trouble. But after spending an hour at the first party, Jeff and Sandy snuck away to the all-night drive-in theatre at the edge of town. They made out, ignoring the sounds of the movie through the speaker attached to the car window, even though it was *Bridge on the River Kwai*, a huge hit that year.

Sandy broke away from their clinch.

"You know I have to go to my youth group conclave in St. Louis next week," she reminded Jeff.

"Why do you have to go?" he whined. "I won't have anything to do all weekend."

"May I remind you I'm the president of the whole region? I have to go to all the conclaves."

"You spend so much time doing that stuff. It takes away from our time together."

"Jeff, you don't seem to understand how important my Jewish youth group is to me."

"It's like you're obsessed with being Jewish, Sandy. I don't get it. I mean, my family, we're good Christians. We go to church on Christmas and Easter and maybe a couple of other Sundays. But our religion isn't our whole life."

"Because you don't have to live in two worlds at the same time like I do."

"Well, OK, but you better behave yourself in St. Louis. "

Jeff kissed her, pinning her against the passenger-side door. Sandy broke away again. She hiked up her uncomfortable bra and smoothed out Joanie's dress.

"I have to go to the conclaves because my parents want me to meet other Jewish kids. Jewish boys."

"You know I don't want you to go out with other guys."

"Jeff, some day, you know…"

He put his hand down her bra and pushed her back against the car door. She extracted his hand from her bra and sat up again.

"You know someday I'll have to marry somebody Jewish. Especially if I ever get to be a rabbi."

"What are you talking about?"

"A rabbi. They're like your ministers."

"I know what a rabbi is. I was at your confirmation, remember? But I didn't know girls could be one."

"They can't. At least not now. But maybe someday."

"There aren't any girl Lutheran pastors, either. That's the craziest idea I ever heard. What kind of girl wants to do that? Those are men's jobs. Nobody would take a girl seriously. Nobody wants to hear the word of God from a girl. And what about me? I love you. I want us to get married after I finish grad school. I'll have a good job, and you won't have to work. You'll be busy taking care of our kids."

"That's a long way off."

"I know. But I'll still love you then. I'll always love you."

"And I'll always love you, Jeff. But I can never marry you."

"Why is marrying somebody Jewish so important? This is America. You know, the melting pot? Everybody's the same here."

"Easy for you to say," Sandy argued. "You don't have to constantly hear about the six million Jews Hitler killed. And how it could happen in America if we aren't careful because anti-Semitism is still around, even here, and it's always growing and getting worse. And how we Jews are dying out because of intermarriage and assimilation, and which movie stars and singers are Jewish and how we hope some big murderer isn't."

"But..."

"...Hitler didn't try to kill all the Lutherans in the world, like he tried to kill all us Jews. You don't have to live with centuries of hatred against Lutherans, with every Lutheran you know always talking about it, saying you're going to disappear off the face of the earth. You don't have to worry about that big eye in the stained glass window in our temple."

"Eye?"

"It's watching me. To make sure I'll be Jewish forever."

Jeff laughed. "You're nuts, Sandy. But I love you."

"Seriously, if I married you I wouldn't be preserving our Jewish heritage."

"Jews would disappear if we got married," Jeff said sarcastically. "It would be the end of the world. You'd be responsible. Sandy, why are we discussing this? This is our prom night." Jeff pulled Sandy's right breast out of her bra as he pushed her back against the car door and mumbled, "Come here."

Two weeks later they graduated. Sandy worked all summer typing three by five cards for new acquisitions in the university library. Jeff went with his family to their vacation cabin in Michigan. They missed each other terribly.

They had both won full scholarships to college because of their high grade point averages in addition to their long list of extra-curricular activities and because both fathers were underpaid college professors. Sandy chose Radcliffe, Jeff chose Wesleyan. They spent many hours on buses traveling back and forth from Boston to Middletown, Connecticut to see each other on weekends, squinting to study by the dim overhead light above their lumpy seats.

Early in their freshman year they decided they couldn't continue the frustrating marathon make out and heavy petting sessions of high school. In spite of the reigning moral imperative of the late fifties that girls remain virgins until marriage, Sandy was ready to go to bed with Jeff. Other couples going steady were doing it.

The privacy of Jeff's dorm room on the Wesleyan campus replaced the front or back seat of Jeff's car and the public places where they parked in high school. Jeff and his roommate worked out some kind of arrangement insuring no one would walk into the room at the wrong time. Sandy was never able to figure out the details.

She and Jeff had loved each other for years. They were ready. It happened. After clumsy beginnings, it was wonderful.

Sandy's parents kept nagging her to break up with Jeff.

"Finish it. So you can find somebody Jewish," Helen lectured when Sandy came home on one of her vacations.

"I know you're right, Mom. But it's so hard."

"Jeff Shoemaker is just a habit," Joanie wrote to Sandy from Los Angeles, where she had migrated after college to conquer Hollywood. *"God, Sandy, you'll be sick of each other before you even get married."*

"You're a great one to be giving me advice," she wrote back. *"Going out with a different jerk every week."*

Sandy didn't tell her parents or sister that frequently she agreed with them, that she had strong doubts about her relationship with Jeff. She couldn't always sweep the differences between their Jewish and Christian worlds under the rug. Differences that became even clearer to her in April of their junior year of college in 1961 when Jews became obsessed with the trial of Nazi war criminal Adolf Eichmann.

After members of the Israeli *Mossad* spirited Eichmann, hiding in Argentina, back to Israel, his trial began in Jerusalem on April 11th. He was charged with crimes against humanity and crimes against the Jewish people, specifically with organizing and implementing operations that transported millions of Jews to ghettos and death camps.

The four-month Eichmann trial was all Jews talked about. They were consumed by the testimony against Eichmann given by one hundred prosecution witnesses, ninety of them concentration camp survivors offering shocking details. The Jewish community argued vehemently about whether or not this unrepentant war criminal should be executed. Israel had a policy of no death penalty. However, most people felt an exception should be made because of the enormity of Eichmann's crimes. The Israelis executed Adolf Eichmann on May 31, 1962.

But Jeff barely noticed the Eichmann trial.

"What's the big deal?" he asked. "The Nazis are in the past. Far away, in another country. It will never happen again. Not in America, anyway."

"I'm surprised you'd say that. You're a history major. Don't we have to learn lessons from our past? So history won't repeat itself?"

In spite of Sandy's reservations about Jeff, things became more intense between them as they neared their college graduations. Jeff won a Fulbright to study Chinese history at Oxford for two years. Sandy wrote to Hebrew Union College-Jewish Institute of Religion in Cincinnati and told them she wanted to apply to rabbinical school. By this time Sandy had told her parents of her wild dream. Helen was surprisingly supportive, but warned her she'd probably not be able to follow her unusual career choice. Leon Miller was appalled, or at least pretended to be.

"You do know religion is all hogwash," he reminded his daughter. "Rabbis don't have mysterious magical powers. This ordination stuff is all nonsense. Laying on of hands. In the twentieth century. It's all magic. There are other ways you can transmit our Jewish culture, if that's what you want."

"Yeah, like baking cookies for the Sisterhood fundraisers? You sound like Rabbi Kahn, Daddy."

She received a polite letter back from the Provost's office of Hebrew Union College. Women were welcome in any of their courses. They would be glad to discuss with her various programs in which she might be interested. *"However,"* the letter continued, *"we feel felt obliged to inform you we do not know what opportunities are available for women in the rabbinate, since no women have yet been ordained. Most women prefer to enter the field of Jewish religious education. Someone from the admissions office will contact you with additional information about this program."*

A few days later Sandy did receive a letter from the admissions office. *"Under separate cover we are sending you a catalog. While there have been women students at the school,"* the admissions officer wrote, *"so far none have taken the full course of study leading to graduation and ordination as a rabbi. The question of women rabbis is one for rabbis themselves to determine, not the school."*

"I guess that means 'no,'" Sandy said to her parents in their next telephone conversation.

"Think about going for a degree in religious education there, as they suggest," Leon advised.

"I don't want to settle for that. I want to be a rabbi."

"But rabbis are just primarily teachers."

"They're more than teachers, Daddy. They're leaders in the community. Surely even sociologists believe in community. Especially sociologists."

"Sandy's always been a natural leader, Leon," Helen chimed in on the extension telephone.

"Don't encourage her, Helen. It's a hopeless aspiration. It'll never happen. There are lots of other worthwhile things she can do to improve the world."

"I don't know how to say this without sounding ridiculous," Sandy said sheepishly, "but I feel sort of compelled to lead our people as a rabbi."

"You mean you've been called by God?" Leon chided.

"No, Daddy. It's just a feeling I have. I can't describe it. An intuition. Something I need to do, or at least try to do."

"Maybe the school will change its policies in a few years," Helen said. "In the meantime you can be a social worker. And, if you ever do become a rabbi, your social work training would mesh well with your rabbinical duties. Especially the counseling training."

Yes, Sandy thought. Going into social work made sense. The eye in her temple would be happy because helping people was important to Judaism. She applied and was accepted into the Masters in Social Work degree at Columbia University.

"Forget about getting an MSW," Jeff said. "At least right away. I want to marry you this summer after we graduate so you can come with me to England."

They were sitting on one of the chintz-covered couches in the lounge of Sandy's dormitory where couples huddled to plan weddings and lives.

"We can't get married. No money. Besides, what would I do while you're at Oxford?"

"You could audit courses. Or just take the two years off. Explore the country."

"I told you, Jeff, I can't marry you. I should never have let this go on so long. I told you this when we first started going together."

"Is that eye in your temple still following you around?"

Sandy knew Jeff was trying to joke, but he wasn't fooling her. He was hurt.

"It's not funny. If all of us Jews married Christians, we'd die out."

"So?"

"So? Hasn't anything I've said all these years sunk in?" She jumped up from the couch. "Don't you know me at all?"

Jeff rose and put his arms around her. The other couples were staring at them now.

"Please, Sandy, I love you."

"I know. I love you, too."

"I just don't understand this Jewish thing. I guess I never will, even if I pretend to. It's just, well, Protestants are so different."

"My point precisely."

"Please don't make up your mind about this until I get back from Oxford. I know two years is a long time to be apart. Wait for me? Please?"

Sandy pondered for a few moments. "OK," she said finally. "I'll be busy getting my MSW. I probably won't have time to even give you a thought."

In the fall of 1962, a few days before her MSW program began, Sandy checked into her little room at Johnson Hall, the graduate women's dorm on the Columbia University campus. Even though she was busy with her classes and training, it was agony being separated from Jeff.

"Why are you waiting for him?" Leon Miller asked her.

"Break it off now," Helen echoed. "Find somebody else."

Her mom didn't need to add "Find somebody Jewish." Sandy knew what she meant. Well, her parents were right. She couldn't argue with them any longer.

But how could she give him up? After all, she loved Jeff enough to go to bed with him. Even so, Sandy decided she needed to break up with him once and for all.

She wanted to end the romance in person, but airplane fares to England cost too much for her to fly there. Jeff couldn't afford to come back to the states, even to spend Christmas with his parents. Trans-Atlantic telephone calls were extremely expensive and connections not always clear. So Sandy wrote what was known in those days as a "Dear John Letter."

She cried after she mailed the letter, even though by now she knew it was for the best.

Jeff wrote a short note back.

"I got your letter. I understand. I knew the end might come some day. You always said it would, and I guess I should have listened to you. Sandy, I love you and always will, but I respect your decision. Good luck. Have a great life. Jeff."

Six months later Sandy got another letter from him, the first time she heard from him after his terse acknowledgement of her letter ending their long relationship. Her hand shook as she sank into the mushy mattress on her narrow bed in her room in Johnson Hall.

She tore open Jeff's letter. Read it quickly.

"Dear Sandy," Jeff wrote. *"I hope you and your family are well. I have something to tell you, and I wanted you to hear it from me first rather than from somebody else. I am engaged. Her name is Eleanor Johnson, she's from Portland, Oregon. She's spending two years at Cambridge. We met in the British Museum in London. She's studying English Lit, specializing in the 18th century.*

As if she needed to know that.

Sandy looked up at the ceiling of her tiny dormitory room. "I hope you're happy now," she shouted to her stained-glass window eye in Illinois. "I hope you're happy now!"

She hurled Jeff's letter across the room and burst into tears.

When Sandy's roommate Lorna Brownstein invited her to what promised to be the most lavish wedding in human history and ordered her to appear with a date, she told Lorna she didn't have anyone to bring.

Sandy was in her second and last year of her MSW program at Columbia University. She had moved from her tiny dormitory cell at Johnson Hall on the campus to a five room rent-controlled apartment on West End Avenue. Lorna was biding her time at Columbia Law School until she met her husband-to-be. Sandy's other roommate was Carolyn Schwartz, a dynamic girl from Cleveland who aspired to be a serious journalist. Carolyn and Sandy shared a bedroom. Lorna's father paid a larger percentage of the rent, so she got the other bedroom to herself. This was fortunate because Lorna retired to bed at 8 p.m. every night, her face swathed in creams and lotions, to get her beauty sleep.

"When does she study?" Sandy had asked Carolyn soon after they moved in together.

"Doesn't matter," Carolyn said. "I think she's bagged her 'Mr. Right'. She told me about him last night. Graduate business school. He'll make enough money to keep her satisfied."

As Carolyn predicted, by the end of the first semester the happy couple was engaged. Lorna dropped out of law school so she could spend time on the telephone with her mother planning the momentous event to take place in late May.

"I've gone out with a few guys since ending things with Jeff, but I don't know any of them well enough to invite them to your wedding," Sandy told Lorna. "I'll go alone."

"You have to have a date," Lorna insisted. "Everybody else will have one." She paused, thought for a moment. "I'll fix you up with my cousin Robert. He just broke up with someone, thank God, we all hated her. Real bitch, didn't deserve him. He's very nice, good looking, and works for a top law firm on Wall Street. Good husband material, Sandy."

Sandy was amazed Lorna's cousin was related to her roommate when he picked her up to take her to the rehearsal dinner the night before the wedding. Robert Brownstein was bright and serious, not crass and materialistic like Lorna and the other members of her family Sandy had met. It was difficult to talk during the noisy rehearsal dinner, so afterwards they went out for drinks at a nearby bar.

"I grew up in Chappaqua," Robert told her. "Dad's a lawyer. I always knew I'd follow in his footsteps. My mother teaches third grade. Really great with kids."

Sandy told him about Elmville and her parents.

"Brothers and sisters?" he asked after they ordered glasses of wine.

"One sister. Joanie. She's out in Hollywood being an agent or manager. Not sure of the difference."

Robert told Sandy about his broken engagement. She told him about her long relationship with Jeff, her complicated childhood growing up Jewish in the Midwest, and about the eye in my temple's stained glass window always watching her. She even confessed her crazy desire to be a rabbi. Robert didn't laugh at her, either about the eye or wanting to be a rabbi, as Jeff had.

"Do you believe in God?" he asked.

"I don't know. I think about it a lot. I don't *not* believe in God. I don't think it's necessary for a rabbi or for any Jew. You have to act *as if* you believe in God. It's about how you act, not about what you believe. It's about transmitting Judaism to the next generation. Keeping it alive. Making the world a better place."

"Social justice," Robert commented.

He signaled the waiter and ordered them another drink.

"Of course, I can't be a rabbi now. But maybe soon."

"You think so?"

"We might be getting there. Slowly. In March my roommate Carolyn's mother clipped an article from *The Cleveland Plain Dealer* and sent it to us. I think the headline said, 'Girl Sets her Goal to be First Woman Rabbi.' It was about Sally Priesand, a girl from Cleveland who was accepted as a special student in the undergraduate department of Hebrew Union College in Cincinnati."

"What does 'special student' mean?" Robert asked.

"The article really didn't say. We read it over carefully. Sally's enrolled for credit, but she's not enrolled as a pre-rabbinic student. But Carolyn, who's a big feminist, says I'm not alone. They'll have to admit women to the rabbinical program soon. We can be anything we want to be now. Carolyn feels there's no turning back."

"Meanwhile you're going to be a social worker?"

"Counseling abused women primarily. I'm not too excited about it, but I know I'm lucky I snagged a good job with The Jewish Board of Family and Children's Services. Most of my classmates would kill for this job."

Sandy was pleased when Robert telephoned the day after the wedding to arrange another date. He was the first boy she thought might replace Jeff in her life.

When Sandy went home to Elmville for a visit before she started her new job, her mother arranged a lunch date with a ninety-year-old man whose family was among the earliest Jewish settlers in Elmville. His father had heard Abraham Lincoln debate Stephen Douglas in front of the courthouse in nearby Urbana in 1858. Helen had told him Sandy wanted to become a rabbi.

"There was a woman in our temple, Ray Frank. Rachel was her real name, I think," the elderly man told Sandy as they ate. "She came here because she married Dr. Simon Litman, an economics professor. Real giant in the field."

"Daddy knew Dr. Litman," Sandy said.

"She died around 1948. He just died, but he preserved his wife's memoirs. Ray was from San Francisco. She attended some classes at the reform rabbinical school, but as far as I know, she never out and out said she wanted to be a rabbi. She was basically self-taught. After she wrote a startling article criticizing the American rabbinate, she traveled to Spokane, Washington, where she wanted to attend High Holiday services. But there was no temple in Spokane, no rabbi. When she complained about this to a local Jewish community leader, the man invited her to lead services. At the Opera House, I think. Apparently in her sermon she convinced the local Jews to build a temple there."

"Wow. She must have been something."

"Throughout the 1890s she wrote extensively and traveled throughout the West preaching," he continued. "A lot of wandering lady preachers back then. Very radical gals. Ray Frank was known as 'The girl rabbi of the golden west'. She conducted services, taught, too. Gertrude Stein and Rabbi Judah Magnes were reputed to be among her students."

How ironic, Sandy thought, that both she and Ray Frank lived in Elmville. Was this a sign she should keep trying to be a rabbi? Maybe Ray's spirit lived on in the stained-glass eye in the Elmville temple's window that was supervising her life?

During Sandy's visit, somehow Rabbi Kahn heard through the grapevine that she really did want to become a rabbi. It wasn't just a childhood fantasy she had expressed to him years ago. Rabbi Kahn was so upset, he came over to the Miller's house to quash her wild-eyed rebellion before it was too late.

"Now that you've grown up, Sandra," Rabbi Kahn said as she poured coffee for him, "I can speak more frankly to you about why there can never be women rabbis." He took a deep breath. "If a woman rabbi put her professional obligations above her family responsibilities, this would set a very bad example for women in the congregation, wouldn't it? It would encourage women to desert their duties to their husbands and children and homes. Mothers are the major transmitters of Judaism to their children. The most important job in the world."

"Umm."

"We Jews have a high divorce rate and low birth rate as it is," he continued. "Having women rabbis would just contribute to this trend. Further undermine the Jewish values of family and childbearing. And other Jewish values. Aren't we having enough trouble nowadays keeping Jews as Jews? Didn't we lose enough Jews in the Holocaust? Must we chase others away with this new feminist nonsense? And it would threaten the authority of all Reform rabbis, lessen the importance of our temples if the rabbinate became 'women's work'. Men would no longer want to be rabbis. Maybe wouldn't even want to participate in temple life. Would no longer feel comfortable there, and might stop attending altogether. There would be a schism in the Jewish community. Bitter conflicts resulting from this radical departure from tradition."

Rabbi Kahn paused his rant to take a sip of his coffee. Sandy seized the chance to counter his arguments.

"We Jews have always fought with each other," she pointed out. "Somehow we've survived. We survived Hitler, I think we'd survive the onslaught of women on the pulpit."

Rabbi Kahn looked at his watch, said he needed to pay a hospital visit, thanked Sandy for the coffee, and fled.

Robert and Sandy married a year and a half after they met. Her wedding couldn't compare to Lorna's, but it was lovely, the best her parents could afford. They were fortunate because real estate prices in Manhattan were low at that time, so Sandy and Robert got a good deal on a great apartment on the Upper East Side, what was called a classic six. Two bedrooms, a formal dining room, and a small room off the kitchen that would be a perfect nursery.

In June 1967 the Six Day War between the tiny Jewish state and its neighboring Arab countries shook up even Leon Miller, who had never given much thought to Israel. Sandy was shocked to discover he led the fund-raising efforts in Elmville to collect money for Israel.

"I thought you didn't believe God promised the land of Israel to us," she teased her agnostic sociologist father over the telephone.

"Jews need a homeland," he answered. "It has nothing to do with God."

Israel's rapid decisive victory in the Six Day War filled American Jews with new respect for the tiny country. Sandy pictured Rabbi Kahn pacing back and forth lecturing to the Sunday School kids, raving about the miracle of Israel's astonishing achievement. The victory filled American Jews with pride in being Jewish. Jews had already taken strong leadership roles in the civil rights and anti-Vietnam war movements. Now Jewish writers and Jewish organizations were more outspoken about their own causes and issues. Sandy felt more at home as a proud Jew in the wider Christian world in which she lived.

In the spring of 1968, Sally Priesand was formally accepted into the rabbinical program at Hebrew Union College-Jewish Institute of Religion. Helen Miller telephoned her daughter as soon as she heard the news.

"Now you can apply, Sandy. If they accepted her for ordination they'll have to accept other women. You!"

"Wow. What I've been waiting for." Sandy thought for a moment. "But it's kind of bad timing, Mom. Robert and I decided it's time to start a family. Anyway, I can't leave my job now. Looks bad on your resume if you leave too soon. Maybe I'd be rejected from rabbinical school and still have to be a social worker. I have to think about it. Maybe in a year or two."

Sandy continued to follow Sally Priesand's story in the press. Reporters gave her a lot of attention. Widespread sympathetic media coverage helped her achieve her goal. Self-effacing and shy, Sally claimed she didn't want to be a celebrity or a role model or symbol. She simply wanted to be a rabbi. She spoke publicly throughout the country, insisting quietly but firmly women had the right to fulfill their potential. She said she wanted to serve our long Jewish tradition, not overturn it as she'd been accused of trying to do. Sally's low-key personality and the fact that she distinguished herself from the controversial high-profile feminists helped win supporters.

Sandy's friend Carolyn Schwartz profiled Sally in an article she wrote about women pioneering in previously male-dominated fields. She introduced the piece by saying she had a friend who had wanted to be a rabbi since childhood and now, thanks to Sally Priesand's persistence, her friend could follow her dream.

"And it's about time," Carolyn wrote. *"The Christian community is way ahead of the Jewish community. Harvard Divinity School has been admitting women since 1955. In 1956, Presbyterians ordained their first woman. In 1967, The National Organization of Women established an Ecumenical Task Force on Women in Religion. At least a dozen other Protestant churches are ordaining women or establishing task forces to study the role of women in their churches.*

"And now the idea of women rabbis seems tame when compared to the other dramatic social upheavals of the late '60s our world has seen. Hippies. Yippies. Anti-Vietnam War demonstrations. Civil Rights demonstrations and bloody battles. Draft card burnings. Catholic priests and nuns and Jewish and Protestant religious leaders radically protesting the U.S. government. Vatican Council II overturning centuries-old traditions in the Catholic Church. The assassination of President John F. Kennedy and the recent slayings of Robert F. Kennedy, and Martin Luther King, Jr. Second Wave feminism. The entire country, indeed the world, has been turned upside down. All forms of authority have been questioned. Why not challenge the contention that women can't be rabbis?"

Sandy applied to Rabbinical School in the autumn of 1971. But now, if accepted, she'd face a real problem.

"Since last year Hebrew Union College is requiring all rabbinical students to spend their first year of the program in Jerusalem," she explained to Carolyn. "They built a beautiful new branch of the school near the Old City. I know Robert won't take a year off from his law firm. He can't jeopardize his career. He's just been made partner."

"Go without him."

"I'm married, Carolyn. Wives just don't do this."

"They do now."

"Go for it," Sandy's sister Joanie said when Sandy telephoned seeking her advice. "It would be so exciting. Those sexy Israeli men are to die for."

"I'm married, Joanie."

"You should go," Leon Miller concurred. "We didn't raise you to be a passive wife. You know how I feel about organized religion and rabbis. But if this is what you want, do it. Don't let this old atheist stop you. Or your husband."

"Times have changed," Helen said. "Women can have their own careers now. Their own lives. Gloria and Betty would want you to go."

"Betty Friedan is divorced, Mom, and Gloria Steinem's never been married."

Her youth group friend from Decatur Susan Kleinman was horrified Sandy would even think of going to Israel without her husband. Susan was, in fact, still horrified Sandy wanted to be a rabbi.

"God, Sandy, get over this already! You have to make sacrifices for love. I quit my teaching job so I could stay home to take care of my twins."

"I haven't been able to get pregnant," she reminded Susan. "I've had two miscarriages."

"You'll get pregnant. But it's for sure not going to happen if you're in Jerusalem and Robert's in New York. Last I checked you have to at least be in the same country. Preferably in the same room."

Her cousin by marriage Lorna Brownstein Weiner, now even richer than when they shared the apartment on Riverside Drive because her husband Mark was already vice president of a big investment firm, was equally horrified.

"Leave a great guy by himself in Manhattan with all those beautiful single women?" she shouted. "Risk your marriage?"

"I trust Robert."

"Yeah. Grow up, Sandy."

Finally she got up the courage to discuss it with Robert. "You're hardly ever home, anyway," she pointed out. "Sometimes I'm asleep by the time you get home at night. During the week we see each other at breakfast for about fifteen minutes."

"What do you want from me? I'm a partner now. We work killer hours. You knew that when you married me."

"And you knew on our first date I wanted to be a rabbi."

Robert sighed. "True. I guess I didn't take it too seriously. You were a bit different. A little weird." He laughed. "I guess that's why I fell in love with you."

"Now's my chance to go to rabbinical school. Maybe my only chance, before we have kids. You can fly over to visit me. Or I can fly home to see you."

Robert thought for a long moment, then said, "Okay, you win. But promise me when you get back we'll start to look into adopting if you don't get pregnant."

"Deal. We'll both be working so hard, the time will go quickly."

"Not fast enough. I'll miss you so much."

"And I'll miss you. But if I do this, I'll be a much happier me. A better wife and mother. You'll see. If I don't do it, I'll always regret it. You don't want that to happen, do you?"

Robert kissed the top of her head. "You'd hold it against me the rest of our lives. I'd never hear the end of it."

At the Isaac Mayer Wise Temple known as the Plum Street Temple in Cincinnati, Sally Jane Priesand was ordained on June 3, 1972.

In the early autumn of 1972, Sandra Brownstein began rabbinical school in Jerusalem.

Liz: 1965-1969

TOM PUT LIZ in charge of their church's interfaith efforts.

On October 7th, 1965, Vatican Council II had released a statement from Pope Paul VI entitled "Declaration on Religious Freedom." This groundbreaking document declared for the first time in history the Catholic Church did not possess the only truth and the only path to God. What the Catholic Church had formerly termed Protestant "communities" that had "separated" from it were now to be called "churches", and Catholics should now study their teachings.

On October 28th, near the close of Vatican Council II, the Catholic Church adopted what they called "Declaration on The Relation of the Church to Non-Christian Religions" urging respect for and dialogue with other religions. It included a specific Declaration on the Jews called *Nostra Aetate* proclaiming anti-Semitism was a sin and clearing the Jews of the charge of deicide. The Protestant World Council of Churches quickly praised the document, affirming that revelation first came through the Jewish people and urging its member churches to undertake interfaith work.

What at that time was called "ecumenism" was in the air. Now every year in Reno there would be a community interfaith outreach at Thanksgiving. Their church in Reno agreed to participate with the Methodist, Lutheran, and Catholic churches in a luncheon the day before Thanksgiving, an American holiday without overt specific religious connotations everyone could all in good conscience celebrate together.

The Jewish congregations in Reno also participated in these luncheons and other programs. Jews had always been a small percentage of the population of Reno, but they had played an important role in the city's history. They had been merchants, part owners of the railroad that had built the wild frontier town, and among the earliest casino entrepreneurs.

At the first interfaith luncheon, Liz met Beverly Cohen. It was an important day in her life because Beverly became her best friend in Reno.

Liz was thrilled. She was badly in need of a new friend. Tina was far away and busy with her new baby. She still corresponded with Alicia, but her marriage to Tom had isolated her from her friend's experiences. Alicia had been wild enough in the sexually repressive 50s, and now she was taking advantage of the exploding sexual revolution to justify her promiscuity. She had started a new life in Manhattan as an assistant buyer at Bloomingdale's after her mother succumbed to her cancer and after she finally realized her well-hung lover in their hometown in New Hampshire was never going to leave his wife. She tried to hide her broken heart by regaling Liz with stories of her crazy escapades in New York City.

Liz felt she could confide in Beverly and relax because she wasn't a member of her church.

"Having friends from your congregation is risky," she explained to Beverly the first time they met for dinner alone.

"Probably especially true for a woman," Beverly commented.

"It's really true for men, too. The person you think is a friend can turn on you when there's dispute about your professional performance. Your best friend can end up in the cabal plotting against you or laying the ground to end your contract. It's a lonely profession."

Beverly's husband Walter taught chemistry at the university. They had a baby son. Fortunately, Tom liked Walter. The Cohen's were as poor as Tom and Liz, so they spent many evenings together putting together huge puzzles as they had with Tina and Charlie at Union Theological Seminary. Beverly shared Liz's love of kitting. They traded new stitches and patterns.

With Beverly and Walter Cohen, Liz suffered through the anxiety of the June 1967 Six Day War between Israel and the large Arab states who fortunately failed in their goal to destroy the small Jewish country. Somehow Tom and Liz as well as the rest of the country made it through 1968, the year cultural historians later called the most traumatic period of social change in modern history. Martin Luther King's assassination in April further ignited the civil rights movement. Bobby Kennedy's killing in a hotel in Los Angeles threw the Democratic Presidential primary season into chaos.

In the spring of 1969, Liz' parents came out to spend Easter with them. After they flew back to New Hampshire, on the Sunday following Easter Liz greeted congregants, then sat in her customary spot on the left side of the sanctuary in the third pew to wait for the service to begin. The choir finished singing "Amazing Grace." Tom rose from his chair and moved to the pulpit.

"My friends, last week we celebrated Easter, the resurrection of our Lord Jesus Christ," he began. "Easter is a time of rebirth and renewal. A time when we rededicate ourselves to our tasks, our families, our lives. Our Savior's rebirth coincides with the coming of spring, the rebirth of nature. Trees and plants burst alive again. The earth in all of its God-given beauty is nourished and renewed. So, too, our lives are nourished and renewed. And our future promise is nourished and renewed.

"From time to time at critical points in our life journey we stop to examine the path we have chosen," he continued, "and we turn our thoughts inward. This is one of the functions of prayer. Yes, some may believe there is someone or some thing listening to our invocations that may or may not answer or help us. I believe there is. But I also believe the real purpose of prayer is to call a temporary halt to our busy lives, to silence our day-to-day frenzy, so we can take time for self-reflection and self-assessment. To listen to ourselves, to pay heed to the dialogue between our inner self and our outer self."

Liz sat up straight in the pew. This didn't sound like the husband she knew. He was, like her, rational and practical. While he believed in God intellectually and let his religion inform his life and his behavior, she never felt Tom allowed his religious faith, strong as it was, to change or overwhelm him.

"I have spent the Easter season," Tom continued, "attempting to silence the cacophony of my outer self so I can listen to my inner self. So I can really hear it. Are my inner and outer selves in harmony? Am I on the right path? Have I made the right choices in my life?"

Oh my God, Liz thought, Tom's going to resign. Without even discussing it with me. We're going to starve so he can go off somewhere to find enlightenment.

They had just heard one of their most promising Union classmates had suddenly bolted from his affluent church in Chicago and run off to join a commune in India...

"...No, I have not made all the right choices," Tom was saying. "None of us has. We are all human. All too human, in spite of our earnest attempts to triumph over our sinful natures. Before it is too late in our personal journeys, some of us need to make important course corrections. This is the meaning of the Easter season. Renewal. A new start. New beginnings. Let us all think about our new beginnings, our new chances in life, and prepare for the changes for us that lie ahead."

When the service ended, Liz and Tom greeted congregants at the door. Then they went to the vestry room.

"What was that all about?" she asked as she watched Tom disrobe. "That sermon didn't sound like you. You're hardly a touchy-feely person. It was very touchy-feely."

"I've been doing a lot of thinking, Liz." He paused. "Re-evaluating."

"What did you mean by 'preparing for changes ahead'?"

"I just want to prepare our congregants. Cushion things so they won't be too upset."

"Upset about what? What are you talking about?"

"Let's discuss this when we get home. This isn't the time or place."

"We're talking about it now, Tom."

Tom carefully hung up his robe, smoothed out the sleeves, scratched at a stain on the collar. He quietly shut the closet door, then turned to her.

"You're leaving the church, Liz. You're leaving Reno. Our marriage is over."

She stared at her husband in disbelief. Had Tom actually just told her their marriage was over? Her calm, well-planned and well-ordered life had just come to an abrupt end?

"What?" she asked.

Tom checked that the door to the vestry room was closed, then said, "It's over, Liz. Our marriage. I'm sorry, I didn't intend to tell you like this."

"*Tell* me? You didn't think about discussing it with me? That maybe we could work out whatever you believe is the problem?"

"There's nothing to discuss, nothing to work out. I've made my decision."

"Why are you doing this? Is there somebody else? You're in love with somebody else?"

"You know I don't believe in that kind of behavior."

"Yes. You are certainly too pure and moral for that," Liz said sarcastically. "God called you, chose you out of all others, to show the superior moral path to the world. Isn't that what you told me the first night we met? The church presents the moral alternative. We are moral. We are above the animals." Liz was speaking more loudly now. She couldn't help it. She didn't care now if others heard them. "Oh yes," she rushed on, "that reminds me. What about God wanting us to be together? What about God or Jesus guiding me to Edinburgh after my brother was killed so we could find each other?"

"Things change, Liz. Maybe God changes, too. Maybe God is not a static being."

"I'm in no mood for a theological discussion." Liz took a deep breath. "What's changed, Tom? What's happened? Why are you doing this to me?"

"I can't put my finger on it. It's just, well, I don't feel we are spiritually compatible any more. Certainly not spiritually unified enough to parent children together in a positive way."

Liz saw it clearly now. Tom never intended to have a baby with her. What a fool she'd been to let him talk her into the abortion. Now maybe she'd never be a mother.

"I'm not metaphysically evolved enough to have your children, is that it?" she shouted.

"This isn't a joke."

"You think I'm joking at a time like this? You're the one always telling me I have no sense of humor."

"I can't help the way I feel, Liz. Or don't feel. Anymore."

"There is someone else, isn't there? Be honest with me, Tom. You owe me that."

Tom sank down onto the old couch in the vestry room and put his head in his hands. He waited for a moment. He looked up at her. "Not yet. But I was afraid there would be. Will be. When she's older."

She sat down next to him, said, "Oh, God. It's a kid."

He nodded miserably.

"One of the youth group girls?"

He nodded again.

"Who?"

"I'd rather not say."

"Who?" she shouted.

"Shh, Liz. Somebody might hear you."

"Who, Tom?"

"Emily Mullen."

Oh, yes. Beautiful blonde, blue-eyed sixteen-year-old Emily. A figure like Marilyn Monroe's. Her Sunday school teacher had warned Liz to keep an eye on this girl at the summer retreat she was planning. It flashed into Liz's mind that now she wouldn't have to worry about the damned summer retreat, and she was oddly relieved. She hadn't been looking forward to policing a bunch of teenagers with raging hormones.

She won't be in charge of that retreat, Liz realized, because Tom just announced she's leaving their church. Leaving Reno. Tom wants her to leave her job here. *He's* not leaving. No, Liz realized quickly, we certainly can't continue working together. And, she thought, she can't remain at this church and in this insular community without him. Even if he left, she'd have to leave, too.

"Emily Mullen," Liz repeated flatly. "You'll be convicted of statutory rape."

"Nothing's happened. I haven't touched her. I won't until she's older."

"Nothing better happen," Liz warned him. "The Presbytery could question your ordination. Chastity in single people, fidelity in marriage."

"Emily and I don't need to have a physical relationship to express our love. We are united spiritually. I can't explain it. We are as one. I've never felt this way before." Tom paused, realizing he shouldn't have said that. "I'm sorry, Liz. I never meant to hurt you."

"How could you think I wouldn't be hurt? I'm you're wife. You've ruined my life, that's all. I've planned everything, my whole life, around you. Being with you, together, a team. A family. We had everything planned out."

"*You* had everything planned out. Maybe you can't always plan your life, Liz. I've learned this. Well, you always wanted your own church anyway. This is your chance."

"Oh, yes, I can see this is all for my own good."

Liz didn't have the nerve to telephone her parents right away. They'd be shattered. There had been only one divorce in her family, when her father's Uncle Eustace had run off with a deceptively virtuous-appearing spinster schoolteacher right after World War II. It was the only family scandal Liz knew of.

She badly needed to talk to someone about this. Could she confide in Tina? But maybe Tom had told all this to their friends from the seminary and Tina knew about it before she did and had been sworn to secrecy. Liz hesitated to tell her friend Beverly Cohen. She wasn't in their congregation, but in Reno gossip traveled at lightning speed and crossed all denominational lines.

Alicia.

For the first time since Liz had known her, her friend didn't make sarcastic comments or jokes. Didn't berate Liz or tell her it was her fault because she was so drab, should have worn sexier nightgowns or more makeup. Alicia listened patiently on the telephone to the entire story without saying a word, then said, "The fucking self-righteous bastard. You're well rid of him, Liz. You have your own career, you can earn your own living, and someday you'll find somebody else."

"That's the furthest thing from my mind."

"Come and visit me in big bad New York City and I'll fix you up with one of my castoffs."

A week later Liz did telephone Tina. Her friend seemed genuinely shocked.

"No, I don't think Charlie knew anything about it," she said when Liz asked her. "He would never keep anything that important from me."

But Liz could hear a strain in Tina's voice. Clearly this was going to be an awkward situation for Tina and Charlie. They'd probably have to choose between she and Tom. Liz knew this often was the case when couples split up. It had happened when some of their friends from Union had gotten divorced. She didn't want to lose Tina as a friend.

Finally she could put it off no longer, and she telephoned her parents. Her father exploded, the first time she ever heard him lose his temper.

"We thought he was so solid and dependable," her mother said. "We thought he'd never let you down."

"How could we have been so wrong?" her father shouted.

"Maybe now you can give up this silly idea of being a minister," her mother said hopefully. "That notion was all tied up with Tom."

"No. I want to serve God. I have a calling. And this is my profession. It's what I'm good at. What I've trained for. And," Liz added, "I'll have to support myself now."

"You can always come home to live with us," her mother offered.

"Thanks, but I have my own life now. Not what I'd planned. But I'll have to work it out myself."

"Well, Elizabeth, retain your dignity," her mother advised. "Don't grovel. Don't stay where you're not wanted. Don't stay too long at the ball. Above all, remember, you must always be a lady."

They needed to deal with many practical details. Liz wanted Tom out of their cottage as soon as possible. They didn't have enough money to pay rent on another house or an apartment, so he moved into a tiny grim room in the YMCA. He'd return to the parsonage when she left. Feeling sorry for Tom and not knowing the full story, congregants took turns inviting him to dinner and preparing food he could eat in his room. Liz noticed no one invited her over for dinner.

They spoke to each other only when necessary to settle practical details about their lives or to fulfill their responsibilities at the church. Liz would work at the church until the end of May, and as far as she was concerned, the end of May couldn't come fast enough. Her relationship with the congregants was awkward. She knew they were dying to know why she and Tom were splitting up, but of course couldn't ask directly. Liz was sure they were all speculating and the dissection of their marriage was the gossip tidbit of the year in Reno. Several women expressed their sympathy. One in her weekly bible study group hugged her and said, "Reverend Hagerman, I am so sorry. Nobody had any idea. We're all in shock."

They were in shock! So was she. Liz realized no one must ever know this had been a surprise and shock to her, too.

"It's for the best," she managed to answer.

"You're young. You have your whole life ahead of you," the congregant assured her.

"I appreciate your support," Liz said. "I'll miss you all."

The elders decided they wouldn't hire another pastor to replace Liz. Tom would have to step into her duties. She'd always sensed neither he nor the congregation appreciated or understood how much work she did there, so no one seemed concerned the education and youth programs might suffer in her absence. Probably, Liz speculated, the Presbytery was glad they could save the money they spent on her salary.

As Liz tried to put her life back together, she began to pray more often. She needed the comfort of prayer now that her life was in disarray. What would she do now? Where would she go? For the first time in her life, Liz didn't know what her future would be. When she married Tom she thought her path had been secure. Now she saw stretching before her only a dark void. Emptiness. Chaos. Her life was slipping out of her control.

And she needed answers to important questions. Was this in Your plan, God? What have I done wrong? What did I do to deserve this? Did I misinterpret Your plan for me? Was I wrong when I believed You guided me to Edinburgh so You could bring Tom and me together? Did You really call me to serve You that day at Jack's grave, or, did I just imagine the whole thing? Was the strange feeling I had that day simply a chill from standing in the cold rain?

Are You even here?

Yes, God was here, Liz decided, even though perhaps she'd never get satisfactory answers to her questions. Yes, God had called her to serve Him, whether or not it was through that mystical experience at her brother's grave or just because of the way He had created her with her conscience and sense of duty and desire to bring the world to Him.

There were more practical matters for Liz to think about than God's role in her life. Now she needed to find a new job. She had to update her personal information form on file in Louisville, Kentucky so the search committee of another church looking for a pastor could peruse it. She'd have to explain on the form why she was leaving her present position.

"Just tell them the truth," her friend Beverly advised her. "The truth is always the best way."

"You don't understand," Liz said. "The Presbyterian Church frowns on divorce."

"It's allowed isn't it? Not like the Catholics."

"Yes. But it's considered a moral failing. And for the pastor herself to be getting divorced…"

"…It's not your fault," Beverly, who now knew the entire story, argued.

Beverly was right. On her personal information form Liz had no alternative but to give the real reason she was leaving her present job. She could no longer work with her husband due to the termination of their marriage. Also, Liz added, she was ready for a solo congregation. Which was true.

The best way to get a new job in the Presbyterian Church after one's first pulpit was via the grapevine. Fortunately Charlie Bell, who grew up in Maine, heard the pastor in a church in the small town of Stewart planned to retire in two years because he had just had a mild heart attack. He needed an assistant to help him now and to be his successor if things worked out.

"The guy they thought would take the job turned it down because a church in a warmer climate made him a better offer," Tina told Liz. "The congregation's been left in the lurch."

Liz assumed the church's search committee would contact her elders and Presbytery to find out more about her. Word of mouth was very important. After all, congregations couldn't be too careful these days. She was afraid her impending divorce might preclude the search committee from even considering her for the position. And would they hire a woman?

Apparently by 1969 the feminist movement had reached even Maine. Or, perhaps the church was just desperate. The congregation sent a representative to Reno to interview Liz. They asked her to visit their church, meet Reverend

Billingsley, the senior pastor, and preach a sermon. She did. They liked her; she liked them. The church's Stated Clerk of the Session, George Peck, recommended offering her a contract. The congregation and the Presbytery agreed. Liz was delighted. As a bonus she'd be near her parents in New Hampshire.

By September Liz had gotten the divorce underway and packed up her clothing, books, knitting yarn and needles, files, typewriter, the pewter collection she inherited from her grandmother, and most of the wedding gifts. Tom was letting her take the Chevy they had bought when they moved to Reno. His parents had given him their old Ford when they bought a new car. Beverly was going to drive with Liz as far as Chicago so she could visit her family there and so Liz wouldn't have to make the long drive to Maine alone.

The morning Liz and Beverly left Reno at 7 a.m., Tom helped them pack up the car. Liz settled into the driver's seat, Beverly into the passenger seat. Liz rolled down the window. Tom leaned in and attempted to plant a kiss on her cheek. She turned away.

"Be careful, Liz. It's a long drive," he warned.

"I'm glad you're so concerned about me," she commented sarcastically.

"I'll always care about you. I'm grateful to God for the time we had together."

"You leave God out of this, you bastard!" Liz shouted.

Beverly laughed and applauded as Liz rolled up the window, put the car into gear, and careened away from the curb.

Part II

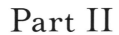

Mona: 1967-1968

IN DECEMBER, A month after Mona's sister Muriel married her Joe, Mona's brother Sluggie announced he was moving to Canada to avoid the draft. Patrick Sullivan was outraged.

"You're running away. No Sullivan has ever run away," he shouted at his son. "It's your duty to serve your country if you're called. Like your brother."

"Guess I can never live up to Rory."

"Now, son."

"That was Rory's choice. If he was dumb enough to sign up for another tour of duty…"

"…Dumb?" Mona's father shouted. "How dare you say such a thing about your brother. He's serving his country. The country that's been so good to us."

"Well, I'm not going to be cannon fodder in an immoral war. We shouldn't be there. We're interfering in a civil war."

"We're fighting there to keep the world from going Communist. If Vietnam goes, the rest of the world could fall. That Father Berrigan. A Catholic priest breaking the law and pouring blood all over government property. Getting himself arrested. I'm ashamed. For the first time in my life I'm ashamed of being a Catholic. What's this world coming to?"

"Many good Catholics are against the war now, Dad," Mona gently pointed out the next time she saw him. "They feel it's their duty to oppose the government if it's doing something they feel is wrong. They believe Jesus would want them to follow their consciences, to fight for a better world. Some parishes are even sponsoring draft-counseling programs. Don't forget, last year the Pope called for an end to the war."

Sluggie told his father again that he was going to Canada and nobody could stop him. Vivian convinced Patrick he must let his son go. Sluggie was twenty years old and no longer a baby. But Patrick Sullivan felt he was losing his family.

"First you, to the convent, Sister Thomas Marie," he complained to her, "though at least I can see you more now than before, and it's an honor to give over a son or a daughter to the Church. Then Rory on the other side of the world in Vietnam. Muriel getting married. I like Joe, but it's hard for me."

"I know, Dad."

"Worst of all Peggy going out with a Jew. What's the world coming to? They don't believe our Lord is the Savior. I've never understood why they don't."

"The Vatican Council says we have to respect all religions now," Mona said. "Other faiths have some truth, too. Our Church no longer has a monopoly on the truth and the only path to salvation."

"Well, that doesn't mean my daughter has to marry a Jew."

Mona sighed, tried a new tactic. "Peggy's a grown woman now. She has to lead her own life. We all of us are leading our own lives. We're all changing. Things change."

"Too fast for me."

"Change is painful," she said. "It's normal to be afraid of it. But we have to learn to cope with it."

"Our Church was never supposed to change. That's what I could always count on. I'm losing my Church, the Church I knew. Having the Mass in English instead of Latin. It's just not the same. Doesn't sound as good in English. Takes away the mystery I loved."

"The Vatican Council wants us to go back to our Church's beginnings, when things were more pure," Mona tried to explain. "They want to make our rituals easier to understand so we'll think about what we're doing instead of just receiving the Eucharist without thinking about it. There's more responsibility on each of us. More for the laity to share in and do."

"Well, they're ruining everything. I guess fasting for one hour now instead of three before going to confession's better, but it's strange to stand while we take communion instead of kneeling. Father Connell doesn't put the wafer on our tongues anymore. Now he looks out at us during Mass instead of facing the altar. They did away with the Index, and we can eat meat on Fridays now. It's all just too much for me."

Mona understood her father's feeling of loss. She too felt the family she had known was slipping away. And she felt she was losing some of her friends in the convent because of the bitter arguments they had in their meetings.

These contentious community meetings now took place nearly every night. The women scrutinized every detail of their lives. Conservative sisters such as Novice Mistress Sister Agnes Brigid and Sister Madeleine John fought all changes. Other sisters just wanted to slow down the pace. Still others eagerly welcomed and embraced the changes. Mona was somewhere in the middle. She could see the need for changes, but she still longed for the serenity and security of their old routines and procedures.

They spent weeks arguing about how to change their traditional habits. Many orders had by now discarded it completely. Mona's community finally voted to continue wearing one, but to do away with the scapular and wimple, shorten the skirt, and replace the large crucifix swinging from their waists with small pins with the order's insignia to be worn on their collars. They would now have to carry purses because they could no longer stash things in the large pockets inside their scapulars.

Decisions about changing their veil, the most important part of their habit, were more difficult.

"We can never discard our veil," Sister Agnes Brigid shouted. "It gets at the very core of our existence. Our veils are the most powerful symbol of our vow of obedience, our separation from the secular world. We've worn them since medieval times."

They compromised. They would continue to wear their veils, shortening them to a more manageable shoulder length.

They abolished their rigid prayer schedule except for the early morning and evening gatherings before and after they left the convent for their work. They had already done away with their periods of silence. Now they abolished prohibitions against "Particular Friendships." In fact, friendships were encouraged, now seen as essential to their wellbeing. They were no longer restricted in their interaction at their convent with what they had called "seculars." They did away with formal penance procedures. Instead, they'd write down their infractions in small notebooks and comment on them during their community meetings.

Sister Theresa James caused a sensation when she took time out from her work with Sister Margaret Traxler in Chicago to visit the convent. Sister Agnes Brigid was appalled when she saw Mona's friend dressed in street clothing. Her cardigan sweater with their order's insignia pin on it was the only indication she was a sister.

"It's easier for me do my work in these clothes," she explained to the others during the community meeting. "I don't need to broadcast who I am on a billboard." She tapped her heart. "My identity is inside me. Now that I know what African - Americans struggle against every day, I can fight against the control the male hierarchy has over me. Those men can no longer tell me what I can or cannot wear. And I've gone back to my former name. Makes me more part of the real world. Sister Luella McBride. Much better. Lots of us are doing it, you all should go back to yours." She paused, took a breath, then announced, "As important as my civil rights work is, I'm leaving it to devote all my time to stopping this immoral and illegal war in Vietnam."

"You are joining those dirty hippies?" Sister Agnes Brigid asked. "We cannot question our government. We have to preserve law and order. And, Sister Theresa James..."

"...Sister Luella."

"Whatever you call yourself now, you cannot decide on your own what work you will do. Did you ask Mother Patricia Luke's permission for this?"

"We can choose our own paths now. With all due respect to our Reverend Mother, I believe she no longer has the power to approve or disapprove what I do. I am no longer ceding her this power over me."

"What about your vow of obedience?" Sister Agnes Brigid asked.

"I'm redefining my vows. Now I see that vow as obedience to my own conscience. To what *I* feel is right."

Sister Agnes Brigid, her face now beet red, leapt out of her seat. "Our vows are inviolate," she shouted. "They are the very foundation of our religious life. This is a veritable slippery slope." The Novice Mistress turned to Mother Patricia Luke. "How can you allow this outrage?"

"To tell you the truth," the Mother Superior said, "I don't know how much authority I have anymore. I'm no longer sure of my place in the new way of doing things. The policy of Permissions and my Grace of Office seem to have gone by the wayside."

"Reverend Mother, you get your authority as you always have," Sister Agnes Brigid insisted. "From the authority of the Pope and our hierarchy."

"Now authority is coming from a different place," Mother Patricia Luke responded. "From the mystical Holy Spirit inside each of us and from Jesus instead of from Church law and the Vatican. We're asserting our individuality now at the cost of defying authority. We're answering our own wants and needs. Sister Luella is answering her own needs."

Mona could no longer remain silent. "But our Sister Formation trained us to deny our own wants and needs," she pointed out. "To deny even our own personhood."

"Yes, I know," Mother Patricia Luke admitted. "It's confusing. At the same time we must look upon these changes and new times as an opportunity. We must be optimistic. A new day dawning. A search for our own spirituality. It's rather exciting, don't you think, Sister Thomas Marie?"

"I don't want excitement, Reverend Mother. I want certainty and peace of mind. That's why I chose the religious life. This is not what I bargained for."

"This is not what any of us bargained for," Mother Patricia Luke said gently. "But we can't have certainty anymore. God is in a constant fluid state of Becoming rather than in an unchanging state of Being. So is our Church. And now our own lives as women religious."

Mona was stunned. Was Mother Patricia Luke really this uncertain about her role in religious life? Was she doubting and questioning herself? Could Mona no longer rely on her, as she had in the past? If her wise Reverend Mother couldn't be sure of anything, then who could be?

At their next convent meeting Mother Patricia Luke announced that Sister Marcella Paul left their community that day. "She's fallen in love, and she's going to get married. A very nice widower, the father of one of her students. She brought him here and introduced him to me."

"But Jesus is our bridegroom," Sister Agnes Brigid protested. "Doesn't this count any more? Doesn't anything count anymore? That girl. I spotted her from the beginning. A silly girl. Too soft. I knew she'd never make it. Never had a real vocation."

"We can't judge too harshly those who are leaving us," Mother Patricia Luke admonished the Novice Mistress. "We must try to understand this is a difficult time for us all and learn from those who have chosen to take another path. Some because, like Sister Marcella Paul, God has opened their hearts in new ways. Or because having so many new choices is confusing us. Now we can forge a productive life outside of the Church. There's a whole new world open to us now."

"I wondered why I didn't see Sister Marcella Paul at supper tonight," Sister Madeleine John said.

"These days you don't know who's going to be at the supper table and who isn't," Sister Agnes Brigid complained. "Even if they've been at breakfast in the morning."

"Yes," Mother Patricia Luke admitted. "It's like the floodgates have opened. We're losing our best and our brightest. Many of our strongest leaders trying to navigate the Church's painful transition to the modern world. To make matters worse, as you know, fewer girls are coming into religious life. Soon we're not going to be able to bring in enough money to support our retired and ill sisters. Or staff our schools or hospitals or social agencies. The hierarchy has always taken advantage of us women. Operated with our free labor."

There was total silence in the parlor.

"Don't look so shocked, sisters," Mother Patricia Luke said. "That's what we women religious have been for centuries. Free labor. The Church could never have flourished or even survived without us. Though the men won't ever give us the credit."

Mona had never heard Mother Patricia Luke criticize the church hierarchy so harshly. She had often argued with their bishop and sometimes outsmarted him, but she had always done it with grace and humor. Now Mona detected a new tone of bitterness.

Was Mother Patricia Luke questioning the authority of the Church hierarchy?

If so, she wasn't the only Mother Superior doing so.

Conflict between the Church hierarchy and sisters was coming to a head in the struggle between the order of Immaculate Heart of Mary, a community of over six hundred sisters in Los Angeles, and their supervisor James Cardinal McIntyre. This battle was the first public challenge to Vatican authority by sisters. It was also the first public pushback from the hierarchy to the changes we women religious were making, had been instructed by Vatican Council II to make.

When the Immaculate Heart of Mary sisters, known as IHMs, cast off their formal habit, sharply curtailed their daily prayers, and asserted their right to choose their own work, Cardinal McIntyre forbade them to teach in the Los Angeles Dioceses' parochial schools unless they reinstated their traditional clothing and prayer schedule. What had been an excellent school system was crippled because the IHM sisters had always operated and staffed it, as well as running their own college.

Neither the Mother Superior nor the Cardinal would back down. A special committee of The U.S. Conference of Catholic Bishops examined the dispute. The Pope sent a delegate to investigate. The Vatican supported Cardinal McIntyre's position by demanding the IHM sisters either go back to their formal communal life or seek dispensation of their vows. The hierarchy made it clear it had had enough of those sisters' steps toward independence.

The dispute captivated the country's attention. Most lay Catholics supported the IHM sisters. The conservative women religious who opposed Vatican Council II changes supported the Cardinal and Vatican hierarchy. Those who welcomed changes in their lifestyles cheered on the IHMs. Most Mothers Superior backed the IHM sisters, but the Conference of Major Superiors of Women failed by one vote to officially back the rebellious women.

In March 1968, due to the increasing opposition to the Vietnam War, President Lyndon Johnson announced to a stunned nation he would not run for another term. Less than a week later, Reverend Martin Luther King, Jr. was assassinated. In early June, Senator Robert Kennedy was shot in a hotel kitchen in Los Angeles.

A week after that traumatic assassination, Mona graduated from St. John's University. She was allowed only two tickets for the large graduation ceremony.

She gave them to her dad and to Mother Patricia Luke. Her stepmother Vivian threw a big party for her afterwards. Sluggie was in Canada and Rory in Vietnam, but Muriel and Joe came, and Peggy brought her Jewish boyfriend David Greene. It was the first time he met most of the Sullivan family and the family's first chance to get to know him. Mother Patricia Luke and all Mona's friends from the convent were there. Sister Luella couldn't come because she was organizing a big anti-war rally on the West Coast. Kathleen's mother babysat Kathleen's three children so Mona's best friend from childhood could help her celebrate.

When Kathleen could get Mona alone she pulled her aside and dragged her into one of the bedrooms. Kathleen closed the door.

"I'm pregnant again," she said, starting to cry. "Dickie found my secret stash of birth control pills under my underpants in my dresser. He flushed them down the toilet, slapped me, told me I'm going straight to hell."

Mona hugged Kathleen as she sobbed.

"This will be your last baby, Kathleen. The Pope's birth control commission has recommended approving the pill as a contraceptive. Dickie won't be able to stop you from using it anymore. It won't be going against the Church."

But Mona was wrong. On July 24th Pope Paul VI promulgated his Encyclical *Humanae Vitae*, rejecting his birth control commission's recommendations that the Church change its teachings. In the 7,000-word Encyclical the pontiff declared each sexual act must be open to bringing a new life into the world.

Again Kathleen sobbed in Mona's arms the next time they were together. Mona couldn't console her friend with her usual explanations of Church doctrine. Kathleen had been right. Mona could see for herself the harm the hierarchy did to Catholic women. Why were they so insensitive to their needs? Why did women allow the Pope and the male hierarchy to make these important decisions for them that deeply affected their lives? If God loved His creatures, didn't that include women, too?

Kathleen and Mona weren't the only ones enraged over *Humanae Vitae*. The Encyclical created a firestorm of reaction. While most of the Church hierarchy supported it, a few European prelates didn't. Catholic academics and theologians harshly criticized it. Catholic University's Father Charles Curran led 172 theologians and other Catholics, including all six American lay members of the Pope's birth control commission, in their rejection and call for Catholics to follow their own consciences regarding birth control use. The secretary of the World Council of Churches in Geneva declared the Encyclical "disappointing." An Anglican Bishop called it "Ecumenically, a disaster for Christianity."

At the core of public discussion was the growing question of the Vatican's authority over Catholics. "The Pope is afraid if he accepts change on this one point, birth control, he'll be vulnerable to changing other things," Mother Patricia Luke explained one night at supper. "Rather like the domino theory Vietnam War supporters cite. If the Church changes one doctrine, then anything and maybe everything can be changed. All Church authority could be toppled."

In mid-August, Dickie Donavan came home from work and found a note from Kathleen on the kitchen table. The children were at her mother's house. They'd all had their baths, so he could just pop them into bed when he brought them home. Don't forget to give Dickie Junior his Teddy Bear and their beautiful daughter her new doll when he tucks them in. There was leftover chicken and macaroni and cheese in the refrigerator for his dinner.

Dickie walked into the bathroom and found Kathleen lying on the floor in a pool of blood.

She had slit her wrists.

Sandra: 1972-1974

SANDY'S OBSTETRICIAN CLAIMED it was because she was relaxed. Her friends and professors at Hebrew Union College in Jerusalem swore it was because she waded into the Jordan River, a legendary source of fertility. Sandy thought perhaps it was because she had inserted a note into a crack in the Western Wall in Jerusalem asking God to give her a baby. Whatever the reason, she became pregnant during her first year of rabbinical school.

"Must have been the night before my sister Joanie's wedding," she wrote to her friend Carolyn. *"The day Robert and I met in Los Angeles for the wedding and saw each other for the first time since I went to Israel. We left the rehearsal dinner as early as we could and rushed upstairs to our hotel room to make up for lost time."*

Joanie had married a would-be movie actor. Unemployed of course, and not Jewish. Her parents were horrified. After all their nagging Sandy to break up with Jeff because he wasn't Jewish, Joanie had fallen in love with a Southern Baptist.

"Is he nice?" Sandy had asked her mother as they waited for her luggage at the baggage claim at the LAX airport when she flew in for the wedding.

"Pleasant enough," Helen had answered. "He is handsome, I'll give him that."

Handsome was not the word. Chad McGrew, real name Timmy Tom Higgenbottem, was gorgeous. Joanie's wedding was exciting because she was now a successful talent manager. Many of the big stars she represented were there. Sandy tried not to stare at them, but she couldn't help it, she was thrilled. When Leon Miller toasted the couple at the dinner following the ceremony, he delivered a ten-minute speech detailing the sociological conditions in America paving the way for young people of two such different backgrounds to meet and marry. He stopped talking and sat down only when Helen tugged at the hem of his rented tuxedo jacket. The family joked about it for years afterwards.

A month after Sandy returned to Israel, she realized she had missed a period. Her menstrual cycles had always been irregular, so she didn't think too much about it. When she called Robert to tell him the wonderful news after the young Israeli doctor confirmed her pregnancy, he said, "Take care of yourself, and be careful."

"I'm trying. But I'm working harder than ever before. And every day I have to endure a crowded, lurching bus ride for a mile and a half to and from the school and our apartment."

"Maybe you should walk."

"Well, you know Jerusalem. The hills only go up, never down."

"How do you feel?" her husband asked.

"Tired."

"Take care of yourself," Robert repeated. "We don't want another miscarriage. Don't work too hard."

"Ha. I have to, Robert. Rabbinical school's more difficult than I anticipated."

"It's what you wanted for so long, Sandy," he pointed out. "And a baby, too."

"I know, I know. I shouldn't complain."

Sandy confined her complaints to her letters to her parents. *"You know I don't have much facility for learning languages,"* she wrote. *"We have to learn both modern and Biblical Hebrew, including Biblical grammar. Reading Aramaic is even more difficult, but important prayers such as the Kaddish are written in it. Other subjects come more easily. We're studying Prophets, Writings, medieval Jewish history and thought, modern Jewish history, Hebrew poetry, and the Talmud, Midrash, and Mishnah, commentaries on the Hebrew scripture. Of course we're also learning how to write and deliver effective sermons. And basic psychology for counseling. Not in the same league as my social work training, of course.*

"We women rabbinical students emotionally support each other. The women in the education program cheer us on, too. As for the male faculty members -- and there

are no female faculty members -- most can barely hide their discomfort with our pres-
ence or mask their outright hostility. They are, to say the least, not welcoming."

The mysterious fertility powers of the Jordan River or her prayer at the Western Wall or perhaps just good medicine triumphed. Sandy gave birth to adorable Joshua in late August after she returned home to continue her studies at the Manhattan branch of Hebrew Union College.

Fortunately she and Robert could afford a full-time baby sitter and twice-weekly cleaning woman. Sandy interviewed four women to care for Joshua. They hired one from Jamaica with an accent they could barely decipher. The woman worked for one day, but didn't return the next morning. Sandy and Robert laughed, trying to figure out what they had done to scare her away so quickly.

After three additional interviews, Sandy hired Marielle, a Haitian, who agreed to cook and do light housework in addition to caring for the baby. Although she spoke no English, they managed to communicate via the high school French Sandy miraculously remembered. Marielle was devoutly religious. She was amazed when Sandy managed to convey to her she was studying to be a rabbi. Like a Christian preacher, she explained. Marielle made Sandy's hectic life possible. She prepared dinner every night, which was great because Sandy didn't like to cook. And didn't have the time.

They installed Joshua in the second bedroom and Marielle in the small room off the kitchen, called a "maid's room," left over in old apartments from the days when maids lived with their employers. Sandy set up her study in a crowded corner of their master bedroom. She had wanted a baby for so long, it was difficult for her to ignore the crying and gurgling sounds she heard through the wall adjoining their bedroom and Josh's nursery. But Sandy disciplined herself to let Marielle care for him in the daytime while she was there. She realized it was going to be difficult to juggle parenthood with her school and future professional life, a problem Sandy never managed to resolve.

Just as Sandy got into the rhythm of attending classes, studying, taking care of her new baby after Marielle left for the day, and stealing a few moments for her husband, on *Yom Kippur,* Judaism's holiest day, October 6th, 1973, Egypt and

Syria led a coalition of Arab States in a surprise attack on Israel. The United Nations brokered a ceasefire on October 22nd. It didn't hold, and the UN brokered a second ceasefire on the 25th, ending what was afterwards called "The *Yom Kippur* War."

The school required rabbinical students to take student congregations in their second year in order to supplement their incomes and get on-the-job training as well as help out Reform congregations unable to afford full-time rabbis. The women in Sandy's class had trouble finding congregations that would accept a woman or even grant them interviews.

A congregation in New Jersey finally granted Sandy an interview. The three men and one woman on the search committee stared coldly at her as they sat at a round table in a conference room near the temple's social hall.

"Mrs. Brownstein, I feel it my duty to tell you most people in our congregation do not want a woman," one of the men began. "Many don't want a student rabbi at all, don't think we can afford it. We've always made do with lay leaders conducting services. So I don't know why we're even here with you today."

Sandy forced herself to smile. This was not promising.

"I personally do not believe women should be rabbis, and many others in our congregation agree," the woman on the committee said. "It's just not in the normal scheme of things. We should be home with our children. Instilling our Judaism in them. Always so much to keep us busy, cooking, cleaning, preparing for the holidays. Setting a good example for our daughters. Being on important committees at our temples, like I am. This committee."

"You girl rabbinical students just want to bring attention to yourselves. You're all just frustrated feminists," the second man volunteered. "And anyway, women aren't up to the rigorous demands of the rabbinate. Maybe you'll cry when somebody criticizes you. Male rabbis will have to protect you in confrontational situations that will undoubtedly arise. And I worry perhaps a woman won't want to leave her home and family responsibilities at night to oversee a temple function. Certainly the male rabbi would hesitate to ask her to do that."

"Maybe they'll be afraid to go out alone after dark?" the third man asked. "Or hesitate to drive at night? My wife never goes out alone at night. And a woman rabbi's voice won't be loud enough to carry through the sanctuary. Perhaps she won't be able to hold the heavy *Torah*. She might drop it, which of course would be a sacrilege."

Everyone expressed horror at this ghastly possibility.

"Women speak too softly," the first man said. "No one would take their authority seriously. They couldn't wield any power. No charisma. No mystique. And even if they do succeed, which is highly unlikely, it will reflect poorly on the men rabbis. In fact, I don't think women should even be in rabbinical school. Just taking up the spot a man needs who'll have to support his family."

"And distracting the boys trying to study there," the woman added.

"Only there to get husbands," the second man added, "and then they'll leave the rabbinate. If they even get that far. Sending them to rabbinical school is a waste of their parents' money." He paused. "I grew up in an Orthodox home, Mrs. Brownstein. I received a thorough Jewish education. Many of our laws are in the *Torah* and oral tradition in order to monitor the effect of the presence of women among men. To curb the bad consequences of mixing men and women together. Sexually, I mean."

He stared at Sandy's breasts. She slumped to make them appear smaller.

"You're a real looker," he continued. "Way too pretty to be a rabbi."

Sandy tried to keep shock from registering on her face.

"As I'm sure you know," he said sternly, "according to the bible, women are the root of sexual temptation. Their presence on the pulpit could sexually arouse men."

Ah, the *Yetzer Hara*, Sandy thought. The evil impulse. The unruly male sex drive must be protected from the constant temptation of women. It is the woman's fault. Their very presence is a danger that must constantly be controlled because women's sexuality is always a threat. According to the bible and commentaries, society must always monitor this *Yetzer Hara*, control it through the Jewish tradition's legal system, because preventing sin is preferable to punishing people for it afterwards. Women are responsible for the sin. The source of it.

"That's why there's a *mehitzah* in Orthodox synagogues," the man continued, lecturing to Sandy as though she knew nothing about Judaism. "The Reform movement has done away with this curtain dividing men and women during worship. But the basic psychology behind the prohibition of worshipping together still stands."

"The *mehitzah* is a symbol of exclusion of women," Sandy said. "Times have changed. Not all of our Jewish laws are equally applicable to today's world."

"The laws of Torah and precepts of Judaism are still psychologically valid," the man countered. "Amazingly so. The authors of the bible and the rabbinic commentators were way ahead of their time in their insights into the human mind. They didn't have Sigmund Freud or our modern terminology, but the basic psychology of people and relations between the sexes was the same then as it is now. Having a woman in our pulpit would be a serious distraction."

When Sandy returned home and told Robert about the interview, she said, "I wanted to shout, 'Hey, why aren't we women hopelessly sexually aroused by male rabbis on the *bema*? We have a sex drive, too, you know.'"

Robert laughed.

"But of course I didn't. I just smiled, thanked the members of the committee for their time, gathered my purse and briefcase, stood up, and left the room with my head held high."

In Sandy's next interview with the search committee of a small congregation in Philadelphia, one of the men repeated many of the same arguments against women rabbis. The other committee members must have disagreed with him, because a week later the chair informed Hebrew Union College they wanted to hire Sandy. Eventually, with great difficulty, the other women in her class obtained student pulpits also.

Before they began their assignments, the women discussed at great length what to wear. They knew their physical appearance would be under constant scrutiny, especially when conducting services on the *bema*. Rabbis had always worn robes over their clothing during services, but this was beginning to change, and eventually robes were nearly abandoned altogether except for the High Holidays. Their skirts needed to be longer than styles of the early 1970s dictated. They could never show their legs above the knees. Pantsuits were out. People already thought they were trying to take jobs rightfully belonging to men. They didn't want them to think they were trying to look like men, too. Or, that they were all lesbians, which they knew many suspected. No bright colors even in spring and summer. Suits, definitely. Brown. Navy blue. Grey. Black. Perhaps beige in warmer weather. Low chunky high heels or flats.

"I'll go back to my glasses instead of my contacts," Sandy told Robert. "And we can't look sexy. I'll have to buy some bras that hide my breasts as much as possible. Flatten them."

"Too bad," Robert said. "I like your breasts."

"We must never be seen flirting with men in our congregations. Actually, any men. Ever. Anywhere. I'm the only married woman in the group, so I'll be somewhat immune from this problem."

Every Friday after her morning classes at the seminary and a quick lunch, Sandy took the train to Philadelphia. A congregant picked her up at the station and drove her to a different house each week for home hospitality. She preferred to stay in a motel, but it was a small congregation with a tiny budget. It could barely afford to pay for a student rabbi, let alone a motel room.

Most of the time the congregants Sandy stayed with left her alone in their spare room to rest and prepare for the evening's worship service, summoning her when the *Shabbat* dinner was ready. But sometimes, perhaps feeling compelled to entertain their guest, they trapped her in their living rooms to confess how lax they had been in their own Judaism but wanted to provide a good religious background for their children. Or how they regretted never having a *Bar* or *Bat Mitzvah*. Or, although they didn't believe in God and thought the whole organized religion thing was a big waste of time, they liked being part of the Jewish community, and so they joined the synagogue anyway.

During one visit Sandy's host steered her into his den, closed the door, and whispered, "Rabbi, I have something to tell you...no one else must ever hear about this."

She nodded solemnly.

"I'm, well, I'm having an affair with my secretary. I know it's wrong, but I just can't help it. I love my wife. I don't want to hurt her or lose her. I'm trying to end the affair, really I am, but now the young girl is threatening suicide. What should I do?"

"I don't need to know these things," Sandy complained to Robert when she returned home. "Why do they tell me these things?"

"Because you're the closest thing they have to a real rabbi. And rabbis listen to secrets. You're a social worker, you're trained in counseling. So, what advice did you give him?"

"I said he should be very careful. Let the secretary down slowly. Play up to her higher instincts. She has to realize he must preserve his family, can't hurt his wife and kids. Make the girl see the noble aspects of giving up their relationship."

"Good, good," Robert said.

Personal counseling was just one of Sandy's duties. In her first year she prepared two boys for their *Bar Mitzvahs*, ran the religious school with only one part-time teacher, conducted services every Friday night, led a model Seder in a congregant's large dining room with card tables extended into the living room, presided over small *Purim* and *Chanukkah* parties, visited people in hospitals and nursing homes, and officiated at three funerals. She met the most resistance doing those funerals. However, the mourners knew she was their only choice, unless they went to a commercial funeral home and got stuck with whatever mediocre rabbi its staff provided.

Most people in the synagogue accepted Sandy. But there was subtle sexism, especially, ironically, among the women. There was the time the very peppy woman who always organized the annual potluck dinner asked her to contribute a vegetable or meat dish. Sandy didn't say what she wanted to, which was, "You'd never ask a male rabbi to do this." Instead she answered, "It would be hard to schlep the food from New York. And cooking is not my claim to fame. Believe me, you wouldn't want to eat what I make."

"How do you feed your family?"

"My baby sitter is an excellent cook. We pay her well," Sandy added quickly.

"You're cheating your husband and your son."

Sandy smiled sweetly and said, "Sounds like you enjoy cooking more than I do. I envy you. It's just not my thing."

"But the kids seemed to accept me without question," Sandy told her former roommate and best friend, Carolyn Schwartz. "One adorable six-year old girl missing two front teeth told me she wants to be a rabbi, too, when she grows up. Her Sunday School teacher showed me a drawing of God she made. Big breasts, like mine."

Carolyn laughed.

"And little Richard Skolnick, he's about ten, asked me if boys could be rabbis. I was stunned by his question, then realized maybe he's never seen a male rabbi."

"Things are changing, Sandy. I told you things are changing. We can never go back."

Sandy immediately got her student congregation involved in the Soviet Jewry movement pressuring the Communist government to allow Jews in the Soviet Union to celebrate their heritage or else let them move to Israel. She outlined the history of struggle in a sermon.

"In 1964, two young men Cleveland founded an organization to make Jews throughout the U.S. aware of the situation of the Soviet Jews," Sandy began. "That same year in New York City Jacob Birnbaum organized the Student Struggle for Soviet Jewry.

"The Jews in the Soviet Union don't know much about Judaism, and they aren't allowed to learn anything more about it or to follow their traditions, even the little they know. The Soviet government has closed down synagogues. They've distributed virulently anti-Semitic books. But after Israel's rapid and decisive victory in the 1967 Six Day War, many Soviet Jews developed a deep sense of pride in being Jewish. They began to secretly study Jewish history and texts in small groups in various apartments and attended *Simchat Torah* outdoor celebrations that became rallies demanding the right to freely pursue their Jewish heritage.

"To suppress this growing unrest," Sandy continued, "the Soviet government imprisoned important leaders of this movement or sent them to labor camps, even mental institutions. If Jews apply for permission to move to Israel, they wait for years. If they ever get to leave at all. They lose their jobs or are demoted, unable to get other employment. Then they're accused of 'parasitism', not having jobs, which is illegal, and living off the government, a crime there. They can't get into universities. Entire families' lives are virtually ruined because they're forced to live at the edge of society and just wait for what might never happen, a chance to leave the country.

"In 1970, nine Jews who had been arrested for attempting to hijack an airplane at the Leningrad airport in order to fly it to Israel received the Soviet version of a trial. All were sentenced to prison terms, two given death sentences. Furious international public opinion, including a strong statement from the Pope and criticism from Communist parties outside of the Soviet Union, forced the government to commute the death sentences to fifteen years in prison and to reduce the other sentences. The strong public opinion forced the Soviet Union to admit it went too far in its punishment of the would-be hijackers and also proved protests do affect their policies and actions.

"In February, 1971, the first World Conference on Soviet Jewry in Brussels, Belgium was attended by 800 activists from thirty-eight countries. Now there's a strong interreligious effort. In March of 1972, seven hundred Protestant, Catholic, Evangelicals, Greek Orthodox, and Jewish leaders met at a conference organized by the American Jewish Committee and the National Catholic Conference on Interracial Justice. A formidable nun, Sister Margaret Ellen Traxler, headed the conference. Convened as the National Interreligious Consultation on Soviet Jewry, Ambassador R. Sargent Shriver, founder of the Peace Corps, was Honorary Chair of the event held at the University of Chicago on March 19th and 20th. Highlighting the mission of this new group, Shriver said, 'It's too late to help the Jews in the Holocaust but it's not too late to help the Soviet Jews, and it's not too late to turn the direction of history.'

"In April of '72, Protestant, Catholic, and Jewish clergy participated in the first annual public demonstration at United Nations headquarters on what's now known as Solidarity Sunday. Because of the pressure put on the Soviet regime by activists in the United States and Israel, for a time conditions appeared to be improving for the Jews there. In 1972 the number of exit visas granted to them to leave the country rose to approximately 31,000, more than twice the number dispensed in the previous year. They were allowed more contact with foreign journalists and Western Jews and Christians. Knowing outsiders were cheering them on apparently encouraged the Soviet dissidents to keep up their struggle.

"But in the summer of 1972, the Soviet government imposed what they called an 'Education Tax' or 'Diploma Tax' on would-be emigrants," Sandy continued. "This came to be known as a 'Ransom Tax' because Jews who wanted to emigrate would have to first reimburse the Soviet Union for what the government spent on their education. This tax, based on a sliding scale depending on the amount of schooling, could be a huge fee, as much as $36,000 for someone with a Ph.D. As part of this Ransom Tax, would-be émigrés also were required to give up their apartments, government pensions, and Soviet citizenship. The imposition of this Ransom Tax and additional restrictions on the lives of dissidents prompted leaders of the Soviet Jewry movement to increase the number of marches and demonstrations in order to pressure the Soviet government and to pressure the Nixon administration into making this human rights issue part of the political agenda in its diplomatic relations with the Soviet Union.

"Jews all over America are joining in the struggle, and so should we in this synagogue. We must fight for the liberation of Soviet Jews because of *Tikkun Olam*, our duty repair the broken world and help bring about justice and a better life for all. In the words of *Mishna Sanhedrin* 4:9, 'Whoever destroys a soul, it is considered as if he destroyed an entire world. And whoever saves a life, it is considered as if he saved an entire world.'"

In 1971, Carolyn Schwartz had helped found a new Jewish magazine, *Davka*, which, for the first time dealt with issues regarding Judaism's views of and treatment of women. The most important article in the first issue, written by scholar Rachel Adler, was "The Jew Who Wasn't there: *Halacha* and the Jewish Woman." The following year a counter-culture Jewish publication *Response* published a special issue devoted to a discussion of the Jewish woman. Jewish women all over the country formed *Rosh Chodesh* and *Chavorot* groups. Carolyn invited Sandy to join hers.

"What's all this belly-button examining stuff?" Robert's cousin Lorna, her former roommate, asked when she and Robert met Lorna and her husband Mark for dinner in Greenwich Village.

"*Chavorot* are informal worship and discussion groups," Sandy told her. "From the Hebrew word '*Chavarim*', friends. They grew out of those '60s consciousness-raising groups."

"You mean those things out in California where everybody sits around in hot tubs nude?" Lorna asked.

"We study Judaism from the woman's perspective. *Rosh Chodesh* groups of women meet at the beginning of every month, at the new moon. Women have always had a special relationship with the moon. Especially a full moon."

"Whooo," Mark said, waving his arms at Sandy, "I'm a werewolf."

Sandy ignored his joke and explained how, according to Jewish tradition, *Rosh Chodesh* is a special holiday given to women as a reward for refusing to turn over their gold earrings Aaron ordered the husbands to collect in order to build the golden calf while wandering through the desert after the Exodus.

"Women are exempt from work on this day," she continued. "Rashi claimed women would be renewed in the world to come as the moon renews itself every month. It was an important festival in biblical times. We get in touch with our own experience as women instead of seeing our lives through men's eyes. It's liberating. We're trying to put ourselves and our bodies back into harmony with nature."

"Oh, my God," Lorna said. "You talk about your periods or what? How disgusting."

"Well, we are inventing new rituals for women for important milestones. Grounding these new rituals in the past, for things like menopause. Divorce. Pregnancy, labor, miscarriages, even adoption. One woman in my group wants to have a ceremony for when she weans her baby."

"God," Lorna said. "I just don't get it. Why doesn't Carolyn just find some nice guy and get married and stop all this man-hating stuff?"

"Lorna, I don't know how to break this to you, but there's more to life than babies, cooking, and shopping."

"My life is very complete. Three kids, a wonderful husband, a beautiful house in Katonah."

Lorna nuzzled her face into Mark's shoulder.

"Well, I'm glad you're happy, but it's all about choices now. You made a good choice for you. Carolyn is making a choice for Carolyn."

"She isn't even dating anybody," Lorna pointed out. "No wonder she's so unhappy."

"Needs a good lay," Mark offered. "All those bra burners need a good lay. Shut 'em up."

Sandy didn't want to tell Lorna and Mark that Carolyn was having an affair with a married man, a prominent best-selling author. Carolyn had sworn her to secrecy.

She changed the subject.

"In fact," Sandy announced, "I'm now going to use 'Ms.' instead of 'Mrs.'"

"What?" Robert shouted. "That's news to me. You *are* married, you know. To me, in case you've forgotten. I don't know, Sandy. This feminist stuff is just getting out of hand. And taking too much of your time."

"It's important to me, Robert. I thought you understood that. I'm an independent person outside of our marriage. A woman's standing shouldn't be defined by whether she's married or single. Why should the whole world know immediately whether or not I'm married just by what precedes my name?"

"I should never have let you fall into the clutches of Carolyn Schwartz," Robert said.

"May I remind you I knew Carolyn before I met you?"

"Yes. Unfortunately that is true."

When Sandy told the nine other women in her *Chavarah* group she'd never had a *Bat Mitzvah* because it wasn't done in Elmville when she was growing up, they insisted she plan her own ceremony with them. Sandy borrowed a *Torah* from Hebrew Union College's chapel and chanted the portion allotted for that week. Her unique *Bat Mitzvah* ceremony was written up in the *New York Times* feature section.

Two weeks after the *New York Times* article appeared, Sandy returned home from classes and rifled through the stack of mail her baby sitter Marielle always threw into a large glass bowl in the middle of the dining room table.

A letter from Jeff Shoemaker lay on top of the pile.

Sandy grabbed it, kissed her two-year-old on the top of his blond head, then ran into the master bathroom. She locked the door.

In the thirteen years since she and Jeff had broken up, Sandy's parents frequently ran into her ex-boyfriend's parents on the campus or in the supermarket or at movies or restaurants. Helen Miller kept Sandy up to date on Jeff's life. He had earned his Ph.D. in history from Harvard and now taught Chinese History at the University of Chicago. An Associate Professor already, his proud father boasted. A rising academic star.

She ripped open the envelope with Jeff's handwriting on it and began to read.

"Dear Sandy, I saw your interview in The New York Times. I want to congratulate you for pursuing your dream of becoming a rabbi. I guess I never took your ambition seriously. The world has certainly changed since we were together..."

Sandy grabbed onto the basin in the bathroom for support. Tears came to her eyes. She had never forgotten Jeff. Never really gotten over him, even though she loved Robert and they were happy together. She took a deep breath, sat down on the side of the bathtub, and continued reading.

"...And all things are possible for you women now. My wife Eleanor, who you may remember I met when I was in England, has taken a break from her Ph.D. work in English lit to raise our two kids, Gail, seven, a real beauty, and Jeff Jr., five. A little devil, but my pride and joy.

"I'm sure you're wondering how I got your address. After I saw this article about you my mother called yours. Asked for your address so I could write to you to offer you my congratulations. Well, I wish you much luck. I expect great things from you. Fondly, Jeff."

Sandy didn't tell Robert about the letter. She stashed it away in a shoebox on the top shelf of her closet. She knew she should have thrown it out or else told Robert about it. But somehow she thought it best to keep the letter a secret.

It was the first secret Sandy ever kept from her husband.

But it was not the last.

Liz: 1969–1973

"HOW 'BOUT YOU get us both a cup of coffee?" Reverend Frederick Billingsley asked Liz when she reported to her first day of work as his assistant pastor in the First Presbyterian Church of Stewart, Maine. "The coffee pot is in what passes as our church kitchen. Down the hall that-away." He pointed to the left. "I take mine with two packets of sugar, no cream. Mean heart doctor says I can't have cream anymore."

Liz set down her briefcase, smiled wanly, then found the tiny kitchen. She took two mugs from the shelf above the coffee maker and poured the coffee she assumed the church secretary had made that morning. She returned to his office. He pointed to a chair next to his desk, and she sat.

"Welcome, Elizabeth."

"Thank you, Reverend Billingsley. I usually go by Liz."

"Liz. Yes. Well, I'm afraid we can't give you your own office. I think this was explained to you during your interview here. We've never had an assistant pastor before. Never needed one, and to be completely truthful, I don't see why we need one now."

Liz smiled wanly again.

"This nonsense about training somebody to take over when I retire. Nonsense. Nobody every trained me after my stint in the seminary. You learn on the job, that's the best way. Yes?"

Liz nodded.

"Yes. Well, where shall we start? First of all, your office, so to speak. I've cleared off a small desk in the church library. Occasionally people retrieve books from there, but not often. And sometimes we hold classes there. But for the most part you will have peace and quiet. I had a telephone installed for you."

"Thank you. I'm sure it will be fine."

"We're cramped for space here. As I think you were informed, we are exploring the possibility of building a badly needed new wing onto the church. Main problem is getting the money, naturally. Takes a lot to get people to part with their money around here. This is Maine, not your free-wheeling Reno with your gamblers and gangsters." He paused to sip from the cup. "Well, next item of business. My wife Blanche runs the ladies' book club, we have a group of really smart ladies here, read only the best new books. None of this garbage passing for literature these days. Well, Blanche needs more cookies for next Monday. The gal who usually bakes them is off visiting her daughter in Boston." He glanced down at notes he had scribbled onto a yellow lined pad. "Make about two dozen. That should be more than enough."

"I'm afraid I can't do that, Reverend Billingsley."

"Blanche says she heard you bake a mean cookie."

"Yes, I do like to cook. But I don't believe you'd ask a male assistant to provide refreshments for a meeting."

"Men have no time for baking cookies."

Liz smiled, said gently but firmly, "I don't believe I'll have time, either, Reverend Billingsley. I intend to devote myself solely to my pastoral duties and learning how to best serve our congregants. Not by serving cookies, but by addressing their personal and spiritual needs."

Reverend Billingsley grimaced a bit, then apparently decided to move on. "Of course you're in charge of all of the youth work and Sunday School education."

"Of course," Liz echoed, hoping she didn't sound as sarcastic as she felt. Of course. She was the girl. Just like in her church with Tom.

"Well, let's talk about our Sunday morning routine," he continued. "We have two services, 9 a.m. and 11 a.m. It's a bit of a strain, but I'll handle both services. You'll do the Scripture readings and commentary, same one of course for both services. The choir will just have to suffer through it twice." He laughed at his own joke. "And the weekly announcements before the final hymn. Very important. You'll do sermons once a month at both services. Of course, you will clear the topics with me ahead of time. And the text."

"I was shocked," Liz said to Beverly when she telephoned her that night to report on her first day of work in her new job. "Does he not trust me because I'm a woman? Or because he's never had an assistant before?"

"Sounds like a control freak," Beverly said.

"I could complain to the Clerk of the Session, but I don't want to cause trouble in my first real job on my own. Anyway, I won't be saying anything in my sermons he'll disagree with. I've just gotten here, but I can see how conservative this town and congregation is. I'm used to keeping my political views to myself, like Tom and I did in Reno."

Even though Reverend Billingsley vetted her sermons ahead of time, occasionally Liz saw him sitting in his pew on the Sunday mornings she was allowed to deliver them shaking his head in apparent disagreement at something she said. She knew the rest of the congregation noticed, too, and she felt he was undermining her authority. Also he popped in unannounced to the bible study classes she had taken over to lighten his load after his heart attack.

"Spying on me?" she wrote to Beverly. *"Afraid I'm giving the New Testament a radical feminist twist?"*

But after six months in her new job, Liz had larger worries. Reverend Billingsley suffered another heart attack. Fortunately, he'd recover, but his cardiologist wanted him to retire a year ahead of schedule. She had only six months to prepare herself to take over the pulpit of the First Presbyterian Church of Stewart, Maine.

Liz was elated, but also frightened. Would she be ready for this new responsibility?

They were planning to hold Reverend Billingsley's retirement party outside on the back lawn of the church. They had enjoyed two weeks of perfect weather, but at two o'clock it started to rain, so the janitor helped the hospitality committee quickly move the tables and chairs inside into the church's social hall. Liz was in her office putting the finishing touches on her speech. She needed to strike just the right note. She didn't want to sound like she was too happy Reverend Billingsley was leaving.

Which of course she was.

She didn't want to seem too eager to take over from him. Yet she had to appear prepared to assume her new duties. The congregation had to feel confident Liz was up to the task of her first solo congregation, even a full year before she'd been scheduled to become the senior pastor.

Liz reread her notes. Yes, she had struck a good balance. Sorry to see our beloved Reverend Billingsley leave but let us thank God for the blessings of his many years of wonderful service and let us wish him a happy, healthy, productive retirement. And let me personally thank him for his year of kind mentorship to me, helping me to prepare myself to become ready, willing, and able to take charge.

The telephone in her office rang. Liz picked it up.

"Reverend Adams speaking."

"Your very best friend in all the world Alicia speaking."

"Can't talk now, Alicia. I have to go home and get into something decent. Billingsley's farewell party." She lowered her voice in case the church secretary was loitering outside her door. "Thank God."

"From what you've told me I thought you'd have to call the police to drag him away."

Liz laughed. "His cardiologist insists he stop working. Billingsley's a little, shall we say, reluctant to relinquish his position to me."

"'Cause you don't have the right equipment down below."

"Probably part of it. Well, whatever the reason, I know he's never quite approved of me. He probably can't stand the fact I'll actually be in charge."

"Wasn't that the agreement?" Alicia asked. "When they hired you as his assistant, you'd take over for him?"

"Yes. Unless I disgraced myself."

"Which you will never do 'cause you're such a prude."

Liz sighed.

"Well, that's about to end," Alicia continued. "I've found the perfect guy for you. It's been long enough since that SOB of a husband dumped you. Time to move on. There's no one to go out with in the God-forsaken hick town you live in, so it's up to me to troll for men for you. Believe me this one's perfect for you."

Liz sighed again. "Okay. Give me the scoop."

"Banker. Big bucks. Prim and proper, like you. Maybe not Presbyterian, but some kind of respectable Protestant, so you could dwell in heaven together forever."

"I'm not interested, Alicia. I barely have time to sleep, let alone a social life. Sometimes I'm so busy with a million details I forget completely about God, and I lose sight of what all this is really about. It'll get worse after Billingsley leaves. Sunday offerings are down, and they can't afford to hire an assistant for me. Or they don't want to because I'm a capable woman and they think I can handle everything myself. Women can, but men can't. They're entitled to have assistants. You have no idea, Alicia. It's endless."

Alicia finally persuaded Liz to take a few days off, and she drove down to the city. The blind date Alicia arranged was a disaster. The banker was actually a stockbroker. Although Liz didn't understand or care about the financial world, she tried to appear interested. But not only was he not interested in Liz's life and career, he was appalled. Apparently Alicia hadn't told him the truth.

"You're a preacher?" he gasped between bites of his shrimp cocktail at the expensive restaurant on the East Side where they had arranged to meet.

"What did my friend tell you?"

"School teacher."

"Does it matter to you what I do?"

"You'll only be working until you get married, anyway."

"I've been married," she snapped. "I guess Alicia didn't tell you that, either. And I've absolutely no desire to try it again."

Another dating disaster.

All the dates Alicia arranged for Liz turned out badly. There was no reason to think they'd ever improve. It wasn't just her profession that scared off men. She had to face it, Alicia was right. She was drab. No sex appeal. She still didn't make enough money to go to a beauty salon, so her brown hair was always frizzy no matter how often she brushed it. She never seemed to pick out the right glasses frames. Her wardrobe consisted primarily of LL Bean turtlenecks or crew necks or cardigans and wool skirts. A brown and navy blue suit to wear under her vestments when she conducted services. Shirtwaist cotton dresses with button-down collars for the few hot days in the summer. Liz had heard stories from other women pastors about men in their congregations making lewd remarks to them or making passes. This hadn't happened to her, probably never would. Not that she cared.

"Why don't you just give up," Liz suggested to Alicia. "I'm not ready to date yet. Maybe I'll never be ready."

Divorce was rare and frowned on in those days, but Liz wasn't alone in the early demise of her student marriage. She knew four of her Union Theological Seminary classmates had dumped their spouses immediately after they finished school and no longer needed to rely on their wives' incomes.

She didn't mind being alone. Mathilde, the affectionate black and white cat Liz had rescued from an animal shelter when she first moved to Stewart, kept her warm in her bed, purring and nuzzling her feet. Mathilde sat on her lap the few nights Liz could relax watching TV on the small black and white set in the living room of the little yellow Cape Cod-style house that was her manse. In the little free time Liz had she knit sweaters for her parents, Beverly, and even for Alicia, even though she knew her style-conscious friend would never wear them.

And, as Liz had told Alicia, she was deluged with endless work at the church, especially after Reverend Billingsley's heart attack. She loved the weddings and baptisms and other happy occasions. But she also had to deal with tragedies. Funerals and hospital visits were the worst.

Liz usually managed to cope with the pain and sadness her congregants experienced, believing she was helping them. But after her hospital visits to five year-old Samantha Curtis who was dying a slow and painful death from child-hood leukemia, Liz railed at God as she had when that drunk driver killed her brother Jack.

When little Samantha died, Liz went to the Curtis' house several times to console the family as much as she could.

"We can't know why God allowed this to happen to your Samantha," she told the devastated parents. "I asked the same question when my brother Jack was killed in an automobile accident when he was seventeen."

"Oh, Reverend Adams, we didn't know you lost a brother," Samantha's father said. "Do you believe our baby is resting in the loving arms of Jesus now?"

"Yes," she said, though Liz was far from sure. Then she regurgitated all the phrases Reverend Davis, her childhood pastor who had gone on to bigger and more prestigious congregations, had recited to her when Jack was killed. Liz realized once again how little Reverend Davis' platitudes helped. How meaningless were the intellectual arguments she studied in her seminary classes dealing with the theological Problem of Evil. The stock phrases and rational explanations brought no comfort.

For weeks afterwards Liz was depressed. God had been unspeakably cruel in taking this small child's life. If there was a God. If there was, He didn't seem to have a plan. Liz once thought God had a plan for her. Well, if He did, it certainly hadn't worked out. She had had to make her own plan. Now she wasn't sure there was a plan for anyone or anything. Maybe existence was all fate, circumstance, chance, or, worse yet, simply meaningless chaos. Not since her brother Jack's death had she experienced such a crisis of faith.

Liz speculated she was looking for another tangible sign from God, like the voice or whatever it had been at her brother's grave. She kept thinking if God spoke directly to her once, maybe He'd speak to her again. Give her some kind of signal.

But there was only silence.

Could she go on?

"But of course I have to go on," Liz wrote to her friend Beverly in Reno. *"It's more than my job, it's my purpose in life. I put on a good show when I officiate at worship services, lead the prayers and preach. I try to be positive when I counsel people. I can't let my congregation know I'm harboring doubts. After all, they look to me for guidance. I can't let them know I'm no more certain of my faith than they are. Sometimes, Beverly, I feel like a complete fraud."*

To pull herself out of her depression, Liz focused on caring for people and trying to improve the world. The social activism she had developed at Union Theological Seminary and had changed American life in the '60s was still very much a part of her, even though she knew she had to be careful to not appear too politically liberal.

She organized ecumenical activities in Stewart as she had in Reno. Her congregation co-sponsored interfaith programs with the tiny Conservative Jewish synagogue two blocks away headed by Rabbi Herman Brill. She worked also with the other local Protestant denominations. Except for the Lutherans. That church's pastor, Karl Steinbrink, refused to work with Liz, probably, she assumed, because she was a woman. Handsome young Father Anthony, known affectionately in Stewart as Father Tony also participated, implementing the Vatican Council's recent encouragement of interfaith dialogue.

Liz became active in the wider national scene. As more women were ordained, questions regarding the role of female clergy in the Protestant churches and the special problems they faced came to the fore. In 1967 the Presbyterian Church's General Assembly had established a Committee on the Status of Women. In 1969 it established a Task Force on Women to discuss how to integrate women clergy into the church and how to deal with bias against them. Liz was asked to join the Task Force.

Her friend in Reno Beverly encouraged her to expand her horizons to wider international events. Beverly was active in the burgeoning movement in the American Jewish community demanding Jews in the Soviet Union be allowed to study and practice their religion there or else be granted permission to leave Russia and immigrate to the Jewish homeland of Israel.

"Many prominent civil rights leaders are involved," Beverly told Liz in one of their many telephone conversations. "We have Evangelicals and Catholics on board because Christians in the Soviet Union are also being persecuted. The Soviet Jewry movement has developed into an interfaith endeavor. There's a National Interreligious Task Force on Soviet Jewry. Its director is Sister Ann Gillen, a feisty nun from Texas you wouldn't want to get on the wrong side of, believe me. Her office is in Chicago. She's not afraid to speak truth to power either in the U.S. or in the Soviet Union. She's enlisted Catholic priests and scholars as well Protestant clergy in the difficult battle. We need a smart young dynamic woman mainline Protestant minister in our movement. You!"

"Beverly…"

"…Your people will be thrilled. They hate the Commies up there in Maine, don't they?"

"Beverly, I love you, but I don't think I can take on one more thing," Liz protested.

"But this is important. We can't remain silent in the face of persecution of Jews like we did during the Holocaust. Can we?"

"Well, this is an argument I can't win." Liz said. "I'm in."

Liz helped persuade her own national church leadership to take an interest in the Soviet Jewry issue. On May 21st in 1971 the General Assembly of The United Presbyterian Church in the U.S.A. sponsored a fascinating speaker at its session in Rochester.

This 183rd session of her church's governing body was already noteworthy because it was to be chaired by its first woman moderator in history, Lois Stair. The American Jewish Committee, an important human relations organization headquartered in New York City, arranged for a Russian Jewish woman, Rivka Aleksandrovich, to speak about the plight of Soviet Jewry and to appeal for help for her daughter. It was the first time a representative of the Russian Jewish community would be addressing a major Christian denomination.

Liz drove to Rochester to witness the important event.

Just three and a half weeks before this appearance, Mrs. Aleksandrovich received permission to leave the Soviet Union with her son. Her husband remained in Riga to be near their twenty-three-year old daughter Ruth who suffered from asthma. In three days the girl was to undergo a secret trial after being arrested in October for trying to leave the Soviet Union to move to Israel after authorities had refused her permission to emigrate four times.

"I am deeply moved by your willingness to hear me, a mother," Mrs. Aleksandrovich told the audience. "I have a moral right to appeal you; my daughter is religious. Help me to save my daughter who stands accused of undermining and weakening the power of the Soviet Union. This is because her only fault is that she is Jewish and wishes to lead a national cultural life which corresponds to her beliefs, her religious beliefs."

Three days later, Ruth and the three young men with whom she was put on trial were found guilty. She was sentenced to a year in prison. Rivka Aleksandrovich and her daughter's fiancé Isai Averbush coordinated a lobbying effort for the young girl's release.

In March of 1972, Beverly encouraged Liz to join the National Interreligious Task Force on Soviet Jewry. Father Tony and Rabbi Brill also joined. They circulated petitions within their respective congregations demanding Soviet Jews be allowed to emigrate. On the evening of April 29th, they held an interfaith service at the temple in Stewart on behalf of the Soviet Jews. The service incorporated the Statement of Conscience that had been adopted at the Consultation conference in Chicago. At the service they circulated additional petitions. Earlier in April, Liz and ten others from her church traveled in a chartered bus to New York with Rabbi Brill and fifteen of his congregants and five Catholics from Father Tony's church to participate in the first annual Solidarity Sunday demonstration at United Nations headquarters.

"The strong support by we Christians of National Solidarity Day for Soviet Jews has been hailed as a major achievement in interreligious relations," Liz told her congregation in her next Sunday sermon, hoping to convince some still-skeptical congregants this was an appropriate use of her time and energy. "Bishop Joseph L. Bernardin, general secretary of the U.S. Catholic Conference, claimed the event 'draws United States Christians and Jews into even closer fellowship, in the knowledge that Soviet restriction of religious and civil liberties extends not only to Jews but to Christians as well.' Presidents of three Baptist conventions issued a joint statement supporting the observance and asking President Nixon to intercede on behalf of Soviet Jews during his upcoming May visit to Moscow. The Texas Conference of Churches has echoed this request."

In early June, the Reform branch of Judaism ordained its first woman rabbi, a quiet unassuming girl from Cleveland named Sally Priesand. Liz mentioned it in her next sermon.

"I wonder what took our Jewish friends so long," she said. "We Protestants aren't usually considered cutting edge in anything. But we've been way ahead in ordaining women." Liz paused for effect, looked out at the crowd. "And so far, so good. The world has not yet come to an end."

She heard nervous laughter from her congregants. They weren't used to humor coming from Liz from the pulpit.

"Actually," she continued, "the struggle to ordain women rabbis has been going on for a long time in the Jewish community. Rabbi Priesand researched this history for her thesis last year. She discovered that the long debate in the United States over whether women could be rabbis began as early as 1889 when journalist Mary M. Cohen first raised the question, 'Could not our women be ministers?' in the Philadelphia *Jewish Exponent*. Mary argued women could preach and teach as well as men to both women and men, and cited many Biblical women as examples, such as Miriam, Deborah, Hannah, Huldah, and Esther.

"The lively discussion was revived in the 1920s. In 1922 the Central Conference of American Rabbis, the organization of Reform rabbis, declared, 'Women cannot justly be denied the privilege of ordination.' Martha Neumark was the first woman rabbinical candidate at Hebrew Union College, but the school's Board of Governors voted against ordaining her. She left her studies at Hebrew Union College after nearly eight years. Irma Levy Lindheim, Dora Askowith, and Helen Hadassah Levinthal also studied at Hebrew Union College in the 1920s. In 1938, Tehilla Lichtenstein took over as rabbi in her husband's congregation after he died, and in the 1950s, Paula Ackerman took over her husband William's Mississippi temple after his death.

"Also, through her research," Liz continued, "Rabbi Priesand discovered she would not be the first woman rabbi after all. In Germany in the 1930s, Regina Jonas studied theology at the Berlin Academy for the Science of Judaism. Although the school's faculty accepted her dissertation, her professor of Talmud refused to ordain her. Rabbi Max Dienemann privately ordained her, but others didn't recognize her legitimacy. She taught in an Orthodox Jewish school in Berlin and worked primarily in a home for senior citizens. Ironically, she had more opportunity to function as a rabbi when the Nazis deported male rabbis to concentration camps. Regina Jonas was sent to the Theresienstadt concentration camp in 1942 where she met transports at the railway station to help others deal with their terror and shock when they arrived at the camp. She taught, lectured, and worked with the famous psychologist Victor Frankl there until she perished in Auschwitz in the autumn of 1944.

"Let's offer our congratulations to Rabbi Sally J. Priesand for breaking down this barrier for our Jewish friends."

Even though in mid-June Liz had attended a conference at a Catholic retreat center called Grailville near Loveland, Ohio titled "Women Exploring Theology", at this point in her life she didn't really consider herself a feminist. Her unusual career stemmed from her belief that God called her to serve Him, not from a conviction that women can and should be able to do any job men can. Her disagreements with Tom about their roles in their congregation in Reno had been based on violation of her sense of fairness, not on feminism, as much as Tom had tried to blame Betty Friedan. Liz had assiduously avoided joining those women's empowerment groups so popular in the '70s even in the Presbyterian Church. She wasn't one to share her inner self or air her grievances to a bunch of strangers. And she didn't agree with the radical ideas some of the women in those groups espoused.

But Liz rejoiced when on January 22, 1973 the U.S. Supreme Court Decision Roe v Wade legalized abortion. She was happy other women wouldn't have to experience the anxiety she felt when she had undergone her illegal abortion ten years earlier. She immediately joined the new Religious Coalition for Abortion Rights, an interfaith group of clergy and laypeople dedicated to insuring the constitutional right to privacy in decisions about abortion, which they sensed would face future legal threats.

She knew legalizing abortion would never remove the sorrow she felt at ending the life of the child she would never know and be able to love. The Roe v Wade decision would never remove the bitterness she felt at having been forced to end her baby's life because her selfish husband, even in their first years of marriage, had no intention of spending his life with her.

It was beginning to look as if she'd never have a baby. She was thirty-three now, and no new husband in sight. While she wanted children, she didn't particularly want the father that would have to come with them. This made her regret her earlier abortion decision even more. Liz wondered if she'd ever be able to forgive Tom for what he had done to her. Liz' mother and her friend Alicia were also well aware of her rapidly ticking body clock and still constantly nagged her to find someone.

"Your father and I are concerned about your happiness, that's all," Liz's mother said during one of her visits home.

"I'm doing fine. I don't know when I'd even have time to be married. We're having meetings several times a week because we're definitely building an addition onto the church for our schoolrooms and a new office if we can raise the money. Of course I have to help. Confirmation class. Sermons, funerals, counseling, preparing scripture readings, the youth group. Golden Age Club."

"What about your personal life?"

"I don't need one, Mother."

"What about your sex life?" Alicia asked her over the telephone. "Or should I say lack thereof."

"Doesn't bother me."

"You're running out of time," she argued "All the best men are married."

"I don't care. I don't want to find anybody. I'm happy."

"Yeah, I guess knitting is better than sex."

"Not everybody's as lucky as you, Alicia."

"It's not just luck. You have to make your own opportunities. When I spotted Harry I went right after him. Didn't leave anything to chance."

Alicia was now happily married to wonderful Harry. He was handsome, kind, had a great sense of humor, and was rapidly scaling the heights of the banking profession. They were going to be very rich. Not to mention, Alicia went out of her way to tell Liz, absolutely fabulous in bed. Further proof perhaps there is no justice in the world, Liz decided, because Tom had been right. Alicia always had been a bit of a slut.

"Who," Liz wrote to Beverly, *"can comprehend the workings of God? Whatever the deal is, it's not a straight reward-punishment system. Not in this life, anyway."*

The recent Roe v Wade decision stirred memories, and Liz thought about Tom frequently. Beverly kept Liz up date on his life. From what her friend could gather Tom seemed to be managing his heavy church workload. His congregants appeared to be satisfied with him. And, so far they hadn't found out about his love for Emily Mullen.

But in early February, nearly four years after Liz and Tom separated, Beverly telephoned to announce that, as she put it, "The you-know-what has hit the fan. Your virtuous ex-husband's relationship with his little Lolita has not been purely spiritual. Emily's father got suspicious because she was coming home from college too often. He pressured her until she confessed their affair to him. Daddy told the Church board. Tom was canned on the spot. Yesterday."

"Wow. He's in big trouble. He'll probably never get another church."

"You should feel vindicated, Liz."

"I don't."

"You're a saint."

"No. Just living without illusions now. I'll never lean on anybody again. I've learned a bitter lesson. You can only rely on yourself. You can't count on anyone else. You have to steer your own course in life. I'll never place my life into anyone's hands."

"From now on," Liz said emphatically to her friend, "I'll go it alone."

Mona: 1968-1970

ACCORDING TO THE Catholic Church's catechism, one cannot end one's own life because God is the sovereign master of existence. We must accept life gratefully and preserve it for God's honor and for the salvation of our souls. We are only stewards, not owners, of our lives.

Before Vatican Council II, Mona's friend Kathleen would have been denied a funeral Mass and burial in a Catholic cemetery because the Church considered suicide a mortal sin. But by 1968, many priests had modified their stance regarding these prohibitions. Fortunately, Mona's childhood parish priest Father Connell was one of them.

"We must give our Kathleen's soul the benefit of the doubt," Father Connell told her distraught parents. "I will provide your daughter a burial service, though it won't be a full funeral Mass. And I will allow her to be interred in our cemetery."

Mona was relieved in death the Church hadn't let her best friend down as completely as it had during her brief life. Kathleen's parents took charge of her three young children. Dickie didn't fight his in-laws. He sank even further into his alcoholism.

Mona's family faced its own tragedy. Two days before Christmas they received word that Rory had been wounded in battle in Vietnam. Doctors in the field amputated his right leg immediately. There was brain damage. They weren't certain of the extent of it. They were testing him. After four months in a military hospital in Germany, the physicians transferred Rory to the Veterans Hospital on Twenty-third Street in Manhattan. Since Mona wore what was still recognizable as a religious habit, the Veterans Hospital allowed her to visit Rory whenever she wanted. She took the subway from Queens to Manhattan every day after she finished teaching her fourth grade class at her parish school.

As Mona walked down the long hospital corridors toward her brother's room, she passed sitting in wheelchairs in the crowded hallways and lounges with stale air and the stench of hospital food and urine the human wreckage of was what was left of these brave young men. Mona had struggled with whether or not we should question our government and our President's judgment, but now she agreed with her brother Sluggie. U.S. troops had no business being in Vietnam.

But her father still insisted we must see the war through to the finish. "Rory was doing his duty," he said one night at supper. "If he could talk to us I'm sure he'd say he was proud to fight for his country and he'd do it all over again if he got the chance." Patrick Sullivan fought back tears. "My poor boy. My poor brave boy."

Gradually her father didn't argue his support of the Vietnam War as vehemently, and Mona detected uncertainty and confusion in his eyes. Vivian no longer echoed his sentiments. By her silence and meaningful glances Mona inferred Vivian was beginning to share her opposition to the war.

When Mona visited her wounded brother she wasn't sure he knew who she was. But she believed Rory was aware someone was there with him, holding his hand, caring about him. That was enough for her. She placed Momma's rosary into his hands and knelt with him in prayer every time she visited. This seemed to bring Rory some comfort.

As Mona sat there with him day after day and even as she prayed with Rory she wondered, "Why?" Why did God let her young handsome brother be maimed in body and mind? First Kathleen's unhappy life and terrible death, and now Rory. Why were these tragedies part of God's plan? Were they part of God's plan? Why was there evil in the world? Was evil part of His plan?

Did God even have a plan?

"God has a plan," Mona's friend Sister Luella wrote from California, *"but it's up to us to act to bring goodness and justice into the world. To bring Jesus'*

teachings to fruition in the world. God gave us brains and the moral compass to do the right thing. That's why I'm battling to force our government to end this immoral war. That's why you have to stop burying yourself in a musty classroom in Queens and get out there and roll up your sleeves and work in the trenches for progress and justice."

"Teaching children is important," Mona wrote back. *"These youngsters are the hope of our Church."*

"Yes," Sister Luella answered, *"but there are children elsewhere who need you far more. Children like the ones I met in Chicago at the Cabrini project. Destitute kids in what pass for schools in the rural south. You'd be doing God's work there. Remember what Dorothy Day says about social justice? 'We cannot live alone. We cannot go to heaven alone. Otherwise God will say to you where are the others?'"*

"I have to admit I don't feel I'm doing enough for God and the world by confining my life to my parish school in Queens," Mona responded. *"I've expanded my horizons over the past few years by going to college. Now I've closed my life up again by going back into the elementary school classroom. You're right. I have more choices now."*

Mona went to Mother Patricia Luke's office to discuss her decision. The sisters no longer needed appointments to see their Mother Superior. Now they could approach her whenever they wished, and to encourage more casual communication in the convent now Mother Patricia Luke rarely closed her office door.

But today Mother Patricia Luke's door was closed. Mona pushed it open. Mother Patricia Luke looked up from a book she was reading, startled. "Sister Thomas Marie. Come in." She snapped shut the book.

"Am I disturbing you?"

"No."

Mona's eye wandered to the book on Mother Patricia Luke's desk. It was upside down, but she could make out the title. *The Church and the Second Sex* by Mary Daly, a lesbian feminist theologian who claimed religion is a patriarchal trap for women. Everybody was talking about this radical controversial new book that later came to be seen as the beginning of the Catholic feminist movement, as important as Betty Friedan's *Feminine Mystique* was to secular feminists.

Mother Patricia Luke saw the shock on Mona's face and said, "Please don't tell the others I'm reading this. Now, what's on your mind, dear?"

"I'm thinking about leaving our school and using my teaching skills in the South," Mona began. "There's so much poverty there. So much need. I've been reading the *Nuns Newsletter*. There are many opportunities."

"I'd be sorry to lose you here. You're an excellent teacher. However, you must go and do this if you feel you are called." Mother Patricia Luke smiled. "I sense your friend Sister Luella behind this move."

Mona laughed.

"Think about this decision carefully," she advised Mona. "It's a big step for you to go so far from your family."

Mother Patricia Luke was right. Things were difficult for her father at the moment. Rory was not improving. After his physical and vocational therapy sessions he just sat and stared at the TV set in the Veterans Hospital lounge. He still couldn't speak, perhaps never would. The physicians couldn't predict his outcome. Each case, they explained to the Sullivan family, was different.

They were worried about Sluggie up in Canada. They didn't hear from him often. He worked at a menial job and was living with friends in a shabby house. He'd gone through several girl friends. He told Mona in his letters he relaxed and partied with marijuana. Everybody did, this was the Age of Aquarius, she shouldn't worry, but please don't tell Dad. Mona did worry because she suspected he dabbled in more serious drugs.

And Patrick Sullivan was furious with her sister Peggy. She hadn't ended her romance with her Jewish boyfriend David Greene.

"I think she wants to marry David," their sister Muriel told Mona. "But it's against Church teachings."

"Not anymore," Mona said. "The Vatican Council changed that in 1964."

"The Jews killed our Lord," Mona's father insisted when Mona discussed her sister's romance with him.

"Dad, you know the Vatican Council absolved the Jews of their guilt. Even if it hadn't done that, David Greene didn't kill Jesus."

"True," he admitted.

"The deicide charge has generated centuries of anti-Semitism," Mona explained. "The Pope has declared anti-Semitism is wrong. Even a sin, especially after the Holocaust. We're supposed to reach out to people of other faiths now. Especially to Jews. We must realize David's religion is probably as important to him as ours is to us. His parents are probably upset he's marrying a Catholic."

Mona was getting tired of trying to solve her family's problems. Dad had Vivian now to take care of him. He and his new wife and her brothers and sisters would have to work things out for themselves. There would be telephones wherever she went if they wanted her advice.

Now Mona needed to chart her own new path. She needed to begin her own new life.

Mother Patricia Luke put Mona in touch with Sister Margaret Traxler, who headed the organization that had placed Sister Luella in Project Cabrini in Chicago. Funding from the Office of Economic Opportunity was drying up, but this remarkable woman always found ways to squeeze out money from various sources for her many projects.

"A fine physician, Dr. John Stevens, is starting a women's health clinic on a large compound in the Appalachian Mountains in West Virginia," Sister Margaret told Mona in their first telephone conversation. "It will be part of a center including a soup kitchen and a shelter for the homeless. The project is a real interfaith effort. A Baptist woman has donated her farm. The Jewish community and Protestant churches in the area are also contributing money and sending volunteers. You'll live in the large farmhouse on the property. They desperately need help in all the areas of services they'll be providing there."

"I intended to teach."

"Without a place to live or adequate food or healthy mothers the children cannot learn," Sister Margaret pointed out. "You'll be paid a modest salary." She chuckled. "Very modest."

Mona thought it over for a moment, then said, "Yes. Yes, I'll do it."

"You'll need time to get organized. I'll tell them you'll be there in a month. Buy yourself some new clothes. You can't wear your habit there, even your modern version. It puts up a barrier between you and those you're trying to help. And go back to your former name so you can blend in as much as possible."

"I don't think I can do that. I did away with Mona Sullivan when I took the name Sister Thomas Marie."

"Yes, yes, I know why we took new names," Sister Margaret said impatiently. "To kill our old selves. Well, now we must bring our old selves back to life."

Before Mona left Queens to begin her new adventure in West Virginia, she endured her convent's most dramatic meeting yet. It lasted for two straight days. Mother Patricia Luke had just returned from another of her many networking conferences with other Mothers Superior.

"I'm no longer going to use the title 'Mother Superior'," she announced at the beginning of the meeting. "I'll be known as Administrative Director of the convent. You won't call me Reverend Mother anymore. You will call me Sister Patricia Luke. A team of five will help me make decisions. You will elect these representatives and they will advise me, taking into account your input. In addition, I'm replacing the title 'Novice Mistress' with the term 'Spiritual Director.'"

"What?" Sister Agnes Brigid shouted. "I will not permit this usurpation of my position."

"I am not usurping your position. This change in title reflects our new inner spirituality. Our new focus on inner spiritual development as opposed to strict discipline imposed from the outside."

"That's it!" Sister Agnes Brigid jumped out of her seat and rushed toward the parlor door. "This is the last straw! I'm going to find an order that still has some sanity and respectability."

She stopped at the doorway, spun around, and glared at Sister Madeleine John. "Well, are you coming with me?" she shouted.

Sister Madeleine John threw a pleading look to the woman they were now to call Sister Patricia Luke.

"It's up to you to make the decision, Sister Madeleine John," Sister Patricia Luke said gently. "You haven't been happy here for a long time. Go with my blessing and seek out a more conservative order where you will be more comfortable."

Sister Madeleine John looked from Sister Patricia Luke to the Novice Mistress. After a few moments, trembling, she rose and followed Sister Agnes Brigid out of the room. The next morning they walked quickly together through the doors of the convent for the last time.

Mona's congregation's internal clashes reflected a larger battle raging in the Catholic Church. Things had come to a head in the bitter dispute between the Sisters in the Immaculate Heart of Mary order and Cardinal McIntyre in California.

Ninety percent of the IHM sisters had refused to return to their traditional habits and to once again let the hierarchy choose their work and set their prayer schedule, as the Cardinal had demanded. Cardinal McIntyre suspended them from teaching in and operating the Los Angeles Archdiocesan schools and gave them dispensation from religious life.

The conflict generated headlines throughout the country. It was the most controversial thing that had ever happened to the Church in America. Twenty-five thousand lay Catholics signed a petition on behalf of the IMH sisters. The bitter confrontation split the order. Forty of the sisters obeyed Cardinal McIntyre and returned to the fold. Some left religious life altogether. Most of the remaining approximately 550 dismissed sisters immediately formed a new Immaculate Heart of Mary order, a non-Canonical community with no formal ties to the Church.

Via this very public dispute Rome was sending a strong and unmistakable signal to women religious: stop the changes you are making. In 1969 a series of Papal directives tried to reinterpret the confusing *Perfectae Caritatis* in order to reverse some changes women religious had made as a result of it. Rome instructed them to go back to the pre-Vatican Council II way of life and to submit to authority.

Tension between women religious and the hierarchy grew. Sister Margaret Traxler refocused her energy away from civil rights and other general social programs to promoting the rights of women religious within the Church. She transformed her influential Department of Educational Services into the National Coalition of American Nuns, dedicated to publicly speaking out against male hierarchical interference in the lives of sisters.

"Rome is trying to stop the hemorrhaging," Sister Patricia Luke said. "But they can't control us anymore. They opened up Pandora's Box. Well, they can't put the toothpaste back in the tube now. It's too late."

It was certainly too late for Mona's friend Sister Luella.

"I'm in love," she confided to Mona one night over the telephone. "Father Peter. I've told you about him. We met at the trial of the Baltimore Four. We didn't mean for it to happen."

"Our vow of chastity! Have you…"

"…I've reinterpreted that vow. It has to do with the authenticity, integrity of personal relationships. We must place morality in the realm of contextuality."

"You *have* had sex with him," Mona whispered into the telephone.

"Made love. Love. It is in God's plan for humankind. 'Male and Female created He them.' It's wonderful. I hope you find out someday for yourself."

"I have no intention of breaking my vow of chastity. The original version. Are you going to get married?"

"Next week."

"You're leaving religious life?"

"It's not our desire to leave the Church. It's the Church that's leaving us, forcing us to make a cruel choice. Peter's best friend Father Steven understands our situation and will marry us. He'll admit us to the other sacraments, too. We can continue our anti-war work outside of our vocations, even more effectively because we'll be freed up from these old-fashioned restrictions."

"Old fashioned? These are the foundations of our religious life."

"Mona, you have to get with it. Like Bob Dylan says, 'Times they are a changin'."

"What are you going to do for money?"

"We'll get by. Friends will help us. Other ex-priests and sisters. There's a sort of underground network." Luella paused. "Please don't tell anyone else we're going to repudiate our vows. We haven't told our families yet. We don't want it to get back to them before we figure out a way to break the news. They'll be devastated."

"Where are you going to live? Will you be able to get jobs?"

"Peter might get a teaching position at Cornell. Don't worry. I'll keep you informed."

Love was in the air. Mona's sister Peggy and her Jewish boyfriend David eloped.

"We went down to city hall," Peggy told Mona and Vivian. "Then we splurged on an expensive dinner at a great Italian restaurant in Greenwich Village. It was so romantic."

"Not my idea of a wedding," Vivian commented. "But we wish you best of luck. Do you have enough money to live on? Because you must know your father will never give you a cent. Not that we have much to spare."

"I'm making good money as an emergency room nurse and David just got promoted. We'll make out okay."

"David's parents in Milwaukee have written a gracious letter to us," Vivian told Mona a week later. "They seem to be very nice and more accepting of our Peggy than we are of their David. Your father will just have to make the best of it."

One more family problem for Mona to worry about. It was time for her to leave.

She drove to a nearby thrift shop. With the small amount of money Sister Patricia Luke gave her from the convent's coffers Mona purchased a navy blue skirt, black cotton skirt, three white blouses, a navy blue cardigan sweater, and a heavy wool jacket. She replaced her clunky black oxford shoes with Keds sneakers. Sister Margaret Traxler told her it rained heavily in the area of West Virginia where Mona would be working, so she also bought high rubber boots.

Mona would no longer be wearing a veil. For the first time in twelve years her hair would be showing. One of the new postulants who had gone to beauty school cut it very short. It curled naturally around her ears. Mona rather liked her new look, even though the red hair she was always so proud of had faded to a dull reddish-brown.

She paid a last visit to Rory in the Veteran's hospital. She explained to him she was leaving New York and couldn't come to see him every day but would visit him when she could. Mona didn't know if her brother understood her, but she saw tears in his eyes when she left him that day.

On Mona's last visit to her house, Vivian prepared a delicious roast beef dinner. Vivian and Mona's father and Muriel and her husband Joe and their cuddly baby, Mona's first niece, and Peggy and David and Mona sat around the mahogany dining room table eating in glum silence.

"I'm not going to Siberia," Mona commented. "It's only West Virginia. I'll be coming home to see you. You can even come down to visit me."

Goodbyes at the convent were equally solemn.

Mona packed up her few belongings, including Momma's rosary that had always comforted her, into the small suitcase she had brought with her from home when as a frightened new postulant she passed her first sleepless night in that small curtained-off space.

Sister Patricia Luke drove her to the airport.

"Write often. Telephone when you can," she said after she parked at the curb near the entrances to the terminal.

"Yes, Reverend Mother."

"Sister Patricia Luke now. No more 'Reverend Mother', remember? God be with you, Sister Thomas Marie."

"Sister Mona Sullivan now."

They laughed.

"I have to get used to that," Sister Patricia Luke said.

"I'm not used to it yet, either. It feels strange to be going back to my former name. No more Sister Thomas Marie."

"No. A *better* Sister Thomas Marie."

They hugged.

Mona took one last look at the woman who had been her rock for twelve years in the convent, and, pushing the heavy glass revolving doors, marched bravely into the airport lobby.

Sandra: 1975-1977

Jews believe that God works in human history, and that this history, albeit with its ups and downs, moves slowly in a positive direction. At this time in Sandy's life she thought human history was indeed progressing on an upward course. America had lived through the turbulent 1960s. The terrible Vietnam war had finally come to an end. America was making progress on the social front. Lyndon Johnson had shepherded his Civil Rights Act through Congress in July 1964, officially ending racial discrimination in the country. Title VII of the act prohibited discrimination in employment on the basis of sex as well as race, a victory for the feminist movement. The Economic Opportunity Act established the Office of Economic Opportunity to fight the Great Society's War on Poverty. The Catholic Church was modernizing itself through decisions made at Vatican Council II. The Supreme Court via Roe v Wade had legalized abortion throughout the country. Activists were finally making progress on the Soviet Jewry front. Judaism was not dying out, as Rabbi Kahn and Sandy's parents and everyone else in Elmville had predicted throughout Sandy's childhood. Anti-Semitism had not yet wiped the Jews out. Israel, though troubled from within and threatened constantly by its neighbors from without, was here to stay. No Holocausts for the Jewish people were looming.

But Sandy's optimism, and that of the entire Jewish community, turned into shock when on December 10th, 1975, the United Nations voted seventy-two to thirty-five, with thirty-two abstentions, that Zionism, the nationalist movement that had restored the Jewish homeland in what became Israel, "is a form of racism and racial discrimination." This official resolution was preceded the previous summer by the Declaration of Mexico passed at a conference held in Mexico

City where over 1,000 women gathered at the first United Nations International Women's Decade Conference. According to the American Jewish women who had attended that conference, although the Zionism is racism resolution was officially referring to the state of Israel, they felt that the hostility and anti-Semitism was aimed at all Jewish women there.

Sandy recalled her mother's advice to her when she was eight years old after her friend Betsy Smith had spewed anti-Semitic statements she had heard from her parents. "Lots of people don't like Jews, hate us, even," Helen Miller had told Sandy that day. "Unfortunately, that's the way it's always been and probably always will be. We just have to learn to live with it."

Well, times had changed, and Jews no longer had to learn to live with it. Jews in the 1940s were hesitant to speak out on their important issues, especially right after World War II, because they didn't want to make trouble by calling attention to themselves. But now they had Jewish organizations such as the American Jewish Committee, the American Jewish Congress, and the Anti-Defamation League, and articulate spokespeople who vociferously protested the United Nations' biased resolution.

But the anti-Israel and anti-Jewish leanings of the United Nations, which had miraculously voted to create the state of Israel in 1948, once again reinforced Sandy's childhood instinct that Jews would always live apart from others. As her parents in Illinois had conveyed to her, and as she had learned just by growing up in that small town in the Midwest, they could never really be accepted or comfortable in the larger outside world. This was something Sandy now realized she'd always have to contend with as a Jew and especially as a rabbi.

In February of 1976, the few women rabbis and women rabbinical students from Hebrew Union College in New York and the Reconstructionist Rabbinical College in Philadelphia had met together to discuss their special concerns. By the end of this meeting, they had formed the Women's Rabbinical Alliance. Now they had an official structure for sharing their issues and advising and encouraging each other. Their discussions about how to balance a demanding rabbinical career with motherhood turned out to be especially valuable to Sandy because in October of 1976 she discovered she was two months pregnant.

"It's a shock. I had so much trouble getting pregnant with Josh, I never dreamt I could get pregnant again so easily," she told Carolyn. "We're thrilled, but the timing's tricky. My due date is May 15th. Ordination's only a few weeks later."

"You'll manage," Carolyn said. "You always do. You're amazing."

Trying to accomplish everything she had to do while pregnant made Sandy's life even more difficult. This pregnancy was more exhausting than her first. Her feet and back ached. Her energy gave out in the middle of the day, and she had to take quick catnaps, often by putting her head down on a desk in the library at Hebrew Union College.

Sandy and Robert agreed the new baby's name should start with a "B" to honor the memory of his father's cousin Boris who had recently died. Robert suggested Benjamin. Barbara, if it was a girl.

"I'd like to name her Beruria," Sandy announced.

"Are you kidding?" Robert shouted. "God, the child would be a laughing stock. She's not going to have enough trouble being a rabbi's daughter? A woman rabbi at that? That's not weird enough for the poor kid? On top of that you're going to stick her with a name like Beruria?"

Next Robert and Sandy argued about whether or not to have a special baby-naming ceremony if the baby was a girl.

Jews celebrate the birth of a boy with a *Brit Milah*, a circumcision, a symbol of our continuing covenant with God as commanded in the *Torah*. Observant Jews also symbolically redeem first-born sons from dedication to service at the ancient Temple in Jerusalem by a ceremony known as a *Pidyon ha-Ben*. Both events are followed by a party. But the birth of a female baby was much less celebrated. If the girl was formally named at all the brief ceremony took place during *Shabbat* services in the synagogue, not even necessarily near the time of her birth. Sometimes the baby wasn't even present, depending on if the rabbi and the congregation could deal with the possibility of a screaming child on the *bema*. Sandy wanted a special baby-naming ceremony to be held in their apartment eight days after she was born.

"No," Robert protested. "We'll name her in the synagogue when the time comes. You're probably making yourself crazy over nothing, Sandy. It might be another boy. You complained when we had Josh's *bris,* said the last thing you wanted to do eight days after having a baby was put on makeup and dress up and put out a lot of food and smile at everybody. Why would you put yourself through that again if you don't have to?"

"It's the principle of the matter."

"Nobody ever noticed these things before you women got together to dig up things to bitch about," he grumbled.

"This is about our daughter and her status as a Jewish woman. The covenant wasn't just between God and men. It was between God and all Jews. Including women. We've been excluded from performing important commandments, from total participation in *halachah.* We have to reclaim the *Torah* for women. We shouldn't be marginalized even when we're born."

In January of 1977, the Rabbinical students began to interview for prospective full-time jobs for the following year. According to policies of the Central Conference of American Rabbis, the organization of Reform rabbis that controlled the job placement process, rabbis just out of school could be assistant rabbis only. Assistantships usually lasted for two years, three at the most, and then they would move on to their own small congregations.

It was difficult for the CCAR's placement director, a gentle chronicler of American Jewish history named Malcolm Stern, to even procure interviews for the women. As was the case when they applied for student congregations, often it was women on the search committees who objected most to hiring them. Rabbi Stern finally got Sandy an interview in late January to be the assistant rabbi at a small congregation in a nice Westchester suburb.

At the interview Sandy was, of course, obviously pregnant.

"While our congregation is not entirely against hiring a woman, as you can see by the fact that we're here with you today," the chair of the search committee began, "we were not told you are expecting a second child."

"We know how difficult it must be for you to work and be a good wife and the mother of one child," the woman on the search committee added. "It will be more difficult with two. I know. I have two kids. It was like having five. I was exhausted all the time, could never have held down a full-time job. You ought to stay home and devote yourself to your family. You're making a big mistake. All you young girls are. You buy into this feminist nonsense that you can have it all. Well, take it from me, you can't."

"Women shouldn't even be in rabbinical school," one of the men chimed in. "Just bothers the boys there. And takes good jobs away from the men."

Sandy didn't get that position.

"There's nothing else available in the New York City area, Sandra," Rabbi Stern told her.

"You mean no congregation that will consider a woman."

"There's a very nice one in a Milwaukee suburb. They're willing to interview you."

"Robert's law firm is in Manhattan. We can't move to Milwaukee."

"Interview for this Milwaukee position anyway. It'll be good experience for you to go through the process. If they do want you and you want them, you can discuss it with your husband then. He might surprise you."

Two weeks later, after Sandy promised Marielle pots of extra money for her additional babysitting and housekeeping duties, she grabbed her small overnight bag and her briefcase with two books she needed to read for her Talmud class, the roomy heavy wool coat that covered her expanding belly, and a wool scarf, hat, and mittens to ward off the bitter Wisconsin cold. She rushed to make the flight to Chicago's O'Hare airport, where she was scheduled to change planes for Milwaukee.

The pilots guided the plane through the clouds down into snow flurries, but by the time they deplaned, the flurries turned into a blizzard and all flights from O'Hare were cancelled. Thousands were trapped. Sandy waited in the long line for a pay telephone to notify the search committee in Milwaukee she wasn't going to arrive the time they planned. It was snowing there, too. They understood, wished her luck.

All the waiting area chairs were filled, the mobs of frustrated travelers now reduced to scrounging space on the floor to claim as their own. Sandy stuck out her stomach, hoping someone would take pity on a pregnant lady. It didn't work. She found an empty spot, slid down onto the floor. Leaned back against her overnight bag. She reached into her briefcase and pulled out one of her books.

"Sandy? Sandy?"

She looked up. She couldn't believe it. Jeff Shoemaker was looking down at her. Sandy tried to appear cool, but she felt faint and disconnected from reality. Hoping she would be able to form words in spite of her shock, finally she blurted out, "Jeff! Oh my God! Jeff."

She stuffed the book into her briefcase, and with Jeff's help, struggled up from the floor. They hugged awkwardly. She hadn't seen her high school and college boyfriend in nearly fifteen years. Jeff wore different glasses. His hair was longer -- crew cuts had long since disappeared -- and a darker brown. He had grown those terrible sideburns men wore in the '70s.

A hundred thoughts raced through Sandy's mind. Was she still so gorgeous he was sorry he lost her? Of course not. She looked like a blimp. Seven months pregnant, and she'd been ten pounds overweight to start with. Her boobs were humongous. Oh God, she thought, I'm not even wearing lipstick. Eye makeup's probably smudged. Not wearing my contact lenses. Hair is a disaster.

"Gosh, Sandy, you're pregnant," Jeff said as they stepped back to look at each other. "But you look great."

"Number two."

"Nobody got up to give you a seat?"

"Chivalry appears to be dead."

"Are you on your way to visit your parents?"

"No. I'm supposed to be interviewing for a job in Milwaukee. It's a miracle they even agreed to meet with me, and now this."

"I'm on my way to a conference in San Diego. I'm the keynote speaker. Was."

They stared at each other again for a few moments. Then he gently helped her back down again on the floor, slid down beside her.

They caught up with each other's lives. Jeff was now a Full Professor at the University of Chicago and finishing his third book on Chinese history. Sandy told him she'd be ordained in the late spring.

"Wow, Sandy, so you've finally achieved your goal. I know I laughed at you in high school. I'm sorry about that."

They talked about their parents, siblings, spouses, children. Pulled out photographs of their gorgeous and brilliant offspring. His Gail was ten, son Jeff Jr.

eight. Sandy showed him a picture of three and a half-year old Josh grinning as he sat on his new tricycle.

"I admire you. How do you do it? A kid and a husband and school. My wife Eleanor couldn't manage it all. She stopped work on her Ph.D. when the children were small. She regretted it, I know. She was depressed. I was pretty worried about her. She was on heavy medication. Sometimes when I came home she wouldn't even talk to me."

"Wow. Tough."

"Watching Eleanor go through this made me realize what difficult choices you girls have to make. I can see how boring and frustrating the housework and diaper changing stuff was for her. For any woman. How difficult it is to be a good mom. She's back at work on her Ph.D. now. English Lit. But she feels she's lost valuable time she can never recoup. The others in the field her age already have tenure, maybe even full professors by now. It's been hard on her."

They talked all night. Sandy knew she'd be sorry the next day when she got to Milwaukee and went through her important interview on no sleep. But there was so much to talk about, and somehow they still felt the same emotional connection as in high school and college. They still communicated honestly and completely and effortlessly.

They stared into each other's eyes as they talked and laughed all night. Sandy realized she still felt the same strong physical attraction for him she had years before. She felt like she was back in high school on the night of their prom at the all-night drive-in in Elmville, backed up against the car door battling her uncomfortable strapless bra as she and Jeff ignored *Bridge on the River Kwai* and made out like mad.

He was the same Jeff, but also a different Jeff. He was still the all-American Protestant Midwestern boy. Obviously still a jock. At the same time he seemed more mature and sensitive now. Sandy could see that his wife's emotional difficulties had affected him. Changed him.

As the sun came up, the snow stopped. Marooned travelers stretched out on seats or crunched up on the floor trying to sleep fought their way back to consciousness. The airport was coming to life. The boards began to light up with re-scheduled flights. Sandy's plane to Milwaukee was scheduled to leave in two hours. She needed to telephone the search committee there to tell them when her new flight would arrive. She'd have to walk a long distance to another gate. Grab breakfast if possible.

"We better say goodbye now, Jeff," Sandy said as she stood up, straightened her clothing, and gathered up her belongings.

"It's been great seeing you," Jeff said. "You have everything?"

"Yes."

They looked at each other for a long time. Neither knew what to say. He took her face into his hands, bent down, and kissed her. Sandy wanted to back away but couldn't. They kissed again, their arms around each other as much as her big belly would allow.

"I better go," she said.

"Good luck with the new baby. I hope you get the job. Keep well." Jeff looked into her eyes. "I'll always miss you, you know that, don't you?"

"Me, too."

He took a deep breath, then said, "I never stopped loving you, Sandy."

She stared at him again.

"I love my husband, Jeff. But I'll never forget you." She was afraid to tell Jeff she still loved him, too, afraid to admit it to herself. Instead she mumbled, "Got to go, or I'll miss my plane."

Sandy picked up her things, and, with one last look at her childhood sweetheart, stepped out into the throngs of delayed travelers hurrying to make their new connections.

Sandy snoozed on the way to Milwaukee, then drank tons of coffee in spite of her obstetrician's instructions to give it up. So she wasn't entirely comatose when she finally did have her interview in the afternoon in the synagogue library.

"I apologize for my appearance," she said as she shook hands with each member of the search committee. "I've been up all night at the airport in Chicago."

They commiserated. Then brought up the difficulty of combining motherhood and career. The woman on the search committee who introduced herself as Judith Gravison interrogated her on this point. How on earth could she do justice to this important job while taking care of her growing family? Sandy gave Mrs. Gravison the same response as in her last interview. Excellent baby sitter. Good cleaning woman. Husband is a busy attorney but always pitches in when he can, kids' baths on weekends.

"That's another thing," Judith Gravison said. "Would your husband be willing to change his job for you? Move here? Being a lawyer is an important job. That's a lot to ask of a man. You know how men are. Stubborn."

Everyone laughed.

"In short, Mrs. Brownstein…" Judith Gravison glanced down at Sandy's *curriculum vitae* on the table in front of her. "Excuse me, *Ms.* Brownstein, we feel a bit uncomfortable hiring you. Even though you are obviously a good student and highly qualified. Your recommendations are sterling."

They finished up the interview politely. Then the synagogue administrator led Sandy into Rabbi Gerson Wenick's office. The man for whom she'd work if she got the job rose from his desk and greeted her warmly. He was just approaching middle age. Good looking. Salt and pepper hair. Warm grey eyes.

"You must be exhausted after your night at the airport," Rabbi Wenick said. "I won't keep you long. I see you lived through my search committee's inquisition. If you can survive Judith Gravison, you can survive anything."

"They were very thorough. As they should be."

"Yes. They're being careful. Last year my assistant rabbi was forced to leave under shall we say unpleasant circumstances. Caught by the police in a raid on a homosexual bar downtown. The president of the congregation bailed him out of jail the next morning."

"Yes. I heard about it."

"No secrets in our small world. Sandra, I think you're a great candidate, and I know you'd fit in well with our congregation. But I must be frank with you. I hope you won't be offended and think I'm being sexist in saying this, but I was hoping you'd be less attractive."

"Is that a compliment?"

"I like your sense of humor. You'll need it in the rabbinate. But Milwaukee is a small town, especially the Jewish community. One reason I hesitate to hire a woman as my assistant is because of the gossip mill here. We'd be working together a great deal. I worry people would start rumors about us. You know. And," he added, "I'm not sure how my wife would react to my working closely with an attractive woman."

Sandy left Milwaukee feeling discouraged. They weren't going to hire her. Nobody was going to hire her. Or the other women in her class. They had all wasted their time going to rabbinical school.

Happily, she was mistaken. A month later, the CCAR placement director telephoned to tell her the Milwaukee synagogue wanted to hire her as their Assistant Rabbi. She was shocked and pleasantly surprised.

Now Sandy and Robert needed to make a big decision.

His large law firm had a branch in Chicago.

"Do you think they'd transfer you to the Chicago office?" Sandy asked her husband.

"I don't know. Probably. Reluctantly, but they would if I insist."

"Are you willing to make the long commute from Milwaukee to Chicago every day? Maybe accept a lower salary?"

Robert frowned, finally said, "I guess so."

"You'd be uprooting your career so I can pursue mine. The job in Milwaukee will only be for two years, three at the most. Then we'll have to move again."

After much discussion, they decided Sandy would accept the Milwaukee job. Robert worked out a satisfactory arrangement with his law firm. Once again she told herself how fortunate she was to have this husband. Many men in those years would not have accommodated themselves to their wives' careers. He was a gem, the other women rabbinical students agreed. A keeper.

Robert's cousin Lorna and her husband Mark were appalled.

"You're really hurting your career," Mark warned Robert during a dinner date. "Ruining your future."

"You should give up your career now you're having a second child, Sandy," Lorna said.

"I am not going to give up my career. After all I've been through? Are you kidding me? Don't you know me better than that by now? "

Robert's parents in Riverdale took the news well and said they'd miss them but they'd fly out frequently to see Josh and the new baby. Leon and Helen Miller in Illinois were thrilled. They could see their daughter and her family more often.

In early April Sandy, Robert, and Josh, flew out to Elmville for Passover. The baby wasn't due for another six weeks, and her obstetrician said it was safe for her to fly. They arrived a few days early so Sandy could help Helen with the Seder preparations. Her parents knew Sandy now adhered to the Passover food restrictions. Helen wanted to accommodate her, though Leon argued the Passover laws of *Kashrut* were simply primitive superstition.

"Don't worry about the right food," Sandy told her mother.

"The great omnipotent deity knows we're doing our best, Helen," Leon said. "If he's not too busy running the cosmos to notice."

Sandy was just happy her parents were finally having real Seders. The Miller family tried to have them when she was growing up after they realized they should be celebrating Passover instead of hunting for Easter eggs like their Christian neighbors. But Joanie would get telephone calls from her friends in the middle of them. Leon was always reluctant to take this or any other ritual seriously. And those old *Haggadot* written in antiquated English distributed primarily by the Kosher wine companies were terrible. By now the *Haggadot* had improved, and Sandy would be leading the service before the dinner instead of her dad.

The night before the Seder was the eve of *Shabbat*. Rabbi Kahn had invited Sandy to deliver the sermon that night at services. She was surprised when she received a letter in January from her childhood rabbi inviting her to share the *bema* with him.

"You know I still don't approve of women becoming rabbis," he wrote. *"For all the reasons I've told you. Please don't take this personally, Sandra. You were my brightest and most capable student. However, I still worry this radical stuff you feminists are proposing to change our liturgy and customs will only drive all men and sensible women away. This nonsense about changing the gender of God, for example. And if we chip away at the basic tenets and principles of Judaism, what would be left? Where would it stop? Would there be any Judaism remaining?*

"Be that as it may, I invite you to speak from the pulpit as our guest if you plan to come to Elmville in April to celebrate Passover with your parents. By the way, how is your father taking your becoming a rabbi?

"Sandra, where have the years gone?" Rabbi Kahn continued. *"It seems like yesterday when I heard you give your sermon at the youth group sermonette contest, which you won, as you will remember. It was a pretty good little speech, as I recall.*

Sandy smiled when she read the last two sentences. Of course she remembered the sermonette contest. How could she forget how empowered she felt when she stood up to deliver that speech when she was sixteen years old? That was the day she decided to become a rabbi.

Helen Miller discovered later through the grapevine that Rabbi Kahn had been pressured into inviting Sandy to give the sermon during her visit to Elmville by the widow of the man who'd been president of the congregation when she was a little girl. The man whose booming voice always frightened her as a child was still pulling strings from the grave through his wife who continued to donate large amounts of money to the synagogue. She knew it was wrong, but Sandy took pleasure in knowing their spoiled daughter who always got to be Queen Esther at the Sunday School Purim parties was now a drugged-out hippie in Haight-Asbury.

The night before Passover, as Sandy sat through the *Shabbat* service waiting to deliver her sermon, she looked up at the eye in the stained glass window. But now she was no longer frightened of it. Now she proudly sat upright in her chair on the bema and bravely met its gaze. I am keeping my promise to you, she said silently to it. Being a good Jew. Transmitting our Jewish heritage as I promised you when I was a child.

But the Reform Jewish heritage Sandy was transmitting had changed over the years. The *Shabbat* service she participated in that night in Elmville was a concrete illustration of this. Sandy felt trapped in a time warp.

Rabbi Kahn was still using the old black Union Prayer Book published in 1940, the year Sandy was born, full of "Thees," "Thous," and "Thines." Most Reform congregations used the new *Gates of Prayer* available for two years now. And this congregation still sang the old hymns, many crafted from German marching songs. Now most congregants in synagogues across America, including Sandy's in Philadelphia, were beginning to enjoy lively music written by a young woman named Debbie Friedman. Influenced by folk singers such as Peter, Paul and Mary and Joan Baez, Debbie Friedman's songs were popular also in Jewish youth groups and camps, bringing the ancient religion to life for a new generation.

As Sandy sat on the *bema*, she realized how much the passage of years and the new Jewish feminism's ideas had transformed her Judaism and how far she had moved beyond the world of her childhood and her child's version of Judaism that was an integral part of it. She could see how much she had changed also. She was evolving, developing the strength to forge her identity as a person and as a Jew. The Judaism she promised the stained-glass window eye she'd preserve and transmit was no longer to her just an intellectual heritage of morality and social justice. Now she understood that rituals and symbols concretized feelings and held Jews together as a community.

The moment for Sandy's sermon arrived.

"Little Sandra Miller," Rabbi Kahn began as he introduced her, turning to look fondly at her for a long moment. "Yes, this is how I remember her. A brilliant child always asking excellent questions, many difficult to answer. Now she's Sandra Brownstein, a star in our congregation. The first potential rabbi to come out of Elmville, as far as I know. Some of you remember her as a child, and you will realize how quickly time passes. Others are meeting her for the first time tonight. A hometown girl on her way, no doubt, to success and a modicum of fame in spite of my objections to her unusual career choice, the reasons for which I will not go into tonight." Rabbi Kahn looked at Sandy again, hoping she was taking his last comment with humor. "I do need to say, however, the sight of a pregnant rabbi-to-be is not something I will ever adjust to."

There was a ripple of laughter from the congregation. Sandy made an effort to smile. She was tiring of pregnant rabbi jokes.

"Yes, a pregnant rabbi," Sandy began after she thanked Rabbi Kahn for his introduction and expressed how pleased she was to be back in her hometown synagogue. "Yes, this is indeed a change for our tradition. It's been a long and difficult road to obtain ordination for women. I am one of the three beneficiaries in my class of Sally Priesand's tenacity and courage.

"Some people are finding this change difficult." She threw a long glance at Rabbi Kahn. "Change is always difficult. Many find it painful. But we must deal with it. It's the only true constant in life. The pre-Socratic Greek philosopher Heraclitus taught that everything is in flux, there is ever-present change in the universe. He famously said, 'You cannot step twice into the same stream.' This is true for Judaism as for everything else. When God told Abraham to 'Go forth from your native land and from your father's house to the land that I will show you,' He was forcing Abraham to leave his familiar world and venture out into the frightening unknown. The injunction to 'Choose life' entails taking risks.

"Judaism would not exist today if not for changes instigated when the Romans destroyed the Second Temple and the priestly caste could no longer perform rituals in its sacred space. We were forced to find new ways to survive. Through the Talmud and other commentaries, the rabbis devised ways to maintain the core of our religion and yet make changes necessary when, in our people's first holocaust we were brutally thrown out of our homeland into the Diaspora. We were forced to adjust to the customs and ways of life of the various societies and times in which we found ourselves, or else perish. This was true throughout our long Jewish history. Once again we needed to adapt to new environments when we were thrown out of Spain and Portugal in the fifteenth century.

"If not for the changes made by the Reform movement in Germany in the early 1800s, Judaism wouldn't have successfully made the transition to America. In their eagerness to adjust to new possibilities of their new lives, our immigrant families would have been forced to choose between the old and the new ways, and most would have cast off what they perceived to be out of date old-fashioned, even embarrassing laws and practices they believed would hold them back in their new lives. Reform Judaism allowed them to select and modify their practices so they didn't have to make this stark either/or choice.

"But we must be careful when we make changes in our religion that we keep the essence of the religion intact. Improve, modernize our tradition without destroying the core of it. This can be a delicate balancing act. Now one of the major changes we are witnessing is the advent of women rabbis such as myself. Among the objections to us raised is the fear that if we chip away at *halachah* and important traditions, there may be no Judaism left." She threw another look at Rabbi Kahn. "And, indeed, we must be cautious when we make changes in our tradition.

"There's a folktale I love called 'Shrewd Todie and Lyzer the Miser,' retold by Isaac Bashevis Singer. Shrewd Todie, a poor man who can barely feed his family, borrows a silver spoon from Lyzer the Miser, his rich neighbor, explaining that his daughter is being courted and he has no good silverware with which to impress the suitor. A few days later, when Shrewd Todie returns the spoon to Lyzer the Miser, he brings back with it another silver spoon from the small collection of three silver spoons he used only for Passover Seders. He tells Lyzer that the spoon gave birth and he's returning the baby along with the original spoon. Two more times Shrewd Todie borrows a silver spoon to impress new suitors, and each time returns two spoons, explaining that the spoon gave birth. Lyzer the Miser is of course delighted.

"Shrewd Todie then borrows Lyzer's entire silver spoon collection, claiming the best suitor of all must be impressed. But Shrewd Todie returns only one. Lyzer is angry and asks, 'Where are the other spoons?' Shrewd Todie tells him the other spoons died. Lyzer, now furious, says this is nonsense, everyone knows spoons are not alive and hence cannot die. Shrewd Todie tells him, 'If you believe a spoon can give birth, you must believe it can die.'"

The congregants laughed.

"While one point of this story is you shouldn't value or hoard your material things," Sandy said, "the other lesson is if your treasure can change and grow, it can also wither and die." She paused. "By the way, *halachah* itself does not forbid women rabbis, as some maintain. And I'm telling you tonight there *will* be Judaism left. It will be a different Judaism. A stronger Judaism.

"Tomorrow night we hold our Seder to celebrate Passover, the liberation from slavery of the Israelites from Egypt. Slavery need not be physical bondage only. It can also be psychological bondage to old ways. This new freedom was terrifying to the former slaves. Wandering through the hostile desert they complained and whined. They wanted to return to their more secure lives in which they knew what to expect. With liberation and freedom comes fear of the unknown, yet also the possibility and promise of a new and better way. Ordination of women will transform Judaism for the better. We cannot go back. We cannot step twice into the same stream."

Liz: 1973 - 1977

LIZ HAD NEVER told anyone about her abortion, not even Alicia. So she surprised herself when she blurted out the whole story to Inga Hansen just one week after they had met.

Inga had stopped by The First Presbyterian Church to explore whether or not to join. Since the church secretary was out for lunch, Liz showed her around the building. Inga told Liz she had just moved up to Stewart from Manhattan.

"I got tired of the city," she explained. "Thought I'd give Maine a try. I need some birds and grass and trees and flowers in my life."

"Perhaps you'd like to join our church gardening committee," Liz suggested. "They've done wonders with our back lawn. We have picnics and services there in good weather."

"I don't garden. I'm a painter. I needed a larger studio so I moved here. I do big canvases. I've bought a house with a barn I paint in. I'm going to knock out part of the southern wall to get more light."

"The old Ball place?"

"How did you know?"

Liz laughed. "There are no secrets in this town. You'll find that out soon enough."

"I have to say, I do feel like a bit of an outsider here."

"You're an outsider in Maine unless you've lived here your entire life. Preferably also your ancestors. I've been here over four years, but they tolerate me only because they know I grew up in New Hampshire."

"I'm a Lutheran, not a Presbyterian," Inga confessed as they walked back to Liz' office. "I tried out the Lutheran Church last Sunday. I didn't like Reverend Steinbrink. Grim."

"Oh, God, yes, that he is."

"And I'm impressed your church hired a woman."

"I'd love to see your work. Are you going to display in Trish Flanagan's gallery downtown?"

"Not enough wall space. Trish says if I did smaller paintings she could hang them. But I'm a big canvas kind of person. Can't seem to box myself in. Come to lunch at my house next week and I'll show you my paintings then."

The following Monday, the one day of the week Liz took off, Inga prepared lunch at the Ball place as it would always be known in Stewart no matter how many years somebody else owned it. As Liz sipped a glass of white wine, rare for her especially before sundown, Inga told her about her life. Raised in northern California, Inga was forty-five now, had never been married.

"I came close twice when I was young," she said. "I left one of them at the altar.   Caused quite a scandal."

"I bet."

"One of my lovers left me money. So I was able to quit my job as an art teacher and focus on my painting." Inga swept her arms, indicating the beautiful rolling hills buried in snow Liz could see from Inga's dining room window. "And live like this."

When they finished eating, Inga took Liz out to the barn she had converted into a studio. She displayed her paintings, wild abstracts in vivid colors.

"They're wonderful," Liz said. "I don't know much about art. But I know I love these."

"You don't 'know' about art intellectually. You follow your instincts. Your feelings."

"Whenever I've followed my feelings they've led me into disaster," Liz said as they hurried through the cold on the stone path back to Inga's house.

"Really? You seem pretty successful to me."

It was then Liz told Inga the entire story of her marriage to Tom. How they met because the voice at her brother Jack's grave told her to get on with her life and so she went to the University of Edinburgh with her friend Alicia. How she and Tom so carefully planned their lives together. How he ended the marriage so abruptly. Was fired from his church because of his scandalous affair with the young girl.

"What's he doing now?" Inga asked.

"My friend Beverly in Reno says he's a therapist. Tom trying to help people have better lives? God help us all. He's living back in Indianapolis with his parents. That's all Beverly knows."

Then, for some reason Liz didn't understand, she told Inga how Tom pressured her into having an abortion when they were students.

"Please don't tell anyone about the abortion," she pleaded. "Occasionally I have to counsel a family with a pregnant teenager, and I don't want them to think my own experience influences my advice. And I might lose my job if it got out. You know what it's like for clergy. Especially for a woman."

"My lips are sealed. But you shouldn't blame yourself for the abortion. Or the bad marriage. You were young."

"I tried to blame God. I felt He had betrayed me."

"You wouldn't be human if you didn't have doubts. Like everyone else."

The two women spent as much time together as Liz's heavy schedule allowed. Although she'd always been wary of getting too close to congregants, somehow she felt comfortable with Inga. She didn't criticize her as Alicia always did. Inga seemed to accept her the way she was, even though they were so different. Inga was an artistic free spirit, Liz straitlaced and rigid. Inga wore brightly colored flowing dresses and what was known in those days as "important" jewelry. Liz still dressed mostly in her conservative LL Bean wardrobe and wore only small cultured pearl earrings or the tiny gold hoops her parents gave to her as a college graduation gift. Alicia had long ago given up trying to change Liz' appearance.

Inga was filling a gap in Liz' life. While she was friendly with Rabbi Brill and Father Tony, these were professional relationships, mostly breakfast or lunch meetings to plan their interfaith services or Soviet Jewry activities or to compare horror stories about their frequently thankless professions. Alicia was so absorbed in her new happiness with Harry, decorating their spacious Fifth Avenue apartment and planning dinner parties and great vacations, she was drifting away from Liz. As Liz had feared, her friendship with Tina and Charlie Bell from her seminary days had become strained since she and Tom had split up. Now Liz rarely heard from Tina except those cheerful Christmas cards with color photos of beautiful daughter Charlotte and darling son Charlie, Jr. Beverly was out in Reno, and now when they wrote each other or talked on the telephone it was primarily about the progress of the Soviet Jewry movement.

Sister Ann Gillen, Executive Director of the Interreligious Task Force, had stepped up the number of her speaking engagements throughout the country. Liz invited her to speak at her church in Stewart. Inga put her up in the cheerful comfortable guest room at her house. This saved Liz's church money for a hotel, which was good because George Peck, the Clerk of the Session, objected to the cost of bringing Sister Ann to Stewart to speak as it was.

"You know, Reverend Adams, we're trying to accrue funds to build the new classroom wing," Peck had said. "Forget about this Communist Jewish thing. It's not our problem. Jews have always suffered wherever they find themselves. This is nothing new. In my opinion they rather enjoy it."

As they ate dinner before her speech, Liz told Sister Ann about the resistance of her elders and others in the congregation to her Soviet Jewry work. Sister Ann assured Liz in her talk that she'd emphasize that religious freedoms and human rights were being denied to Christians in the Soviet Union as well as to Jews and that this joint interreligious effort was cementing bonds between Christians and Jews in the United States.

That night at Liz's church, the short stocky nun wearing a Jewish star around her neck spoke from Liz' pulpit at the First Presbyterian Church about how discouraged the Soviet Jews and activists throughout Israel, the U.S. and Western Europe clamoring for their release had been.

"A nine-day fact-finding trip to the Soviet Union to be taken by ten prominent American Protestant, Catholic, and Jewish leaders was cancelled because the Soviet government claimed the reserved hotel rooms in Moscow were suddenly unavailable," Sister Ann explained. "Massachusetts Congressman Robert F. Drinan, a Jesuit priest who headed the mission, declared at a press conference called after the trip's cancellation that denying the ten church leaders the ability to travel to the Soviet Union showed the government there didn't want the outside world to know how it treated its three million Jews.

"But now progress is being made with the Soviet government because of our interreligious efforts and other public pressure. Telephone calls and letters from Christians as well as Jews to these brave Soviet dissidents have kept up their spirits and inspired them. The USSR is accountable to no court, holds no agreement as binding. But still, it wishes to have good public relations, build up its image as a great humanitarian power.

"In the court of world public opinion, we charge the leaders of the Soviet Union with the deliberate destruction of dissidents' families, with a policy of cruelty which is causing the loss of human lives, not only the denial of human rights. We are appealing to the highest levels of American government, to the religious and political leaders of the West to make massive interventions for the persons and families presently threatened."

Sister Ann summarized how the dissidents' lives had been marginalized, how they had become an economic underclass with no jobs, schooling, means of supporting themselves and often no medical care. "Families are separated forever when some members get permission to emigrate and the others are left behind. Yet they have organized underground schools and seminars held in secrecy in various apartments. This seriously jeopardizes the safety of the family offering its home for this purpose. They surreptitiously study Hebrew, the language of the bible now revived and spoken in Israel, a miracle in itself. They study Jewish art and history and other aspects of their faith, organize kindergartens and activities so Jewish teenagers can meet. They celebrate Jewish holidays, especially *Simchat Torah*, which marks the end of their reading of the first five books of the bible. These *Simchat Torah* celebrations are becoming major events them to meet together, primarily at the main synagogue in Moscow."

After the program at the church ended and they were enjoying a glass of wine at Inga's house, Sister Ann invited Liz to attend the Second National Interreligious Consultation on Soviet Jewry.

"It will be May 14th and 15th in Washington instead of Chicago where we held last year's meeting," Sister Ann said, "so national experts can brief us and we can meet with Congressional leaders and officials at the State Department. Congressman Drinan will lead an Interreligious Evening Vigil outside the Soviet Embassy."

"I'd love to go, but I don't think my church will give me the money."

She was correct.

"Reverend Adams, we feel you are spending entirely too much time and energy on these international issues," George Peck admonished her when she requested funds to attend the Consultation.

"I'll use some of my vacation days to go to the Washington meeting."

"You would have to get the approval of the Presbytery to do that. And this isn't what we hired you for. We need our pastor to tend more to our local needs, the needs of our congregation. The thirty days of vacation time we give you is for you to relax and refresh yourself. You'll wear yourself out with all this, and our church will suffer."

Inga offered to pay all expenses for the trip to Washington for the Consultation. Liz accepted her generous offer even though she felt uncomfortable taking money from her.

Optimism about the fate of the Soviet Jews and the dissident Christians grew when, bowing to public pressure from the outside world and in deference to President Nixon's upcoming trip to Moscow, in March the Soviet Union abolished the Ransom Tax.

The Second National Interreligious Consultation on Soviet Jewry was a great success. The delegates met with Senator Henry Jackson who had sponsored what came to be known as the Jackson-Vanick Amendment contained in Title IV of 1974 Trade Act legislation. Jackson had designed his amendment to deny most favored nation trading status to countries that did not respect human rights and the freedom of its citizens to emigrate. The delegates presented to Senator Jackson letters and petitions supporting his legislation signed by thousands of Christians.

Sister Ann asked Liz to help her plan future Interreligious Coalition's national events. At one of the planning meetings, Sister Ann introduced Liz to a rabbinical student named Sandra Brownstein, also active in the Soviet Jewry movement.

"Sandy," her new friend said. "Please call me Sandy, not Sandra. And not 'rabbi'. I'm not a rabbi yet. Tell me, how did you get involved in this issue?"

"My Jewish friend in Reno, Nevada talked me into it. I served a congregation there with my ex-husband."

"We should plan some joint programs together. About Soviet Jewry. And other interreligious things, too."

They exchanged contact information and promised to keep in touch.

On April 7th, 1974, the second night of the Jewish holiday of Passover, Rabbi Brill's synagogue, Liz' church, and Father Tony's congregation held a joint Freedom Seder. In this symbolic community dinner they dramatically connected the Jewish Passover Exodus story in the Old Testament to the desired exodus of Jews and religious Christians from the Soviet Union. Liz and Sister Ann planned a special Holy Week program for Christians in Washington D.C. entitled "Exodus '74" held by many congregations in that city. There was a Seder on Palm Sunday at New York Avenue Presbyterian Church. On Easter Sunday there was a procession and Silent Prayer Vigil for Soviet Jews across the street from the Soviet Embassy.

In the summer Liz travelled to Philadelphia to attend what the Episcopalians termed the "irregular" ordination of eleven women by four retired Episcopal bishops. There she met another activist nun, Sister Mona Sullivan, a prominent leader in the movement pressing for the ordination of Catholic women as priests. To show further support to these Episcopalian women, in October Liz drove to Manhattan's upper West side to watch three of them serve Eucharist at the famous Riverside Church. This was the building from which the organ and those melodious chimes on Sundays and Christmas and Easter mornings had awakened Liz and Tom in their small apartment in the adjacent McGifford Hall when they were students at Union.

"These Episcopal women's ordinations are not sanctioned by that church's governing body," the Stated Clerk of the Session said to Liz when she returned to Stewart. "Reverend Adams, may I remind you we were not aware we were hiring a women's libber when we chose you. This is not what we want or need. This is Maine, not San Francisco or Manhattan. Perhaps you would feel more comfortable serving a congregation in those hotbeds of radicalism?"

His veiled threat did not escape Liz. She needed to be more cautious.

"You catch more flies with honey than with vinegar," her mother advised when Liz told her parents about this disturbing conversation. "You can never go wrong if you act like a lady, Elizabeth."

"I've come too far in my life to go back to 'acting like a lady,'" Liz complained to Inga later. "I guess I've evolved too much. I can't go back to being the nice respectable passive girl I was brought up to be who believed in steady order and upward social progress. Now I think God wants us to be active and fight to bring justice into this messy world. Jesus was a social revolutionary, after all. The Romans killed him because they saw him as a political threat."

Liz continued her Soviet Jewry work. In December the Jackson-Vanick Amendment passed both houses of Congress unanimously. On January 3, 1975 Gerald Ford, now President since Richard Nixon resigned the previous August because of the Watergate scandal, signed the Trade Act into law with that amendment as part of it. The Jackson-Vanick Amendment holding the prospect of free and open trade over the heads of the Soviet regime was in large part responsible for the eventual success of the Soviet Jewry movement. On August 1st the President signed the Helsinki Final Act calling for all countries to allow free contact with others, free movement, and the reunification of divided families as basic human rights. This document became a vital means for pressing for human rights in the Soviet Union and for free Jewish emigration.

In 1976 Liz was one of 1,000 delegates to the Second World Conference of Jewish Communities on Soviet Jewry held in Brussels. They were moved when Sister Ann Gillen presented to former Israeli Prime Minister Golda Meir the document "Call to Christian Conscience" her Interreligious Task Force had issued to Christians throughout the world at the Brussels International Conference on Soviet Jewry in 1975.

In the summer of 1977, Sister Ann invited Liz to attend the Belgrade Conference on Security and Cooperation sponsored by her organization.

Representatives of the thirty-five nations that had signed the Helsinki Final Act of 1975 were planning to meet to review the record of compliance and to make new proposals to improve the Act.

The conference in Yugoslavia was scheduled for Thanksgiving week. This was a problem for Liz. That week was very important in her church in Stewart. It always participated in the local interfaith luncheon. The Sunday school kids always put on a sweet pageant celebrating God's blessing on America. The women's auxiliary distributed food and clothing to the needy. Also, Liz generally tried to make it home to New Hampshire to celebrate at least part of the holiday with her parents, who, she noticed, were beginning to age. But Sister Ann convinced Liz this was a key moment in the Soviet Jewry struggle. At last the U.S. had a tool for forcing the Soviet Union to comply with human rights.

When Liz told her elders she would again use her vacation time to go to the conference, one of them said, "You took vacation time to go to the Brussels conference last year. Wasn't that enough? Where is this going to end? And we gave you money to go to that. We're not going to give you church money to go to Yugoslavia."

Again, although Liz felt uncomfortable about it, Inga paid for her trip. The conference in Yugoslavia was indeed exciting. Seven Hungarians attended, the first time delegates from an Eastern block country met with an inter-religious group. The delegation from the U.S. met with Senators Robert Dole and Claiborne Pell and Representative Millicent Fenwick. Afterwards the group went to Rome to meet with Vatican Officials.

Two days after Liz returned home, Reverend Billingsley died in his sleep. A final heart attack. Everyone knew he'd been living on borrowed time, but the congregation was devastated.

"I'm grateful the end for him came peacefully," Billingsley's wife Blanche told Liz when she went immediately to their home the following morning to pay her condolences and plan the funeral with the widow. "I believe my dear husband is now with our Lord," she added as Liz gave her a hug. "My faith is a great comfort to me."

Liz spent the following day in her home study trying to write the eulogy for Reverend Billingsley's funeral. She just couldn't get it right, no doubt because he'd been her nemesis. When Rabbi Brill telephoned to express his condolences Liz told him she had hit the wall on the eulogy.

"Ask the children to talk about him," the rabbi suggested. "This is what I do when I'm stuck. Or lay people. And then there's good old Psalm Twenty-three. Include one or two more psalms. Or, you can ask your congregation to each recall their own personal good memories of him. This can take up two minutes. We Jews are very big on the power of memory."

"Would you say a few words at the service?"

"Of course."

"I'll ask Father Tony, too. I have to get my eulogy just right," Liz confided. "It's politically very delicate. A lot of people never wanted a woman here. They certainly weren't ready for me to take over from him as soon as I did."

"Feel free to come to me and *kvetch*," the rabbi said. "I'll always be here for you."

"It was a lovely funeral," Inga assured Liz after she had officiated at Billingsley's church and burial services. "Why were you so nervous about it?" They were sipping wine before dinner at their favorite restaurant. "You're the pastor of the church now. You've been there for eight years. They can't take that away from you."

"Yes, they can."

"But not just because you're a woman. They can fire anybody. Why are you pussyfooting around? It's 1977, not 1957. You're not in the kitchen in your little lacy apron dispensing milk and cookies to your kids and waiting for hubby to come home from work in the city so you can hand him a martini. You don't need to apologize for yourself. You don't need to be subservient to men anymore."

"I'm not subservient to men. I don't have a man in my life."

"That is fortunate. You had really bad taste." They both laughed. "But you still have that old mindset. Relish your womanhood, Liz. Enjoy it. You don't see me apologizing for my existence."

Liz grinned. "You're the strongest, most independent, most free woman I've ever met."

"Let's have another glass of wine."

"You know I never have more than one. I don't want to wrap my car around a tree on the way home."

"I'll drive you home," Inga said. "Your car will be safe in the parking lot here. I'll bring you back here in the morning so you can pick it up."

Inga signaled the waiter and ordered the wine. They drank it in silence. Already Liz could feel a bit of a buzz. Inga leaned across the table and took Liz's hand. Liz furtively glanced around the restaurant searching for people they knew. She drew her hand away from Inga's and placed it in her lap.

"Somebody could misinterpret your gesture of friendship," Liz whispered. "You know how gossip spreads in this town."

"They wouldn't be misinterpreting it."

Liz stared at her.

"Liz, I thought you figured this out by now. Everything you admire about my strength and independence and freedom is because I'm comfortable with who I am. A lesbian. After a lot of therapy forced me to confront my pattern of running away from men, I realized I always have been. The person who left me the money I live on was a woman I was with for over ten years. Maddy. The love of my life." Inga paused. "Until now."

Speechless, Liz continued to stare at her friend. Somewhere, as though from a far distance, she could hear the clatter of dishes and the conversations of other diners. But it seemed to her time had stopped.

The waiter brought their dinners. Liz stood up. Pushed her chair back from the table. "We can't talk about this now," she whispered. "Someone might over-hear us."

"Come back to my house."

"No."

"We're going back to my house, Liz. Now."

Inga drew out her credit card and paid the bill for their uneaten food, adding a generous tip for the confused waiter.

Liz silently followed Inga out to her canary yellow Karmann Ghia.

Part III

Mona: 1970-1972

CLARA MCKITTRIDGE WORE jeans, a baggy t-shirt, and a soiled University of Texas sweatshirt as she escorted Mona around the farm in West Virginia on the first day of her new life there.

"You won't want to wear skirts here, Sister," Clara warned, critically scrutinizing the carefully chosen clothing Mona had bought at that thrift shop in Queens. "Basically, nobody cares what you wear, so you might as well be comfortable. You don't have worry about looking respectable here. Nobody has time to notice."

The pretty young girl pointed to a battered pick-up truck parked at one side of the farmhouse. "After you get settled you can drive into town and buy yourself a sturdy pair of jeans at Sears. And shorts while you're at it. It gets very hot here in the summer. Take money out of our petty cash if you need it."

"I don't know how to drive."

"You're kidding."

"Never learned. My family didn't have a car in Queens. Then I went into the convent."

"I guess you nuns think you can just pray and God will provide?"

Mona didn't know how to answer her. Sister Margaret Traxler, who had connected her with this project, had warned her others here would doubt she'd be up to doing her job. That she'd have to work twice as hard as everyone else to prove herself.

"Can I walk into town?" Mona asked Clara.

"Too far. I'll drive you in later. When we have a free second, which will probably be never, I'll teach you how to drive. Sometimes we have to pick up our 'clients' and drive them home. They don't have money for food, let alone automobiles. Come on, I'll show you where you'll be sleeping."

They trudged toward three old trailers parked side by side in a field behind the farmhouse.

"I guess they told you you'd be living in the farmhouse," Clara said. "Well, it's already stuffed to the gills with volunteers, and believe me, it's no bargain. Someday we're going to give it a fresh coat of paint when we're finished with everything else for the day. Which will probably be never. Your trailer isn't bad. It leaks when it rains. We put a plastic sheet over the roof. Helps a bit, if we have time to tie it down before storms come. Weather changes quickly here."

They climbed up three steep crooked steps of the smallest trailer. Clara pointed to a couch in the back, yellowed peeling sponge rubber stuffing poking out from its broken springs. "The deluxe guest suite," she joked. "All yours, Madame. Just ring for service. You can stash your belongings in the cabinet under the sink. You're a holy woman, so I guess you're used to living simply. Some of our northern college do-gooders whine and run home to mommy quick as they can. Just drop your stuff. I'll take you to meet Dr. Stevens now. He's a real dreamboat," Clara said as they entered the modest new building housing the women's health clinic. "Single, too. All the girls have the hots for him. But he won't faze you. You're a nun."

"There's a rumor going around we're human, too," Mona responded.

John Stevens was indeed great looking. Not since that afternoon in high school when Mona fought off Will Matthews in the movie theatre so Kathleen and Dickie Donovan could be together had a man so affected her. He was tall and blonde. His deep blue eyes looked right into Mona's as he welcomed her with a strong handshake.

"We just opened the health clinic a month ago, Sister Mona," Dr. Stevens said. "The homeless shelter and battered women's facility and food pantry are due to get up and running this week. You've come at a good time. We need all the help we can get. You'll work in the clinic."

"I have no medical training."

"Not necessary. You'll be doing patient intake. Check what other social services they might need. Send them to the homeless shelter or abuse facility if called for when we get them set up. Problems of poverty are never merely medical. Every aspect of their lives comes into play."

Later, Clara drove Mona into the small town. Three churches, four bars, a diner advertising in its window it served the best barbeque in the universe, a branch of Montgomery Ward, and a tiny general store selling cigarettes, milk, Wonderbread, and CocaCola. In the Sears, Clara helped Mona select Levis to try on. Mona didn't even know what size to look for. Mona explained to Clara she'd never worn jeans.

"We wore uniforms in my Catholic schools. Ugly maroon and navy plaid skirts, white blouses, and red bow ties. Except in May and October when we wore blue ties in honor of the Blessed Virgin Mary."

After Mona struggled into a pair of Levis, she stared into the mirror of the Sears dressing room at her unfamiliar reflection.

"Not bad," Clara said. "You could almost pass for a regular person."

"Are they ignorant about sisters or just anti-Catholic?" Mona asked her new roommate Sister Olivia Marconi from Chicago that night as she settled into her quarters in the trailer.

"A little of both," Sister Olivia answered. "There aren't many Catholics in West Virginia. They think we're here just to convert lost souls to the one true faith. They still call us papists behind our backs, and sometimes even to our faces. They're stuck in their old-fashioned concept of sisters."

"I hear the nearest Catholic Church is an hour away," Mona said. "Do you go there for Mass?"

"Nope. Too far, and I don't like the priest. When he heard I was working here, he assumed I'd be a house nun. Come on my day off and cook his meals and clean his rectory and teach catechism classes to the kids in my spare time. I told him I came down here to help people, not to be a servant for a male chauvinist pig priest."

"You didn't!"

"Well, I didn't actually call him a male chauvinist pig, but I did tell him God didn't steer me down here to wait on him. We're going to set up interfaith services every week, in the dining room or outside in good weather in the garden I plan to start. That'll have to substitute for Mass for me."

"Who will hear my confession?"

"You won't have time to commit any sins here, not even the sin of pride," Mona's new friend joked. "Believe me, you won't have anything to confess."

The first Sunday after Mona learned how to drive the pickup truck and had managed to get her driver's license, she did drive to the Catholic Church. Sister Olivia was right about the priest. He was condescending. But she couldn't not go to confession. There was no way she could live with that. So Mona made the long trip to his church on Sundays for the seven a.m. Mass. He agreed to hear her confession immediately afterwards so she could return as soon as possible to the farm.

Mona's primary responsibilities were in Dr. Stevens' clinic. She did whatever else they asked. Everyone worked to clear out the barn that was going to shelter the homeless. Strong local young men and volunteer college boys divided the large space into smaller rooms. The rest of them painted the new plywood walls, scrubbed the cement floors, and set up as many cots as they could squeeze into the spaces there. In the little spare time Mona had, she worked in the garden Sister Olivia planted in the back of the farmhouse. She enjoyed working the land, as she had enjoyed working in her convent's garden briefly when she was a new postulant.

Mona distributed clothing and food in the food pantry they set up in one half of the barn. Twice a week the "clients" came jammed in old cars or pickup trucks and gathered their clothing, food, and paper goods. One of Mona's tasks was to look them over as others processed them in order to spot medical problems. You didn't have to be a physician or nurse to determine when someone here needed medical care. Dr. Stevens taught Mona to recognize skin rashes and other signs of malnutrition or infection.

And you didn't need to be a trained medical professional to spot pregnancies. A look of desperation in the eyes was one tip-off. Or, more accurately, an expression of emptiness or resignation. At least half the girls, some as young as twelve or thirteen, came into the clinic pregnant.

"I hand out condoms, but I can't get them to all the girls quickly enough," John Stevens told Mona one night as he spooned macaroni and cheese onto his plate in the dining room. "Anyway, most of the boys won't use them. It's a macho thing. Sure, the girls' mothers help raise the kids, but most of them are only in their thirties themselves. The new babies just add to their burdens and downward spiral of poverty. I know you probably buy into all your Church's teachings, Sister Mona, but now do you see the need for free and accessible birth control?"

"I've been questioning our stand on artificial birth control for a long time," she confided. "My best friend killed herself when she couldn't cope with so many children and another one on the way and a rotten alcoholic husband. I saw what having so many kids did to the mothers of the students I taught in Queens. And maybe to my own mother."

"There's a lobbying group in New York State pushing for women to have legal access to abortion," he said. "Catholics for the Elimination of All Restrictive Abortion and Contraceptive Laws. Naturally the Bishops Conference has condemned the organization. You should come on board."

"I can't sanction abortion. Only God can take a life."

"That depends on how you determine what is a life. When it begins."

"The Church says life begins at conception."

"Oh, so now you agree with everything your Church teaches? Isn't it more important now to follow your own conscience?"

Mona had little time to mull over conflicts between her conscience and the dictates of her Church. She was too busy working endless hours in the medical clinic or the homeless shelter or handing out food or running errands in the truck or preparing meals in the kitchen for thirty or forty volunteers and staff and scrubbing dishes and floors afterwards. And laughing and drinking a glass of wine or beer with the others in the kitchen or out on the porch or under the stars on warm evenings when they finally finished their work.

Romances flourished. Mona wondered how these couples found the energy. She barely had time to collapse onto her lumpy couch in her trailer and try to sleep through Sister Olivia's snoring before it was morning and time to get up and begin the exhausting routine all over again. Her life here was as nearly grueling as her days in the convent. And she had little time for formal prayer. Aside from the early Sunday Mass she attended and the farm's interfaith service, during the week Mona settled for rushed personal prayers in the morning before breakfast and at night before she fell asleep as she clutched Momma's rosary in the dark.

Sometimes Mona felt as confused and frightened as she had that first night in the convent over twelve years ago. She was on her own for the first time since she had taken the veil. She had to interact with different kinds of people, deal with new situations, devise solutions to difficult problems sometimes on the spur of the moment. Although sisters had been allowed to carry money after Vatican Council II, now for the first time in twelve years Mona managed her own finances. She put herself on a strict budget so she could stretch her small salary to cover her personal necessities and still send a portion of her earnings back to Sister Patricia Luke every month.

Mona could no longer rely on Sister Patricia Luke to provide for her personal needs out of their convent budget or to guide her life. No longer could the rules of her order prescribe her behavior. Mona found this new freedom and independence frightening as well as exciting. She wasn't as brave or adventurous as her friend Luella McBride in embracing a new life with new possibilities.

But she was trying.

Either as an expression of her new freedom or because she felt like an insecure teenager desperately wanting to fit in with the crowd, Mona started smoking again. Nearly everyone on the compound smoked. Even Dr. Stevens bummed cigarettes on his few breaks from his exhausting work. Her childhood friend Kathleen would have gotten such a kick out of her lapse. Mona often thought back to the night before she entered the convent when Kathleen hard warned her she'd never be able to give up cigarettes.

Mona thought of Kathleen frequently. She missed her so much. Her dad's wife Vivian wrote that Dickie was still drinking heavily and now no longer even tried to hold down a job. He was living with his parents. They had dragged him to Father Connell for counseling, but their parish priest couldn't help him. No doubt Dickie blamed himself for Kathleen's suicide, Vivian speculated, and probably couldn't live with the guilt.

Mona's stepmother kept her up to date on her own family. There was no change in Rory's condition and probably never would be. Peggy and David seemed happy together. Muriel and Joe went up to Canada to check on Sluggie because he was writing home even less often than before, and the family was worried. They suspected serious drugs were the reason he couldn't hold a job.

"Dad's against the war now," Muriel wrote. *"He won't admit it, but he's changed his mind since he's realized Rory will never get better. Don't mention it to him. He doesn't want to talk about it. You know Dad. Never could admit he's wrong about anything."*

The one person Mona didn't hear from was her friend Luella. Although Luella had assured Mona she'd let her know what and how she and Peter were doing after they had married and left religious life, Luella didn't contact Mona again for several months. When Mona finally did get a letter from her, it was strangely vague.

"Something's the matter," Mona wrote back to her. *"You don't sound like the Luella I know."*

"Nothing's wrong," Luella answered. *"Our plans are just a little up in the air right now. Don't worry. And please don't call me."*

Now Mona was really worried.

Finally, Sister Patricia Luke, who knew all the gossip, telephoned Mona and told her the FBI was tapping Luella and Peter's telephone and monitoring their mail. "Following them around, too," she told Mona. "They found out Peter and Luella hid Father Berrigan in their apartment in Ithaca. I guess they think they'll lead them to Father Dan so he can be brought in to serve his prison term."

During one of their smoking breaks at the clinic, Mona told John Stevens about Luella and Peter's experience with the FBI and about their marriage.

"It's great they found each other," he said. "It's normal. Natural. Why shouldn't you be allowed to experience human love? Haven't you missed it?"

"I have my family's love. And God's. It's more powerful than any human love."

"You know what I mean."

John stared directly into Mona's eyes. She looked away, made a big show of flicking ashes from her cigarette onto the ground. "I gave all that up when I chose the religious life," she said finally. "I knew what I was doing. I'm married to Jesus."

"You still believe that?"

Mona nodded sheepishly.

"Well, I think it's a waste," John continued. "You would have made a great wife and mother. Don't you ever miss having children?"

"I raised my brothers and sisters after Momma died. That's what good Catholic girls do. Catholic women care for others. And I had the children in my classrooms. All the kids here." Mona paused. "What about you? All the girls are madly in love with you, I'm sure you know that."

"I was married for three years. My wife died in childbirth. Yes, I know what you're thinking. In this day and age with all our technology, every physician in the hospital working frantically to save Alice. The baby was stillborn and the placenta seeped into my wife's bloodstream and poisoned her."

"How terrible for you."

"People don't realize having a baby is still dangerous. Which is why I'm so concerned about these girls down here getting pregnant. No proper nutrition or medical care. No way to support them once the children are born. And why it's so hard for me to believe in the God you're so sure of. What kind of God takes away the woman you love at age twenty-six? And all this terrible poverty. Child abuse or child neglect at best. The lives these people lead. No hope for a better future. What can God be thinking? So much suffering. They're so passive, especially the women. Please don't be offended, but I'm convinced their strong religious faith contributes to this attitude of hopelessness. It seems to sanction their suffering. God's will, these women tell me when they talk about their troubles… The good Lord doesn't give us any burdens we can't handle. I hear this nonsense all the time. Sometimes I think religion does more harm than good."

"Maybe it seems that way. But look at how many people the Church helps. Jesus teaches we must help the poor, feed the hungry. That's why we set up huge networks of hospitals, schools, and charities when we came to this country. And missions around the world."

"I envy your commitment, Sister Mona. And your certitude of faith."

"My faith's not so certain anymore. I have my doubts, too, sometimes. I used to think I knew the answers. That we can't question God, that He knows what is best for us. Now I'm not so sure."

A tragedy a week later confirmed Mona's doubts. And changed her mind about birth control and abortion.

John ran into the homeless shelter where Clara and Mona were serving breakfast and told them to drive the pickup truck as fast as they could to bring Patty Thompson into the clinic. The thirteen-year-old girl was bleeding profusely after an illegal abortion.

"I guess I should have called you sooner," Patty's panicked mother said when they arrived at the isolated cabin. "She was doing OK 'till this morning. I know you good Catholics are against abortion, Sister, but no way did she want this baby. She's nothin' but a child herself. Did I do the wrong thing, taking her to…?"

"…I don't want to know who did it," Mona said. "Just help me get her into the truck."

Patty continued to lose even more blood as they sped on the back roads. Clara took over the wheel so Mona could try to stop the bleeding with her recently acquired first aid skills. The girl was unconscious by the time they reached the clinic. She died an hour later.

"It's my fault," Mona sobbed as John comforted her in his arms. "I didn't get her here fast enough."

"You did everything you could," he assured her. "We all did."

The following Sunday in the garden Mona conducted a memorial service for Patty.

"Now I see there must be alternatives for women and young girls like Patty Thompson," Mona proclaimed. "She probably didn't even realize submitting to whoever it was, whether voluntary or involuntary, could result in a pregnancy. She shouldn't have had to put her life at risk. Even if she had successfully given birth, this youngster's future shouldn't have been defined by this one event. One mistake should not have ruined her chances of breaking out of her cycle of poverty and building a productive life for herself, with family to come only when she was ready. Or choosing to forego a family, if this is what she wanted.

"The Catholic Church needs alternative points of view on the important issue of birth control," Mona continued. "Four years ago the Pope missed a chance to forge positive progress and instead took a step backwards when he refused to accept his commission's recommendations for changes in our Church's position. My childhood friend Kathleen Donavan, who tragically took her own life when she couldn't face raising another child in addition to the three she had, once asked me, 'Why do a bunch of celibate old men get to decide how many kids I'm going to have?' Why, indeed.

"My Church has transformed itself on many important issues since Vatican Council II ended seven years ago. Why not give fifty percent of its adherents a means of controlling their own futures? In addition to having a choice regarding birth control," Mona continued, "I'm beginning to believe Catholic women should be able to make their own moral decision about abortion and should, like all women, have access to legal procedures performed by qualified doctors in sterile conditions. Patty Thompson would be alive today if this had been the case."

Mona cried a month later when she told her sister Peggy the story of Patty Thompson's death. Peggy had come down to visit Mona before she and David moved to Milwaukee. David had obtained a good position in a bigger accounting firm there. They looked forward to living near David's parents. Mona showed Peggy around the farm, and then drove her in the truck into town to dine at the local barbecue joint.

"Delicious!" Peggy said as she licked her fingers after devouring a messy pork sandwich. "I can't believe I'm eating food like this at a place like this with you. Though you'd hardly know you're a sister anymore. Your hair."

Mona's hand reached up to touch her hair, now nearly as short as the crew cuts the boys sported when she was a teenager. "Clara McKittridge chopped it off," she explained. "No time here to fool with hair."

"The sin of vanity," Peggy said dryly. "Well, it suits you. So do the sloppy jeans. And do I detect a bit of lipstick and eye makeup? And what would Momma say if she saw you smoking again?"

"She never knew I smoked."

"We all did. We could smell the tobacco on your breath even though you tried to hide it. And a nun bopping around in a pickup truck. When I told David's parents about it they laughed. They picture you lighting candles in a chapel in your full habit with a halo hanging over your head. They have a pretty old-fashioned view of sisters. Of all Catholics."

"How have they taken to having one in their family?"

"Whatever they really think they've been good to me. Especially since I agreed to raise our children as Jews. "

"Does Dad know this?"

"Don't tell him. He'd have a fit."

A week later while Mona was doing intake for a new patient at the clinic, Clara McKittridge announced she had another visitor.

"She wouldn't give me her name. Said she wanted to surprise you. You expecting more family?"

"No.

"Friend?"

"I don't have any friends down here except you all."

"Well, she looks like an aging hippie who ought to know better. She's outside on the front porch. Go on out. I'll cover the desk for you."

Mona hurried out to the porch. In the driveway she spotted a mud-spattered pea green Volkswagen van plastered with yellow and white daisy and peace symbol decals. Leaning against the van was a heavy woman wearing black orthopedic sandals and a purple and chartreuse-flowered ankle-length Hawaiian muumuu swigging a Coke and taking long drags on a cigarette. A large floppy straw sun hat hid her face, so Mona couldn't see it at first. Then she whipped off the hat and looked up at Mona, shouting, "Mona! Mona, dear!"

She threw down her cigarette and ran up the porch steps toward Mona, arms outstretched. Mona met her halfway down the stairs and hugged her.

"Sister Patricia Luke!"

"It's Sister Phyllis Wartofski now. I've gone back to my former name." Mona's Mother Superior stepped back, held Mona at arm's length, said, "Well, well, look at you."

"Look at *you*," Mona countered.

"I know. I look like a flower child. A wilted flower child, ten years too late. I've always been too late for everything. Well, I have a lot of lost time to make up for now."

"What are you doing here?"

"Road-tripping. All over the country. I turned down an offer to be Executive Director of NETWORK at the Washington office we just opened. We elected Sister Ellen McCarthy to be Acting Administrative Director of the convent while I'm gone. I decided to get out and see the world we've vowed to be part of and improve. I never travelled before I entered religious life. I never did anything before I entered religious life. I've come to take you with me. I'm stopping all over the country to visit as many orders as I can. See what they're doing, how they're handling transitions. You can be my personal assistant again."

"I can't leave here"

"I know you're doing wonderful work, Mona dear. But others can do what you're doing here. You're limiting yourself. You need to widen your horizons, step onto the national scene if you want to make a difference. You're too good to bury yourself in this place. You need to get out. Face some new challenges."

Mona thought for a moment. "I don't know," she said finally. "Traveling with you would be a drastic change for me. I mean, I'm not living in the convent anymore, but I'm still doing God's work down here."

"You'd be doing God's work if you come with me. A different kind of work."

"Can I change my life so drastically?"

"You've already changed your life by coming down here. And you won't exactly be going off on your own. I'm asking you to do this. To help me bring our convent into the modern world. It's a different kind of apostolate."

Sister Phyllis fanned herself with her straw hat. "Got a drink in this place? Somewhere an old lady can put up her big fat smelly feet and relax?"

Sister Phyllis settled into a spare room in the farmhouse and helped out wherever she could. She told everyone she'd stay at the compound as long as it took to convince Mona to come with her on her cross-country journey.

On the first Sunday she was there, she attended the interfaith service Mona had volunteered to organize. Every week Mona prepared a short sermon and a scripture reading and commentary from the Old or New Testament, connecting those messages to their mission of battling poverty in Appalachia and working for social justice throughout the world.

"Your remarks today were eloquent," Sister Phyllis told Mona after the service. "Your scriptural exegesis was far more interesting than Father Vertucci's, that's for sure. Of course, that's not difficult. But you have real presence. You've broken out of your old role, become a stronger presence. Are you doing pastoral counseling here?"

"I guess I've become sort of an unofficial personal counselor and spiritual leader to the volunteers. And to local 'clients' who come to the compound for health care and social services. We haven't been able to get a real social worker or psychologist down here yet. Of course, to the kids here I'm an old lady. But I suppose they think because I'm a sister I possess some special secret wisdom." Mona laughed. "If they only knew how confused about life I am. But I like the counseling. And the scripture readings. And writing and delivering sermons. I'm questioning God intellectually now, but somehow I feel closer to Him. I feel the Holy Spirit is inspiring my creativity, guiding me. I believe I have something valuable to say."

"You'd be a wonderful priest."

Mona stared at her mentor.

"How did you know I've been thinking about it? Wondering if God is calling me to do that? But," she added, "you know that's never going to happen."

"'In Christ there is no Jew or Greek, slave or citizen, male or female. All are one in Christ Jesus.' Galatians 3:28," Sister Phyllis quoted. "And Genesis 1:27. God created both man and woman in his image. We have to adjust our concept of creation in the image of God. Women can image Jesus also, so why can't women be priests?"

"It'll never happen," Mona repeated.

"We can't be so sure. You know women played a much larger role in the Church in the middle ages. We had real spiritual authority. And women were important in the Gnostic texts. We were teachers, wandering preachers, prophets, healers, missionaries, priests, even bishops. There are growing rumblings for our ordination. In that 1970 survey, half the Catholics polled said they'd accept women priests. A quarter said they wouldn't. The other fourth said they weren't sure. A huge change.

"Two years ago a priest in Czechoslovakia secretly ordained that woman Ludmila Javorova," Sister Phyllis continued. "Though those old buzzards at the Vatican claims it's not valid. *Gaudium et Specs* from the Vatican Council says the Church must adapt to the modern world. And Pope John said in *Pacem in Terris* women should be able to fulfill their potential. Since we've become more conscious of our dignity, we should demand our rights in both our personal and public lives. Be able to choose freely. The Holy Father even said everyone should have the option of choosing to be priests." She sighed. "What a loss his death was for us. We didn't appreciate how forward looking he was."

"No, we didn't."

"The Protestants are ordaining women now, except for the Episcopalians. And a Jewish girl just became a rabbi. You always displayed excellent leadership qualities, Mona. I had my eye on you from the beginning."

"You're tempting me with the sin of pride," Mona responded, laughing. "I suppose that doesn't count for much anymore. I don't know anymore what *does* count."

"Nobody does. I don't want to be a priest, but I'll fight for your right to be one, if that's what you want."

"How do I know if this is what God wants for me? If that's His plan?"

"Mona, dear, surely you've moved past that. Surely you've learned something with all the changes we've been through. You must take charge of your own life now. You can no longer depend on God to tell you what to do. He wants us to use our brain. Even women. Yes, even sisters. No matter what those grumpy old men at the Vatican say."

"I don't think I could ever make such a radical decision," Mona told her. "My family would never get over it. If I left the Church it would kill my father."

After a week of thinking it over, Mona decided she'd leave her work there and go with Sister Phyllis. It took her another week to wind up her work on the Appalachian compound.

"I don't want you to go," John Stevens said as they hugged goodbye after Mona and Sister Phyllis had packed up the green VW van. John looked toward Sister Phyllis, sitting in the driver's seat, frowning and tapping her fingers on the steering wheel. "But I can see your Mother Superior's determined to drag you off."

"We don't call them that anymore. But she's right, John. It's time for me to move on."

As if on cue Sister Phyllis honked the horn, stuck her head out of the window, and shouted, "Let's get the show on the road. We haven't got have all day."

John hugged Mona again and then kissed her. She was startled. She hadn't been kissed since that afternoon when she was in high school at the movie theatre with Will Matthews.

"Well, that was interesting," Sister Phyllis said after Mona settled herself in the van. "That gorgeous fabulous doctor likes you."

"Just as a friend."

"You're so naïve, dear. Well, that's going to change. You're venturing out into the big world now. A rather handsome truck driver made a pass at me at one of the rest stops on my drive down here. Can you imagine? He must have been desperate. Or drunk. Or stoned."

Sister Phyllis backed out of the driveway leading up to the farmhouse and headed toward the highway. Mona clutched her momma's rosary she always wore under her T-shirt and recited a silent prayer as Sister Phyllis pulled onto the Interstate and revved the old Volkswagon van up to eighty miles and hour.

Mona was venturing out into the world. What lay ahead for her now?

Sandra: 1977–1978

IN MAY AS the due date for her second child approached, Sandy researched baby-naming rituals for girls. Toby Fishbein Reifman had just edited a collection, *Blessing the Birth of a Daughter: Jewish Naming Ceremonies for Girls*. Sandy stole some ideas from her book but also wrote her own ceremony. If the child turned out to be a boy and she didn't need it, she'd give what she had written to her *Chavurah* group for someone else to use. And her friend Carolyn could probably get it published.

As Sandy had predicted, Carolyn Schwartz was by now famous in Jewish and general feminist circles. Last year she had been one of the founders of *Lilith* magazine, named for the rebellious first woman God created, who, according to Jewish tradition, was replaced in the bible by the more compliant Eve. Carolyn was a founder and contributing editor to *Ms Magazine*. She had just published an important collection of feminist essays about which a long and controversial article had been written in *The New York Review of Books*, ensuring Carolyn's entree into the Upper West Side's star literary intelligentsia.

To Sandy's delight her new baby was a girl. Blaming Carolyn Schwartz for her feminist metamorphosis as he always did, Robert gave in to Sandy, and they named her Beruria. He also reluctantly agreed to a baby-naming ceremony.

Sandy's sister Joanie flew into New York for the celebration a few days early. It had been a long time since the sisters had spent any time together. Sandy sensed immediately something was amiss. Joanie had always been so sure of herself, always so bombastic, always tearing Sandy down with her sarcastic humor. But now she was subdued.

"What's the matter?" Sandy asked.

"Chad."

"Yeah? You getting tired of supporting him?"

"He's gay, Sandy."

"That gorgeous hunk?"

"Ninety-nine point nine percent of the gorgeous hunks in Hollywood are gay. It's all a big secret or their careers would be finished. God. I should have known better. Our sex life was never too great, but I figured it was me."

"How did you find out?"

"A week ago I didn't feel well, so I came home early from the office and found him sucking a guy's dick. In our bed. On my new satin sheets that cost a fortune."

Sandy tried not to laugh, but couldn't stop herself. Joanie started to laugh, too.

"I thought this stuff just happened in bad movies." Sandy said.

"My life has turned into a bad movie."

"What did you do?"

"Screamed like a maniac. The guy threw on his clothes and bolted. I pulled out all Chad's drawers and opened his closet and threw all his expensive clothes onto the front lawn. Told him to pack up all his shit I had by the way paid for and get out. He's staying at the guy's beach house in Malibu now. Big producer. Brad just got a role in his next movie." Joanie laughed bitterly. "Now I know why. Even I can see he's totally talentless."

Eight days after Beruria's birth five of Sandy's classmates from Hebrew Union College, three professors, six women from her *Chevurah*, Robert's parents and brother, Lorna and Mark and three other Brownstein cousins, Leon and Helen Miller, miscellaneous friends, and neighbors from down the hall gathered in the Brownsteins' apartment. Sandy gave Marielle strict orders to take Josh into his bedroom if he caused a disturbance, but she hoped he'd be able to participate in the happy event.

As she held beautiful little Beruria, for the moment happy and quiet, Sandy said, "Before we begin the naming ceremony, I will say a few words about Beruria's story, because we have so few women's stories in our tradition. She was the daughter of Rabbi Hananya ben Teradion. The Romans burned him to death along with Rabbi Akiva, whose legal decisions formed the basis of the *Mishnah*, wrapped in Torah scrolls, in 135 C.E. Their crime? Teaching *Torah*, which was forbidden. Beruria was the wife of Rabbi Meir, a disciple of Rabbi Akiva. Her husband probably was her unofficial teacher, but nobody knows for sure.

"She is the only woman," Sandy continued, "whose teachings are recorded in rabbinic literature. We have *Perkei Avot*, Teachings of the Fathers, but where are the Teachings of the Mothers? Beruria had no official teacher and no official students because as a woman she was left out of this teacher-student transmission system of study. Even if she had been exempt from the rule that women couldn't study *Torah*, she was not allowed into the study building where the exchange of knowledge took place. She was excluded physically from the transmission process. A woman's role was to wait at home for her husband to return from the study house. So Beruria's teachings fell into a void because as well as being excluded from the men's system of transmitting them, there was no women's scholarly network for passing them on to others. Women didn't have to be taught, so they didn't have to teach others.

"Even with this limited scholarly role for Beruria, men still felt it necessary to discredit her. If they didn't defame her memory, they'd have had to change their views of women's ability to be scholars. So they probably invented a sordid tale of her downfall as one possible explanation for her husband's mysterious flight to Babylon. They told a story that Beruria was tricked into allowing herself to be seduced by one of her students and, ashamed, committed suicide.

"Whatever the real reason for her husband's escape to Babylon and whatever the real fate of Beruria, these are the lessons I draw from her life and these are the hopes for the daughter, her namesake." Sandy spoke firmly now. "My daughter will not be shut out of the study house. My daughter will not be shut out of the transmission process from teacher to student. She will be part of a community of women who will transmit their knowledge. She will not be shut out of the real community and network of Jewish life. She will not be marginalized."

Two weeks later Sandy was ordained.

They processed down the long aisle of the cathedral-like Temple Emanu-El on Fifth Avenue and 65ᵗʰ Street. There were thirty rabbinical students, fifteen male and two women cantorial candidates, and eleven women receiving degrees in Jewish Education.

Sandy walked slowly to the music, her black robe fortunately hiding the weight she had gained during her pregnancy. She passed Robert holding Josh on his lap. He was prepared to quickly take their son out of the sanctuary if necessary. Marielle was home with little Beruria. Leon and Helen Miller and Joanie beamed from their aisle seats.

After long speeches, the women in the education program received their Masters in Jewish Education degrees. Next the cantorial students were invested. Then, following the tradition traced back to Moses when he passed his leadership on to Joshua so the line of the authority of *Torah* would not be broken, each rabbinical student received *smichah* through a laying on of hands by Rabbi Alfred Gottschalk, the German-born president of Hebrew Union College.

During this emotional moment Rabbi Gottschalk whispered a personal message to each of them. "Well, the day has come at last, Sandra," he said as he placed his hands on her head. "Congratulations. You have embarked on a brave path, and you've worked hard and accomplished your goal. But the way ahead will not be an easy one. The victory of being granted ordination is not the end of the road. Sandra, your voyage will often be a lonely one. You will need to be a role model, with few of your own to follow. You will constantly struggle to break down long-held stereotypes and blaze new paths. May God be with you on your arduous but, I pray, rewarding journey."

Sandy was pleasantly surprised to receive a letter from Rabbi Kahn congratulating her on her ordination. He was trying to be gracious, she could tell, but it was grudging. *"While I still don't approve of your decision,"* he wrote, *"I'm proud of you, Sandra, for pursuing and achieving your challenging personal goal. Please let me know if I can be of assistance to you in any way. Hannah and I wish you well."*

A brief congratulatory note from Jeff Shoemaker also arrived. She read it quickly, then, without telling Robert, tossed it into the shoebox in her closet where she had hidden his other letter.

Now Sandy needed to focus on their move to Milwaukee where she was to be an assistant rabbi.

While Josh was in the 92nd Street Y day camp, Sandy weeded out the belongings they had accumulated in more than eleven years in their apartment. She and Robert flew out to Milwaukee to look at four houses a real estate agent in her new congregation had narrowed down for them to rent. On the airplane as they flew home Sandy raised an issue she knew might upset her husband. But she wanted to get it settled before she started her new job.

"I'm going to hyphenate my last name. Combine my maiden name with yours," she announced.

"You're going to confuse people," Robert protested. "You're already known as 'Brownstein'. You *are* married."

"Why should I negate my previous identity by no longer using Miller? The combined name would be a more accurate description of who I am. Women shouldn't have to wipe out their past when they get married. Men don't."

Robert laughed, said, "We've been married for eleven years. I hardly think you've negated your previous identity or wiped out your past. Far from it."

"It's the principle of the matter. And I'm doing it."

The woman sitting in the row ahead of them turned around and said to Sandy emphatically, "Good for you, dear."

They moved at the end of July. Before Sandy began work in mid-August she wanted to have a new baby sitter lined up. She hired Leana, a gorgeous Indian girl from South Africa with that fabulous accent.

Rabbi Wenick devised a strategy for warding off possible gossip about them he had warned Sandy about during her job interview. "You and I will never meet together alone behind closed doors, Sandra. We'll always leave the door to my office open a little so the secretary or whoever's passing through the outer office can see and hear us. I make it a point never to be alone with a woman in my office, and I advise you to do the same. Early on in my career I went to a woman's house after she telephoned to tell me she was going to kill herself that night. She met me at the door in one of those black negligees you can see through. I fled. Fortunately she didn't harm herself, or I might have been in trouble."

Sandy and Rabbi Wenick divided up their duties. She'd officiate at one *Shabbat* service a month, more often in the summer when he and his family went on vacation or if he was away for other reasons. She would plan all adult education programs. A Jewish education specialist ran the religious school, but Sandy would supervise her. She was in charge of Sisterhood, the women's organization that raised money for social action activities and the religious school. Sandy took charge of their chapter of *Hadassah*, a Zionist women's organization that supported a large hospital in Jerusalem and other medical services in Israel. She'd be responsible for the youth group, a chapter of the National Federation of Temple Youth that had been so important in her life and had helped her hone her crucial leadership skills.

They would share hospital visits and personal counseling. Rabbi Wenick would officiate at funerals unless he was out of town or ill. He would conduct three *Shabbat* services a month and at all other life cycle events, with her assistance at the *Bar* and *Bat Mitzvahs*. They divided up the liturgy and sermons for the exhausting upcoming autumn holiday marathon of *Rosh Hashona, Yom Kippur,* and *Sukkoth,* the harvest festival that was a precursor to the American Thanksgiving.

On the afternoon of the eve of *Rosh Hashona,* a week after Sandy officially began her duties, a young woman in the congregation shot her three children, ages six months to four years, as they slept. Then she shot herself in the head. Rabbi Wenick telephoned Sandy three hours before the High Holiday's evening service began to tell her the terrible news.

"She had the best psychiatric treatment available," he said. "I counseled her for years. Her husband and family did everything they could for her. Sometimes people just can't be helped. Maybe they don't want to be. We have to learn to live with that."

From the *bema* later that night Rabbi Wenick told a somber audience listening in complete silence, "On *Rosh Hashona* and *Yom Kippur* we scrutinize our lives. Every year as we recite the *Unataneh Tokef* prayer in our *Rosh Hashonah* liturgy we wonder what lies ahead for each of us. We ask, 'who shall live and who shall die? Who by water? Who by fire?'

"We live with uncertainty and with the knowledge that at any moment our lives can change irrevocably and perhaps tragically," he continued. "Yet the *Unataneh Tokef* prayer declares we'll keep going in the face of all difficulties and trials. That life is ultimately good. We're constantly struggling to believe in good overcoming evil, that life is worthwhile even in the face of contradictory evidence and experience. Deuteronomy 30:19 tells us, '*Ovacharta bachayim.* Choose life.'

"Tomorrow afternoon we will blow the *shofar* in both short and long bursts. The short bursts signify the interrupted, unfinished, frustrated acts of life. The long blast at the end of the *shofar* service signifies the steady enduring worth of life, the arc of overall accomplishment. Blowing the ram's horn is a positive statement. We proclaim we will keep going in spite of our uncertainty. That we're determined to push ahead with life in spite of our doubts. It takes great courage to affirm this position in the light of grief. This is the beauty of Judaism. This is the meaning of the High Holydays. In the uncertainty and sometimes apparent randomness of existence, and in spite of it, we proclaim God and His power."

After this difficult start to Sandy's new life in Milwaukee, things settled down into a routine.

The first night she officiated at *Shabbat* services, at the *Oneg Shabbat* afterwards a young man and a middle-aged woman approached her.

"I'm Miriam Greene," the woman said. "This is my son David."

They shook hands.

"We're members of another synagogue but we have a problem, and we hope you can help," Mrs. Greene explained. "David is married to a Catholic girl. She's wonderful, we're very fond of her, like a daughter to me. She's kept her promise to raise their two kids as Jews, though she comes from a devout Irish Catholic family. One of her sisters is a nun."

"Now Peggy wants to convert to Judaism," David said. "We're thrilled. I didn't pressure her," he was quick to add. "She came to this decision on her own. We were wondering if you might do the conversion. Our rabbi has been cold to Peggy, and she feels she's not wanted in that congregation."

"I'm sorry about that," Sandy said. "As you know, we Jews don't seek out converts. Sadly many congregations are not as welcoming to non-Jews as they should be. Fortunately, this is beginning to change."

"My mother and I want Peggy to have a good experience."

"You'd have to join this synagogue."

"We're more than willing," Mrs. Greene said. "I liked your service tonight. Everybody was involved in it. I think Peggy would be happier with a woman rabbi. Seeing a woman up on there makes you think about things differently. Makes you think about God differently. Someone you can have a relationship and dialogue with, not just a stern judge. More inclusive, somehow."

"She'd have to take several classes and work her way through a challenging reading list," Sandy warned.

"Peggy is very bright," David assured me. "She'll be able to handle the workload, even though she's a nurse."

Sandy set up an appointment to meet Peggy. She was indeed a sweet woman, Irish to her core. They worked out a schedule for their meetings and her reading assignments. Peggy Greene was amazed Jews didn't have a set doctrine of beliefs one has to adhere to, as Catholics did.

"We don't have a catechism like Catholics or what Christians call a systematic theology," Sandy explained. "Theology plays a limited role. What's important in Judaism is deed, not creed. But you can't make a distinction between the two. The rabbis who passed down their commentaries on our *Torah* claim you can't separate morality and religion. They form a single whole. If you're good, it's because you believe in God. If you're not good, it's because you don't believe in God. On the other hand, being bad produces a denial of God. And denial of God produces bad behavior. You can't separate them. Of course, you have to believe in one God, not many. That's the importance of the *Sh'ma*, where we proclaim 'Hear O Israel, the Lord is God, the Lord is One.' And, you have to realize, we Jews are a people, not a set of beliefs or religion."

"I've never understood that," Peggy said. "Can you explain it to me?"

"Well, it's difficult. We're a specific people Israel. That's the Jacob story of wrestling with the angel. At the end of the struggle he was called 'Israel,' reborn with a new name. In Judaism relationship with God comes with being part of community. We're a people even though we're every nationality and we live throughout the world. It's a miracle, really, and a miracle we've survived the temptations to assimilate into the larger culture and the many attempts to wipe us out. My father, who's a sociologist and cynical about religion, explains our survival through rules of how societies work or don't work. To me that's not enough. Now I believe maybe there's more at work than just good social organization or luck. Something mysterious. Maybe it is God."

"How have you Jews survived without certainty?" Peggy asked.

"You're right, we don't have the certainty you Catholics do. I've always admired your strong faith. It helps you deal with life's adversities. Jews have to be able to deal with uncertainty and ambiguity. We're encouraged to question, even challenge God."

"We Catholics don't have much certainty anymore. So many changes since Vatican Council. Some of them are good, but what we used to think was set in stone forever's been changed. When my sister Mona was just out of high school she went into a rigorous old-fashioned convent. She's had to totally change her life, and now she's pretty radical. A real pioneer, like you. I can't wait for you to meet her. I know you'll hit it off."

Sandy was happy to see the Milwaukee congregation had always been involved in social justices issues, especially the Soviet Jewry struggle. This battle with the Communist government was at a low point. Rabbi Wenick also encouraged the congregants to participate in local interfaith projects such as the shelter for abused women and a food pantry.

Sandy didn't want to limit the activities of the bright, capable women in her new congregation to Sisterhood and *Hadassah* and the usual potluck dinners and *Oneg Shabbat* baking. She had come too far in her thinking from being part of her Manhattan *Chavurah* and *Rosh Chodesh* groups and following Jewish feminists such as her friend Carolyn Schwartz. Sandy wanted to start *Chavurah* and *Rosh Chodesh* groups.

"We need to take things a bit slowly," Rabbi Wenick advised her. "We're not so backwards out here in the Midwest, you know, but I do have to think about our more conservative members. We don't want to drive people away."

"I won't rush things," Sandy assured him. "Won't have them dancing nude on the *bema* to greet the new moon. At least not right away."

Sandy introduced her feminism gradually. At their first *Rosh Chodesh* meeting, well attended, somewhat to her surprise, by older women also, they discussed language and liturgy. Sandy pointed out how the language of prayer forms our concept of God and defines women.

"As you may know," she began their first session, "when feminists at Brown University recently instigated their own Sabbath Services, two years ago two of those women, Maggie Wenig and Naomi Janowitz, wrote a prayer book called *Siddur Nashim* in which they use the female pronoun for God throughout. We know, of course, that God is neither male nor female. But because God has always been assigned the attributes of a powerful and often stern male -- father, king, lord, etc. -- we've come to think of God's realm as a patriarchy with a hierarchical structure.

"This defines all of humankind and all Jews in terms of maleness," Sandy continued. "In this construct women are the alienated Other. A prominent Catholic feminist, very radical, Mary Daly, analyzed this for the Catholic Church in her famous book about ten years ago called *The Church and the Second Sex*. As you can gather from the title, Daly utilizes the language and theories of Simone de Beauvoir. The Catholics got this concept of women as Other from us Jews. This was one of the major reasons, by the way, women were kept from becoming rabbis. Being a Jew is defined in terms of being a man, so people couldn't envision us in that role. But this restrictive concept affects all Jewish women, not just the crazy ones like me who want to be rabbis."

The women laughed.

"Because we aren't men through whom God and all of Jewish life have been defined, women have been either omitted altogether or relegated to the lowest rung on the cosmological ladder. The mechanism for suppressing women has had divine sanction. In order to correct this, we now want to use feminine pronouns when we talk about God. Not that God is a she, anymore than God is a he. But in doing this we hope to counterbalance the effects the hierarchical patriarchal structure has had on our tradition and life. To break the gendered pattern of authority."

The group decided to order copies of the *Siddur Nashim* to study it and, working with the synagogue's ritual committee, to adapt some of the gender-neutral language into their own services.

Not all the changes Sandy tried to make were as well received. In fact, *she* wasn't entirely well received. How else could she explain why one of the members of her congregation's board of trustees, sitting in the front row directly in her line of vision, clutched a stopwatch in his hand and timed her sermons?

When Sandy complained to her Senior Rabbi, he laughed. "Just ignore him. He loves to play power games with this congregation. Retired. Nothing better to do."

Once the man realized Sandy was keeping her sermons down to twenty minutes he tried another means of distracting her. He always purposely lagged one or two seconds behind everybody else in the responsive readings, ruining her concentration.

"Try to ignore him," Rabbi Wenick advised her again.

"It's making me crazy."

"That's what he wants. Don't give him a victory. *Hazak, Hazak, V'Nithazak.* Be strong, be strong, and let us strengthen one another!"

Sandy shared these stories with other women rabbis and rabbinical students through their network of the Women's Rabbinical Alliance at a special meeting in February 1978. She felt better when she realized she wasn't the only woman being hassled.

In late spring, after Peggy Greene completed her challenging conversion requirements, on *Shabbat* from the *bema* Mona blessed her with the three priestly benedictions from Numbers 6:23-27. "May God bless you and keep you," she said to Peggy as they stood facing each other, Sandy's hands on Peggy's head. "May the light of God's presence shine upon you and be gracious to you. May God bestow favor upon you and give you peace."

Sister Mona Sullivan, sitting in the front row of the sanctuary, smiled up at them as Sandy's congregation formally welcomed her little sister into the mysterious and miraculous people Israel.

Liz: 1977-1978

Liz's well-ordered, well-planned life had been thrown into chaos again.

Of course. She should have realized Inga was a lesbian. All her life Liz had enjoyed close friendships with women. Alicia. Tina. Beverly. She had assumed Inga was just the next in line. But she should have sensed her friendship with Inga was different, Liz berated herself. Should have realized Inga was falling in love with her. And she with Inga.

Over and over Liz thought about what had happened to her the night she had dutifully followed Inga out of the restaurant and into her sports car and into her house and into her bed. There had been feeling of inevitability about it, as if Liz had no choice in the matter, no will power to resist. As if it was predetermined. Predestined by God. That night no amount of reasoning or arguing or thinking would or could change the course of what was happening.

Liz always been a control freak, afraid she'd lose power over her life. As she looked back on it, she realized that had been the worst thing about the end of her marriage to Tom. No say in it, no control over those events. Her carefully planned life with him had suddenly been demolished by forces outside of herself over which she had no power. Suddenly her secure life had been opened up to endless possibilities. And that, to Liz, had been frightening.

But the sensations of helplessness and surrender Liz felt that first night with Inga were not fear of loss of control and fear of disorder. No, her feelings were happy ones. A sort of blissful relaxation. Yes, this surrender was meant to happen. And yes, it was good.

It wasn't until the next day when reason once again took over, that Liz was horrified. What had she done? What happened to her vow to go it alone, to never again let her life fall into the hands of another who could hurt her?

And she had jeopardized her job. Her entire career.

A recent incident in Stewart confirmed this danger. The board of the synagogue had fired her good friend Rabbi Brill after his love affair with his cantor became public.

Rabbi Brill had hired one of the first women cantors ordained by Judaism's reform movement in 1975. Liz would never have expected her good friend, a solid family man of integrity, to fall prey to temptation. But he and the young cantor fell in love and into a serious affair. No one in the congregation or in Stewart knew about it until the romance broke up, as tempestuously as it apparently began.

One Sunday afternoon Rabbi Brill and the cantor were scheduled to perform a wedding ceremony, the second marriage of an important synagogue board member. The couple, their children, and other close family members were waiting for them downstairs in the modest sanctuary when suddenly everyone heard escalating shouts coming from the rabbi's office. The groom ran upstairs to the office and discovered the rabbi wiping red wine from his face that the cantor had just tossed at him. The rabbi quickly changed his shirt. The three took the elevator downstairs to the sanctuary together, the cantor still shouting at the rabbi. Everyone waiting for them could hear everything. They performed the wedding ceremony, but the cantor was fired the next day and Rabbi Brill's contract terminated a month later. His wife left him. The scandal threw the small Jewish community in Stewart into an uproar.

If Liz lost this job because her relationship with Inga became public, probably she'd never get another church. Her congregation couldn't fire her without the approval of the Presbytery that governed it, and the charges against her would have to be well documented. But Liz had violated her ordination pledge: fidelity if married, chastity if single. Her Presbytery could challenge her ordination. Her fate would be decided by the Presbytery's judiciary committee. If its decision went against Liz, she'd be allowed to appeal it, but the chances of reversal would be slim to non-existent. Not only had she broken her vow of chastity as a single woman, they'd perceive her to be a corrupting influence in any congregation. Especially to the youth. Liz had sinned against nature. Against God.

And what if Liz's parents found out she was in a lesbian relationship? They'd be appalled. Certainly not dignified behavior. Certainly not ladylike. They wouldn't be able to hold their heads up, face their friends. It would shatter her parents' respectable world.

So she told Inga the next day, "What happened last night must never happen again." She listed all the reasons.

"You can't always live life rationally, Liz."

"It's the safest way."

"You lived safely and look what happened with Tom. That's not living. You want to deny yourself what we had last night? Your religious experience at your brother's grave wasn't rational. You based your entire future on it. You said that was your destiny." Inga moved toward Liz and took her in her arms. "This is our destiny."

Liz gave up trying to end their relationship. She realized she was powerless to control her actions. Inga had awakened in her all the sexual feelings she never knew with Tom, never even dreamt were possible. She had turned Liz's world upside down.

Tom was the only man Liz had ever slept with, and she had no desire to have a sexual relationship with other men she had met. Perhaps she was a lesbian and always had been. In those days no one discussed this openly. Few then dared to admit it even to themselves.

This went against everything Liz had ever believed, against the way she had always run her life. Being sensible. Thinking. Planning. One foot in front of the other, building her life methodically toward reaching carefully thought out goals. Living a moral life according to the Judeo-Christian ethical system. But now Liz realized Tom had been right when he confessed his love for Emily Mullen: You can't always plan out your life.

Liz and Inga focused their efforts on being discreet. They stopped going out in public together. Inga never came to her house because Liz's congregants might see Inga's automobile parked there. And Liz knew members of her church's pastoral housing committee drove by the manse at all hours of the day and night to make sure she wasn't wasting electricity by leaving lights on in rooms she wasn't in. The committee possessed a key to her house, so sometimes its members even came in to inspect the premises when Liz wasn't there. What if they walked in on Inga and Liz making love?

"You have to change churches," Liz announced to Inga.

"But I like yours."

"This is not a joking matter. You better join the Lutheran church."

"Reverend Steinbrink's gloomy personality depresses me. I want to kill myself when I'm around him."

"Inga."

"OK. You're right, Liz. I guess we can't take any chances."

As the months passed, Liz began to speculate that perhaps her strong friendships with Alicia and Tina and Beverly had been indications of latent homosexuality. Maybe this was the reason she had never had a good sexual relationship with Tom, why she'd never even tried to improve their sex life. Perhaps she just wasn't attracted to men?

And as the months passed, Liz began to think perhaps labels didn't matter. Yes, the bible preached against homosexuality, but she knew those documents were codified in a specific cultural context, and scholars were beginning to question those interpretations. Jesus never mentioned homosexuality, in fact preached tolerance for those who are "weakest among us". And what she had with Inga felt so natural and good and right, how could she be committing a sin? If she was, now Liz understood how weak humans are. How we need God and Jesus to help us and, through their grace, to save us and bring us redemption. Jesus forgives all our sins. We can all be redeemed.

Inga and Liz had more than a sexual relationship. They were soul mates. Liz was really happy, she realized, for the first time in her life. Her new joy in living brought her closer to God. Was her love for Inga what He wanted for her? How much control did she have over her own life, anyway? How much control did God have over it? In the theological struggle between freedom of the will and predestination so important to Presbyterians, now predestination seemed to be winning out in her life.

If this was her psychological and physical makeup, maybe Liz couldn't fight it. Didn't God create her, Elizabeth Adams, as He had created everything in the cosmos? Didn't He want her this way, plan for her to be what she is? If He hadn't, wouldn't He have created her differently?

Liz was powerless to struggle against this new path. She had changed irrevocably. Her life had been transformed.

Fortunately Liz's mother and Alicia had by now given up trying to set her up on dates. They had reconciled themselves to her being alone, probably for the rest of her life. People in Stewart probably assumed Liz was too plain to attract men and, anyway, no doubt far too busy for a love life. They knew she had her precious cat for company. Years ago people would have called her an old maid, but now with the new wave of feminism fifteen years old, they probably saw her as one of those new liberated independent women.

Her biggest regret was now she'd never have children. She felt wistful whenever she conducted a baptism or visited the children in her Sunday School or watched them perform in the church's Thanksgiving pageant or saw them running and laughing at their annual spring picnic. Her parents would never have the grandchildren they desired. Liz had cheated them as well as herself.

A year passed since Inga and Liz had embarked on their relationship, and so far so good. No one seemed to suspect anything.

The spontaneity and joy Liz discovered with Inga both sexually and emotionally carried over into her service to her church. As their love opened Liz up she became a better pastor. She was changing both personally and professionally. No longer so rigid, she developed a better understanding for the problems of her congregants and a warmer relationship with them. Although she was constricted by the necessity of keeping her relationship with Inga a secret, Liz felt personally freer than ever before. She even gave up her conservative color scheme and started wearing reds and yellows and pinks. Experimented with more daring jewelry. Allowed her frizzy hair to grow long and run wild. She no longer tried to brush it straight, just let nature take its course, reveling in the chaos framing her face.

As Liz put her trust into another human being again she gained more confidence in herself. She developed a stronger feminism, even though she still had to be cautious at her church. But she sensed the women in her congregation gained from her strength even though she didn't express it publicly.

This confidence carried over into her social action work. She no longer feared the criticisms of the Stated Clerk of the Session and the other elders and congregants who felt she was devoting too much time to outside projects. Now she believed she possessed God's mandate to forge ahead and do what was right to help improve the world. And now she was confident she could bring her congregation along with her.

Liz increased her interfaith programs with Father Tony, other Protestant churches in the area, and the new rabbi of the synagogue in Stewart. Rabbi Sandra Miller-Brownstein, her new friend Sister Ann Gillen had introduced her to, brought her out to her synagogue in Milwaukee for an interfaith panel discussion. She was appointed to an important commission sponsored by the National Council of Churches to brainstorm ways women clergy from various denominations could network to discuss their common problems and manage and solve them.

These trips down to Manhattan for those commission meetings allowed her to visit her old friend Alicia, who now had two adorable children. Also, this commission work brought her to the attention of prominent feminist Catholic theologian Rosemary Radford Ruether. Dr. Ruether asked Liz to write a chapter tracing the history of ordination of women in Protestant churches for an important anthology she was co-editing, *Women of Spirit: Female Leadership in the Jewish and Christian Traditions*, scheduled for publication the following year.

And with Inga's encouragement she publicly rallied for ratification of the Equal Rights Amendment passed in both houses of Congress. Deadline for expiration of the proposed constitutional amendment if not ratified by all fifty states was June 30, 1982, just four years away.

Sister Ann Gillen had gone to the Soviet Union in 1974 to encourage Jewish and Christian dissidents. Now she was planning a second trip with Sister Gloria Coleman, a friend from her order, Sisters of the Holy Child Jesus in Rosemont, Pennsylvania.

Sister Ann invited Liz to accompany them.

"Soviet dissidents and activists for their cause throughout the world need encouragement now more than ever before," Liz told her congregants in a sermon informing them she planned to go with Sisters Ann and Gloria to the Soviet Union. "We're at a low point in our struggle. In March last year Anatoly Scharanksy, known as Natan, was arrested on charges of treason and spying for the U.S. He awaits trial and a possible death sentence. This brilliant young mathematician and chess champion has become a symbol of the entire Soviet Jewry movement. The important leaders are being arrested, imprisoned, or exiled. New leaders of their stature are not stepping up, understandably so in light of the personal sacrifices they must make and the danger they place themselves in.

"The Jews in the Soviet Union are simply amazed," Liz continued, "that a Catholic nun, Sister Ann Gillen, cares so much about them. They are astonished that she spends her life lecturing about their situation, picketing Soviet embassies, going to the United Nations and the White House and Congress to petition leaders, and rallying support from Christians such as ourselves to 'Let My People Go.' These Jewish and Christian dissidents rely on activists throughout the world to keep up pressure on the Soviet government. When Sister Ann visited the Soviet Union in 1974 and met Vladimir Slepak, one of the leading dissidents, he told her the fate of the Soviet Jews depended on outside activists. 'When you are strong, we are strong,' he said to her. 'When you are silent, we can be sent to Siberia.'"

Liz described to her congregants the conditions the "Prisoners of Conscience" face. "They're allowed little or no contact with their outside families and must perform at least nine hours daily of heavy labor in these prison camps near a city called Perm in central Russia. Or they are sent to camps in Siberia. Breakfast typically consists of one slice of black bread, one cup of hot water, and one ounce of herring. Lunch might be two thirds of a cup of cabbage or potato soup or gruel. Dinner three and a half to five ounces of watery mashed potatoes or one cup of cabbage and tomato soup.

"God and my conscience compel me to make this trip with Sisters Ann Gillen and Gloria Coleman. As the Prophet Isaiah intones in Chapter 42, Verses 6-7, 'I the Lord have called you for the victory of justice, I have grasped you by the hand; I formed you and set you as a covenant of the people, a light for the nation. To open the eyes of the blind, to bring prisoners out from confinement, And from the dungeon, those who live in darkness.'"

Liz justified the time away from her church by claiming it as her two-week study leave to which she was entitled according to her contract. The additional few days of the trip she'd subtract from her vacation days.

In order to prepare herself, Liz read the *Briefing Kit for Travelers to the USSR* published by the American Jewish Congress for American Jews going to the Soviet Union to meet secretly with dissidents. The authors advised travelers to memorize its contents and not take the booklet with them into the country.

They said travelers should bring with them Jewish prayer books both for daily use and the Jewish High holidays, Passover *Haggadot*, prayer shawls, bibles, Jewish calendars, yarmulkes, Russian-Hebrew dictionaries, and phylacteries, small leather boxes containing scripture passages Jewish men wear during their morning prayers. They warned these items could be confiscated, so people should take just one or two of each. They should also bring copies of Leon Uris' novel *Exodus* and James Michener's *The Source*, outstanding fictional accounts of Jewish history. And blue jeans and rock and roll or country music items. No one, they warned, should bring anti-Soviet propaganda. When people meet with dissidents they should not take written notes. They must be careful because their telephones would be tapped, hotel rooms bugged, and KGB agents would probably be following them.

The booklet gave instructions for using the difficult Russian telephones and provided quick and easy answers to questions about Jews in the US and about Israel the Soviet Jews might ask. This was especially helpful to Liz.

Her friend Rabbi Brill, now living in Manhattan and working for a Jewish organization there, helped Liz gather the items she planned to sneak into the country.

"There's a huge black market in the Soviet Union," he told her. "Give these things to those no longer allowed to work. The money they get for selling them, especially the jeans, will help them survive. Take as much medicine as you can. Ulcer medicine."

The sixteen-day journey into the Soviet Union began after a long flight on Air France. So everyone there would know they were nuns, Sisters Ann and Gloria donned small headpieces and veils, leftovers from full habits they no longer wore.

Exhausted from the flight, the three women disembarked at the chaotic, noisy smoke-filled Moscow airport. They waited in line for an hour to pass through customs. The officials stared at Sisters Ann and Gloria because of their clothing. One man grabbed the Jewish Star of David Sister Ann wore around her neck and peered at it. Another examined Sister Gloria's order's emblem. Shook his head, muttered. Fortunately the men were too busy shouting at each other and smoking vile-smelling cigarettes to look through the luggage in which the women had hidden their smuggled goods under their clothing.

One of the dissidents Sister Ann had met during her 1974 trip to the Soviet Union greeted them after they passed through customs. He drove them in his old broken-down car to an Intourist hotel on Gorky Street in the center of Moscow. They dragged their luggage up to the rooms, passing an ancient wrinkled woman sitting on a chair in the dark smoky corridor glaring at them.

"KGB," Sister Ann whispered. "To see who goes in and out of your room."

Liz desperately needed sleep and a bath. But they changed clothing quickly and walked to the home of Vladimir and Masha Slepak also on Gorky Street and very near the Kremlin. Now in their eighth year of what the Soviet Jews called "refusal", the Slepak's flat was usually the first stop visitors made when making contact with the dissident network. As the women tried to enter the building three burly men with bulging jackets stopped them. Liz' heart stopped. She wasn't in Maine anymore.

"Ladies, you cannot go there," one of the men said to them in Russian-accented broken English.

"We intend to see Mr. Slepak," Sister Ann announced defiantly.

"He is under arrest," the man answered. "You must leave here now."

They rushed to the home of another dissident to find out what had happened. He told them a group of women refuseniks had planned a protest for the day before they arrived, a holiday in the Soviet Union known as International

Children's Day. The women were going to display banners from five balconies in various parts of Moscow at approximately half-hour intervals to protest the emigration policies of the Soviet government. But some backed out because police cars surrounding their apartment buildings the night before frightened them. The remaining protesters gathered in one woman's flat.

The Slepaks hadn't planned to take part in the demonstration, but after secret police came into their home, pushed and shoved them and taunted them, they decided to participate. They painted on a sheet, "Let Us Go To Our Son in Israel" and draped it over their balcony's railing. A large crowd gathered in front of their building on Gorky Street, one of the busiest in Moscow. Traffic was blocked. Eventually nearly 1,000 people congregated. Some in the crowd shouted anti-Semitic slurs. A few urged the police to use firearms on the Jews.

As both Slepaks clutched the sheet, police poured scalding water onto their heads from a balcony above. The police used axes to destroy the front door of their apartment and rushed into it. They yanked the banner from the Slepaks' hands, took them outside, and threw them into a prison van. The police also took into custody the eleven women and thirteen children gathered in the other flat.

Liz was shocked. She had heard about these brutal tactics in the Soviet Union for years, but witnessing them almost first-hand was a different matter.

That night they attended a press conference given by Masha Slepak at the home of prominent dissident Dr. Alexander Lerner. Western reporters stationed in Moscow the Soviet government had allowed into the country for public relations purposes were also there. The officials had released Masha from custody for medical reasons.

Mrs. Slepak described what had happened at their flat, then talked about her overnight ordeal at the police station.

"I did not give testimony or answer questions," she said, "because I refused to cooperate with fraud, to recognize false accusations. We refuseniks are hostages. Commodities to be sold. I ask our government to sell us before we spoil. We are ageing and ill. The price is not money but something else. My family has been destroyed."

After Masha Slepak spoke, reporters urged Ida Nudel to tell them about her experiences in the protest. But Ida modestly answered, "No, one story is enough."

Sisters Ann and Gloria and Liz heard Ida's story when they visited her in her flat the next day.

"I applied for an exit visa in May 1971," the small woman with wire-framed glasses began, "but my request was denied. In 1972, I was forbidden to work as an economist. I kept reapplying for exit visas, but was continually refused.

"I became known in the dissident community as it's Guardian Angel because I corresponded with the Prisoners of Conscience, sent them food, medicine, and books, and took them into my home when they were released. I visited prisons, camps, and transport points. I brought to public attention the violation of the prisoners' rights through my demonstrations, correspondence with Westerners, and frequent meetings with visiting activists. For these activities Soviet authorities constantly harassed me.

"At six in the evening of these latest protests, unaware the others had been arrested," Ida continued, "I attached my banner to skis on which I wrote, 'KGB, Give Me My Visa for Israel'. From an adjoining apartment's balcony the KGB pulled down the banner with metal rods. I made another sign, fastened it to the skis. When the agents tried to destroy this banner, I threw water at them. The agents went to an apartment above mine and, I suppose encouraged by cheers from the crowd gathered below, with a wrench they shattered my window. As the police pounded on my barricaded doors, I lay down on my couch and went to sleep."

"You what?" Liz asked, incredulous.

Ida laughed. "I went to sleep."

She became serious again. "But before you came, I just received the summons to go to the police station to have the file of charges being brought against me read." Ida paused, moved closer to Sister Ann. She picked up the necklace around the nun's neck, peered at it, and asked, "You wear our Star of David?"

"Yes," Sister Ann said. "To show support for you."

Ida's face lit up with joy.

"Imagine. Two Catholic sisters and a Protestant pastor work together to help me! In my country Jews and Christians do not work together."

Ida looked up at the ceiling, pointed to it, indicating to the visitors what they already knew, that the KGB was bugging her flat and listening to everything that transpired there. "The government here does not like any religion," she whispered. "It has shut down nearly all our places of worship." Ida proudly pointed to a large Star of David made from paper in her window. "I made this to fill the hole in the window the police made."

As they talked, Ida began to mend a pile of clothing. "Soon I will be on trial," she explained. "I will need this clothing when I serve the prison sentence I know they have already decided to give me."

"Aren't you frightened of going to prison?" Liz asked her.

Ida raised her head and fist toward the ceiling and shouted, "I am ready for prison, even for death."

Sister Ann shouted up to the ceiling, "You have many friends in the West who will work to help you."

Liz was moved to tears by Ida's bravery and Sister Ann's resolve. She would remember this moment forever.

When they left Ida's building it was still light because in June in Moscow the sun didn't set until nearly midnight. The women saw a long black car barrel toward them. When it stopped, two men jumped out, grabbed them, and ordered them to come with them.

Liz was terrified, sure the three of them would spend the rest of their lives in a Soviet prison. Perhaps even be sent to Siberia. She'd never see Inga again. Her parents. Who would take care of them? What would happen to her cat? To her church? Could the U.S. government intervene and get them released?

"You have no authority over us," Sister Ann stated quietly but firmly.

What guts, Liz thought. Nothing frightens this woman. Liz was sure if she had tried to speak at that moment no words would have come out of her mouth.

"You come now," the man repeated, now shouting.

The men pushed them into the car. The driver sped recklessly through chaotic traffic to a police station. They waited there for an hour, not allowed to speak to each other. Finally an important KGB official arrived and asked for their photographs and notes from their meeting with Ida Nudel.

"We have no photographs or notes," Sister Gloria said.

"If you do not give them to us we will search you. I assure you, ladies, it will not be pleasant."

"We are Catholic Sisters," Sister Ann reminded them, nodding toward Sister Gloria. "We have dedicated our lives to our Lord Jesus Christ. Reverend Elizabeth Adams is also a woman of God, a Presbyterian pastor. We will take great offense if you touch us."

The men grunted, then took each of them into separate small rooms. Liz closed her eyes and held her breath as the KGB man roughly patted down her body with his thick hands. Obviously frustrated because they found nothing on the women, the officials informed them a car would take them back to their hotel. Sister Ann said resolutely to one of the KGB agents as he wrote up charges against them, "Now I know in some small way personally what Soviet Jews suffer to a far greater degree. This is contrary to the Helsinki Agreement, which is supposed to guarantee the freer flow of persons and information."

For the remainder of their stay in the Soviet Union they were constantly followed. It was even more difficult than before to have conversations with the total of thirty Christians as well as Jews in refusal they met with.

At the airport before their departure Sisters Ann and Gloria and Liz were again taken into separate tiny rooms. This time, knowing, Liz assumed, she was not a nun, she was given a full body search. The uniformed woman stared at Liz coldly as she ordered her in broken English to unbutton her blouse and remove her brassiere. Then she told Liz to pull up her skirt and lower her underpants to her knees. She invasively poked at Liz's breasts, crotch, and anal area with her fingers. Liz closed my eyes and said a prayer to block out the pain and humiliation. The woman muttered something in Russian, then gruffly signaled Liz to put on her clothes.

The officials confiscated whatever notes and photographs they had managed to take. The three women would have to rely on their memories when they reported at home on their trip.

As they were being harassed, Liz kept looking at her watch, afraid they were going to miss their flight. Finally the officials grudgingly released them, and they ran with their luggage through the long corridors to the gate. They endured one last search of their luggage, then rushed onto the plane and sank into their seats in relief.

"Thank you, God," Liz said silently as the airplane took off. "Thank you, God, for letting me return home to our wonderful free land of America."

Mona: 1978 - 1990

MONA WATCHED FROM her pew in the synagogue in Milwaukee as Rabbi Sandra Miller-Brownstein blessed her sister Peggy and formally converted her to Judaism. She envied this woman.

If Sandra Miller-Brownstein could be a rabbi, why couldn't she be a priest?

Mona's longing for ordination had grown over the six years since she had left the West Virginia compound to drive across the country with Sister Phyllis. The two women had continued to discuss Mona's growing desire to become a priest and the possibilities of it happening as they visited various orders, stopped at the office in Washington of the activist sisters' organization NETWORK that Sister Phyllis had helped found, attended meetings and conferences, and visited Sister Margaret Traxler in Chicago and Peggy and David in Milwaukee. They had hours, days, weeks, and months on their journey to think and to talk.

Mona's father would never know if she disgraced her family by leaving the church to become an Episcopal priest. Patrick Sullivan had died in 1976. Vivian had found him at 7 a.m. sprawled out on the floor of the upstairs bathroom. A fast, painless massive heart attack, the doctor assured them. A good way to go, we should be grateful for that, everyone agreed. Mona was devastated, but comforted knowing he was with Momma now, probably complaining to her about all the changes in their family and in their Church since she had passed away twenty-three years ago.

Dad would be telling Momma now you don't have to go to Mass anymore on Sunday mornings, you get to pick your own time. Muriel and Joe go on Saturday nights now so they can sleep in on Sundays. Whoever heard of such a thing? Like going to church is some kind of hobby. Hardly anybody's going to Mass anymore, anyway. Hardly anybody listens to the Pope anymore or does what he tells us to. And now women are taking part in the Mass as acolytes, even the scripture readings. They've removed the communion rail. You wouldn't believe some of the ridiculous things they're experimenting with to get people more interested in coming to church. Folk singers and guitars. Like we're supposed to be entertained, like we're going to the movies or going bowling.

And Dad would be complaining to Momma their Peggy married a Jew and the children were Jewish, not Catholic, and he didn't care what that confusing Vatican Council said, it was a fact Jews cannot be saved and go to heaven because they deny our Lord, and he was sorry about that because he liked Peggy's husband and his family very much.

Dad would be telling her how Mona left her convent and her school teaching and went down to some God-forsaken hippie farm in West Virginia to try to help those poor people who couldn't help themselves and had no desire to improve their lives anyway so she was just wasting her time. And then how she left there and wandered all over the country with that crazy hippie Mother Superior or whatever they call them now, can you imagine? Both of them smoking and drinking and acting like wild teenagers, not like respectable nuns from the old days. And trying to persuade the Pope to change his teachings about birth control and abortion! Why, the Supreme Court has even said women can kill babies by getting abortions. What's the world coming to?

Surely, Mona thought, Dad would be complaining to Momma about Sluggie. How he rarely heard from him up in Canada and how worried about his youngest son he was. Unfortunately Mona's father died before President Jimmy Carter declared amnesty for those who had gone to Canada to avoid the draft just one day after he was inaugurated in January 1977. Patrick Sullivan never knew his beloved younger son finally came home to them.

Vivian had tried to help Sluggie move forward with his life. In Canada Mona's brother had worked only at odd jobs and never built up any skills or a career. Vivian offered to pay his college tuition, he could at least enroll in a technical training program, she told him. But after Sluggie's first visit to Rory in the Veterans' Hospital in Manhattan, he had returned home and climbed into bed, so depressed he didn't emerge from his room for three days. Mona wanted him to get counseling, but the bishop had transferred their neighborhood priest, Father Connell, to another parish, and Vivian didn't like his replacement. Getting professional counseling through the Veterans' Administration required navigating miles of red tape and long waits. Unable to work and realizing he was imposing on Vivian, Mona's brother moved in with her sister Muriel and her husband Joe.

As Mona watched Rabbi Miller-Brownstein bless her sister and welcome Peggy into the Jewish fold, the Sabbath service came to an end. They ate delicious cookies, cakes, and fruit in the temple's social hall. Then Rabbi Sandra Miller-Brownstein invited her back to her home.

The rabbi's husband, Robert, a lawyer, greeted them warmly. One and a half year old Beruria was asleep. Their beautiful five-year old son Joshua was still awake, waiting for Rabbi Sandra to come home so she could say goodnight. She hugged and kissed him, then Robert carried him off to bed. The rabbi sank down into an easy chair and kicked off her shoes.

"You have a full plate, Rabbi," Mona said. "I don't know how you do it. Husband, children, career."

"Precisely what the search committees asked when I was applying for pulpits. Their excuse for not hiring me. Motherhood is a full-time job. I'll have to go through the whole interviewing thing again in two years when it's time to get my own congregation. If I can get one. We women are having a hard time. Well, they're not entirely wrong. Motherhood is demanding. I'm always behind on everything. I feel like I'm drowning. Always feeling guilty, that I should be working when I'm home with the kids and I should be home with the kids when I'm working."

"Peggy tells me you're brave. You helped break the sex barrier for rabbis."

"Peggy says you want to be a priest."

"I'm still struggling with that decision. It would mean going against the Church."

"Do you think your Church will ever ordain women?"

"Probably not in my lifetime. But we're working on it. So are the Episcopalians. Four years ago four retired Episcopal bishops 'irregularly' ordained eleven women. Two weeks later the ordinations were declared invalid. That September another retired bishop ordained four more."

"I remember reading about all this," Rabbi Miller-Brownstein commented.

"Three of the women, one of them nearly eighty, caused an uproar when they served Eucharist at Riverside Church in New York that October. My Mother Superior and I attended each ceremony to support them. The Episcopalian House of Bishops brought charges against the dissident bishops. They tried to prevent the women from serving. Finally two years ago in Minneapolis the Episcopal General Convention voted to approve ordination of women and to make those earlier ordinations official. But this change in canon law was not made compulsory for all American bishops, so an Episcopalian woman priest could find herself in a position of not being valid in some places."

Over decaf coffee Mona described how this upheaval in the Episcopalian Church resulted in the founding of Priests for Equality.

"The organization sponsored a conference, Women in Future Priesthood Now: A Call to Action, over Thanksgiving weekend in 1975 in Detroit. There was room for only 1,400 people. Nearly 2,000 came. We had to turn away 600 people."

"Wow."

"Nearly a year later, Pope John Paul II released his encyclical saying the Vatican is not authorized to admit women to the priesthood. Women can never be ordained because priests participate in Christ's priesthood. They act for Jesus, the pontiff said. Jesus was a man, and therefore women can't reflect his image. Jesus himself established the tradition of a male priesthood. Being a priest is not just a function, it's a spiritual state of being. So, he claimed, even if women were ordained they wouldn't really be priests. The Church could never make this doctrinal change. The key issue is the Eucharist, it's validity and who can serve it.

"The Women's Ordination Conference grew out of that 1975 event and the Vatican's response to it," Mona continued. "We're based in Washington. I'm the Executive Director. We're organizing liturgical protests around the country. There's a flood of new Biblical scholarship arguing against the Pope's encyclical. We're planning another conference this November in Baltimore, enough room this time for everyone who wants to attend. We're expecting about 3,000. Of course there's the usual politics and infighting."

"Oh, you Catholics have that too?" Rabbi Sandra Miller-Brownstein asked, laughing.

Mona looked at her watch. "It's getting late. I need to go and let you get to bed," she said. "And I have an early flight back to Washington."

"Will you keep in touch? Let me know how your battle is progressing? I'll be cheering you on from the sidelines."

"I'll write you and phone often. Thanks. I'll need all the encouragement I can get."

In late September, a month before the Women's Ordination Conference, Pope John Paul I died suddenly of an apparent heart attack after being in office just thirty-three days. On October 16th the College of Cardinals elected Polish Cardinal Karol Jozef Wojtyla, the first non-Italian Pope since the 1500s. To honor his predecessor, he took the name John Paul II. The new Pope was known as a theological conservative, so Mona realized the path to ordination of Catholic women would be even more difficult.

The Women's Ordination Conference at the Baltimore Civic Center displayed a banner, "New Woman, New Church, New Priestly Ministry." The motto, "It's time to lay to rest the heresy that women cannot image Jesus in the priesthood," was a response to the Pope's Encyclical. They held a religious service at the Baltimore Harbor the night before the formal opening of the proceedings. Many of the sisters and Catholic laywomen in the huge crowd wrapped themselves in a large grey plastic chain symbolizing chains oppressing women.

"We have to fight for ourselves before we can fight for social justice for others," Mona proclaimed in her speech at the harbor. "We can't insist on equality in society at large until we have equality and justice within our own Church."

After the conference, a group gathered up the plastic broken chains left over from their demonstration and drove to the Bishops meeting in Washington. TV cameras were present. Their protest appeared on the major evening news broadcasts.

"I saw you on TV," Rabbi Sandra Miller-Brownstein wrote to her. *"Keep up the good work!"*

The struggle for women's ordination in the Catholic Church once again hit the national news when Sister Teresa Kane confronted Pope John Paul II on the podium of the Shrine of the Immaculate Conception on October 7, 1979.

Men and women wearing blue armbands to protest sexism in the Church had greeted the pontiff at every stop on his first trip to the U.S. When he came to Washington Mona and two other WOC members held an all-night vigil outside where the Pope slept. As he emerged early that morning, Mona's friend Ruth Fitzpatrick held her candle above her head and shouted, "Ordain Women." The Pope just smiled, shook his head.

Although many in the hierarchy had tried to keep her off the program, the event's organizers chose Sister Teresa Kane, president of the Leadership Conference of Women Religious, to deliver official greetings to the Holy Father at the National Shrine of the Immaculate Conception program. Mona stood throughout the entire proceedings with twenty-nine other women in the audience wearing blue armbands so the television stations would cover their protest as well as her speech because by now the sisters were aware of the power of the media to help shape public opinion.

"As I share this privileged moment with you, Your Holiness," Sister Teresa Kane began, "I urge you to be mindful of the intense suffering and pain which is part of the life of many women in the United States. I call upon you to listen with compassion and to hear the call of women who comprise half of humankind. As women, we have heard the powerful messages of our church addressing the dignity and reverence for all persons. As women, we have pondered these words. Our contemplation leads us to state that the church in its struggle to be faithful to its call for reverence and dignity for all persons must respond by providing the possibility of women as persons being included in all ministries of our church. I urge you, Your Holiness, to be open to and respond to the voices coming from the women of this country who are desirous of serving in and through the church as fully participating members."

The Pope sat expressionless in total silence. As everyone applauded wildly, Sister Teresa Kane walked across the altar and greeted the pontiff. He wouldn't shake her hand. She knelt for his blessing. Later she wrote to Pope Jean Paul II asking to meet with him, but never received a response to her request. This very visible protest by Sister Teresa Kane connected the Catholic feminist movement with the general feminist movement. It also generated support from some men headed for ordination.

Mona traveled with her assistant throughout the country to protest at various ordinations. Some of the male candidates wore blue armbands or blue ribbons to show solidarity with them. In a standard ordination ceremony as the bishops called men forward to be ordained, they would reply, "I am ready and willing." Now in some of the ceremonies as the last man was called, women in the congregation would stand one by one and call out, "I am ready and willing" and remain standing throughout the ceremony. If they couldn't get inside the church, they marched outside wearing blue armbands and distributing leaflets.

On September 9, 1980, Mona's friend Luella and her husband Peter, along with Daniel and Philip Berrigan and four others, broke into the General Electric facility in King of Prussia, Pennsylvania where nose cones for nuclear warheads were manufactured. They acted out the biblical injunctions of the prophets Isaiah and Micah to "Beat swords into plowshares" by bashing the metal cones with hammers and pouring blood over documents in order to protest war and the build-up of nuclear weapons.

Luella and Peter and the other six, who became known as "The Plowshares Eight," were tried, convicted, and sentenced to prison terms ranging from a little over one year to ten years. Because Luella and Peter had a child, Luella was sentenced to only eighteen months. Peter was sentenced to two years. Mona offered to care for their two-year old Marianne, but the child stayed with Luella's parents. All the cases were being appealed. Everyone was dismayed, but Mona and Sister Phyllis doubted their friends and the others would have to complete their sentences. Luella only served six months, and vowed to devote the rest of her life to prison reform.

By now sisters were crafting their own final vows, often not even recited during a Mass. Some were replacing the vow of poverty with a promise of responsible stewardship, the vow of chastity with a promise of responsible intimacy, and the vow of obedience with a commitment to make responsible decisions. Some sisters and laywomen were abandoning the# Church so they could be ordained in Protestant religions, especially as Episcopalians.

"You could do that," Sister Phyllis reminded Mona often.

"No. We need to reform the Church from within," Mona always responded.

"We'll never get it to change," Sister Phyllis argued. "It's hopeless. We have to create a new structure. Mary Daly's right. We can't operate within the old hierarchical patriarchal system."

As much as she argued with Sister Phyllis about this, Mona knew she was right. Nothing was the same as before.

"The life I yearned for when I entered the convent twenty-two years ago no longer exists," Mona wrote to her new friend Rabbi Sandra. *"My old world is gone forever."*

In 1984, Frances Kissling, the Executive Director of Catholics for a Free Choice, asked Mona to publicly include her name on a full-page advertisement entitled "A Catholic Statement on Pluralism and Abortion" to appear in *The New York Times* on October 7th.

The statement was designed to boost Catholic Vice Presidential candidate Geraldine Ferraro's election chances after New York City Archbishop Cardinal John J. O'Connor said Catholics should not vote for a pro-choice candidate, as he considered her to be. Also to defend New York Governor Mario Cuomo, who had come under attack by the Church when in a speech at Notre Dame University he had argued, "There can be different political approaches to abortion besides unyielding adherence to an absolute prohibition."

The ad appeared on what American Bishops had declared "Respect Life Sunday". It brought to the general public's attention the dispute between the Vatican and growing numbers of pro-choice Catholics in the U.S. The ad proclaimed, "Statements of recent Popes and of the Catholic hierarchy have condemned the direct termination of pre-natal life as morally wrong in all instances.

There is the mistaken belief in American society this is the only legitimate Catholic position. In fact, a diversity of opinions regarding abortion exists among committed Catholics." It quoted a recent survey reporting only eleven percent of Catholics thought abortion was wrong under all circumstances. There should be a "candid and respectful discussion" within the Church in which there is a diversity of opinion on the issue.

Ninety-seven people signed the advertisement. Sixty-seven were lay people, including Luella and Peter and Catholic theologians. The rest were two priests, two lay brothers, and twenty-six sisters -- including Mona -- from fourteen communities. Others supported the statement anonymously, fearing if they signed their names they'd lose their jobs.

The U.S. Conference of Catholic Bishops denounced the ad as contrary to the Church's teachings. In December the Vatican's Congregation for Religious and Secular Institutes directed the Mothers Superior of the sisters who had signed the advertisement to tell them if they didn't publicly retract their signatures they would face immediate dismissal from their orders. After they recanted the Mothers Superior were to write letters to the Congregation for Religious and Secular Institutes saying the sisters for whom they were responsible were once again in line with the Church's teachings on abortion. If these supervising women did not do this they'd also be guilty of disobedience and, it was implied, might be replaced by men chosen by Rome.

"It's a threat to the independence of women religious," Sister Phyllis fumed. "Coming right when we're struggling to renew our constitutions. They're trying to dictate sisters' lives. Repress us. They didn't ask the laypeople to retract their signatures. They're treating them differently. That just proves this is not about the morality of abortion, it's about making sisters obey."

"Maybe I will withdraw my signature," Mona offered. "Then you can write the Vatican to tell them I'm back in line again. This would get you off the hook. It's just a formality. I can keep fighting from behind the scenes."

"Just a formality?" she shouted. "Are you out of your mind? If you do recant, you'll be folding under their pressure. It would go against everything we've fought for all these years. Our rights as women in the Church, our dignity as sisters able to determine our own lives. Against everything I've taught you. To stand up for yourself as a person and as a woman. Our right to follow our consciences, to dissent when Church teachings are wrong. And the Vatican is wrong on this. They've never declared the Pope infallible on this issue. They have no right to force you to recant, no right to put me in this position. This is outrageous. I will not force you to retract your signature. Even if I agreed with them, I wouldn't force you. They can't make me do it!"

It was the last straw for Sister Phyllis. She resigned as Administrative Director of Mona's convent. And the following day she renounced her vows.

"Well, that's it," she told Mona. "I feel strangely relieved. Free. I've been a sister since I was seventeen. For the first time in my life I have an open future. I'm going to backpack through Asia and Africa. I'll send you all postcards of Buddhist and Hindu temples and African churches."

Mona was shocked. How could she face the future without this woman's firm guidance? Sister Phyllis had steered Mona's course as her Mother Superior since the day she had walked tremulously through the gates of their convent.

Mona prayed harder than she had in years for God to guide her decision regarding The Catholic Statement on Pluralism and Abortion. Should she publicly retract her support? She wanted to follow her conscience, but she also wanted to remain a sister. She couldn't do both. Which should she choose?

In December, thirty-five signatories of the controversial ad met in Washington to discuss what to do. They released a statement saying the ad had not called for women to have abortions, it had merely asked for an open discussion. They maintained that the Congregation for Religious and Secular Institutes' ultimatum that they withdraw their signatures or be ejected from their religious orders did not follow the spirit of Vatican Council II which had declared, "Let there be unity in what is necessary, freedom in what is unsettled, and charity in any case."

The group met twice again in January. The two priests, two lay brothers, and many of the sisters publicly retracted their signatures. The media hounded the sisters who had not yet given in to the Vatican. Mona's group of holdouts even appeared on the Phil Donahue show on January 28th. After that TV exposure Mona gave ten press interviews.

"I didn't take the veil to become a media star," she complained to Luella on the telephone.

"I didn't take the veil to go to prison," her friend responded.

The Vatican kept its pressure on them to recant. The battle dragged on for another year.

In March of 1986, the Vatican's Congregation of Religious and Secular Institutes sent Archbishop Vincenzo Fagliolo and Sister Mary Linscott, at that time the highest ranking woman in the Vatican, to Washington D.C. to meet with Mona and the two others, Sisters Barbara Ferraro and Patricia Hussey, who had also not yet withdrawn their names from the *New York Times* abortion statement. The meeting would take place at Trinity College of Catholic University.

Adhering to her father's advice to always keep smiling no matter what, Mona tried to be polite as Archbishop Fagliolo and Sister Mary Linscott told the three women they couldn't remain in religious life if they continued their dissent. Their cases wouldn't be resolved until they pledged adherence to the Church's teachings on abortion. They gave Mona and Sisters Barbara Ferraro and Patricia Hussey until April 4th to submit their written statements of obedience.

Thirteen days.

"I want to follow my conscience and do what's right," she told her friend Rabbi Sandra on the telephone. "Abortion can't be wrong all the time. But I don't want to be thrown out of my congregation if I don't retract my signature. I always wanted to be a sister. I still want to be. I'm a Catholic. I want to be a Catholic for the rest of my life. Maybe they'd excommunicate me."

"What does your former Mother Superior think you should do? Where is she?"

"She's wandering around Asia. I've heard she's in China now. She doesn't have a schedule. But she does write me long letters, not just the exotic postcards she promised everybody when she left. She knows the Vatican is still pressuring me and I'm still agonizing about my decision. She usually offers me words of encouragement. But in her latest letter, she printed in bold letters, 'If you do withdraw your signature from the ad, if you do recant, I will never forgive you.'"

"Ouch. You think she means it?"

"Phyllis always means everything she says." Mona paused, fought back tears. "I don't know if I can survive without her respect. She's been my mentor. My surrogate mother. Now she's also my friend."

On April 3rd Mona sent a letter to the Congregation for Religious and Secular Institutes withdrawing her name from the advertisement.

Immediately she bitterly regretted her decision.

Why didn't she have the courage Sisters Barbara and Patricia had shown when they had once again refused to withdraw their names? Well, now it was too late to change her mind.

Luella and Peter were disappointed in her, Mona knew. After all, hadn't they both spent time in prison to uphold their principles? Mona didn't know how Phyllis, somewhere in Asia, heard about her decision. But she knew she must have, because Mona never received another letter from her.

Mona deserved Phyllis' contempt. She was a coward. She had not followed her conscience. She had failed her biggest test.

When Mona went home to Queens for Thanksgiving in 1988, she ran into Dickie Donavan, Kathleen's widower. He was sober now, still going to Alcoholics Anonymous. He had remarried, finally forgiven himself for Kathleen's suicide, and reconnected with their children. Mona's brother Sluggie was now married to wonderful Janet. He had a good job and had legally adopted Janet's two children from her first marriage. Muriel and Joe's daughter was in college. Their son had made the high school honor roll. They missed having Vivian with them for the holiday. She had gone down to Florida to celebrate it with her sister. But they were able to bring Rory home from the Veterans Hospital for the day.

Via convent gossip, Mona heard Phyllis had returned to the States and taken up sculpture. She now owned a New Age art gallery in Sedona, Arizona. Mona also heard John Stevens and Clara McKittridge, who had married after Mona left the West Virginia compound, had two children. John was in private practice in Atlanta. Mona was happy for Clara, but also, she had to admit, a bit jealous. She could easily have fallen in love with John and married him. Been a wife and mother. A good one, as John had assured her.

Had she made all those personal sacrifices to be a sister for nothing? Had she lived her life for nothing? She didn't even have the courage to live up to her convictions.

In early January of 1990, Mona received a letter from the president of a prominent interfaith women's organization called WomanSpeak: Voices of Women of Faith.

"Dear Sister Mona: We are pleased to inform you that our organization, WomanSpeak: Voices of Women of Faith, wishes to honor you with its WomanSpeak Let My Voice Be Heard Award," the letter began. *"This recognition is given annually to individuals whose outstanding work has advanced the role of women in religion and in society. Your award will be presented at our banquet on Thursday March 22 nd, 1990 at the Plaza Hotel in Manhattan.*

"We will honor two other women, Reverend Elisabeth Adams, Pastor of the First Presbyterian Church of Stewart, Maine and Rabbi Sandra Miller-Brownstein, spiritual leader of Temple Beth El in Chicago. Please let us know as soon as possible if you will be able to attend the dinner to accept this honor."

"It will be wonderful to see you again at the dinner," Mona told Rabbi Sandra on the telephone. "Didn't Reverend Adams work with Sister Ann Gillen on the Soviet Jewry struggle?"

"Yes," Rabbi Sandra said. "She went to the Soviet Union with her."

"Oh yes, I remember. She got strip searched. Big brouhaha. And she's a friend of yours, isn't she?"

"Yes."

"I think I met her briefly at the Episcopalian women's ordinations in 1974." Mona paused. "But why would this organization give me an award? You and Reverend Adams deserve it, but I don't. I didn't stand up for my principles. I wasn't brave when I most needed to be. Played it safe so I could keep the life I was accustomed to. I should never have withdrawn my signature from that *New York Times* statement."

"Don't be so hard on yourself," Rabbi Sandra said. "You had a lot to lose."

"And I still haven't changed. Eighteen years now I've been grappling with the possibility of becoming a priest, and now more than anything that's what I yearn to do. It's ironic. Every day as Executive Director of the Women's Ordination Conference I fight for the right of Catholic women to be ordained. But I don't have the guts to leave the Catholic Church and seek ordination for myself outside its structure. Don't have the courage to leave my order and leave my church and follow where my heart leads me, to a denomination in which I can become a priest and fulfill my potential and complete the destiny I now believed God has planned for me. And now it's too late. I'm nearly fifty. Middle aged. Past middle age. More of my life behind me than ahead. My journey should have been completed long ago."

"Our journeys are never completed, Sister Mona. Haven't you realized this by now? It's not really too late for you. You can still change your life."

"You think I have enough time left? I'm up to the challenge? I can still become the person God wants me to be?"

"Of course. But you need to make up your mind once and for all," Rabbi Sandra advised. "Before it really is too late. Give yourself a deadline."

"Yes. You're right." Mona thought for a moment. "March 22nd. The night of the WomanSpeak dinner. I'll make my decision by then."

Two and a half months away.

Two and a half months to choose her future.

Sandra: 1980 – 1990

In February of 1980, along with twelve other women rabbis and twenty fourth- and fifth-year female rabbinical students, Sandy attended a meeting of the Central Conference of American Rabbis' Task Force on Women in the Rabbinate. The topic discussed was "What Gives – Home, Career, or Sanity?"

Well, Sandy could certainly relate to that topic. She was having more trouble than ever juggling the different aspects of her life. The demands on her time from her children were endless, although of course she loved being with them, watching them grow and change. Her rabbinical duties were also endless. And in the spring, Sandy's tenure as Gerson Wenick's Assistant Rabbi would end. Her three-year contract was nearly over. Now she needed to get a job in another congregation, hopefully as Senior Rabbi. But nearly all reform congregations still resisted hiring a woman for the top position.

Once more Sandy went through the torturous process of job interviews. Same sexist attitudes and questions. At least this time she wasn't pregnant, so she avoided the pregnant rabbi jokes and comments. Finally she received word from the CCAR placement director that a mid-sized congregation in a Chicago suburb wanted to hire her. He thought it would be a good fit. She agreed.

But Sandy was nervous. Jeff lived in Chicago.

"I'm afraid if I take that job I might run into him again," she confided to Carolyn. She had told her best friend about seeing Jeff at O'Hare airport during the snowstorm on her way to her job interview in Milwaukee and about the letters he'd written to her. "Jeff and I can never plan to see each other. We can never meet again."

"Did you tell Robert about that night? Or about his letters?"

"Are you kidding? Course not. You're not married, you don't understand husbands. Why upset him? Those letters and our encounter at the airport meant nothing."

"Hmm."

"And everybody knows you never quite get over your first love. It's silly to even think about that night. I'll forget about it completely, so why make Robert anxious? He's such a good father and husband. Robert and I have a good marriage and I'm happy with him." Sandy paused. "But what if Jeff and I accidentally run into each other again? What if he deliberately contacts me? Would I be able to resist him?"

"I think you would. You're a strong woman."

"Well, anyway, I've got no choice. This Chicago congregation is the only one offered to me. There are fifteen women rabbis now, but I'm lucky to get a solo pulpit. Albeit," Sandy added, "at a lower salary than a man would get."

"Of course."

"And I had to pressure them into including a clause about maternity leave in my contract in case I have another baby. Unlikely, but, then, you never know." She paused. "Jeff is in my past. My life is going well. Nothing will change that."

The transition to the family's new location in Chicago where Sandy would be heading her own congregation was difficult. Josh had adjusted well to his elementary school in their Milwaukee suburb. Now in the second grade, he'd be starting a new school. Packing up the family's possessions was a huge undertaking.

Fortunately their terrific live-in baby sitter Leana was moving with them. Robert was happy he'd no longer have to commute from Milwaukee to his law office in Chicago. An added bonus was that Sandy's youth group friend from Decatur, Susan Kleinman, had moved to Chicago after her divorce, now balancing raising her twins and attending medical school. She and Sandy looked forward to seeing each other more often.

Sandy's parents drove up to Chicago and Joanie flew out from LA for Sandy's formal installation as the congregation's new rabbi in mid-October. The president of the congregation invited Rabbi Kahn from Elmville to speak at the installation as well as Rabbi Wenick from Milwaukee. Sandy was afraid Rabbi

Kahn wouldn't accept the invitation because he didn't approve of women rabbis. Or, worse yet, if he did, in the installation ceremony he'd list all the reasons why women shouldn't be ordained.

Sandy was pleasantly surprised.

"I have to admit I was wrong," Rabbi Kahn said from the *bema* on the night of her installation. "I tried to discourage Sandra because I thought it would harm Judaism to have women rabbis. Now I can see I shouldn't have tried to talk her out of it. Now I can see our religion will be transformed by the introduction of new blood into our leadership. Our Sandra Miller-Brownstein is just one excellent example of the contributions these courageous women are making." Rabbi Kahn turned to her. "Sandra, *Mehayil el Hayil*. May you go from strength to strength."

That night Sandy's father also sort of admitted maybe he had been wrong all these years about religion. "I guess institutionalized religions have a legitimate place in the world," he said to her afterwards at the reception. "As long as people like you are guiding them."

As they said goodbye the next morning before the Millers drove back to Elmville, Leon said to her, "I'm proud of you, you know that. You are really making a difference. I'm so proud to be your father."

"And I've always been so proud to be your daughter," Sandy said as they hugged. "I love you, Daddy."

"I love you, Sandy."

Those were the last words Sandy and her father spoke to each other. Joanie telephoned Sandy two days later to tell her he had been hit by a car while crossing Main Street in downtown Elmville to meet their mother for dinner.

"Killed instantly," Joanie sobbed into the telephone.

Sandy and her mother and Joanie recited the *Kaddish* as they stood at Leon Miller's gravesite. Sandy knew the Jewish prayer for the dead does not mention death and instead affirms the greatness of God even in the face of great personal loss. But as she put her arm around Joanie and her mother to comfort them and they gazed at the casket, Sandy thought, If God is good and all-powerful He wouldn't have taken Daddy away from us. How can we praise God's greatness in this prayer when

He can snatch someone we love away so suddenly? How can I be positive and affirm the greatness of God in the face of such pain? How will I be able to tell my congregants to do this when I can't do it myself? How can I comfort my congregants when I can't comfort myself? Who comforts the comforter?

After they buried Leon, they went back to the Millers' home to sit *Shivah*. Neighbors and friends who came all week to pay their condolences prepared and brought food Joanie and Sandy set out on the dining room table.

On the third night of their *Shivah*, Jeff Shoemaker and his parents appeared at the front door. Sandy was so happy to see her childhood sweetheart, she ran into his arms, faintly aware of everyone's stares and the startled expression on Robert's face.

"I'm so sorry, Sandy," Jeff said. "I just happened to be home visiting my folks when we got the terrible news."

After Sandy recovered her composure, she introduced Jeff to Robert and their children. Robert stared at Jeff as he shook his hand and said coldly, "Yes, I've heard about you."

"Eleanor's not with you?" Sandy asked Jeff.

"No. She's on a long trip. For her dissertation research. My mother-in-law from Oregon has come out to help me with the kids."

Jeff quickly changed the subject. He and Sandy talked about her father, how wonderful and funny he was. About Jeff's work at the University of Chicago, his latest book on Chinese history, and Sandy's new congregation. Jeff had heard she had moved to Chicago.

"How did you know his wife's name?" Robert asked when they were alone later in her childhood bedroom. "How did you know so much else about him? You two have been in touch over the years."

Sandy nodded sheepishly.

"You never told me. You must feel guilty about it. Is there a reason you feel guilty?"

Robert had never interrogated her before. She told him about Jeff's letters and the O'Hare airport encounter nearly four years ago. She assured her husband it all meant nothing.

"Please tell me you'll never keep secrets again," Robert said. "It's not like you. You aren't living up to your high standards. I'm disappointed in you."

"I'm angry with God," Sandy wrote to her friend Sister Mona Sullivan two weeks later to tell her that her father had died, *"but I can also now see for myself how important Judaism's prescribed mourning rituals are. Knowing what's expected during this time guides people through the following difficult days. For seven days, Jewish mourners remove themselves from all other obligations so they can devote themselves to their sorrow and loss. The word 'Shiva' means 'seven.' At the end of that time, one must go back to life."*

"Yes," Sister Mona replied. *"Religious ritual is rooted in psychological benefits. Though sometimes I think we Irish Catholics drag out the funeral stuff bit too long."*

After the blow of her father's death, Sandy tried to return to her normal life, as Judaism prescribed. She needed to muster her energy to work hard to make her first year in her new job a success.

"I've got to get myself going again. A lot of people in this synagogue didn't want to hire a woman rabbi," she told Joanie over the telephone. "After all, it's only been eight years since Sally Priesand's ordination. I don't want to confirm their opinion that women aren't emotionally suited to the pressures of the rabbinate. But I can't seem to pull myself out of this depression. I still can't believe Daddy is dead, can you?"

"No," Joanie agreed.

"I've always told my congregants the mourning process takes time. You need to be patient. Now I'm not following my own advice. But how can I continue to give others advice about how to lead their lives when I'm not leading mine well? I have to keep up this façade of self-confidence. But I feel like I'm cheating my congregants. Telling others how to live their lives, when I can't even manage mine."

And, Sandy could no longer deny it. She kept thinking about her encounter with Jeff in Elmsville. She wanted to see him again. At times she caught herself thinking of nothing else. At those times she forced herself to concentrate on her work.

Being in charge of everything at the synagogue was more difficult than being an assistant rabbi. The buck stopped with her. Now they could blame her for everything that went wrong in the religious school, the services, the life-cycle events, the adult education programs, and the community outreach.

She needed to be extremely careful. She made a point of memorizing names of her congregants, putting names to faces. She was always on time for meetings and appointments, usually even early. Always paid close attention to what she wore, especially when on the *bema*. She wrote down names of a baby she was naming, names of the bride and groom, and the name of the deceased at funerals. She was especially careful about this after she heard one of her classmates from Hebrew Union College blanked on the name of the congregant he was burying and the board almost fired him.

Sandy couldn't ignore the fact many people in her congregation did not share her love of all things Jewish and didn't want to be there. Especially the children, most of whom were forced by their parents to attend religious school as she had been in Elmville so many years ago. And spouses of enthusiastic congregants who didn't want to be there. She tried to ignore the boredom or pain in their faces she could easily see from the *bema* during her services or classes.

The rabbinic liaison committee communicated the congregation's "issues" to Sandy.

"A fancy word for complaints," Sandy explained to Robert. "Apparently lots of people don't like me wearing a a *tallis* and *yarmulke* on the *bema*. Think they're for men only. But other people seem to like them. A couple of women are wearing them themselves."

Her clothing was too stylish, the liaison committee members told her. Perhaps they were paying her too much? Her clothing wasn't stylish enough, she needed to attend to her appearance more. After all, the synagogue had an image to keep up in the community. Her skirts were too long. Her skirts were too short. The *Shabbat* services were too long. The *Shabbat* services were too short. The temperature in the sanctuary was too cold. Too warm. Too much music in the services. Not enough music. Rabbi Miller-Brownstein spoke too softly, could she please raise her voice? This is what they had worried about when they hired a woman rabbi, her voice wouldn't carry, nobody would be able to hear her, there were a lot of old people in the congregation with hearing problems, after all. Rabbi Miller-Brownstein spoke too loudly, she didn't need to shout, did she think they were deaf? She should give her opinion about current political issues, people wanted to hear her opinion, especially about what was going on in Israel. Don't let anyone know your political leanings from the pulpit, you'll alienate half the congregation.

The congregation's "issues" were endless.

Being a public role model put Sandy under additional pressure. She was a constant source of curiosity in the press, the subject of several feature articles in the Chicago papers and in the national press and on TV. How did she do it all? Could she as a woman have it all? Could any woman have it all? What was her advice for girls wanting to pursue her unusual career path? Are women rabbis treated differently than their male counterparts? The answer, though she didn't say it, was a resounding "yes." Given equal pay? The answer, again, was "no," but of course Sandy didn't complain publicly. She saved her complaints for the Women's Rabbinic Network, the new name for the Women's Rabbinical Alliance, at sessions now held at every gathering of the Central Conference of American Rabbis.

As with Helen Gravison when Sandy was an Assistant Rabbi in Milwaukee, she had one special nemesis in her Chicago synagogue whose major aim in life was to make hers miserable. Herb Klausson. A board member, because he was a prominent CPA he headed the finance committee and monitored every cent the congregation spent. The synagogue owned the house Sandy's family lived in and paid for all expenses involved, so Herb Klausson was obsessed with how much everything in the house cost.

The usual difficulties faced by all rabbis were complicated by the fact that Sandy was a woman. People seemed to be constantly testing her to see if she was strong enough, tough enough, up to the challenge. To see if one day she'd collapse and just throw in the towel and stay home and bake cookies. She had to work twice as hard as a male rabbi to constantly prove herself. As in her tenure as Assistant Rabbi in Wenick's congregation in Milwaukee, many resisted having a woman officiate at funerals of their loved ones or counsel them during hospital visits. One man threw Sandy out of his wife's hospital room when she stopped in to see how the patient was doing.

Then there was the question of Robert's role at the synagogue.

"If I were a man, my wife would be expected to attend all services and events, smiling up adoringly at her spouse on the *bema*," she told Robert.

"Well, you're not a man, and I'm not your wife. I just don't know what your congregation expects from me. I wish somebody would tell me. Or you."

"They probably don't know, either. It's new territory for them. When you come to *Shabbat* services, everyone seems surprised you've taken time out from you busy and important life. Like my life isn't busy and important."

"I hate it when they ask me if I want to be called 'Mr. *Rebbitzen*,'" Robert complained. "Then they chuckle over their brilliant joke. Like they're the first person to think that up."

Finally Robert stopped coming to synagogue events, limiting his appearances to the High Holidays or family *Yartzheits*. No one criticized him, whereas a male rabbi's wife would have been strongly condemned for her absence.

Although by 1982 there were fifty women rabbis and nearly one third of all Reform Rabbinical students were women, they still struggled with different requirements in their role as rabbis because of their gender.

"We first women rabbis have to create our own role models, because we don't have any," Sandy told Reverend Liz Adams in a telephone conversation.

"I know. Presbyterians were ordaining women for only nine years before me, so I didn't have many role models either."

"We have to carve out our own role. I mean, we're at the helm of an organization, so we're CEOs. We need to use good leadership and management skills. We have to be confident enough to lead aggressively, but at same time we must be thoughtful and sensitive. I'm a rabbi, after all, not the head of IBM. We need to be good executives but at the same time we have to, well, sort of listen to God. Maybe not literally, but try to ascertain moral principles and guidance from the Bible and our traditions."

Sandy also faced special difficulties as a woman because apparently some men thought she was an attractive one. Although she'd done her best to dress conservatively, always wore her glasses at the synagogue instead of her contact lenses, and found bras that as much as possible flattened the ample breasts she had so longed for as an adolescent, occasionally men in her congregation made inappropriate comments. Sandy pretended to laugh them off.

But she couldn't pretend to ignore the president of her synagogue when he tried to grope her in his automobile.

Unfortunately, Sandy hadn't followed the advice Rabbi Wenick had given to her when she was his assistant in Milwaukee to never be alone with a male congregant.

They had just finished a long exhausting evening board meeting in the library. Sandy's car was in the repair shop. Robert had driven her to the synagogue. She planned to telephone him when the meeting was over and he would pick her up.

"I'll take you home, Rabbi," The president offered. "Save your husband a trip. It's not much out of my way."

The president waited for Sandy to gather up her things from her office. By the time they got out to the dark parking lot it was empty. When they got into his car, he leaned over to Sandy.

"Rabbi. Sandra. I have to be honest with you. I can't keep this to myself any longer. I'm in love with you. I know it's wrong, but I can't help it."

Sandy moved away from him as far as she could, saying, "That's ridiculous."

The president moved toward her again and tried to kiss her. She turned her head away quickly. He grabbed her breast, then lowered his other hand to her knee and stroked it. She pushed him away and tried to open the car door, but it was locked. He put his head in his hands and rested it down on his steering wheel.

"Rabbi, I'm so sorry," he mumbled. "I...I don't know what got into me. I'll never step out of line again. Please don't ever mention this to anyone? Please forgive me."

"Of course. It never happened, and I won't say a word about it."

She wanted to suggest he bring it up to God on *Yom Kippur*, the Day of Atonement, but she couldn't let he sardonic sense of humor ruin her relationship with this man who had such power over her life.

Sandy did break her promise and did bring it up at the next meeting of the Women's Rabbinic Network. Her story of inappropriate behavior toward female rabbis was only one of many. Together they devised strategies for dealing with these delicate situations.

"Take advantage of what happened in that car," one of the other women rabbis advised Sandy. "The president knows what happened. He knows you know what happened. So he can't say anything if you make the most of it."

"I can't," Sandy protested. "He'll know I'm doing that."

"What's he going to do about it? You've got him by his balls."

Although Sandy was a bit ashamed of herself, she did follow her colleague's advice and took full advantage of the president's guilty secret. She felt certain that incident was the reason he convinced the board to endorse most of the changes in the synagogue she introduced. She and the cantor agreed to include more Debbie Friedman music and that of other contemporary composers into their services. Sandy encouraged the education director to make the religious school fun and meaningful, not the bore it was when she was a child. She included gender-neutral language she developed with the women in her Milwaukee congregation into their liturgy.

Having made the leap of hiring a woman, most of the congregants seemed amenable to Sandy's feminist perspective. The women eagerly came to the *Rosh Chodesh* group she started. They devised feminist Seders. Sandy initiated support groups for women for miscarriages and other birth losses, menopause, divorces, and bereavement issues.

And now no one complained when Sandy talked about God more in her sermons, in a less intellectual and more spiritual and emotional way. In spite of her anger at God for taking her father from her, she somehow felt herself developing a more personal relationship with Him.

"God is to me no longer just the arbiter of social justice and preserver of the Jewish people, as He was in my childhood," she confided to Sister Mona in one of their now frequent telephone conversations. "Somehow, I feel I'm listening to God. That I can somehow hear His voice. My father would laugh at me. 'Nonsense', he'd say. 'Magical thinking.'" She paused. "Oh, how I miss our lively discussions."

Sandy was thinking about her father, missing him as usual as she sat in her office at the synagogue staring into space, when the telephone rang. The secretary was on her lunch break, so she answered it herself.

It was Jeff Shoemaker.

"I hope you don't mind me phoning you, Sandy. I was wondering how you're doing. Since your father died."

"Well, it's been difficult. Thanks for asking. I've moved on with my life, but I miss him. I guess I always will."

"I read about you in the paper. My pastor came to your last Thanksgiving interfaith service. I was visiting my parents in Elmville, or I would have come."

"How are they?"

"My father's retiring this spring. They're thinking about buying a house in Florida. How's your mother doing?"

"It was a big shock to her when Daddy was killed, but now she's doing better. She still has her job at the university, her friends, bridge. She comes to Chicago to visit us. Always here for the kids' birthdays. She flies out to LA to see Joanie. My sister remarried, you know. A Jewish guy who actually works this time. Manages millionaires' money."

"Children?" Jeff asked.

"Joanie's totally wrapped up in her career. And her husband has two kids from his first marriage. He doesn't want any more."

"Sandy, could we meet? Lunch or something?"

"I don't think it's a good idea, Jeff. Do you?"

"Probably not."

"Thanks, anyway."

"Yeah."

They wished each other well, said goodbye. After Sandy hung up the telephone, she stared into space. She thought she had pushed Jeff out of her thoughts --and her life -- forever.

But she hadn't.

Two weeks later Jeff telephoned her at the synagogue again.

"Please have lunch with me, Sandy? You're out of excuses."

She thought for a long moment. What could be the harm? It was twenty years since their split in 1963. A lifetime ago. They were adults now, with families and careers and responsibilities. She had a husband and a good marriage. Nothing could threaten that.

"Ok," she said finally.

They set a time and place, a restaurant across town where chances were slim they'd run into anyone they knew or any of her congregants.

"Actually, I didn't tell you the whole truth about Eleanor when I saw you in Elmville when your dad died," Jeff confessed after they ordered their food. "She's wasn't off doing research for her thesis. She gave up her Ph.D. work a long time ago. She's in Hawaii. Searching for her inner self in a commune. Her folks think it's some kind of cult. I don't know, and, frankly I don't care. I just wish she hadn't deserted our kids."

"How terrible for you."

"Things weren't good between us for a long time. Hitting forty threw her for a loop. She needed to take some time to reevaluate her life."

"Must be difficult for your children."

"It's hardest on Gail. She's a teenager. Girls needs a mother. I'm doing my best, but it's not good enough, I'm afraid. My teaching, writing the new book. My mother comes up to help, interviewed housekeepers and baby sitters for me. I started divorce proceedings a year ago."

"I'm sorry to hear that."

He took her hand. "Are you, Sandy?"

She removed her hand from his. "Jeff, I don't think we should see each other like this again."

"I guess you're right. Yes. That's the right decision."

But they didn't stick to that decision. A month later they met for dinner at the same restaurant. As they said goodnight in front of the restaurant he kissed her. She pulled away, looked around hoping no one they knew had seen them. She told Jeff they couldn't let this happen. He agreed. They kissed again and parted.

As they had resolved, Jeff didn't contact her. But two years later he telephoned her. They met for lunch again. Then dinner. Then another dinner. That night they couldn't fight their desire for each other any longer. His children were visiting Eleanor's parents in Oregon. They went back to his empty house. Everything they had felt for each other over so many years exploded in their lovemaking. It was better than when they were kids. Their love had grown and matured and settled.

Sandy was consumed by guilt. Was the eye from her childhood synagogue still watching her? Was God watching her?

This affair was against everything she had always believed in and stood for. While she didn't think the Seventh Commandment prohibiting adultery was literally handed down to Moses by God on Mount Sinai, she did believe breaking marriage vows was a serious infraction of personal integrity and of the rules which, as her sociologist father had pointed out, kept society running smoothly. Judaism believed in family. The *Torah* and Talmud preached honesty and truth in relationships. Above all Judaism taught moral values, and to be a good Jew meant living these values. The ancient Israelites had agreed to carry God's moral message into the world. Jews were obliged to live this moral code. She was a rabbi. How much more, as a rabbi, she personally was obliged to live it.

And Sandy was jeopardizing her career. Even if her congregation didn't fire her, having an affair was a violation of the ethical code of conduct of the Central Conference of American Rabbis. The CCAR could conduct an investigation. Perhaps suspend her from the organization. Then she'd never get another congregation through their network.

Yet, she was happy. She couldn't help it. Sometimes she wondered if her happiness was written on her face as she sat on the *bema* where everyone could see her.

Above all, she was confused. Could Robert sense this? Could her congregation sense her inner conflict as she conducted services and preached and gave them personal advice? Could they see into her soul? See what a hypocrite she was?

But ironically Sandy felt her affair with Jeff was making her a better rabbi. She was more compassionate. Less judgmental when congregants confided their transgressions – often of a sexual nature – to her. She no longer saw life in blacks and whites. Things were not always so cut and dried, especially in the realm of ethics. She realized how complicated human beings are and how well the rabbis in their tradition understood this. Now when Sandy counseled people she tried to help them find their inner voice to guide them. And now she felt things more deeply, somehow felt a closer connection to God even though she knew He wouldn't condone her behavior.

This deepening of her emotional life and constant inner conflict sapped Sandy's energy. Keeping the affair secret required a great deal of time and planning. She and Jeff perfected a routine, meeting once a month at a hotel in a Chicago suburb where no one they knew would see them. They never entered or left the hotel together.

Along with everything else going on in Sandy's life, now she was planning her son's *Bar Mitzvah*.

As was common during the 1980s, Josh "twinned" with a boy from the Soviet Union who couldn't have his own coming of age ceremony. They got his name from a list prepared by The National Conference on Soviet Jewry. They placed an empty chair on the *bema* bearing a sign with the Russian boy's name on it. During his *Bar Mitzvah* speech, Josh talked about why the youngster in the Soviet Union was not permitted by the government there to celebrate his Jewish heritage and how we in America must appreciate our freedom of religion here and always continue to celebrate our Judaism. Sandy hoped her childhood synagogue eye was watching and was as proud of her fine son at that moment as she was.

In 1988, former Congresswoman Bella Abzug chaired a committee organizing the First International Conference for the Empowerment of Jewish Women to be sponsored by The American Jewish Congress. It was to be held in Jerusalem in December. Carolyn was very excited about it. She insisted Sandy go with her.

"The plane fare and hotels will cost a fortune," Robert shouted. "Add in the conference fee. You can't ask your synagogue to pay for it. And you shouldn't leave the kids. You can't delegate parenting to a babysitter like when our children were small. Motherhood isn't just one more of your many projects. Josh will never admit it, but he needs you, and Beruria's getting even more rebellious. I'm really worried about her. You're confusing her. Filling our daughter's head with these unrealistic feminist goals. Telling her she can do things she can't, or will cause her trouble if she does." He took a deep breath. "In fact, I forbid you from going."

"Oh, really?"

"This feminist stuff has just gotten out of hand, Sandy. I used to joke about it, but now it's not so funny anymore. You've gone way beyond the call of duty."

"This is an important conference. And I haven't been back to Israel since rabbinical school. I'm going."

After the long flight and Sandy had checked into the hotel in Jerusalem, she wandered around the city revisiting places she frequented as a first year rabbinical student sixteen years before. She took a bus to the apartment she had shared with two other female classmates, explored the markets and cafes where they hung out. She went to the *Kotel*, the Western Wall inside the gates of the Old City that is the holiest site in Judaism.

Composed of large stones from the rampart wall left over from the Second Temple destroyed by the Romans in 70 C.E., the Wall was a tangible symbol of the glory of the First and Second Temples and of Jews' return to the Promised Land. Under Arab rule Jews were allowed to pray at the Wall, then a garbage-strewn ruin, only at limited times and with great difficulty. When the Israelis liberated it after the 1967 Six Day War, it was put under control of the Orthodox faction. Immediately they installed a *mehitzah*, a high fence made of fiberglass panels to separate the women's section from the men's. Women were allotted one third of the wall, the men two thirds.

Sandy entered the large open plaza leading to the Western Wall. She went into the women's section, approached the Wall, and inserted into a crack between the stones a tiny folded paper upon which she had written a prayer asking God to protect her family and guide her children through their difficult growing years. After all, the prayer she inserted into a crack in the Wall her first year of rabbinical school asking God to let her become pregnant had worked, hadn't it? Maybe this one would work as well?

The conference began the next day. Six hundred women came from throughout the world and every religious and secular ideology, and every economic group. On Wednesday November 30th, Orthodox activist Rivka Haut raised the idea of a group of women at the conference worshipping together at the Wall the next morning. Those interested met together that night and engaged in a prolonged emotional discussion. If they went, would they bring a *Torah*? If they did, would they read from it? If they did read from it, would they be safe? Women were permitted to pray individually from their prayer books at the Western Wall but were forbidden by Israeli law to pray aloud as a group, sing prayers, wear prayer shawls, blow *shofars*, or carry the *Torah* and read and chant from it.

They decided they would bring a *Torah*. For their protection they'd stand throughout their service with arms linked tightly in a circle surrounding it. They would post lookouts to signal them if they needed to close the circle around the *Torah* and leave quickly. Although the women came from Orthodox, Conservative, Reform, and Reconstructionist branches of Judaism, they decided their service would strictly follow *halachic* guidelines established by the Orthodox Women's *Tefilla* Network, an umbrella organization of Orthodox women's prayer groups. This would allow the Orthodox women to participate and would also help to deflect later criticism.

At seven a.m. the next morning, seventy women boarded buses taking them from their hotel to one of the gates of the Old City. They walked to the Western Wall, prominent feminist Francine Klagsbrun proudly carrying in her arms a *Torah* borrowed from Hebrew Union College. They set up a small folding table, which would have been automatically provided for men in their section of the Wall, and placed the *Torah* on it.

They conducted their service quietly, singing blessings softly, the first time a group of Jewish women from every branch had ever prayed together. Things went peacefully until they opened the *Torah* scroll and Rabbi Helene Ferris started to chant from it the opening words of the *Torah* portion for that day, *Vayeshev* --"Now Jacob was settled in the land where his father had resided, the land of Canaan". An Orthodox Israeli woman watching pounded on the shoulders of a woman on the outside of their circle, yelling, "Women are not permitted to read from the *Torah*! The *Torah* is not for women!"

Her shouts alerted Orthodox men praying in their section, who climbed onto chairs to peer over the *mehitzah*. The men cursed, jeered, shouted threats and violently shook the *mehitzah*. The rattling sounds were terrifying. Sandy's delegation quickly concluded the *Torah* chanting and service. They rushed away from the Western Wall plaza, forming a tight circle around the *Torah* to protect it, and climbed onto the buses waiting for them outside the gate of the Old City. The buses sped away.

As they drove to the hotel, on the bus Sandy tried to absorb what she had just experienced. The hostility of the Orthodox men and women frightened her, but at the same time, she was elated. She had been deeply moved that morning as she prayed with this diverse group of women and read from the holy scriptures at the holiest site in Judaism.

"Some of those women never read from the *Torah* before," Sandy told Robert when she returned home. "Their faces reflected their joy. I felt solidarity with them. And I saw myself in a new, more powerful way. I experienced a vivid spiritual awakening. We all felt we were transformed by this momentous event."

Robert didn't seem interested. He was still angry Sandy had gone to the conference over his strong objections. He rebuked her for putting herself in a position of danger that morning at the Wall.

"You are the mother of two children. You had no right to endanger yourself."

Ironically, Jeff seemed to understand her powerful spiritual experience better than Robert did.

Sandy and Carolyn joined other prominent feminists to establish Women of the Wall, known as WOW, the organization stemming from their controversial experience with the *Torah* that morning at the Western Wall. WOW was the first and only organization made up of Jews from every background, ultra-reform to ultra-Orthodox and representing views from the entire political spectrum, praying and working peacefully together.

Carolyn returned to Israel to teach for a semester at Hebrew University. She described in a letter to Sandy in great detail what happened when women went back to the Wall to worship during the *Rosh Chodesh* holidays in January and February of 1989.

"One of the women borrowed a Torah from her Yeshiva. They brought it to the Wall in a Guatemalan backpack," Carolyn began. *"When we took it out of the backpack and opened it, all hell broke loose. The Orthodox women tried to grab our prayer books and throw them to the ground. They whispered through the mehitzah to the Orthodox men, and about fifty rushed over to the women's section. They pulled at our prayer shawls, threw two of us to the ground. The Orthodox women shouted, 'The Torah belongs to men' and called us 'Reform women.' As you know, the worst insult they can think of.*

"The men spat on us," she wrote. *"One kept screaming 'I denounce!' Some of the women laid their hands on us and cursed us, saying things like, 'May you never have children. May you die young in accidents.' They called us whores, Nazis, witches, and dogs. Pushed us, dragged us away from the Wall. Men on the other side of the mehitzah threw metal chairs at us. All this time the police just watched, and did nothing to protect us.*

"We clung together in a tight circle. As we rushed out of the Wall plaza, we lifted the Torah and sang from Proverbs, 'She is a Tree of Life for those who hold onto her.' Lots of media people were there, but they said later we had provoked the attack."

In March, when approximately 150 women and 100 male supporters tried to reach the Wall to pray during Purim, Orthodox men blocked their passage. The police cleared their way but the Orthodox cursed and spat at them. When the women began to pray, the men threw metal chairs and tables at them. One woman's neck bled after a chair hit her head, and she was rushed to a hospital. The police just watched from their vans.

Finally the police threw heavy canisters of tear gas into the crowd to disperse it. An Orthodox man redirected the canister toward the women. The women gagged and coughed as the tear gas burned their throats and eyes. Four WOW activists proceeded immediately directly from the Wall plaza to their attorneys' offices to prepare a petition to go to the Israeli Supreme Court.

During Sandy's next *Shabbat* sermon, she told her Chicago congregation, "Purim, the holiday we just observed, celebrates Haman's failure to kill all the Jews in Persia. But now, such disputes as women enjoying equal rights at the

Western Wall in Jerusalem are killing the spirit of the Jewish people by dividing us. Prejudice is transforming the Wall from a symbol of unity into a symbol of hatred. We must not allow this to happen.

"Why," she continued, "has the attempt of women to pray as a group at the Wall, to read from the *Torah*, and to say aloud the prayers and sing together so upset the Orthodox? Because they see our activity there as a violation of the Protection of Holy Places Law put into effect immediately after Israel regained control of the Wall in 1967. It states that measures will be taken to prevent desecration of holy places or behavior that might offend people to whom the site is holy. I think the men are 'offended' because they see women invading their territory, invading their psychological as well as physical territory. Men have always been territorial. They see this as a conflict over holy space.

"But there's a deeper reason for the outrage of the Orthodox when they hear us singing at the Wall. According to our tradition, women's voices are disturbing. Our singing distracts men when they pray. Our voices are sensual. Seductive. Cause men to be lustful. Remember the Sirens of Greek mythology?

"And why are our *speaking* voices not allowed to be heard as we pray at the Wall? Because women should be quiet. Modest. If we are heard we are being rebellious, provocative, arrogant, dangerous. According to Proverbs 9:13, 'A foolish woman is noisy; she is wanton and knows no shame.' Women should be silent and private. Know our place. Women may pray quietly and privately at the Wall, but the prayers can't take on the trappings of an official public religious event. We must not enter the public arena because this would give us the authority and power that comes from spiritual knowledge.

"In short," Sandy concluded, "our 'forbidden' activity at the Wall threatens male authority. Once this crack opens, the entire patriarchal system could collapse. They cannot allow that to happen. Well, this is what I cannot allow to happen. I will not 'stay in my place.' I will not remain quiet. I will not be shut out of the triumph of worshipping at Judaism's holiest site because I am a woman. I will not be shut out of full participation in Judaism because I am a woman."

In April WOW petitioned the Supreme Court on behalf of all Jewish women for the right to pray together at the Western Wall. In May the Israeli Supreme

Court heard the case. The state was given six months to make a decision, an unusually long period of time. In August the Israeli government hired women sentries to eject women who sang at the Wall. The harassment from the women sentries caused WOW to urge the Supreme Court to speed up the date of its ruling.

Sandy also helped organize the International Committee of Women of the Wall, ICWOW, to support WOW's efforts in Israel. She and Carolyn served on the board of directors. Robert was furious about the amount of time Sandy spent on the telephone arguing with board members throughout the world at all hours of the day and night. For the remainder of 1989, Carolyn traveled throughout the country on behalf of The International Committee of Women of the Wall speaking to synagogues and women's groups to raise money to purchase a *Torah* for WOW in Israel. The organization finally got enough money to buy the sacred scroll. Sandy was chosen to be part of the small delegation traveling to Israel to present it to WOW in December. Again she argued with Robert about making the long trip, but he relented when she promised she'd return home immediately after the *Torah* dedication.

Things were in a state of chaos when Sandy arrived in Jerusalem. They planned to hold the dedication ceremony at the well-known Laromme Hotel after an evening outdoor prayer service at a nearby park and candlelight procession to the hotel. But the Jerusalem rabbinate threatened to withdraw the Laromme's kosher food certificate if the hotel allowed them to hold the ceremony there. The hotel cancelled the ceremony. They held the *Torah* dedication in a nearby school.

On December 31, 1989, the Israeli Ministries of Religious Affairs and Justice prohibited any religious ceremony at a holy place "not in accordance with the custom of the holy site and which offends the sensibilities of the worshippers at the place." It assigned a penalty for violation of six months in jail and/or a substantial fine.

"We're further away than ever from reaching our goal of enabling women to worship on an equal basis with men at Judaism's holiest site, the Western Wall," Sandy wrote to her friend Reverend Liz Adams. *"I'm disheartened. Has our struggle*

for equal rights for women at the Wall and in Israel and throughout the world been fruitless? Has my work, all I've stood for and fought for all these years, my personal transformation, my journey, come to nothing?"

Jeff was pressuring Sandy to leave Robert and marry him.

"We were meant for each other," he said. "We always have been."

"I can't do that."

"Because I'm not Jewish? After all this time, it's still an issue? I'll convert if you want. I understand you now. I know how important your religion is to you, and I'm sorry I was such a jerk about it before. I'm sorry I never understood why the Holocaust is so important to Jews. I even get your feminism. I see how the old system destroyed Eleanor, and how I contributed to that. I've learned my lesson. I'd never stand in the way of your work."

"Robert's been a good husband. If he wasn't, I'd be justified in leaving him. I couldn't do that to him and live with myself. Couldn't do it to my kids, not at such a vulnerable time in their lives. You see how your daughter was affected when Eleanor left you. Rabbis are supposed to be living examples of our Jewish values of love and fidelity and family. I'd be a horrible example."

"I won't wait much longer, Sandy," he warned. "You have to think about my feelings, too."

"Can you wait for my decision until after Beruria's *Bat Mitzvah?* Next May?"

Jeff sighed. "You're always going to have a reason to delay your decision. You're the busiest woman I've ever known. We both have kids to think about, careers and lives. You have to decide if you're going to make room in your life for me. Permanently. We're running out of time. I'm running out of time. I won't wait much longer."

Sandy could no longer keep her secret to herself. She needed to confide in someone. The only person she could trust was Carolyn Schwartz. Carolyn would understand. She was teaching at Barnard College as well as writing books and speaking about women's rights all over the world. The next time she came to Chicago, they met for lunch. Sandy told her friend about her affair with Jeff. How she had fought it but had lost her struggle.

"It's like a battle between my *yetzer tov*, my inclination for good, and my *yetzer hara*, my inclination to be bad. I feel so guilty. Now Jeff's getting impatient. He's pressuring me to leave Robert and marry him. Can I risk losing my synagogue if I do?"

"I don't think you'd lose your job," Carolyn said. "It's 1989. Things have loosened up. Adultery's not such a sin anymore."

"It is for rabbis. Men get fired for it, so imagine what they'd do to a woman. I'll always be under the microscope, even more than a man. If people find out about Jeff, it could destroy my life. And to be marrying a non-Jewish guy after all my lecturing about preserving our Jewish heritage? Carolyn, this is like when I was a kid in Illinois, torn between my Jewish world and the Christian world."

"I've taught you to be strong. To live by your own convictions."

"That's good feminist ideology, but it isn't always possible. Besides, I'm nearly fifty. Too old to make such a drastic change in my life."

"No, you're not. But soon you will be."

Carolyn was right, as usual. Sandy didn't have that much time left in her life. Soon she'd have to make a painful choice.

She would have to make her choice sooner than she anticipated.

One of Robert's clients saw Sandy and Jeff having a drink together in a hotel bar. The client mentioned it to Robert casually. It didn't take Sandy's intelligent husband much time to figure it out.

"How long has it been going on?" Robert shouted.

"About six years."

"Six years? You've been lying to me and deceiving me for six years? How could you do this to me? To the kids? I don't believe it. You! The great rabbi! Miss Jewish ethics. Miss God and family. Miss virtue."

"I never claimed I was virtuous. I'm a human being, and I'm sorry. Jeff and I tried to fight it. For many years. We knew it was wrong, but we couldn't help it."

"Don't you think I've had my temptations? Clients throwing themselves at me, beautiful young paralegals? Secretaries? Working alone together, late into the night. But, oh, yes, I forgot. Jeff Shoemaker is your great childhood love. That's different." Robert paused to take a breath. "It's all that feminist crap, isn't it?"

"My relationship with Jeff has nothing to do with my feminism. Although, I would like to point out, he seems to understand it better than you do."

"I just can't believe it, Sandy. I just don't know what to say. You better promise me you'll never see him again."

"I have to think about that."

"Then our marriage is over. If you can't promise me right now you'll end it immediately there's nothing more to talk about."

"Stop talking like a lawyer."

"Either you break it off with him for good or our marriage is finished."

A few days later Sandy received a letter from an organization called WomanSpeak. *"Dear Rabbi Miller-Brownstein: We are pleased to inform you that our organization, WomanSpeak: Voices of Women of Faith, wishes to honor you with its WomanSpeak Let My Voice Be Heard Award,"* the president of the organization wrote. *"This recognition is given annually to individuals whose outstanding work has advanced the role of women in religion and in society. Your award will be presented at our banquet on Thursday March 22nd, 1990 at the Plaza Hotel in Manhattan.*

"We will honor two other women, Sister Mona Sullivan, Executive Director of The Women's Ordination Conference, and Reverend Elizabeth Adams, Pastor of the First Presbyterian Church of Stewart, Maine. Please let us know as soon as possible if you will be able to attend the dinner to accept this honor."

Everyone in Sandy's congregation was thrilled. Mom would fly out from Illinois for the dinner, of course, and Joanie would fly out from LA. They regretted Leon Miller hadn't lived to see her receive this honor.

Robert refused to come to the dinner. He wouldn't let the children come, either.

"How could I go?" he said. "Sit there and listen to them heap praises on you when I know what a hypocrite you are? Besides, we may not even be together by then. It depends on whether or not you've decided your boyfriend is worth destroying your life for. Listen, Sandy, I should kick you out of the house right now, but we have Josh and Beruria to consider. So I'll give you two months to make up your mind. Until that dinner. You have to make up your mind before you come back to Chicago after that dinner." He paused. "It's your choice, Sandy. Jeff or me. Jeff or our marriage."

Liz: 1978 – 1990

LIZ DIDN'T GO back to Stewart immediately when their airplane landed in New York after the trip to the Soviet Union because the next day she appeared at a press conference arranged by the American Jewish Committee, co-sponsor of The National Interreligious Task Force on Soviet Jewry. Sisters Ann Gillen and Gloria Coleman gave the press details of their trip, talked about the status of the refuseniks in the Soviet Union and about the worldwide efforts on their behalf.

"The KGB followed us everywhere," Sister Ann reported. "They patted us down so they could find incriminating evidence. They conducted a complete body search of Reverend Adams at the Moscow airport before we left the country."

All eyes turned to Liz. She didn't want anyone except Sisters Ann and Gloria to know about the body search. This was just what her congregants and her parents needed to hear.

Her mother was horrified. "How could have you let yourself in for such danger, Elizabeth?" she admonished over the telephone the next day. "That's just not like you. I've always taught you to be dignified. Having some Commie man's hand up your skirt and down your blouse."

"It was a woman, Mother. They sent in a woman."

"I don't know why you're bothering with these Jews over there anyway. It's always best to keep to your own kind."

Alicia was amazed at Liz's bravery in the Soviet Union. She was shocked Liz had even gone on the trip and impressed by all the media attention her friend was getting. Inga was proud of Liz. Beverly Cohen in Reno was ecstatic.

She'd been responsible for getting Liz involved in the Soviet Jewry issue in the first place.

But now that media all over the country was publicizing Liz's intrusive body search, she worried more than ever about the reactions of her congregants. Had she had put her job at risk? Her church leaders didn't like controversy, didn't like the idea of their respectable pastor being so prominently covered by the media. And they still felt Liz was ignoring their church in pursuit of wider glory. An important and wealthy congregant had died while she was in the Soviet Union. Liz had planned for funeral coverage while she was gone, but the man's family still was furious she hadn't officiated.

"You should have been here," one of her elders said. "That family is very important to our church. You must focus on your local duties, Reverend Adams. Those people in the Soviet Union are not our concern. Let these radical Jews take care of their own problems. They got their own country, for heaven's sake, threw out the Arabs. What more do they want? They're never satisfied. Greedy."

"But I've heard through the grapevine other congregants think my radio and TV appearances and those newspaper articles are generating good publicity for The First Presbyterian Church of Stewart," she told Rabbi Sandy Miller-Brownstein in their first telephone conversation since she had returned. "Maybe this will help my church win the membership competition with the Presbyterian Church in the next town?"

Just weeks after Liz's return from the Soviet Union on June 21st, Vladimir Slepak and Ida Nudel went on trial on the same day in the same courthouse, the People's Court of the Volgogradsky Region of Moscow. Both were charged with the same crime of "malicious hooliganism." Neither was allowed to have witnesses to testify for them. The audiences in the courtrooms were hostile. Their supporters, American embassy officials, and reporters were kept outside. At one point when the crowd outside got too close to the courthouse, the Soviet police turned fire hoses on them. After a few hours, Vladimir Slepak was sentenced to five years of internal exile. Masha Slepak received a three-year suspended sentence with permission to join Vladimir in exile and return to Moscow occasionally so she could keep up the claim on their apartment there. This was a trip of 5,000 miles. Ida Nudel received a sentence of four years of exile in Siberia.

When the judge gave Ida a chance to comment at her trial, she said, "I am being tried in fact for the last seven years, the most wonderful years of my life. If I should ever find myself obliged to deliver another final plea, I am absolutely convinced that I shall affirm once again that the seven years which are the cause of this trial were the most difficult but also the most wonderful of my life. During the seven years, I learned to walk with my head high, as a human being and as a Jew. The seven years have been full of daily struggle on behalf of myself and others. Every time that I was able to keep a victim alive, I experienced a rare and intense emotion comparable, perhaps, to the joy of a woman who has given birth. Even if the remainder of my life should turn out to be gray and uneventful, the memory of those seven years will warm my heart and reassure me that I have not lived my life in vain."

Liz was just settling back to her normal routine when one night as she was preparing her Sunday sermon, the doorbell rang. Mathilde leapt off her lap, padded into the kitchen. Liz went to the door, asked, "Who is it?"

"Tom. Hagerman."

She opened the door.

"Liz. I hope you don't mind."

"How did you know where I live?"

"I looked up your address in the telephone book. I knew you were in Stewart. Charlie and Tina told me. And you've been in the news a lot lately. I didn't think you'd get so famous."

"Wow, still putting me down."

"I'm sorry. I didn't mean to. It was supposed to be a compliment."

Liz ushered him into the living room and told him to sit down. Mathilde walked over to Tom, looked up at him curiously, and hopped onto his lap.

"My cat doesn't usually warm up to strangers. Would you like a glass of Merlot?"

"You drink wine? You never drank."

"I'm a big girl now." She poured the merlot and handed it to him. Poured a glass for herself and turned to face her ex-husband. "So. What are you doing here?"

"Just sort of wandering around, trying to sort things out. I've given up my therapy practice. Trying to figure out what to do with my life now. I can't go back to the ministry. I was stripped of my ordination because, well, you know."

"You're living in Indianapolis?"

"After I left Reno I didn't have any money so I moved in with my parents. My father lost his business. Now we all agree I need to get out on my own again. It's been rough on all of us."

"Yes, I can imagine." Liz paused. "Emily?"

"Her father put a quick end to our relationship. Last I heard she married a rich boy from Harvard. It would never have worked out for us. I've been out with a few women, but I'll never remarry." Tom perused the small living room of her modest manse. "I see you haven't." he added, "Gotten married again."

"No."

Liz didn't think this was the time to remind Tom he had destroyed her trust in men. Or to tell him she was in love with a woman.

"Too bad," he said. "I know you wanted children."

"And now it's too late. I'll never forgive you for forcing me to get that abortion."

"I'm sorry about that, Liz. I'm sorry about everything."

"Is this why you're here? To apologize?"

"I don't expect you to forgive me. But I'd feel better if you did. 'For if you forgive men their trespasses, Your heavenly Father will also forgive you. But if you do not forgive men their trespasses, neither will your Father forgive your trespasses.' Matthew 6:14."

"I'm not in the mood for bible games."

"Can I stay the night? I can sleep on your couch. It would save me money on a motel room."

After she settled Tom on the couch, Liz lay awake for hours trying to decide whether or not to tell her former husband she'd forgive him.

Tom was right. Jesus did preach forgiveness, even -- especially -- when it was difficult. People were no different in Jesus' day than they were now. We had automobiles and air conditioning and television, but human nature hadn't changed. You just had to read the bible stories to realize that. Anger and bitterness just poison your life and keep you from moving on, Liz had often told her congregants when she counseled them. She needed to take her own advice.

And, during their marriage Liz had been cold to Tom. Now since she had found such happiness with Inga, she knew why. She just didn't respond sexually to men, and Tom hadn't been experienced enough in sexual matters to help her. It wasn't entirely his fault he had looked elsewhere for love. Liz had been partly to blame.

Since she had fallen in love with Inga, Liz now understood what it's like to be swept away by passion. How difficult it was to fight it, that sometimes you didn't even want to try. Life wasn't always dictated by reason. Some things were out of your realm of control. Tom had been powerless to keep himself from Emily Mullen, as now Liz was powerless to keep herself from Inga Hansen.

At breakfast the next morning Liz said, "I do forgive you, Tom. Let's get past this. We were young. I have a new life now. I've been lucky, I landed on my feet. You will, too."

"You forgave the bastard?" Inga shouted later that day after Tom had left Stewart. "After what he did to you? And he spent the night at your house?"

"Like we were going to tumble into bed? We hardly slept together when we were married, we weren't going to now. My God, Inga, you're jealous? Of Tom?"

"Did you tell him about us? Were you at least honest enough to do that?"

"No. You know I can't take a chance."

"Your rotten ex doesn't know anybody here. Our deep dark secret would have been safe with him. How long is this sneaking around going to last, Liz? When are we going to shout out our love to the world?"

"I can't do that. I've told you the reasons so many times."

"Well, I don't know how long I can take it."

They had the same argument a month later.

Donations for the new wing Liz's church wanted to build for their Sunday School had increased as people gave money in memory of their beloved Reverend Billingsley. They had finally raised enough to build the addition, and they were going to name it after him. The building committee interviewed architectural firms. A Boston-based firm won the contract. The architect they assigned was in his early 50s and recently divorced. He asked Liz out for dinner. She accepted.

"How could you do this to me?" Inga asked.

"He's very nice. It will be a pleasant evening, that's all. I thought it would be good cover. If I'm seen around town with a man, it'll put to rest any rumors about us that might be starting."

"Oh, so you're using him as a beard. You're just going to live your life as a lie."

"You know if they find out about us my career is finished. All I've worked for all these years would go down the drain. It would destroy my parents. I can't allow that to happen."

"That's unfair to that nice architect. And to me. If you truly cared about me you wouldn't be ashamed of our love."

"I do care about you. I'm not ashamed. But you know what's at stake."

They didn't speak to each other for a week. Liz went out with the architect, choosing a restaurant she knew many people in her church frequented so they might be seen together. He was a sweet guy, but he didn't seem much more interested in Liz than she in him. He telephoned her the next day and said he wasn't ready to date yet because it was too soon after his divorce. He hoped she understood. Liz was relieved. It was better this way because they were going to have to work together planning the new church wing. And it solved the problem with Inga for the moment.

Liz's mother telephoned a few days later. Her father had suffered a stroke. She cancelled an adult education meeting and pre-wedding counseling session scheduled for the next day. She packed an overnight bag, then drove as fast as she could to New Hampshire to meet her mother at the hospital's emergency room. They prayed as they sat for hours waiting for the updates from the physicians.

Liz's father pulled through, but he was a very sick man, and he would never recover fully from the effects of the stroke. Now Liz would have to devote a lot of time to her parents. Over the next six months she juggled her church duties with trips down to New Hampshire to help care for him. She tried to persuade her parents to move up to Stewart so she could help her mother and watch over them both.

"Oh, great. Then we'd never see each other," Inga protested. "I hardly see you now as it is."

"That's a selfish way of looking at things. Your parents are dead. I have responsibilities."

Inga didn't need to worry. Liz couldn't talk her mother into leaving the house she and her husband had lived in for over forty years.

"The best I can do is help pay for a health aide so Mother can get out more often to see her friends," Liz wrote to Beverly when she told her friend in Reno about her father's stroke. *"So she can do her volunteer work and go to church. It'll really cut into my salary. I'll pare down whatever expenditures I can. I'll have to ask my church for a raise. Seriously doubt I'll get one."*

Even though Liz drove down to New Hampshire once a week to check on her parents, she still managed to squeeze in her Soviet Jewry work. Sister Ann Gillen asked her to be in charge of a special interfaith women's organization she had started called Women of Faith to help women in refusal in the Soviet Union. In May of 1979, the Interreligious Task Force called for a month-long series of protests against the unjust sentences given by the Soviet government to Ida Nudel and Sister Valeriya Makeeva, a Russian Orthodox nun who had recently been sentenced to a psychiatric institution for selling belts embroidered with the words, "Lord, Thou hast been our dwelling place." Sister Ann declared that on June 21st, the first anniversary of Ida Nudel's sentence, she would renew her efforts to free the brave Jewish dissident.

Ida had been sent for her exile to a Siberian village called Krivosheino built on drained swampland near the River Ob. She couldn't find a job there that didn't involve physical labor, so officials sent her to a land reclamation project three miles away to work as a draftswoman. She was forced to share a barrack with male former convicts who were draining swamps. Constantly fearing sexual attacks, Ida lived behind a closed door in her little room.

Although Liz didn't want to be too far away from her parents, she went with Sister Ann to the 1980 World Conference of the United Nations Decade for Women held July 14th to July 30th in Copenhagen. This gathering of women from throughout the world was a followup to the first conference in 1975 in Mexico City to acknowledge the International Year of the Woman. She shared a hotel room with Rabbi Sandy Miller-Brownstein's friend Carolyn Schwartz.

"There's even more anti-Semitism here than at the first conference five years ago," Carolyn told Liz after a few days. "We Jewish feminists assumed perhaps we'd meet the same hostility as at the 1975 Mexico City conference, and a lot of us hesitated to come. But we're shocked. We never expected the level of hatred spewed by delegates from throughout the world towards us as Jews. We've been isolated, not allowed to speak in sessions, even tyrannized. It's very frightening."

At the Copenhagan conference, Sister Ann Gillen offered publicly to take the place of Ida Nudel in Siberia for the next two years of her sentence. In her formal request in a letter to Soviet Ambassador Anatoly Dobrynin, Sister Ann wrote, "We exchange spies. Why not friends?"

The Soviet government ignored Sister Ann's offer.

Ida Nudel was released from her exile on March 20th, 1982. She was warned to avoid contact with other refuseniks and with foreigners. She wandered from place to place for nearly a year because she wasn't allowed to return to her apartment in Moscow.

Inga complained Liz spent too much time on the Soviet Jewry effort and on her other work and obligations. Liz had stepped up her interfaith efforts in Stewart, planning interfaith Holocaust Memorial Services every year in April. She wrote articles for the national Presbyterian publications, especially the women's magazines and newsletters. Rosemary Radford Ruether asked her to co-edit another collection of feminist essays addressing the role of women in religion. When Carolyn Schwartz read that collection, she asked Liz to co-author a book with her to be titled *Lilith and Eve Revisited: New Jewish and Christian Perspectives*.

"Now you really won't have any time for me," Inga complained.

"I thought you'd be happy about the book. I thought you wanted me to become more of a feminist."

"I don't know why I put up with this. We've been sneaking around like criminals for five years."

"You know why."

"I'm one half of this relationship, Liz. I should have something to say about it, too." Inga paused, then said, "I'm going to move back down to Manhattan. I'm tired of driving down there to visit art galleries. I need to be in the center of the art world instead of stuck up here in the middle of nowhere. It's difficult to get shows in Manhattan while I'm in Maine. Hard to maintain the important contacts I've made. You know how political the art world is. One of my friends there has offered to share her painting studio with me so I can buy a smaller apartment."

"When would we see each other?" Liz asked.

"Well, there's a switch. When do you ever have time for me?"

"There's more at work here, isn't there, Inga? Tell me the truth. What's the real reason you want to move?"

"I can't take it anymore that you're uncomfortable with our relationship. If you loved me as much as I love you, you'd want to shout about if from the rooftops. You wouldn't care if you lost your job. Which, by the way, I don't think you would. If you loved me you wouldn't care about anything except us being together."

"I do love you, Inga. You are the most important thing in my life."

"No. Your career is."

"Don't make me choose between you and my career. I haven't made you choose between me and your art."

"I thought you had grown. Gotten stronger so you could face whatever people say about us. But you haven't. Even if you did get strip-searched by that Russian policewoman and the whole world thought you were a heroine, I don't. I think you're a coward."

Liz burst into tears, devastated. She was even more devastated that she had reneged on her vow to never again let anyone hurt her. To go it alone in life, to depend only on herself.

Inga took Liz in her arms. "I'm sorry, I didn't mean to hurt you. I'm just frustrated having to live a secret life with you. We shouldn't have to do this anymore."

"We shouldn't, but we do. If you move I'll come down to see you as often as I can."

"No. If I move to New York I'm moving out of our relationship, too. It will be over. We'll be over. Finished."

"Is this an ultimatum? You're giving me an ultimatum?"

Liz rushed out of Inga's house, drove home, and cried for an hour. Then she sat down and stroked Mathilde's fur as she thought things over.

If she proclaimed her love for Inga publicly, declared to the world that she was a lesbian, how could she face her parents? Weren't they going through enough as it was since her father's stroke? She wouldn't be able to face her friends. She'd probably lose her job in Stewart. And have her ordination questioned and perhaps withdrawn so she'd never again be given a church.

Ordination and serving her church and God and her Savior was the path God had chosen for Liz. Could she just give up this calling? But hadn't God also chosen Inga for her? Created Liz to love Inga and want to be with her? Wasn't that part of His plan for Liz also? But, Liz reasoned, once she thought Tom was part of God's plan for her. And she had been so wrong.

Her commitments to God and to her church were more important than her personal life. She would have to go back to life the way it was before she met Inga. She had been happy then without her. She'd be happy again.

Liz told Inga her decision. In a week, without even saying goodbye, Inga was gone. She couldn't sell her house in such a short time, so she rented it to a couple with four children. Liz avoided driving past it. She tried to avoid all the places they'd been together, difficult in a small town like Stewart.

It was over. Their love was over.

After Inga left Stewart, Liz went into a depression even deeper than when little Samantha Curtis had died of childhood leukemia. She could barely drag herself through the day. She hoped nobody noticed. She was listless, mechanical. Her housekeeping, usually meticulous, slipped. She lived alone, so who cared, she said to herself. Her mother wasn't there to see it and berate her.

Liz was sloppy in her work at the church. At the end of the day, if she didn't have a committee meeting or other professional obligation, she rummaged up a pathetic snack instead of cooking a good meal as she always had and drank a glass of wine as she watched TV or read. She didn't even feel like knitting.

One glass of wine turned into two. Then three. Sometimes four. Liz remembered the bottle of vodka she had saved from her trip to Russia with Sister Ann Gillen. She found it and discovered it was delicious mixed with cranberry juice. You could barely taste the vodka. How much harm could it do?

One night as Liz lay in her bed, the room spinning because she had mixed three glasses of vodka and cranberry juice with two glasses of wine, the telephone rang. She decided not to answer it. The ringing stopped. Five minutes later it started again. Liz ignored it. Ten minutes later the telephone rang again. She tried to get out of bed to answer it, but couldn't. She was afraid she'd fall. The constant ringing grew more faint as she let herself slip into a deep sleep...

..."Reverend Adams? Liz?"

She opened her eyes. Father Tony and police officer Jimmy Monahan were leaning over her.

"Are you alright?" the Catholic priest asked. "You were supposed to be on a panel at my church tonight. Four hours ago."

"Oh, I'm so sorry. I guess I forgot to put it in my calendar. Not like me. I'm so sorry."

"Are you ill?" Father Tony asked.

"No, just tired I guess. Maybe I'm coming down with something."

"When you weren't at the church and you didn't answer the telephone, I got worried. After we finished up the program I drove over."

"How did you get into the house? Did I forget to lock up again?"

"When you didn't answer your doorbell and I saw your car was here, I got Officer Monahan to break down your door."

Father Tony glanced at Liz's night table, took in the bottle of wine she had left there. He saw that the young police officer had noticed it also. He turned to him. "Thanks, Officer Monahan. I owe you one. You haven't seen anything here tonight. You haven't been here. Right?"

"Right, Father Tony."

"Reverend Adams became ill. She lives alone and she couldn't get out of bed to telephone and tell me she couldn't be on my church program. Right?"

"Right, Father Tony."

"By the way, Sister Angela told me yesterday your little Katy's been moved into the lead for the Easter pageant. The Blessed Virgin Mary herself."

"Katy will be thrilled. Thank you, Father Tony."

After Officer Monahan left, the young priest helped Liz get out of bed and into the bathroom so she could wash her face and brush her teeth. Then they went downstairs. She slumped over the kitchen table as he fried eggs and bacon for them.

"Now, Liz, what's the story?" Father Tony asked when he sat down at the table with her. "What's wrong? You can tell me. Pretend you've come to me for confession. You know I can't tell anyone else what I hear in the confession booth." He delineated four invisible walls around Liz with his hands. "OK, now you're in the booth. You're a Catholic now. I'm behind a curtain, you can't see me." He paused. "Does this little problem you've developed have something to do with Inga Hansen suddenly leaving town?"

It was a relief to get the whole story off her chest.

"You made the right decision," Father Tony said. "I understand, perhaps more than you realize. We were all of us conceived in sin. Our Lord Jesus Christ died so he could save us. We cannot find redemption without the help of God and our Savior."

"I'm horrified. I've always been so disciplined. This just isn't like me. More than anything else I fear losing control of my life. Now I see I have."

"It's not too late. Drinking, drugs don't help our pain and despair. They only mask it for a while, make it worse. You must turn to God and to our Lord Jesus Christ to regain your strength. Let us pray together for their mercy and help."

They prayed for a moment, then Father Tony asked, "So, what are we going to do?"

"Maybe I should go to Alcoholics Anonymous? No, I can't, even in another town. No matter how far away I go, word would get back."

"That's true," he said. "So I'll be your AA. Pretend I'm your AA sponsor. We'll work through it together, with our Lord's help. We can't do it without our Lord's help. Give yourself over to him."

Wonderful Father Tony, perhaps with God's assistance, perhaps not, helped Liz more than he would ever know. He was a great friend when she needed a friend more than anything else. True to the AA model, Liz didn't touch another drink, even an innocent glass of wine with dinner.

The book Liz wrote with Carolyn Schwartz about Lilith and Eve was published in September, 1985. It received a lot of attention from both the religious and the general press, including a long positive review in the Sunday *New York Times* Book Review section. Astonished at her friend's success, Alicia threw a book party for Liz in her large Fifth Avenue apartment. Liz's congregants grudgingly accepted her new notoriety, finally reconciled, Liz assumed, to the fact that feminism was here to stay. Even her mother seemed proud of her, although she admitted she didn't understand what the book was about.

Inga appeared at Alicia's book party. Liz never did find out how she heard about it. Liz intended to ask her, but instead they rushed by taxi to Inga's apartment, rushed into her bedroom, and had an entire night of the best sex they had ever had. Inga moved back to Stewart as soon as she could after arranging to sublet her condo in Manhattan. The large family was still renting her house in Stewart so Inga found a small apartment in town and a larger space for her art studio in an empty warehouse.

She promised she'd never leave Liz again.

On October 2, 1987, the Soviet government informed Ida Nudel she had been granted an exit visa to emigrate to Israel. For sixteen years she'd been waiting for this news, as had Vladimir and Masha Slepak, who received their permission to leave the Soviet Union eleven days later.

The Soviet Jewry movement had been more successful than anyone had thought possible. Now most Jews and dissident Christians who wanted to leave could. To celebrate its success the director of the American Jewish Committee's Washington D.C. office, David Harris, planned a rally in Washington to be called "Freedom Sunday." It would take place on Sunday December 6th, the day before the first Reagan-Gorbachev summit meeting was to take place in Washington.

Harris and the other organizers of the event worried attendance would be low because activists felt their work had been accomplished. But over 250,000 attended the rally, the largest ever gathering on behalf of a Jewish cause. Liz chartered a bus from Stewart for twenty-five congregants. Tens of thousands converged on the nation's capitol by bus, plane and train. Eleven hundred buses were chartered in New York City alone. Three jets arrived from Chicago. Every city in the country with a large Jewish population sent an impressive delegation.

For the first time since 1971 there was no Solidarity Sunday program in New York City the following April. The December Washington Freedom Sunday had marked the beginning of the end of the decades-long movement.

The arguments with Inga began again.

"Why can't I move in with you, Liz? I hate my apartment."

"Kick the renters out of your house."

"I don't have the heart. That's not the point. I want to live with you. I want to be with you all the time."

"You know why we can't do that."

"People would think we're just roommates. They wouldn't have to know we're lovers."

"Women our age don't have roommates. Even in Stewart, Maine."

One night as they were having coffee in Inga's apartment, Inga said, "I can't take it any longer, Liz. If you really loved me you wouldn't care what people say about us. You wouldn't care about your career."

"We've been over this a million times. I thought we had resolved this."

"To your satisfaction. Not mine. This is against everything I've ever stood for."

"What you're asking me to do is against everything I've ever stood for," Liz responded.

Inga stood up, slammed her coffee mug onto the table. "I'm going back to New York. I'm never coming back here."

"You promised you'd never leave me again."

"That's a promise I just can't keep."

Three days before Christmas, Inga moved down to Manhattan again.

Liz drove down to New Hampshire to spend the worst Christmas of her life with her parents. She tried to hide her depression, but her mother wasn't fooled. She asked Liz several times what was wrong, and several times Liz lied to her and said "nothing", then quickly changed the subject. Finally her mother stopped asking. During the holiday season when there was so much drinking at gatherings, Liz battled the urge to have just one little glass of wine or rum-laced eggnog. But she had promised Father Tony she'd never touch alcohol again. She couldn't let him down, and she couldn't let herself down.

To make matters worse, Sister Gloria Coleman telephoned Liz to tell her Sister Ann Gillen had been diagnosed with cancer. They both wondered why God would inflict this terrible illness on this great woman.

"Maybe it's not God's doing at all," she said to Rabbi Sandra when she telephoned to share the bad news. "Maybe Sister Ann feels her life's work has come to an end?"

"Yes. The organization that funds the Interreligious Task Force has closed down her office in Chicago. Our brave outspoken nun's mission has been completed. Perhaps Sister Ann believes soon it will be time for her to take a well-deserved rest."

In early January of 1990, Liz received a letter from the president of a prominent ecumenical women's organization. *"Dear Reverend Adams,"* it began. *"We are pleased to inform you that our organization, WomanSpeak: Voices of Women of Faith, wishes to honor you with its WomanSpeak Let My Voice Be Heard Award. This recognition is given annually to individuals whose outstanding work has advanced the role of women in religion and in society. Your award will be presented at our banquet on Thursday March 22nd, 1990 at the Plaza Hotel in Manhattan.*

"We will honor two other women, Sister Mona Sullivan, Executive Director of The Women's Ordination Conference, and Rabbi Sandra Miller-Brownstein, spiritual leader of Temple Beth El in Chicago. Please let us know as soon as possible if you will be able to attend the dinner to accept this honor."

Liz was happy she'd be able to see her friend Rabbi Sandy at the dinner. She had heard of Sister Mona Sullivan, in fact recalled meeting her at those Episcopal women's ordinations. She was nearly as radical as Sister Ann Gillen. Sister Mona was one of the nuns who signed that statement in *The New York Times* about abortion and was now a leader in the movement for Catholic women's ordination.

And being in Manhattan for the dinner would give Liz an excuse to perhaps see Inga again. She ached for her. She missed her emotional fulfillment. She missed their fabulous sex life. She missed the joy. Liz wondered if she should telephone Inga. She thought about it for two weeks, then mustered her courage, found her number through long-distance information, and dialed it. Liz told her about the dinner at the Plaza and invited her to come.

Inga refused.

"No, Liz. Congratulations, but no. I told you I'd never see you again unless you agree to live the rest of your life with me. Openly. Those are my conditions. You have to make your choice. I won't go back to you the way things were, not compromising my principles anymore. If you do lose your job I can support you for the rest of our lives. My paintings are selling for ridiculous prices. Plus I still have the trust fund Maddy left me."

"You know I don't like to take money from you."

"Don't be ridiculous. You'd let yourself be supported by a man and think nothing of it. Why should it be any different because I'm a woman? You can move down to Manhattan, Liz. Start over. Start a new life. With me."

Inga was giving Liz another chance. Should she grab it? Could she jeopardize her career, live without it if it came to that? After all her struggling to accomplish what she had?

"I'll think about it," Liz said.

"If you have to think about it, then I already know your answer. I don't want the old Liz who lives by reason. I want the new Liz that opened herself up to me like a flower." She paused. "When is this dinner again?"

"March 22nd."

"Okay. That's the date, Liz. That's my deadline. If you want to be with me for the rest of our lives, you will come to my apartment after the dinner. Don't telephone. Just come. I'll be waiting for you. But only if you've made your final decision. For us to be together forever. To let our love see the light of day. If you don't come to me that night," she added, "we'll never see each other again."

That was it.

Two months for Liz to make the most important decision of her life.

Part IV

Mona, Sandra, Liz: March 22, 1990

THE OFFICIAL WOMANSPEAK: Voices of Women of Faith dinner photographer snaps pictures of Rabbi Sandy, Reverend Elizabeth Adams, and me proudly holding up our silver plaques and smiling. He photographs the three of us with the president of WomanSpeak. Then my brother and sisters and their spouses and my stepmother Vivian gather around me on the podium, eagerly examining my silver plaque. The photographer rapidly snaps four photographs of all of us.

"Your father would be so proud," Vivian gushes, tears in her eyes.

"Momma, too," Muriel adds.

My family splurges on two taxis back to Queens. Vivian has invited Muriel and Joe and Sluggie and his wife Janet back to my childhood home to celebrate my award with a glass of champagne, but they decline because they have to get up early tomorrow to go to work. Peggy and David are staying at the house. They'll sleep in Sluggie and Rory's old room. I'm staying in the bedroom I shared with my sisters.

In the kitchen, as Vivian pours the champagne for Peggy, David, and me, she asks, "Your friend Sister Phyllis couldn't come to the dinner tonight?"

"She's just Phyllis now. She left religious life. She's sculpting, huge ugly bronze things, I've heard. Running an art gallery in Arizona. And she has a lover now. A priest in Los Angeles who leads a double life comes to Sedona to live with her on his days off."

"No! What is our church coming to?" Vivian moans.

I don't want to tell Vivian that Phyllis is furious with me for withdrawing my name from that controversial *New York Times* abortion statement. I don't want to bore her with those details, and I know my stepmother disagrees with my liberal stand on abortion.

But Phyllis won't be angry anymore when she discovers what I've planned for my new future. When she learns of the decision I promised myself I'd make by tonight. The decision I made tonight during the dinner as I thought about my entire life.

"Let's go to bed," Vivian says. ""I'll wash up the glasses in the morning."

I climb the stairs to the bedroom I shared with Peggy and Muriel before I entered the convent. It looks exactly the same. Vivian and Dad left our childhood rooms as they had been so we'll always feel welcome when we come home. I undress, brush my teeth, and climb into my bed and think of how many nights I lay here as a child dreaming of becoming a sister.

But now I have a new dream.

I'll contact Phyllis' nephew in Omaha tomorrow morning to get her telephone number in Sedona. To tell her I'm leaving my order and the Catholic Church that has been my entire life. To tell her I'll become an Episcopalian so I can become a priest.

And tomorrow I'll ask Sister Ellen McCarthy, my convent's Administrative Director, to send a request for dispensation from my vows to the Vatican office in charge of religious orders.

My family will be shocked, but they'll come to understand. And God will understand why I'm asking to be released from my vows and leaving the Church. He wants me to follow my new dream. God wants me to serve Him in this way.

As I lie in my childhood bed, as I did at the dinner at the Plaza tonight I think back to my first night in the convent as a postulant. I was young. Frightened. Idealistic. I recall how I had prayed to God that night thirty-two years ago, asking Him if I had made the right decision. Asking Him if I was doing what He had planned for me.

Yes, now I am making the right decision. Now I am going to do what He has planned for me.

I thought I'd find peace when I became a sister. But I never found what I was searching for. I won't have an easy life as Episcopal priest either. It will be a difficult path, perhaps even more tumultuous than my past life has been.

I'm a bit frightened. But I am at peace with my decision. I am at peace with myself.

As I drift off to sleep I think, Yes. At last I have found peace.

Another photograph of Sister Mona, Liz Adams, and me posing near the podium with the president of WomanSpeak. Then two photos of me with Carolyn, Mom, and Joanie. As we smile and I hold up my silver plaque, I hear the remaining dinner guests chat as they meander from the room. Behind the photographer I see bus boys scurrying to gather up the dirty dishes from the tables. Hear the clink of glassware.

I say goodbye to my friend Reverend Liz and remind her to stay in touch. Then I walk with Carolyn, Sister Mona, and David and Peggy Greene to the cloakroom outside of the ballroom. Sister Mona's stepmother and other siblings and their spouses are already retrieving their coats.

"I really miss both of you since I moved to Chicago," I tell David and Peggy.

"We miss you, too, Rabbi," Peggy says.

I pull Sister Mona aside and whisper, "Your decision. Don't forget. Tell me your decision."

"Yes, I will," she says. "Thanks for your advice. I'll phone you tomorrow."

We all say goodbye, then the large Sullivan family leaves together.

"I'm sorry I can't have a drink with you," Carolyn says. "I'm on *The Today Show* tomorrow. My new book. The 7:30 to 8 segment. I need to get to bed."

"I wanted to talk to you about...you know."

"Let me know what you decide," Carolyn whispers as we hug goodbye. "Whether you choose Jeff or Robert, I'll support you. I'll always be there for you. Remember, Sandy, you're in charge of your own life now."

I thank Norma Appelbaum, the obviously overworked Executive Director of WomanSpeak, for coordinating the dinner. Say goodbye to Liz Adams, promising to keep in touch. Joanie, Mom, and I leave the Plaza Hotel and walk a short distance in the damp March air to a less expensive hotel where we've reserved adjoining rooms.

"What's up?" Joanie whispers to me as we drag our luggage to rooms. "Something's going on with you. You could never fool me, Sandy. Let's get a drink in the bar after I settle Mom in."

"Ten minutes," I reply.

I put my suitcase and briefcase in my room, then go back downstairs to the cocktail lounge where a pianist is quietly playing old standards. I order a gin and tonic and wait for Joanie. Five minutes later my sister eases in beside me on the banquette behind the small round table.

"OK," Joanie says after she orders her wine. "Tell me everything."

I blurt out the entire story of my affair with Jeff. How he's pressuring me to leave Robert and marry him. How Robert found out about it and told me I must break it off now and never see Jeff again. My usually loquacious sister doesn't say a word until I'm finished.

"Yikes. God, Sandy, what are you going to do?"

"I had a long time tonight during the dinner speeches to think about my life. To really think about my personal journey. How far I've come. I've achieved my dream, and now I have obligations. A responsibility to the Jewish people." I take a sip of my gin and tonic. "Can I throw all this away? All I've struggled for since I was a weird kid wanting to be a rabbi?" I pause. "Even if I don't lose my job, I'm not sure I could live with my decision if I choose Jeff. It would devastate the kids. And for the most part Robert's been a good husband. After all, he held back his career by switching to the Chicago branch of his firm when we moved to Milwaukee. Not many men would have done that. Not many men could have lived with the turmoil I've put him through. He has every reason to be furious and hurt now."

"But you're in love with Jeff. You always have been. Not everyone finds this kind of love in their lives."

"Love isn't everything. I'm turning fifty. Jeff and I aren't prom king and queen anymore. I don't know if Jeff's up to the struggle that might lie ahead for me. He has evolved, but I'm not sure he really understand us Jews, even after all these years. He says he does, but I'm not sure."

"So you've made your decision, Sandy."

"Have I?"

"Listen to yourself."

The pianist stops playing. The waiter glares at us. Joanie looks at her watch. "God, it's midnight. We have to get up at the crack of dawn for our flights tomorrow."

We sign for our drinks and take the elevator up to our rooms. I open the door with my room key. Carefully put the silver plaque on the dresser. Toss my purse onto the bed.

Joanie's right. I have made my decision.

I sit on the bed and pick up the telephone. It's only eleven fifteen in Chicago. Jeff will still be awake.

I'm calling him to tell him we can never see each other again.

As for my marriage to Robert? I have to think about it. Maybe that's over, too. Maybe it's been over for a long time. That's a decision I'll make later.

But I must give up Jeff. It's the right thing to do. I will continue to serve the Jewish people. To preserve our precious heritage.

I will keep my promise to that eye in the stained glass window of my childhood.

The official dinner photographer snaps photos of Sister Mona Sullivan, Rabbi Sandy, and me posing near the podium on the dais table in the Grand Ballroom of the Plaza Hotel. The three of us hold up our engraved silver plaques from Tiffany's. We smile broadly and lean in toward each other. Another photo of the three of us with the president of WomanSpeak. Then two photos of me with Alicia and Harry.

When the photographer indicates he has all the shots he needs, Norma Appelbaum, the Executive Director of WomanSpeak, leads us to the cloakroom in the lobby outside the ballroom's gilded doors. I thank Mrs. Appelbaum for the dinner. She gives me the light blue Tiffany box with tissue paper in which the silver plaque came so I can safely pack the award for my drive back to Maine tomorrow morning. As we retrieve our coats, I say goodbye to Sister Mona and Rabbi Sandy, promising to stay in touch.

"What a great evening," Alicia says to me. "I'm so proud of you."

"Come on, girls," Harry nags. "Might be hard to get a cab."

Am I going with Alicia and Harry to their apartment to spend the night before I drive home tomorrow? Or am I going to Inga?

If I don't go to Inga's apartment tonight our relationship is over. She made that clear. She will never give me another chance. You're out of time, Liz. This is it. You have to make the decision now.

"I better go to the bathroom first," I tell Alicia and Harry. "In case we don't get a cab right away."

Alicia holds my coat as I trek down the long wide corridor to the elegant ladies' room. No one else is there. I walk over to the large mirror and stare into it.

My fifty-year old face stares back at me.

I peer into its eyes, searching for my soul. Searching for an answer.

What should I do?

During this dinner tonight I thought over my entire life. How God called me to serve Him when my brother was killed thirty years ago. How difficult in those days it was to decide to be ordained. The challenges I've faced as a woman in a man's profession and in a patriarchal religion. How carefully I've led my life. How carefully I've always tried to do the right thing. How I've tried to ascertain what God wants, what God has planned for me. How I've tried to serve Him.

Tonight at the dinner, I thought over again all the arguments I'd debated the first time Inga left me. Can I risk my career? My parents' mortification and rejection? The harsh judgment of my Presbytery? The harsh judgment of the world? Perhaps the harsh judgment of God? But can I live any longer without Inga, the one person with whom I felt emotionally fulfilled? Should I grab this last chance for happiness?

Publicly declaring my love for Inga as she is demanding can destroy everything I've fought for. And I've vowed to never again place my life into the hands of another. I've learned the hard way you can only count on yourself. You have to steer your own course. I can't risk depending on another person who might hurt me and throw my life into turmoil as Tom did.

It's true, I think as I stare at my aging image in the mirror, I have found joy and happiness with Inga. More than I ever thought possible. But will it be worth it in the future if this is all I'm left with? What if this joy fades and I'm no longer fulfilled? What if one day what I have with Inga is no longer enough for me? Or, what if one day Inga announces, as Tom did, that she no longer loves me? She's found someone else?

Can't take that chance.

I comb my hair, put on fresh lipstick. I leave the ladies' room and walk briskly back to the cloakroom where Alicia and Harry wait for me.

"You ready to go back to our apartment?" Alicia asks me.

I ponder for another moment, then say, "Yes, I'm ready."

Yes. I will continue to serve God as He has asked.

I have found my voice. I won't silence it now.

About the Author

Marcia R. Rudin graduated magna cum laude from Boston University. She received a joint MA degree in religion from Columbia University and Union Theological Seminary. She studied for a PhD at the New School for Social Research and taught history of religion at William Paterson College. She was a resident in screenwriting at the MacDowell Colony of the Arts. Several of her plays have received productions.

Marcia is the coauthor of *Why Me? Why Anyone?* and *Prison or Paradise? The New Religious Cults*. Her articles have appeared in the *New York Times*, the *New York Daily News*, and other publications. A longtime expert on destructive cults, she has been quoted by many renowned publications and has appeared several times on national and regional television.

She and her husband, Rabbi James Rudin, live in Manhattan and Florida. They have two daughters and one granddaughter. For additional information, visit www.marciarudin.com.